I0583982

MORE BAD COMPANY

MAX BARRINGTON

Max Barrington

First published in Australia in 2024 by Etteleah Books - Cairns Australia

ISBN: 978-0-9756538-9-0

Max Barrington

Other Books By Max Barrington

Woolgar River Curse: Receiving a phone call announcing that you are the heir to a 70,000 acre cattle property that is complete with a five bedroom mansion would be like winning the Lotto. But to Gus and Lynette Teague, it was the beginning of a discovery into corruption, deceit, tragedy and murder. Was it really an 'Aboriginal Curse' on that property that caused the death of a family of five, or simply tragic events?

Task: I was looking to make a few dollars until my next work project started. "Check out the Air Tasking pages on Facebook," they said. An Australian road trip from Cairns to Darwin turns into Mystery, Intrigue and Life Threatening Danger

Dying to Find Gold:

Fossicking for Gold in Australia is a popular activity. But when Mick West's, best mate goes missing whilst on a fossicking trip The police suspect Mick of murder.

The First Ten Years in Australia From a 10 year old ten pound pom

An Amazing story of a ten-year-old boy's adventure of coming from England to Australia with his parents in 1959.

It tells of the family's ten moves to different New South Wales towns, within ten years, whilst his father sought work, from a ferry skipper to a quarry manager.

It, also tells of a determination, to succeed in a new environment.

A very moving, yet, such an interesting turn of events, of a real family, based on a true story.

You will not be able to put this book down!

Max Barrington

To my inspiration, my loving wife Lynette

Max Barrington

Max Barrington

Contents

Max Barrington

HARRY CROFT

Max Barrington

Max Barrington

Harry Croft

'What the fuck do you mean when you say that I can't work here any more lad, I've bin here since well before you were born' said Harry, or 'Aitch' as all his workmates called him, in his very strong Scouse, or Liverpool accent that he had not lost in the fifty-five years that he had been in Australia.

'It's not my idea Harry, it's the insurance company, they won't insure you for workers compensation because you are now sixty five years old', Simon Drury was trying to explain to Harry Croft the district manager at the south side maintenance depot in the ACT.

'I put you into that fucking job lad, you fucking arse wipe and you have turned into the biggest fucking arse licker and crawler that mankind has ever ad the misfortune of coming across, now crawl back to your little arse licking office with your cock sucking buddies and leave me alone.'

Sadly, Simon had to call the police in to remove Harry Croft from his office. Harry had been the district manager of that depot for the last twenty five years, he was now past the age where he could be covered by workers' compensation, so in accordance with local government policy, he needed to retire. Simon knew that financially Harry was fine with his super and he would be eligible for an age pension, sadly Harry could not see all the benefits that retiring had to offer.

The police entered Harry's office without knocking, a big mistake,

'Who the fuck do you pricks think you are and what, the fuck are you doing in here'

'Sorry sir, but we have orders to remove you from these premises and with reasonable force if required', said the first class constable who had entered the office with a female constable.

Harry started to cool down, he realised that these people were only doing their jobs and it didn't matter what he thought about the system there was nothing he could do about it, plus the fact that he didn't want to make a complete fool of himself.

'Just give me ten minutes son, and I'll get out of your way'. Harry went into the store room and found an empty carton and went back to his office to pack the few things he had in and on his desk, he had a few books on the bookcase which he also took, there were some other books that he decided to leave there.

It had taken him no longer than five minutes and Harry was in the car park with his cardboard box, and then he realised that he only had his govy there, he put his cardboard box down onto the bonnet of the car, a Toyota Corolla poverty pack as Harry called it, Harry took his mobile telephone from his trouser pocket and looked for Simon Drury in his contacts then pushed the button.

'You ok Harry, sorry about all this mate."

'I'm sorry Simon, I just lost it, It's just a shock to me is all I can say', Harry said, although he had known for months that yesterday was his deadline and the last possible day that he could remain in the employment of the department. 'Look I ave only govy car to get home, I'll drop it back tomorrow an', Simon cut him off.

'Just bring it to the Canberra Club on Friday night where your farewell dinner is and leave it in the basement car park and I'll get it sorted from there.'

Harry's wife Val, wasn't surprised to see him come home at ten thirty that Thursday morning. She had warned him this

Max Barrington

morning before he had left to go to work that he was wasting his time going and that she didn't think that they would even let him in the door, he was being just too obstinate, bloody old fool.

'Did they give you that car as a going away present? Or did you knock it off, Harry'?

Harry didn't answer her but went to the fridge instead and took out a stubbie of Carlton draught and just muttered something that was totally beyond any resemblance to the English language and went into the lounge and sat to drink his beer and read the Canberra Times. After about an hour he wandered back into the kitchen where Val wasn't really doing anything, Harry looked around the kitchen as he was sort of hoping that a bit of lunch might have been happening. At this time at work, he would be at the takeaway that was beside the depot and wondering what to have for lunch, it was always either a pie and hot chips, or fish and chips, or sometimes chicken and chips but it was always 'and chips' and he would take it back to the depot and sit in the lunch room with all his workmates to eat his lunch.

The conversation in the lunch room was about the shit food that they had bought from next door and they all agreed that they would find somewhere else to get lunch from tomorrow, but that never happened.

Harry, after realising that lunch, did not look like it was 'on' in the kitchen, asked Val if she would like to walk up to the Statesman Hotel with him for lunch.

'Are you bored Harry? you have been home for all of one hour and one half and you do not know what to do with yourself' Val asked. 'You get up to the pub and have some lunch there Harry and leave me to my work, go and enjoy yourself'.

Max Barrington

And he did go, he wasn't going to, but then he was going to and then he did, so he walked the three hundred metres from their home to the pub. Of course at twelve thirty on a Thursday lunchtime, there was no one there that he knew, they were all at work, there were only old retired blokes and unemployed bludgers, but the place was busy and there was mixed grill on as todays special which sounded pretty good to Harry, but first a couple of beers at the bar.

'What are you having mate' the barman recognised Harry, 'Day off mate?'

'Would you believe it Wal, I am now officially retired, middy of tooth's thanks'

'Holy shit Harry, your not going to be here every day annoying us are you? Have you plans Harry, are you going to move down the coast and go fishing every day?'

'Mate, I don't even eat fish anymore, so why would I want to go and catch the bastards, cheer's Wal', Harry went to find a table, placed his beer on it then went to the food serverey to order a 'mixed grill'. The young girl serving, who looked like she really did not want to be in the pub working and was doing everyone who ordered a meal, a personal favour.

'You right mate?' She asked Harry. Harry turned and looked behind him, then turned back and spoke to the girl.

'Were you talking to me?', Harry asked with indignation, 'I thought you were talking to a dog'.

'Nah, I was asking what you wanted', Harry just shrugged and could not be bothered, but he made a mental note to tell Nick, the hotel manager about this young lady's attitude.

'I'll have a mixed grill please'

'That's twenty dollars, mate'.

Harry passed the twenty dollars to the girl and said 'Thank you very much, and don't ever call me 'mate' again'.

She just gave him a blank stare as a zombie would, but didn't know any different, it was a waste of words from Harry.

Harry went back to his table only to discover his beer was gone, he looked around, which was useless as almost everyone in there had a middy of beer, either in their hands or sitting in front of them. Harry went to the bar and told Wal that his bar hand was a bit anxious in collecting glasses and must have taken his beer. Wal said that Phil, the roustabout hadn't started yet and suggested that it may have been one of the dole wacker's playing pool.

'Don't worry about it Harry, it's not worth it these days, I'll get you another one, back in the old days young pricks like that, I would have thrown through the door with a following boot in their arse and would ban the pricks for a month. If I do that today, those assholes would have me charged for assault'. Then Wal added, 'better get back to your table mate while your meal is still there'.

They both enjoyed a laugh.

Harry arrived back home about an hour after he'd left to go there and Val said to him,

'That didn't work did it Harry, you don't know what to do with yourself do you? What are you going to do, you had the chance to think about it six months ago when they told you, but no, that won't happen to me sez Harry and now what? You don't want to go down the coast and get a place near the beach or the river. You will need to work something out, you can't just mope around here like this.

Harry, was just *not* ready to retire, he had completed his apprenticeship as a carpenter at the age of twenty and then had worked on various construction projects at many levels for ten years. At thirty Harry had joined the ACT Police force and had risen to sergeant within ten years but he didn't feel it was really the life for him and left there to take up the advertised position of district manager for the then, Dept of Housing and Construction.

Self Government had come along for the ACT and things changed slightly with Harry's position with the biggest change being that he was given a much bigger salary and a home garaging Government (govy) car.

Harry had decided that he was too young at sixty five to retire and decided to look for some sort of work, maybe just until he got to around seventy five thought Harry. As fate would have it and before Harry had to do any serious thinking about what he should be looking for in a job at his age, he got a call from one of the other DM's (district manager) at another maintenance depot, not really a friend but they both got on well together, and during the conversation, Harry had mentioned that he would most likely try to find some sort of a job. The other DM said that if he was interested he knew of a position going for a maintenance cell supervisor at one of the large private office buildings in the city. Harry reminded him that he was now sixty five and apparently workers compensation insurance was a problem, whereas his former colleague told him, not in private enterprise. Harry became interested and got the contact details for the position.

Val was quite happy when Harry announced that he intended to apply for the position as a maintenance supervisor with a large company that supplied this type of service on contract, to many private high rise office complexes, and buildings.

Harry had made contact by phone to the contact name he had been provided who in turn did confirm that such a position was indeed available and asked Harry if he could contact the HR manager, make an appointment with him and to bring along his CV , he gave Harry a number for HR manager. Harry thanked the person on the other end of the telephone conversation then hung up.

Harry was a little concerned, he didn't have a CV, as such, back when he applied for his last job, twenty five years ago it was called a resume and he still had a copy of that, he didn't really have much to add to it though. After a long thinking session with Val, Val suggested that he give Gwen, his former secretary a call and ask her about a CV.

Gwen was so delighted that Harry had rang, she wanted to call him but thought that he may have still have been too upset with all the commotion of him having to leave his job. Harry finally, got around to asking her about a CV and that he had nothing really to add to it as he had only been with his last job for the last twenty five years.

"Harry, I have been with you for eighteen of those twenty five years and in that time you have attended at least six courses where you have received a qualification and one that I know of where you received a degree. Give me an hour or so and I will email a list to you, if you like I will prepare an up to date CV, how would that be?

Within an hour Harry had received to new CV from Gwen, It read like some other, somewhat dignified, persons CV rather than his. True he had not really added much weight to all the courses that his former job had required him to attend and complete and now when he thought about it, one of them was a three year part time course.

Harry had always only really regarded the courses as a source of a getaway, staying at flash hotels and enjoying the free, rather expensive and extensive meals at hotels, not to mention the endless free drinks, or simply a couple days off from work each week.

He started to read the qualification that he had acquired whilst in his former position, it was fairly extensive and also seemed quite impressive.

Other than his original former qualification as a journeyman carpenter, Gwen had added Acumen of Business cert IIII, Human Resources Development, Diploma in Management Skills, Diploma in Applied Science Blg, and on and on. After perusing his new CV, Harry now recalled some of the courses, it had been such a long time ago, surely things would have changed so much by now as to make these qualifications obsolete. Anyway, Harry took his new CV with him to his appointment with the HR manager.

He was nothing that Harry had imagined and Harry thought that maybe he was still at school and just here on work experience. The HR manager introduced himself to Harry,

'Joshua Benthall, Harry, pleased to meet you'.

In Harry's experience, people around this age generally addressed Harry as Mr Croft, Harry responded with a 'Good Morning, Josh"

'Joshua, it's Joshua Harry'

'Right, Joshua'

'You have a rather impressive CV Harry, I must say, However, you do realise that we don't really require such qualifications for the position intended, simply your qualification as a carpenter is sufficient, however your strengths are quite apparent through these further education qualifications. Harry, What do you see as your weak point'.

'I don't know that I do have a weak point, Josh..Joshua'.

'Harry, everybody, myself included, has a weak point or weakness, if you prefer, think about it, Harry'.

'Well, I suppose my weak point would have to be my honesty'.

'I don't think that being honest is a weak point, Harry'.

'Well, responded Harry, 'I don't really care what you think, and I did not come here to be belittled by you, now if you have a position for me then tell me so, otherwise we are both wasting our time here this morning'.

Joshua's smugness disappeared instantly, he had been in this position for two months now and he was not prepared for this reaction, from a person seeking employment. His training did not provide for the aggressive behaviour of job seekers but that of a humble and positive nature. He felt a reversal happening and he could not stop it.

'yes,...er,.there is a position available at one of our properties in the centre of civic'

'And what is the role'? Harry asked, 'What is involved and what is the remuneration'?

Joshua, on his back foot now seemed to be going even further back, 'It's a casual rate of sixty dollars per hour, but because of your age, the insurance company place a surcharge against your cover which will reduce the hourly rate to fifty five dollars per hour', he added the last bit somewhat gingerly.

'That will do', said Harry, I can start next Monday, tell me where I have to go, I will be there at nine o'clock'.

Harry had taken over the interview and had awarded himself the position, Joshua had been aware of this and could

Max Barrington

do nothing to stop it from happening. Quite feebly and almost apologetically, Joshua found himself following Harry's directive and had supplied him with a written format of the address to be at on Monday at nine am as Harry had dictated, he was to meet the engineer in charge there who would advise him further. Joshua had also given Harry employee and tax declaration forms to complete and Harry told Joshua that he would pass these to the engineer on Monday.

'Nothing else you want to tell me', asked Harry pausing for a response from Joshua, who just looked at him quite blankly, so Harry said 'Good day'.

Harry was back at his car when he looked at the documentation that Josh had given him. The address of the maintenance cell was the lower level on the corners of Northbourne Ave (North bound) and Alinga Street. The company name was Combined Programmed Building Maintenance. They had contracts around the city at various locations and operated from this cell, it was Harry's job to run the cell. 'Piece of piss' Harry thought to himself.

Harry had met with the company's chief engineer at nine o'clock on the following Monday who introduced himself to Harry as Malcolm Tate, he took Harry down in the elevator, which needed an access card to access the basement, where the maintenance cell office and workshop is located and introduced him to the other three tradespeople, one carpenter, one electrician and one plumber, as 'meet your new boss Harry'.

'Jim, how are you Harry, I'm your sparky', said a fairly slim but tall and lanky dark haired man in his forties.

'Im a Charlie, please to meet with you, I look after the plumbing', said the plumber, shot fat and Italian.

'Roger, Harry, how are you doing', tall and thick set with a moustache and looked authoritative.

'You must be the chippy then', said Harry to Roger as he shook all of their hands.

Malcolm showed Harry to his new office and explained how the computerised maintenance system worked, his role was to physically assess the maintenance requests and to give an indicative estimate for repair costs then create a scope of works and supervise the works. Harry did have a female office assistant named Veronica but she wasn't coming to work today as she was ill. Before Malcolm left Harry as he had other issues to attend to that morning, he gave Harry a keycard for the elevator and the loading dock shutter and also gave Harry his mobile number to contact him for any reason he should need to do so.

Malcolm called out to Roger as he was leaving and asked him to give Harry a tour of the works.

'As soon as you are ready Harry' responded Roger.

Harry said 'Well I have bugger all else to do, let's go!'

Roger showed Harry the other office where Veronica worked, 'when she's here' Roger said with a little sarcasm, then took Harry to the plumbing workshop, a fairly small area of around six metres by eight, Charlie wasn't there.

The electrical workshop was about the same size as the plumbing and Jim was in there setting up a small switchboard, heading in a westerly direction was the carpentry, and joinery workshop which was around two and a half the size of the other workshops. At the western end of the basement was a loading dock with a ramp exiting onto Moore Street, there was sufficient room to park six cars which Harry was quite pleased about as he had left his car, what seemed like miles away that morning for a car park. Back up near Harry's office was the store area's consisting of three separate seven by seven metre lock up stores backing onto the northern end of the basement.

In the centre storeroom on the back, northern wall, was a set of large double doors that were closed with some items leaning on them.

'What's through there?', Harry asked Roger.

'Another set of locked double doors, goes through to the basement of the building next door, the Jolimont Centre I think, I'm not really sure Harry, I have never really been interested'.

Val was happy to hear all about Harry's new job and pleased when he said that he thought it would be quite ok and that he could virtually please himself how many hours a day, or week for that matter, he wanted to work.

'Pretty cruisy and the extra money can be put away to buy a place down the coast for retirement in about five years' Harry had said to Val, 'that'll give us around six hundred thousand extra to add to it'.

Harry was fitting in pretty well with his new role, he found it to be pretty much the same as his old position with the ACT Government, but this was maybe just a bit more involved. Veronica, Harry's assistant seemed a bit dippy to Harry but after a couple of months they were getting on really well and Veronica revealed to Harry that in the two months that he had been running the cell, they had made half as much money again than the previous guy Damien, that was running the cell. Veronica had also let it slip to Harry that Damien was also on a casual rate and was being paid seventy five dollars per hour. This had prompted Harry to give his mate Joshua, the HR manager a call.

'Good morning Josh, it's Harry Croft, trust you are well'.

Joshua's mind was starting to recollect the name Harry Croft and he suddenly sat up in his chair as he realised who it was and he frowned at the shortened use of his name.

'What can I do for you Harry?', Joshua said a bit curtly.

'Josh, my boy', said Harry in his well practised, polished style of voice, 'when you selected me as the incumbent for this position, the remuneration of fifty five dollars per hour, was but for a three month probationary period was it not?'

'I can't say offhand Harry, but I don't think so, I'll have to check your file'...........

'No worries Josh, I'll wait', Harry cut Joshua off very quickly so he would be unable to say that he would call Harry back.

'No Harry, there is not any mention of a probationary period, nor any mention of an increase to the remuneration".

'No worries, then that means that there would be no reason to have to wait for an increase on remuneration to seventy dollars per hour?'.

'I am sorry Harry, I don't really understand what you are saying'.

'I am saying, that you can increase my hourly rate from fifty five dollars per hour to seventy dollars per hour, as from next Monday'.

'I don't have the authority to increase your hourly rate Harry,.

'Then I suggest to you Josh, that you put it to whoever the person is that can make this type of adjustment to my hourly rate and get it all together by next Monday, Good bye Josh'.

Whatever had happened in the interim period between when Harry had called Joshua and Monday morning, Harry had no idea, but he had received a text message from Joshua on

Monday morning advising that his rate of pay was now seventy dollars per hour as from today, 'well done Josh', thought Harry and got on with his work.

Veronica had received a maintenance request from the centre next door and had taken the details and had handed them plus the file on the building over to Harry's in box. Harry had taken it from his inbox sometime later that afternoon and looked at the request that one area in the building at the ground level had moisture forming on the floor.

The following day Harry had visited the next door buildings caretaker and he had shown Harry the area of condensation, it was a very small area, about one metre wide by four metres long on a tiled section. Harry new instantly that it was a dew point cause of condensation, this can generally, only happen when two different temperatures come into contact. As this building, as with many in Canberra, was using a controlled environment system for heating and cooling it meant that the windows in the building were inoperable to stop either cold or hot air entering the building, and as it was now July in Canberra and the system employed was heating the building, then cold air was coming into contact with the hot air from the heating. In this instance, it seemed that below the ground floor slab was a source of cool air within that confine of the condensation.

Harry asked the caretaker how to get to the basement, to which the caretaker responded that there was no basement in this building, well none that he was aware of anyway.

Harry walked around the outside of the building and found on the western wall adjacent to where the condensation was taking place that a surface level vent that had been previously closed off with a one way damper, had somehow now became open to allow air to enter. Being on the west side put it directly

Max Barrington

into the prevailing winter winds of around twelve kilometres per hour.

A Simple job smiled Harry upon his discovery, the vent damper was replaced later that day and Harry had inspected the section of tiled area the next day to discover that the area was now dry. The caretaker was amazed at Harry's instant investigation and solution to what he had imagined to be quite a major problem. Harry was good at his job and there was little doubting of that.

It was November now and summer was starting to happen, Val had called Harry on his mobile one Friday afternoon to ask him if he could get some steak on his way home from work that evening as she had totally forgotten to get it while she was shopping earlier that day and thought that a bbq might be nice for dinner that evening and that their son Scott and his wife Zoe and the grandson Morgan would be coming.

Harry had finished work early that Friday, as usual and had called at the Statesman hotel for a beer, it was very busy in the bar as Harry saw a couple of his old drinking mates and joined in a couple of beers with them. There was some sort of altercation in the pool table area and one of the bar staff was trying to evict two young fellows from the pub, they didn't look to be aged any more than fifteen. They were refusing to leave the hotel amid the jeers of onlookers and maybe, even some of their mates, the bar assistant was being careful not to touch either of the two to avoid any later claims of assault that could be directed towards him, he had called the police twice now but there had been no attendance as yet by them.

Suddenly one of the youths picked up a ball from the pool table and threw it towards the crowded bar, the pool ball hit a drinker who had his back turned towards the bar as he was just paying for a round of drinks, the ball struck him somewhere in the middle of the back of his head. The scream the victim of the pool ball emitted was loud and mournful and caught the attention of everybody in the bar, perfect timing for the two youths to slip outside unnoticed.

The ambulance had arrived and was in the process of removing the victim from the bar when the police, who had been called prior to the throwing of the ball by the bar staff, arrived to look helplessly on.

'Mate we rang you blokes nearly fifteen minutes ago about a couple of young underage pricks that refused to leave, they got the shits and threw a ball at this poor bastard and then they fucked off' said the bar manager Wal.

'What did they look like mate' asked a young female copper with a somewhat smart attitude and strange sounding voice that nineteen year old females seem to display these days.

'And what the fuck do you think they looked like', said Wal who was quite shaken with the event, 'they were wearing those fucking grey or black fucking hoodies that they all fucking wear'.

The other constable with her, a male who looked a bit older but seemed much smarter told her to follow him outside and they would call for backup and do a search of the adjacent shopping centre and then they both left.

Harry, who had witnessed the full event with his drinking buddies, finished his beer and said see you to them and left the hotel to go to the supermarket to get the steak that his wife had asked him to buy on his way home. Inside the supermarket in the lollies and peanut aisle, Harry saw the two youths that had left the pub after one of them had thrown the pool ball, they were laughing and eating a pack of potato chips that each had taken from the shelf.

Harry could not help himself and said to the youths, ' You know that bloke you hit with the pool ball is in a bad way'.

'Who the fuck do you think you are grandpa, fuck off you stupid old cunt before you get the same'. One of the youths said whilst threatening to throw a can of baked beans that he had in his hand at Harry.

Harry had just started his crouch and natural self preservation to hurl himself at the youth holding the can in his hand when both of the constables that Harry had seen in the pub walked into the aisle and called out STOP!....instinctively, Harry stopped, the youths fled.

It was a great bbq, the steaks that Harry had collected from the supermarket, plus all the other condiments that Val had put towards the meal, were just great. Harry had not told anyone about what had happened at the pub, nor what had happened in the supermarket, but he looked at his son and thought thank christ you didn't turn out like those pieces of shit that I saw today, but he knew that would have been impossible because Harry had been his father and had brought up Scott in a way that involved something that is banned today when bringing up children, not just at home, but also in schools, Marshall punishment.

Harry had heard in the news the next day that the fellow in the pub had died from the injury he had received from the pool ball, but that the police had charged two youths aged sixteen and seventeen with his murder, 'well that's good' thought Harry. One month later both the youths were placed on bonds as they had been under the influence of a substance which affected their ability to behave in a normal manner.

Harry could not understand that although an innocent person had been killed for no reason whatsoever, just a thoughtless deliberate act by two children there was no punishment delivered, they had shown no remorse whatsoever, there was no deterrent to any others that may consider similar actions towards their fellow man.

Because nothing happens when you get caught, in their minds, must seem to mean you can do it, you are not allowed to do it, then you will be told not to do it again, but that is about the extent and it does not matter what you did, murder, assault, steal a car, whatever, it's just a game like a video game, you have to start again.

Harry thought that it was also pathetic that these kids that murdered the guy, were also released by a legal representative that the dead guy was also paying towards by the means of taxation, legal aid. The dead guy was also paying towards the psychologist and human rights affiliates that objected to any form of reprimand towards his killers as it may lead to affecting the mental or social way these youths may react later in life, it could fuck their brain in later life, they may become withdrawn and no longer to participate in normal social behavioural activities.

Little thought seems to go to the victim lying dead in the morgue, to the grieving family who have lost their loved father, husband and in many cases, breadwinner. No, all that matters is that these youths don't suffer any mental issues later in life. Unbelievable, and not a good subject to mention to Harry.

Life Goes On

Life does go on and Harry was in his office some weeks after the pub incident, Veronica came into his office and showed to him an invoice that had been rejected from being paid by the company for a 'new vent damper' as it was under the wrong asset charge number.

'Ah shit, sorry said Harry, I do remember that, it was the place next door, Veronica looked it up and inserted the correct asset number so that the sub contractor who completed the job could be paid. Harry thought how strange that although his team could have quite easily have repaired that duct damper, because it was classified as HVAC, heating ventilation and air conditioning, and they did not employ a person qualified in such, then it had to out sourced, hmmm, thought Harry, a new way of life. This little incident, not really an incident, just a little error on Harry's behalf, but it brought back to Harry the day he walked around the building next door and found the air vent with the damaged damper. There would be more of those vents around the base of the building next door, their design is to allow the flow of air as in natural ventilation to the basement of the building, but in the in the event of a fire in the basement, then these dampers within the vent are controlled with a thermostatic device and will shut the damper when triggered.

Harry's mind back to that day and he remembered talking to the caretaker of the building who told Harry that there was no basement in that building. There must be a basement Harry thought, hence the ventilation ducts. He then remembered the double set of doors in the centre storeroom just outside his office, Harry got up from his desk and left his office to look inside the centre store, he went to the double doors and they were locked, reaching into his pocket for the master key to the cell that he had been handed by Malcolm Tate and inserting it into the lock and it turned smoothly and unlocked the doors. Harry opened fully both door leaves only to find another double set of doors set at four hundred millimetres back from the first set of doors, this was to allow for the wall thickness. Harry inserted his master key into the lock but although the key would go into the lock, it would not turn to unlock the doors. Harry made a mental note to find his set of hand picks and the lockaid tool that he had at home somewhere and bring them with him tomorrow to allow further exploration into the mysterious, next door basement. Harry then returned to his office and promptly forgot all about the basement and got back into his work, he was really enjoying this new job, no pressure here, Harry thought, as there was with his former role.

Harry had remembered to locate his lock picking tools from his little workshop he had in the garage and he placed them into the glovebox of his car in order to remember to take them to work with him tomorrow.

That evening following dinner, there was more news about more crime around the ACT, especially car theft, it was now the leading crime around Canberra. Harry thought, other than the politicians who were guilty of taking money under false pretences. Harry had called into the Statesman for a drink on his way home that afternoon and had bumped into an old colleague from his police days, Tony Strause, Tony had been a young twenty something constable when Harry was an 'about to retire sergeant' and he had quite a lot of time for Tony back then. Now Tony was and 'about to retire sergeant' at the age of fifty five and confided in Harry that he was setting up a private enquiry agency just for something to do, he gave Harry one of his new business cards and asked him not to show it around for a while until he had left the force. Harry had wished him luck and suggested they get together more often for a drink and a few yarns about the 'good old days'.

Back at work the next day and Harry had taken his lock picking gear, placed in a small bag, into his office for an exploration adventure later that day when everyone else in the office had left. As an afterthought he took the rechargeable torch, that he had discovered in his cupboard when he had first arrived, he searched for it's charger in every drawer and shelf that was in his office but to no avail, he was about to leave the office in search of a charger when he noticed that one was already plugged into a powerpoint near the door. 'Men's look' Val would say to him if he was at home looking for something, Harry thought, then grinned to himself.

It was three o/clock in the afternoon when the last person had left the cell and Harry was also about to leave and go home when the torch plugged into the charger reminded him of his intending adventure, he grabbed the bag containing the lock picks and also took the torch and headed to the centre storeroom. Removing his lockaid tool and a tensioner from the bag, he then attempted to pick the lock, he wasn't an expert at picking locks but he had enjoyed quite considerable success, that was not to be the case to day however, he had already spent about an hour on the lock when he decided that he would go into the carpentry workshop and find a cordless drill and a six millimetre drill bit, he had one last try and he unlocked the door. You couldn't even make this stuff up, Harry thought as he swung the operable door leaf in towards the pitch black of the mysterious basement.

Shining the torch through the doorway revealed a concrete masonry wall about one point eight meters from the doorway, a corridor Harry thought, the wall went from slab to soffit and was the entire width of the basement, to the right it went for about twelve metres then terminated at the end of the building, to the left it went about twenty five metres and also terminated at the end of the building, but then Harry could just see something along the wall to his left about twenty meters away that had caused a reflection, it looked like a door. Harry walked through the doorway to his left with the torch beam on the wall, as he approached the reflected item he saw that it was a door, not a normal door but a steel door. It was a flat door with two hinge straps, top and bottom running full width from the hinges on the left of the door, there was a single keyhole escutcheon on the right hand side approximately in the centre between the top and bottom of the door with a single latch lever.

Harry shone his torch on the door thinking that this is the end of my excursion, he took hold of the latch handle and pushed it down expecting it to be solid, the handle moved down, the latch was withdrawn inside the steel door allowing Harry to pull the door towards him, leaving the heavy door open. Harry walked cautiously through the doors opening shining his torch quickly from side to side and wishing that he had someone with him, Harry was feeling quite anxious, most likely because what he had found so far was totally unexpected. He was in another corridor and the walls here were also concrete masonry and painted a dark grey, the floor was smooth concrete and the ceiling was metal, pressed metal Harry guessed as he walked very slowly forward, the corridor abruptly ended with a sharp turn to the right and another door that was wide open, this door seemed to be the same as the door he had entered from the corridor. He was in some sort of reception room with a large barred window beside another door to his left.

Harry's torch gave a single flicker then went out without any other warning, the darkness was indescribable. Harry had made a big mistake when the light went out, he had turned around to look behind him, apparently a quite normal reaction when suddenly you are enveloped into darkness, nonetheless a big mistake for Harry as he did not now know which way he was facing. Harry put his hand into his side pocket to retrieve his phone, not there, Hmm it's on the desk he remembered, he held out his left arm fully stretched in front of him and walked slowly until he arm touched a wall, or something, he knew that he wanted to find the doorway that he had just entered which, according to Harry's inbuilt compass, meant following this wall to the left, slowly letting his fingers follow the wall until they came to a doorframe, he now knew exactly where he was, he was now leaving the reception area and into the short corridor that would lead to the first steel door, then he would go left and should then see the light from the storeroom that he had entered from, did he leave that door open? Anyway, he was doing just fine he thought, until he walked into something just below knee height which caused him to fall forward and over an object that really hurt his knees and his head made contact with what he thought was a low shelf.

Startled and bleeding from his head wound Harry felt around at what he seemed to be suspended on and after some time realised that it must be a toilet pan that his knees were now resting on and that it felt like a wash basin that he had struck with his head. He was lost, what a startling realisation it was to Harry, 'I'm fucking lost' he said to no one and Harry then started to feel frightened, he didn't want to keep walking in the dark because he had no idea of what he may walk into, go back! He thought, I must just now go back away from these things, trying to remember that he came through a door just before he fell, wrong fucking door he thought and grinned as he remembered for some strange reason a joke about a Chinese bookshop, 'Wong fukin bookshop', why would he think about such a stupid thing like that at a time like this, as he was feeling the wall with one hand but now putting his legs forward much more cautiously than before. Then Harry felt another doorway and after feeling all around it decided the door was open and that this must be the exit to the second corridor and he started to move much more confidently and quicker and he knew he must now go to the left of this doorway to reach the corner to the left, yes left, or was it right, no definitely left. Harry had to stop and regain his bearings if he could. He had come through the storeroom door and turned to the left, the first steel door was along that corridor on the right hand side and it led straight forward, then it turned to the right and another doorway, he went through this and then blackness,...think... think. How the fuck did I fall over a toilet, I must have gone to the right, there was a window and a door to the left, but no toilet.......I must have gone right. Wait...which way did I turn when the light went out, left or right...left or right.......any other situation you'd laugh,...fifty fifty, ok if I did turn to the right, when I found the wall I went to the left,....so now,... go right, keep going, keep going, keep going, like the breathalyser show, keep going, another door frame, the door is open, no go left, yes left, keep going, keep going keep going, another door frame, door is open,.......let, yes left,....light, there is

Max Barrington

light….walk to the light. He was at the store room and he was as shaky as a shit house rat, Harry was a wreck.

Harry went to the bathroom and got a shock when he saw his head, the blood had run down one side of his head onto his neck and onto his white shirt, fark me, unbelievable. Harry looked at this watch, it was almost seven o'clock. He went back to the store and to the double door in the corridor and closed them, he didn't lock them and then he closed the set of doors on the store side and locked these. He no longer had the torch and he decided that he must have dropped that when he fell, must get another torch he thought, two torches he decided as he made his way home.

'Overstayed at the pub' said Val, then seeing the blood on Harry's shirt, "My god Harry, what has happened to you, here sit here and I'll get something'.

'I'm fine…fine, really it's nothing, really I am good'

'Oh my god Harry, what is it what's going on', said Val whilst getting some water water and detol.

'I only tripped in the car park at the pub, some dick must have dropped his tow bar and I didn't see it'.

Harry was thinking, what a dumb thing to say, someone dropped his tow bar. It was the first thing that came to mind, fortunately Val must have been too concerned with all the blood on his shirt to realise what he had said. Val had bathed his cut, it wasn't bad at all, just one of those that tend to make a mess, they had dinner and watched a bit of television and went to bed, all back to normal. Except Harry could not sleep, what the fuck was in the basement next door to them, he was anxious for tomorrow to arrive so he could do some investigating.

It was a great spring Friday morning in Canberra, except it was bitterly cold and pissing down with rain, Harry's car was booked in for a service at the dealership in Phillip. He had dropped the car off and had decided to walk down to the Woden bus interchange where he would catch a bus into the city centre, civic as it was called.

As Harry approached the bus interchange he saw a police car and two constables were standing out of the car talking to three youths, meanwhile on the opposite side of the road stood about seven youth's jeering at the police and hurling abuse at them, 'fucking useless copper cunt' and 'get a fucking life you fucking morons'.

Harry could see that the two constables were very nervous and he wondered why they had not called for backup and then he realised that it was just a waste of time as these two police just jumped into their car and drove off.

Harry knew that in his day, all seven of the abusive youths would be at the lockup sporting broken ribs and bruised kidneys and would be pissing blood for a week, but they would never, ever hurl abuse at a police officer again. How things have changed.

As Harry was about to get off the bus in the civic centre, one of the youths that had been verbally abusing the police back where he had got on the bus at the interchange, had been travelling on the same bus as Harry and was also getting off at the same stop, as he walked past Harry, just as the bus was starting to brake for the stop. Harry pushed out his right leg and the youth, aided by the inertia of the stopping bus, went flying down the aisle and collided with the handrail at the front of the bus. The youth, bleeding profusely from his nose looked back to see who had tripped him, just as Harry had walked past him with a snigger.

The next day, Friday and it was starting to rain quite heavily and it looked like any plans for the weekend were, in a nutshell, fucked. Harry didn't even notice the weather, he drove to work oblivious to the rain and his cars climate control automatically adjusted its interior temperature to twenty two degree's Celsius, he drove into his basement car park and walked into his office and was onto Google to try to find out what was in the basement next door to him.

He had simply typed in the address as sixty five Northbourne Avenue Canberra and added history and it came up as Jolimont and went on to say that in 1920   a timber building was erected at the site of 65 Northbourne Avenue on the Corner of Alinga Street and bounded by Moore and Rudd Streets, the building was originally constructed in England in 1899 for the use at Jolimont Railway Station in Melbourne and then later transported to Canberra in 1920 and was known as the Jolimont Building, in 1946 the ACT Police had vacated their station in Acton and moved to the Jolimont Centre and remained there until 1966 when they moved into a dedicated constructed complex in London Circuit.

'Well, said Harry to himself, 'I never knew that'. Harry then realised that what he had become lost in the other night in the dark, must be the old ACT Police station prison cells. It seemed, from what Harry was reading that the building suffered fire damage in 1969 and was demolished in 1977, the building that stands there now was constructed in 1981. And by the looks of it, thought Harry, it was built on top of the old police prison cells, wow.

Roger knocked on Harry's door, 'Harry, we have a fire rated partition that needs replacing in the old CBS building, do we have to get that certified?'

'You do Roger, but you also need to make sure that the contractor who constructs the fire rated partition has the appropriate license for fire rated construction and, he will also have to use a tested system for the required FRL'.

'Thought as much Harry, can you designate a system for that, it's 60/60/60 FRL',

'I'll do that for you old son, how soon do you need it?'

'No rush Harry, tomorrow's good, can you certify that also?'

'Yep, I certainly can Roger', Harry wanted to ask Roger a few questions to see if he knew anything about the basement next door. 'Are you a true local Roger?'

'I was born in O'Connor, lived here all my life, why do you ask Harry?', Harry had suddenly decided against asking Roger about the basement next door. 'Just wondered, no reason mate', Harry ended the conversation.

That afternoon, once everyone had gone for the day, Harry took his new rechargeable torch from the charger that was indicating a full charge, he also made sure his mobile phone was in his pocket and fully charged, this would give him a spare light if the same thing happened to the new torch and a way to contact help if he needed to do so. Harry headed off to the centre store room, he had placed the things that were in front of the door on his last visit, back as he had found them and now it all looked undisturbed, he unlocked the storeroom side doors and entered the corridor and followed it down to the steel door, then into the next corridor, he was amazed with the new light, it was an LED and it lit the whole place up. He found the reception room where he was when the light had failed on his last excursion then he found the toilet that he had fallen over with the old torch lying in the toilet pan. He pulled the old torch from the pan and noticed that there was no water in the bottom, he instinctively reached across and pushed the button to flush the pan, once flushed he could hear the cistern refilling, interesting Harry thought that the water was still on and with that thought in mind looked for a light switch, there was one near the doorway and Harry flicked it on, he could hear a light starter somewhere above him then suddenly the room he was standing in was brightly lit up, 'unbelievable' Harry thought to himself, 'why the fuck didn't I try that the other day'. Harry flicked off his torch and now moved around and found more light switches in different areas.

There was a long corridor with prison cell doors staggered on each side there were four doors on one side and three on the other, Harry tried a couple of them to find them to be unlocked. Harry then went completely through the whole complex, he was looking for another way into the basement, there must be one, he was thinking and then found another steel door at the end of the cell's corridor, it was unlocked and it led into a stairwell, Harry flicked his torch back on as there was no light in the stairwell and he couldn't see a switch. The metal stairs went up to about half of the ceiling height onto a small landing and then turned to the left, Harry walked up the stairs his foot sounds echoed and seemed to be quite loud, he slowed down and placed his feet down more gently to avoid making any noise and then saw the doorway at the top of the stairs. The doors opening direction was away from him, Harry slowly turned the cylindrical door knob and gently pushed it, the door did not move, Harry turned off his torch and looked at the bottom of the door, there was no light emitting from the other side.

41 Max Barrington

Strange thought Harry, the only way in and out of here seems to be by our storeroom door, that can't be right.

Harry had thoroughly searched the prison cell area, it was not a very large area and he did not think that it was the full size of the building above, he could find no other entrance, but he did find what may once have been a roller shutter in an open area and he assumed that it was once a small car park area and possibly a ramp up to street level. Harry needed a compass to work out exactly where he was and thought that he would bring one next time, he had tried the one on his phone but he could not get any reception. It seemed that no one had been down here for quite some time but he was sure that the main entry to the cells was by the doorway at the top of the stairs, maybe it was situated within an airlock, that would be the reason for the lack of light under the door.

Harry had returned to his office, placed his torch back on charge and placed the old torch into the garbage bin along with the charger. Harry had gone directly home this night as he and Val were meeting up with old friends, Don and Kathy Freeman, for dinner at the Hellenic Cross Club. Val was waiting for him as he arrived there to tell him that the dinner had been cancelled as Don had been involved in an accident in his car and was in the Woden Valley hospital. Val had told Harry that apparently, Don's car was tee boned at an intersection when a stolen car went through a red traffic light as it was being chased by a police car and into poor old Don, but, according to Kathy, he is alright, just shook up a bit but his car is a write off.

'Fucking kids, I'll bet' said Harry taking off his jacket then quickly replacing it, 'come on, we'll go anyway I'll call a taxi'.

A Night Out

The taxi arrived within twenty minutes and they headed off towards Woden to the club. It was very busy and it was just as well that Val had not cancelled the table that she had booked and she had told the maitre'd, with his enquiring looks, that their friends are running late. It was a bottle of 'La Adeline' rosé for starters while they decided what to eat. A grilled halloumi for two was enjoyed as an entree which finished off the rosé, next they both chose the rib fillet on the bone served medium rare and they selected a bottle of Louis Jadot pinot noir.

It had been an excellent evening and they even had enough of a win on the pokies to cover their costs of dinner and drinks, that wouldn't have happened if the Freeman's had been with them, as they don't play the pokies.

After waiting for about ten minutes in the freezing cold for a taxi, they decided to walk around to the taxi rank opposite the shopping mall on Corinna Street. Almost at the taxi rank when a car travelling towards them at high speed attempted to turn left into the Melrose Drive access, the speed that the car was travelling was much too fast to negotiate the turn resulting in total loss of control of the vehicle. The vehicle rolled a number of times coming into contact with Val and Harry Croft.

'Time to wake up Harry, come on Harry, wake up', a soft voice was calling him, but he didn't even remember going to bed. Harry slowly opened his eyes to Val's voice, but it was not Val's voice, the voice was coming from a young lady in a dark blue, casual type of uniform of a Canberra hospital nurse.

'Well, good morning Mr Croft, how are you feeling?', the nurse in the blue uniform was asking.

' I'm....alrig....where, what is happening" said Harry starting to sit up.

'No, stay down, you're fine', said the nurse re adjusting Harry's drip line and pushing the 'assist' button at the same time.

'You were involved in an accident Harry but you are doing fine' she said as a nursing sister came into the room.

'Good afternoon Harry, how are you feeling, you have been in a coma for a little while, please don't try to get up, the doctor is on his way to see you, please just relax', the sister soothed.

'How, how long have I,......where is Val,.. is Val here somewhere', Harry was becoming distressed, 'where is Val, please go and get Val'.

'The doctor won't be long now, please just stay calm and try not to move your left arm' was the sister's soothing response.

Harry lay still, his mind was trying to put things back together, nothing was working, he was totally blank, it slowly started to come to him, the taxi rank and the speeding car, what happened, they saw the car start to turn and then it seemed to flip up in the air and then over and then......that was it, something must have gone wrong, his legs were hurting, he tried to move them, they moved but painful.

'Mr Croft,..' Said a voice with an Indian accent and Harry looked up to see a dark man wearing a pale blue top. 'My name is David Dharmani, how are you feeling Harry? you have been involved in an accident'.

'I'm not sure, but I want to know how my wife is', Harry was becoming very worried.

'I'm afraid your wife didn't make it, sadly she died early this morning I am sad to have to inform you'.

Harry did not hear any more words from the doctor or from the nurses, he was just in total shock, his thoughts were that maybe they made a mistake and it was someone else but not Val, no no no not Val, it can't be, why, but why why and how, it can't be right. He could feel the tears welling in his eyes, he could see her smiling and fussing about him as she always did, he always said 'what will I do without you' and now it's happened, can't be right, please let it be a mistake, he wanted Val to here with him.

It was three weeks until Harry could be released from hospital due to a hip fracture, his other minor bruises and lacerations had all cleared but it would be another three weeks yet until he could get around more normal and at three months until he would be totally normal. Harry was not looking forward to going home as the first thing he would see there would be signs of Val when she had left with him to catch a taxi to dinner, it was going to be painful and he knew it, but Harry had a much bigger challenge on his mind. Whilst in the hospital, Harry had many visitors and most made him feel very sad whenever they mentioned Val. Harry could not attend Val's funeral as he was confined to a bed but he watched it over and over on the television in his hospital room, first the live service and then the recording.

Amongst Harry's visitors was his boss Malcolm Tate, who told Harry that everything was fine and he still had his job just as soon as he was able. Other visitors were ACT Police officers, Detective John Simms and Detective Sergeant Barry Upfield to take a statement from Harry about what he could remember, which was not very much at all, Harry had thought about it for hours and hours while lying in his bed about what he did remember, what was the last thing he saw but it was all to no avail. The police filled in the blanks for him, one youth aged fourteen, and two youths aged sixteen, the fourteen and one of the sixteen year old's are brothers, were travelling in a BMW that was stolen from the suburb of Hughes about an hour before the accident, the vehicle travelling south on Corinna Street Phillip at approximately one hundred and forty kilometres per hour when the driver, the fourteen year old youth was driving the car, attempted to turn into the Melrose Drive connector and lost control of the vehicle. The three youths were unharmed in the accident and all three fled from the scene, video surveillance was viewed from three adjacent buildings to where the accident occurred resulting in positive identification of all three youths and they were all apprehended two days following the accident.

The youths appeared in the ACT Children's Court charged with Manslaughter, break and enter of premises and theft of a motor vehicle, all were remanded on bail to appear for trial at a later date to be advised.

A shattered Harry had returned to his home and his job and tried to get on with life, his friends could not understand why he had not sold the house with memories and had really retired to somewhere away from Canberra, Harry's response was always 'soon, very soon'. Harry had maintained contact with Sergeant Barry Upfield as he had also been a friend of his late father Ted, (Tiger) Upfield who had been a colleague of Harry's back in his police days, but for a specific reason, Harry wanted to know when the youths would be attending court.

Things were good at work and it did not take Harry long to get his total mobility back, he had brought to his office on the day of his return, his old prismatic compass and his not so old DME, a laser measurement device. He again later that afternoon visited the adjoining building's basement but this time he did a rough sketch as he went from the storeroom door to the extent of the basement and terminated at the stairs leading up to level one of the building next door.

Returning to his office he went to his plan file cabinet and found the drawings for the Jolimont Centre that were kept as part of the ongoing maintenance for location descriptions. After two hours of transferring his rough sketch to drawing film, he could place it on top of the ground floor plan of the Jolimont Centre to form an underlay and locate precisely where the basement stairs rose to the ground floor of the building. According to Harry's calculations, the stairs would be near the Rudd Street end of the building next to a service duct. Harry looked closely at the drawing and made some notes about the service duct and took some measurements. The next day Harry contacted the Caretaker of the Jolimont Centre and made an appointment to meet with him as soon as practicable to inspect an item in the service duct at grid A section 4, the caretaker told Harry anytime, just drop in whenever it suits. Harry had gone to the Jolimont Centre at eleven o'clock that morning, taking the drawings with him for reference and also to make it look a bit official.

The caretaker was holding the end of Harry's tape and assisting Harry to make measurements near the service duct. The caretaker had the utmost respect for Harry since his first visit there when condensation was pooling on a section of tiled flooring and Harry had solved the problem within a matter of hours. Harry had found the entrance to the stairwell was closed in on all four sides by what seemed to be 200 series concrete masonry blocks which just did not make any sense to him, the caretaker told Harry that he had a full set of construction drawings in his office if he needed to check something.

'You're welcome to them Harry, I have never used them, I salvaged them from an old cabinet that was being thrown out'

'Thanks, that would be great if I could take them to my office and get them digitised then I will return them' Harry responded as he rolled up the full set of construction drawings for transit to his office.

Harry was pouring over the drawing in his office and checking each variation as it appeared and then discovered that the existing basement was to have been converted to subfloor parking but it was found that the entrance ramp encroached on the bounding property. It also showed a plan for the demolition of the existing cells and rooms but also showed a very expensive system of replacing these with structural columns and due to cost blowouts, it seems it was all scrapped and that the place was basically sealed off.

Armed with his new information, later that afternoon Harry again visited the basement but this time with some tools to enable the removal of some locks. The prison cell locks were Chubb custodial series mortice locks and Harry guessed that they would have all been 'keyed alike' so that only one key was required to be carried by the officer on duty to access the cells. The other three locks were Chubb vestibule locks that were on the interjoining steel doors and one set of 590 lock cylinders from the doors adjacent to the storeroom doors. These locks Harry took to a Locksmith located in the Fyshwick industrial suburb of Canberra. He instructed the Locksmith to recombinate the five cell locks and to key them alike, the vestibule and the 590 cylinders locks the same.

Harry had driven into the boarding town of Queanbeyan one evening to meet an old mate at Walshes pub, Nick Obodden was from Russia and had been working as a plastering contractor and a roof tilling contractor with his two brothers and four cousins in the ACT for as many years as Harry could remember. You really needed to be on the *right* side of these guys, Harry remembered as he walked into Walshes.

'Dobryy den Harry' shouted a heavy voice, 'your putting on the weight brother'

'Good day to you also' returned Harry, grabbing Nick's outstretched hand. Nick was a very athletic looking man at about fifty years old now, Harry guessed, but if you knew him well he was a good friend, you couldn't be his enemy because, as he had told Harry, 'all my enemies are dead'.

'You remember Bear'? Nick said as a giant of a man with the wildest unkempt dark reddish coloured beard walked up looking inquisitive.

'That's not that scrawny little prick that was your 'gofor' a few years back?' Then Harry started to realise that it was indeed one of Nick's very young cousins holding out his hand towards him.

'Gee Harry, you have changed a bit since I last saw you' said Bear, 'except you've got fatter, a lot fucking fatter actually', laughed Bear, c'mon over here it's my shout, and he ordered three schooners of VB.

'Vomit Bomb, be fucked' said Harry, 'get me a carton'.
The three of them sat at a table in the noisy bar and Nick came straight to the point and asked Harry what it was he wanted because the only time he ever comes to see him is when he wants something.

Magnus McCallum owned the Canberra real estate company known as Capital Real Estate and Auctions and was based in the suburb of Manuka.

'Certainly no lower than one point two million Harry, and I would imagine that it would sell fairly quickly, within two to three weeks, I would imagine' Magnus suggested as he walked through Harry's house.

'It won't be going on the market for that Magnus, try for another four hundred thousand and you can have the listing, I will still expect a contract on it within a month', Harry knew that this old Scott's prick wanted an easy sale for himself, 'and I'm not paying for advertising either you thieving old Haggis'.

Harry had approached Magnus at his office seeking a three month rental residential unit property, preferably furnished. He had also asked Magnus to appraise his home in Curtin and then form a marketing plan.

Magnus had found him a delightful, two bedroom unit on the third floor on Manuka Circuit in Kingston, just around the corner from the 'Kingo', one of Harry's old haunts. It was a fully furnished unit and had a lock up garage.

Harry had cleaned out his house and sold all his memories. His house was sold within three days for one point five million dollars, Harry said farewell to the old home that he and Val had shared for so many years and he tearfully turned his back on it, what a sad and cruel ending it had been thanks to the thoughtless and selfish actions of young irresponsible adults.

These 'young adults' as Harry had referred to himself, were they victims of society? They were brought up in an age where their parents did not believe in any form of punishment, and in fact, if these children were punished then the police could charge the parents for assault. The teachers in the schools that these children attended could not deliver any punishment against the students other than to send them from the class, otherwise, they also could be charged with assault. The police also had very little authority against the youth and were openly and publicly mimicked by these youths, if these people were arrested by the police there was always a good chance that charges would be brought about towards the police for abuse or false arrest by public defenders. The children could not be harmed, their parents would not get them inoculated for various diseases for fear it may harm them in some way or another, it wasn't the child's fault that they suffered from behavioural disorders. The parents would openly abuse the school teachers and accuse them of preventing their children from being responsible and educated young adults.

It was a great Saturday and a great drive out to Gunning to visit Val's sister Sonia and her husband Lex. Sonia was just a little older than Val and was a veterinarian and operated around the area, Lex her husband was more of an odd job man around the area, he had a tractor and slasher and a bobcat and other bits of machinery and did all sorts of work around the neighbouring properties.

Before moving to Gunning they had lived in the Canberra suburb of Duffy in quite an elite house on Eucumbene Drive, Sonia had a vet practice attached to the side of the house and Lex had a subcontract concrete truck that he drove. Lex was an American and a former US Navy seal and just loved fighting. Harry had pulled Lex out of the Canberra police lockup more times than he can remember and Lex was always indebted to him, as he said.

It was Lex's drinking and fighting that had caused them to move to Gunning and live on a property that was away from pubs as it was only a matter of time before Lex killed someone. On this day Harry had a beer with Lex and asked him if he could arrange a 10mm syringe and 100ml of xylazine and not to let Sonia know about it.

Lex told Harry that she left that sort of shit laying around everywhere and went to find some then and there, he was back within a minute with the syringe and a 500ml bottle of xylazine, saying that it seemed to be the smallest bottle of the shit that she keeps, Harry quickly placed it into his car then returned to finish his beer with Lex.

Sonia soon came out from whatever she had been doing in the house to join the boys in a beer.

'Seems you're busy inside there Sonia', Harry mused.

'Just getting three of the best looking rump steaks ready for dinner Harry and fixing the bed in the guest's room for you' said Sonia with a look of 'don't argue with me'.

Harry was expecting it and did not put up any resistance and merely went to his car and grabbed the carton of Great Northern stubbies that he knew that Sonia and Lex drink.

'You're a champ Harry', both Sonia and Lex said in unison, 'but you shouldn't have'.

Harry had replaced all the locks back into the cell doors and communicating steel doors in the basement of the building next door to his storeroom, he had also checked the plumbing in each of the cells to ensure that the toilet pans were flushing and that the wash basin taps were still tamper proof. The old watch house cells were in great condition considering their age, the locks on the doors worked exactly as they should and the acoustic barriers around the cell doors was remarkably intact, Harry had brought down a small radio and had turned it on to full volume and placed it into a cell, he had then close the cell door to find that the sound from the radio was barely audible, good.

The drive down the Clyde mountain was always quite enjoyable to Harry, but when you finally got to the bottom of it and past all the bends, you expected to be on the coast and it was quite a while until the Clyde river came into view and you were finally there, then through Batemans Bay onto Tomakin, a quiet little town on the beach that was once called Sunpatch with all the streets being named after Canberra suburbs. Colin Chrisp had been a fellow sergeant back in the day, although Col was a senior sergeant and quite often an acting inspector, but he did not want to be an inspector and failed every time they gave him the examination to become one. Col was a great mate and a great copper, his only downfall was that he was always finding things that weren't yet lost, he was a procurer, if you wanted something then Col could most likely acquire it for you, but it was always the rule not to ask where it had come from. Even the top dogs at the station would ask Col if there might be a chance at getting a supply of the latest handcuffs that had just come out as their budget was blown out, Col would find a shipment of them and they would become ACT police issue.

Harry had 'self invited' himself to visit Col and his wife Helen, when he had called on the phone, Helen had answered and when he had hinted about coming down for a spell of fishing and maybe a few beers, Helen had said.

'For fucks sake Harry, you don't have to ask, just come on down, you know where we are, we haven't moved, it will be good to get Col out of the fucking house for a bit, he needs motivation Harry, the sooner you get here and the longer you stay the better.'

'See you tomorrow, just after lunch' Harry had replied.

'Good, we'll all go to the sporties for lunch, I'd better wash my hair'.

They all enjoyed a great lunch at the club and a great 'get back together' then continued drinks at Col and Helen's place just down from the club. It was too rough and windy to take out their big boat onto the ocean the next morning so they all went in their smaller, 18ft boat on the river to do a bit of fishing and drinking and eating great oysters from the banks of the Tomaga River. And that night enjoyed a feed of flathead that they had caught in the river that day. Helen had gone to bed at around nine o'clock and Harry and Col had opened a bottle of port and had followed the tradition of 'throwing the top away', which of course mean't, to drink the whole bottle.

'What is it that you are after Harry'.

'What do you mean Col?'

'You know full well what I fucking mean Harry, don't be fucking stupid man, and whatever the fuck you are planning, I do not know and I do not want to know, but be fucking careful Harry, you are not a young man any longer and whatever it is Harry, think about it and plan it properly. Now let's get out the chess board Harry'

They were on their third chess game and had reverted back to beer as the port had diminished totally and out of the blue Harry said.

'Nine millimetre Glock'.

'Ammo too?' Asked Col.

'Don't think that I would really need any ammo Col'.

'Harry, you know the old saying son, if you are prepared to point it, be prepared to use it, a box of fifty'.

'Handcuffs?'

'I only have the old swing type, unless you can wait for a couple of weeks. How many?'

'Four, should be enough, I don't mind the old swingers' replied Harry with a giggle.

'No worries', confirmed Col, 'we can collect that tomorrow if you like, anything else?'

Harry could not believe this guy, he had a storage unit in Moruya, which was about sixteen kilometres south of Tomakin, we arrived there early the next morning and the guy at the storage facility said hello boss to Col. After awhile Harry had discovered that Col actually owned the storage business, what a clever front if it ever got busted how would Col know who the prick was that was storing illegal shit in there. Harry wondered how many other storage lockers Col had his special goods stored in.

Harry was now on a two week break from work and had just arrived at Sydney's Mascot airport in preparation for his flight with Qatar Airways to Palma. After the long, 29hour flight and two stops combined it was good to get to the Hotel Victoria Gran Meliá. Harry checked into his room and then went down to the Terraza restaurant where he enjoyed a black Angus rump steak and a bottle of Can Axartell pinot noir. Harry had an early night so he could be up early for the ferry trip to the Balearic Islands on the northeastern side of Palma. It was a seven hour trip to get there by ferry and he would be staying at the Hotel Catalonia Mirador des Port.

Another long day for Harry and he was relaxing at the bar with a cold beer wondering where to eat that evening. Harry was picked up at the hotel the next morning by the real estate agent who took him to see the house that Harry had found on the web in Cala en Bosch-Serpentona. It was about an hour's drive to the property and Harry just loved it from the moment that he had seen it on the internet. The agent had said the price was £470.000 and Harry offered £400.000 with an instant settlement.

The agent had made some telephone calls and returned to Harry and said 'Trato' meaning deal in Spanish.

'Going to have to learn this lingo' Harry nodded to the estate agent while shaking his hand on the deal, not bad he thought, seven hundred and sixty grand Australian dollars, still left him another seven hundred and fifty to buy a boat and stuff.

The estate agent then took Harry to the Banco Santander in Cittadella, the closest city to where Harry had just bought his house. Here Harry opened a bank account and transferred one point four million dollars into his new account and then transferred the deposit for the house to the estate agent with the balance to follow. The estate agent took Harry back to his hotel in Des Port where he insisted on buying dinner for Harry that night. The estate agents name was Marco, at about thirty years of age, Harry guessed, he looked pretty fit and was extremely polite, he also spoke very good English and told Harry that many British people now lived around Palma and that English was a popular language, so there was no rush for Harry to learn Spanish as most people now speak English.

Marco could not do enough for Harry and told him that when he moves over to live here, that he will meet Harry and help him to move in, not much to do anyway as the house he bought

Max Barrington

is furnished and he would organise the 'residence permit' the only thing that a foreigner requires to buy a house and live permanently in Spain.

Harry had returned to Canberra just in time for the Trial of the three youths who had been charged with manslaughter and theft. Barry Upfield had given Harry the 'heads up' on the court day although he had said to Harry that it was no good to him as it was a closed children's court and he would not get entry. Harry did not need entry to the court, Harry had only needed to know how many juveniles would be attending court that morning as it was a fair bet the the number attending would also be the same number leaving, as rarely were any juveniles held over in custody, it was always either a bond or suspended sentence.

Barry had told him that there would be five youths attending court that morning, the three charged with the manslaughter of Harry's wife and two others that were driving the stolen car that actually tee boned Harry's friend

Don Freeman, who was now a total paraplegic and living like a vegetable, and his wife, Kathy had recently suffered a heart attack due to the strain that had been recently placed on her as she tried to cope with her husband's condition.

Harry had contacted Nick just as soon as he had received the information from Barry and had told him, simply, 'five'.

Harry had listened to the news later that evening in his unit whilst eating a Pizza Hut pizza and drinking a Carlton drought stubbie. One of the boys convicted of manslaughter was placed on a two year good behaviour bond due to his young age. Another of the boys was given a five year prison sentence but wholly suspended on the youth being under parental care and the usual reporting to youth welfare officers due to his age of 17, the remaining boy who had previously offended was given a six year suspended sentence with similar conditions. They had killed an innocent person who just happened to have been there.

The other two boys who had been convicted of car theft both received two year good behaviour bonds. They had maimed an innocent man for life and had caused his wife to suffer a heart attack which she was unlikely to recover from.

What a fucking poor excuse of a justice system, it is not a justice system, these kids have no remorse, they have no respect nor feeling, and they could not care fucking less about what they have done, the lives they have destroyed, the hurt they have created and the pain, the pain that will never go away for so many people, but the courts don't give a fuck, the twenty year old psychologist who looked at and analysed the offences that these 'children' had committed had convinced the judge that they were unlikely to reoffend. How the fuck would she know and what dickhead of a judge would believe her, well fuck me, Harry thought.

Justice

Back at work and Harry had been very busy. Whilst he had been away much had happened and required a fair bit of input from Harry to get things into the 'outbox' and having done that he could now look at the other job he had at hand. Nick had sent Harry four addresses, in one of the addresses he had added the number '2', that would be the brothers thought Harry. Nick and four of his fellow 'bikie' mates had watched on the day of the court case for five youths exiting the court with their parents and then following them until they reached their respective homes and had recorded the addresses. Nick had guessed Harry's motive and had told him that the supply of each address was as far as they would go, no further, stated Nick.

Harry did not waste any time and started on the addresses one by one, his job gave him plenty of cover to be doing building inspections and or certifications so his absence was not going to be noticed. It was a simple thing to follow each youth in the morning to either their school or college, in either car or bus or walking as in the case of the younger brother of the two boys. Then the plan was to take each youth, one by one each afternoon in the same week which would take him exactly five days, just enough time to make it work, any longer could cause problems.

It was three ten on Monday afternoon when the first of the five was intercepted by Harry just as he had planned it, he had chosen the exit of an underpass and as the boy had walked out of the underpass, Harry, wearing a suit and displaying his old and out of date police badge, he stepped from his white Toyota Camry, just as the police were using, and called the boy over to him and then told him that he needed to speak with him at the police station, then simply opened the back door of the car. Harry had 5ml of xylazine loaded in the syringe that he held out of site in his hand that also displayed his badge and injected it into the youth's backside as he entered the car, he then followed by pushing the youth into the car and closing the door simultaneously, the startled scream would have been undetected and should any bystander have witnessed the whole operation, it would have looked like a normal police arrest taking place.

It was just too easy, Harry had in the back of his car the sixteen year old who had been with the brothers the night that Harry's wife had tragically died, he had gone out like a light and lay half and half on the back seat and the floor. Harry quickly slipped a pair of cuffs onto the youth with both his arms behind his back, just guessing with the xylazine dosage Harry estimated about thirty minutes before he may start to regain consciousness.

It was just on four pm when Harry drove down the ramp and through the roller shutter at his maintenance cell workshop and parked as close as he could get to the centre store room, he did a quick check to ensure that every one had left for the day the quickly dragged the youth from the car to the store room then through to the Jolimont basement doors which Harry had left purposely unlocked in order to get through quickly and then down the corridor to the first steel door.

It was at this point that Harry had realised that he had forgotten to bring the lock up keys with him, he had left them in the car. If he left the youth here on his own, he may regain consciousness in the short period that it would take Harry to go back to his car and retrieve the keys, he could not chance that, The steel doors also had a sliding bolt and a hasp to accommodate a padlock on the exterior side of the door and Harry quickly unlocked one handcuff and removed from the youths arm then placed it through the padlock hasp the quickly headed back to his car. As Harry exited the store room and headed towards his car he came to an abrupt halt, there was another car parked next to his in the basement car park.

'There you are Harry' said a cheerful Malcolm Tate, 'just dropped in to see how you were getting along with the backlog, looks like you are certainly putting the hours in old chap, are you coping OK?'

'Good to see you Mal', Harry said whilst trying to compose himself, and thinking fast, ' just came back to get my DME for an inspection tomorrow, I thought I would do it on my way in seeing that I live fairly close by to the site'.

'I just dropped off a memory stick for Veronica, I left it on her desk, it's a new monthly report format for head office', anyway I'd better keep going and let you get home Harry, see you later'.

'Yeah Mal, and thanks for your concern, keep in touch mate'.

Harry felt sick, he had messed up big time, and all his well laid out and time consumed plans had all just gone out of the door. He had never even considered the fact that someone could arrive here after hours and catch him out so easily. Harry knew that if he had not had the keys to the lock up in his car he may well have been caught in the act of imprisoning this youth. As it has turned out it is a good lesson learned, he will in the future lock all doors behind him so that if someone should arrive unannounced then they can't follow him into the lock-up, he would also acquire and install a small wireless camera somewhere in the basement car park tomorrow and connect it to his phone, that should solve those hiccups.

The youth was still slumped against the steel door, hanging with one arm from the hasp, Harry unlocked him from the hasp and then opened the steel door, dragged the youth through it then closed and locked the door behind him, 'no more surprises, Harry thought as he started to shake from the shock of almost getting caught then he turned on the corridor light.

What would he have done, he was thinking, he had been totally unprepared, caught out in total. He would have had to kill Malcolm, it would be the only way and then put his body in the lock-up somewhere, and then Harry realised that he didn't even have the Glock with him to shoot Malcolm with, had it got to that stage, 'must be getting past it old son, maybe nearly time to retire' he said to himself as he dragged the youth into the nearest cell that contained a bed, mattress, table, chair, stainless steel toilet bowl and wash basin. The youth had started to wake up and looked in sheer terror at Harry, he then started to become composed and looked around, in an arrogant voice he said 'What the fucks happening, where am I, is this prison?'

Harry, very calmly said to him while removing the handcuffs, 'Certainly is son, the judge had a rethink and gave you life', Harry laughed as he walked from the cell and then locking it said, 'Good luck'! The youth's screams and abuse were silenced as the door slammed shut. Harry removed the youths school bag from his car and went through it and removed anything relating to him then disposed of the bag in a hopper at the Manuka shops on his way home, exercise books were put through Harry's shredder at his unit and textbooks were dropped into Lake Burley Griffin, one down and four to go.

On reflection of what he had just done, and more to the fact to condone his own actions within himself, Harry knew that he had not physically harmed the boy in any way. He knew that by now the boy was becoming scared and that before very long, maybe five to seven days, the boy would become remorseful. These kids who are offending are aged anywhere between twelve and sixteen, so they were born around the just past 2000 mark. Physical punishment was banned in the ACT schools in 1988, NSW was 1990, SA in 1991 and Vic the earliest in 1985.

By 2006 all types of physical punishment was banned in both public and private schools. The prison population in Australia in 2012 was 29,400. In the year 2022 it had climbed to 40,600, the average age of prisoners is almost equal to the amount of years from 1988 to 2022 being 35.9 years of age.

Once the discipline in schools ceased, so did the respect from teenage children towards adults in general, meaning school teachers, police and parents. In the 1970s and '80s children referred to teachers as either sir or madam, miss or mrs, it is now a first-name basis or a nickname. Family members were called uncle or aunty, mothers were also known as mum, not by their Christian name, as with fathers. In today's society, a mother can be described as a 'birthing person' How gross is that?

In 1990 Australia ratified the United Nations 'Convention on the Rights of a Child'. In doing so the Australian Government agreed to prevent the harm or mistreatment of children, children are now defined in Australia as being under the age of 18. Sadly for Australia, the different states have different laws with respect to the discipline of children. Harry knew only too well what a ruler behind the knee, delivered by a Catholic Nun, felt like, as with six cuts on the fingertips of both hands from a flexible cane that was accurately wielded by a teacher in high school, or a leather strop that father kept for such occasions, not to mention the slap from mother either across the face or applied with great force on the calves of the legs. 'We had a deterrent in those days' thought Harry.

Harry had collected the other four youths in a similar method without too many minor obstacles, one was when two of the youth's friends had attempted to free him from Harry's custody and Harry had pretended to call for a backup with a paddy van, that seemed to scare them off. The situation now was that all five youths occupied all five cells in the old police lock up and it had taken five days to get them. It was by Wednesday that the media was reporting the disappearance of the first youth taken by Harry, his parents had simply thought that he may have just run away from home and blaming the repercussions from the trauma of appearing in court over a minor incident in the last week. Harry did not think that the death of his wife was a minor incident and remarks like this from the parents just demonstrated how incapable and irresponsible they were at being parents.

The youths had been left in the cells in the darkness with only water to drink from the basin. Harry had been taking loaves of bread down to the lock-up and had been placing two slices through the communicating hatch of the door, the sniffling and crying that he heard from each of them moved him emotionally and caused Harry to question himself on his quest for punishment but he convinced himself that no harm would befall the children, children that's a joke thought Harry, although, after three days in the cell, they were starting to sound like children, must be working thought Harry as they no longer seemed to have the attitude of 'you can't hurt me mister' and they had all actually stopped calling him a 'cunt' which Harry was pleased about as it was a word that disgusted him.

He was pretty sure that they didn't know that the others were also in cells beside them. Harry had thought that it may seem worse to each as an individual to think that they were the only ones in the prison, rather than form a bond and gain strength through unity, it best he thought to keep them isolated.

On the following Monday following Harry's capture of the offending youth's, Harry had placed his formal resignation to the company's HR Manager   Joshua Benthall, to take place in two weeks from the date of notice.

'Hello, ..Harry, it's Joshua here, the HR Manager'.

'Who, sorry...', joked Harry, he just could not help himself.

'Joshua, the HR manager' Joshua repeated,

'Ah yes, Josh, what is that I can do for you'.

'It's about your resignation Harry, just wondered why you might be leaving, maybe there is something more that the company could do for you, perhaps more money or a company car'.

'Josh, my dear Josh, if it were a case of more money you would be much too late, as an HR manager you need to keep in touch with your employees, not just when they tell you they are going to leave. It is your role to maintain communication with your people and develop a relationship with each and every one of them so that you will know if there exists any dissatisfaction in any form amongst them. Once they submit the resignation it is usually the end Josh and once you start losing too many of the good hands, then your position may be in danger' then Harry said farewell to Josh, 'yet another lesson for you to learn Josh, and don't forget that you do not stop learning until you are dead, Goodbye Joshua'. Harry hung up the telephone.

On the Thursday prior to Harry's last day with the company, Harry visited the boys in the cells, they were a wreck, each and every one of them seemed that they accepted the fact that they were here to die, Harry opened each access hatch on each door and said in a loud voice so that they could all hear him,

'Today is Thursday, you have been here for a mere two, to almost three weeks, it was only about forty years ago that men in Australia were placed in cells as these for the same crimes that you have committed and left in there for the term of their lives. I do not solely blame you for the crimes you have committed but rather the system, the society but more importantly, your parents. You will be set free in five days, consider yourselves lucky, when you leave here I know you will be different, tell your friends and your families what it had been like to have been here, if only for a short few weeks. I don't think any of you will want to come back and do it again. You may consider behaving like a human once you have been released. Harry then closed all the hatches just as the boys had started to shout out to each other and the room became silent again.

It was Harry's final Friday and luncheon was planned at the Marble and Grain restaurant on Mort Street, just a two block walk from the office. Harry had packed up last week and had vacated his unit, he had been living at the Meriton Suites for the last four days and was due to fly to Palma this evening. He had sold his car to a dealer and it was being collected from the basement car park at two pm that afternoon. At one thirty, following lunch Harry farewelled everyone and said he would send a postcard from the Gold Coast, he told Veronica that he would leave his keys on her desk at the office, together with his garage remote. Harry had also left an envelope on Veronica's desk that contained two Chubb keys and another standard key with a brief letter stating.

Veronica,

could you please contact the police and advise them that the five missing Canberra youths can be found in the old police cells of the Jolimont building.

These are the access and prison cell keys that they will need to release them. They were all in a very good condition when last seen on Thursday.

Kind Regards, Harry.

The police sergeant read Harry's note twice before he called for a backup at the Jolimont centre. He and the constable with him took the lift up to the ground level of the maintenance cell and walked to the main entrance of the Jolimont centre next door and they waited for backup. Detective Senior Sergeant Barry Upfield and his partner Detective Constable John Simms arrived as backup with another two uniformed police. Barry read Harry's letter and although he was confused he managed a grim grin, and then all six police officers went into the main entrance of the Jolimont centre. The caretaker was soon found and was told to lead the police to the basement to which he responded that there was no basement. Upfield told a uniformed constable to arrest the janitor and ordered a complete search of the ground floor to find the basement entrance, he then called for more backup.

With the search underway, the backup arrived and with it senior inspector David Prattman, Upfield handed Harry's note to Prattman.

'Where's the basement?' Prattman asked Upfield.

'Can't find it, the janitor said there is no basement', replied Barry Upfield. 'I've got him detained in the divvy outside'.

Prattman went outside to the police van to talk to the janitor and then told him he was free to go, Prattman then told Barry Upfield to check with the cell office where the letter had come from and ask them where the basement is, apparently, he said that the cell maintained the Jolimont centre so they should know.

'I've never heard of any basement other than this', said Veronica, 'but, let me check with the other guys' and she gave them all a buzz on the intercom and asked them all to come to her office as a matter of urgency as the police are waiting here. They all came around to Veronica's office and as soon as she mentioned the Jolimont basement, Roger said, 'I think that I might know where that is, but it's locked, or should be' and he escorted everyone out of Veronica's office and down to the storerooms area near the basement car park and he opened the centre store room with his key. They all walked in and Roger showed them directly to the double doors at the back and opened them both inward revealing the other set of double doors that opened outward, Roger tried the handle of the doors and demonstrated that they were locked.

Barry took the standard type of key from Harry's envelope and tried it in the door, he was able to unlock the double doors and then he pushed them both open revealing a very dark corridor, In fact, it was black, the only light was coming from the store room where they were all standing, 'Torch anyone' called Barry Upton and two of the four uniformed police came forward with torches from their tools belts. Barry took one of the torches and went through into the corridor and looked to his right where the corridor came to an end.

'This way' said John Simms as he was shining the other constable's torch to the left and down the corridor to another door that could just be seen. They all reached the door and Barry tried one of the Chubb keys in it and it worked, he unlocked the door and they fumbled in through the door, Barry called a halt and told the maintenance cell workers that they would no longer be required at this stage and that the police will want to talk to them later or tomorrow.

Barry shone his torch around but it was John who found the light switch and turned on the lights, they followed the corridor up to where it turned and discovered the the next steel door, the same Chubb key also opened this door and they all passed into the anteroom with the large window looking down another corridor with two cell doors to one side and three cell doors to the other. Barry walked up to the first cell door and tried the same Chubb key, it would not enter the lock, the other Chubb key unlocked the cell and a scream was heard within the dark cell. The light switch adjacent to the cell door was soon found and turned on revealing a youth just standing there looking confused, he mumbled something about how he had been waiting for them and then started crying uncontrollably and asking for his mother. They then unlocked the remaining cell doors to find the five boys all safe but very shaken up and none were feeling well, ambulances were called and the cars parked in the basement car park were moved to make way for them. Amazingly all five youths that had been missing for nearly three weeks had been found alive.

Harry had been shown by one of his neighbours how to brew and keg beer at his new home, his other neighbour wanted to show him how to make wine but Harry decided that beer would be enough for him, although he did admit that the neighbours wine had a very good taste, a very nice burgundy he thought.

Harry had now been back on the island for three months and had heard very little from Australia, the bits of news that he did get did not mention much about the ACT. Harry did not have internet on the island as he did not want to become addicted to it as many people his age tend to do and, anyway who gives a shit about the ACT. He knew he was safe here from the police as Spain has no extradition treaty with Australia, that's why he chose Spain, sure he got homesick and missed watching the NRL but there was plenty to do here, or nothing if thats the way it suits you. Harry's house had a great pool with a huge outside living area and it was a big home with four bedrooms and three bathrooms, much too big for just him but he knew the kids would come for a visit one day.

He had just finished kegging a brew of beer into three nineteen litre kegs and was enjoying his third schooner when a voice called out to him. The home was very secure with a high fence that surrounded the entire property and had a secure double steel bar gate that was securely fixed to the high stone wall, the garage door was always closed and locked,

'Harry, are you here?.....Harry'

'Who is it?' Asked Harry

'Me, Nick, Nick Obodden....'

'Fuck me' called out Harry with glee in his voice, 'you are fucking kidding me mate, what the fuck are you doing here'.

'Long story Harry, but let's have a beer first mate' Nick said looking through the fence at Harry's half finished schooner on the table. Harry went and got his key to let Nick in, he was so happy to see a friend from Australia, it had only been three months but it did seem much longer, Harry grabbed a cold schooner glass from the outdoor fridge beside the kegerator and poured Nick a coldie.

'Cheers Harry', Nick said as the beer glass went to his lips, 'my god, that is good, very good Harry'.

Nick had parked his somewhat large bag on the ground next to the outdoor table and now sat down on a chair next to the table and Harry.

'What a surprise Nick, gee it is good to see you mate, are you going to stay for a bit?' Harry asked, hoping that he was going to stay.

'Mate, if you don't mind and can handle some bad company, then I'd love to stay for a while, like a month or so if that's ok?'.

'As long as you want to mate........'.

'I'll pay my way' interjected Nick, 'I'm not here to bludge on you Harry'.

'I couldn't give a fuck if you did mate, but, tell me....why are you here?' Harry asked Nick.

'The same reason you are here mate', grinned Nick.

'I do not want to know', so what's all the news', said Harry taking Nicks and his glass to refill them.

'That's a nice drop of beer Harry'.

'It's home brew, believe it or not, the bloke next door, whose name I can't pronounce, showed me how to make it and got me started'. Harry went on to tell Nick about the other neighbour who made a good wine, he told him about the good fishing, the cheap, but excellent beef that was available and the general run of the place and he once again told Nick how happy he was to see him and that he could stay as long as he wanted.

Nick did tell Harry it concerned him that he was so easy to find here, in fact, Nick had said, it seemed that everyone knew the new 'Guiri' in town and I had no worries getting directions. Harry said that he wasn't really in hiding as he knew the Australian coppers could not touch him out here, and besides, Harry slipped the Glock out from his pocket and back in. Nick thought that was a good idea and that he was now glad that he had called out.

Harry and Nick had a great time around the island and Nick was most impressed with the quality of the food, he had thought that it might have been a bit warmer but at least it was not cold, Harry had reminded him that it was winter. They had both bought a Vespa moto (scooter) each and Harry could not believe that he had not done that earlier, so much easier than dragging the Jeep out when he needed something from town.

Nick had now been on the island with Harry for about five months and they really got along well, more like a father and son relationship which seemed to work well. Harry was pleased that Nick had turned up out of the blue, he needed someone to talk to at least, but this was good, they took it in turns cooking and even brewing the beer, which could not have been better. Harry had thought that if Nick had have called him first before coming to the island, then he thought he would most likely have told him not to come as he would not be welcome, strange, he thought, how things just turn out.

Visitors

Harry had returned from the town with some beer brew extract and rump steaks. He parked his moto next to Nick's out the front of the entrance to the house and he went inside carrying the bag he used to transport his things on the moto to find Nick inside the house standing in the main reception room with the two detectives that Harry knew from Canberra. Harry's hand instinctively went from the bag that he was carrying to his right side pocket, then to the sudden call from Nick..

'Woha... wo.. wo Harry' Nick called out urgently to Harry, 'It's ok,...it's ok' he said as he moved towards the two detectives and held up their arms to show Harry that they were both locked together with handcuffs.

'What the fuck is going on here' asked Harry, whilst trying to maintain his rage and placing his bag down to the floor, 'are these blokes here for you Nick?', Harry was pretty wild and getting a bit wilder.

'No, no...Harry just settle for a minute', Barry Upton started to plea, 'just listen for a moment.......'

'Just shut up copper cunt, I'll do the talking', said Nick as he pushed both of the detectives to the ground.

Nick went on to tell Harry to relax and get a drink for both of them and he will explain what he knows and not to listen to the lying pricks of coppers. Harry restored his cool and went and came back with drinks. Harry told Nick that he was hoping that what he was going to say would be good. Nick had replied that it was pretty fucking unbelievable. Nick had been in the pool when Harry had gone into town, and after about twenty minutes Nick had heard a noise coming from inside the house and had just assumed that it was Harry back from town, so he stayed in the pool just floating on his back, then he heard the back door open and close, and then open and close in quick succession which made Nick cautious and he let himself sink to the bottom of the pool, he then came up slowly and peeked over the edge of the pool to see the two goons sneaking past the pool to the garage, side by side peeking in the garage window. Nick had then, as he said, simply leapt from the pool and grabbed a head in each hand at each side and just slammed them together and they just fell in a heap, the useless pricks he added. Nick had then found that one of them was carrying cuffs so he cuffed them together,

Barry Upton was looking at Harry and he looked like he did not know what to say.

'I really hope Barry, that you can tell me why you are here, it needs to be good Barry or this is not going to end well' Harry said.

'I can explain, I really can, and we only came here to basically say hello, it's true Harry, as silly as it sounds Harry it's true. Barry said pleadingly. He went on to tell Harry that Canberra had issued a warrant for his arrest and as we had no treaty with Spain, it was decided by the hierarchy that we should just simply come over here and persuade you to come back with us on your own free will so you can explain to the Canberra judges what you thought you were doing by kidnapping juveniles.

'We knew it was never going to work Harry', said John Simms, 'we just came for the holiday and to look you up to tell you that you are a hero in Canberra, to us and the public'. Simms continued to explain to Harry that when the kids were released by the police and had made statements, the media got

Max Barrington

hold of the story, it was leaked actually, Barry Upton had added, and it seemed to have a huge impact on the youth crime in the ACT.

Some Canberra residents were so motivated by the story of a bit of justice that was finally happening to the 'untouchable' youths in Canberra that they formed vigilante groups and started to round up any kids they could find around the suburbs or shopping centres and even pubs, they would then take these kids on a drive down to the cotter and strip them naked and remove their shoes, throw buckets of cold water over them and then leave them to walk back to town.

Some vigilantes, sadly went way too far and actually inflicted injuries to some of the kids and in one incident the kid died. But it had a great impact Harry, juvenile crime almost ceased within a week, stolen cars dropped from around three hundred a week to about five, it was just brilliant what you have started Harry. But the law is the law Harry and some dickhead politician decided that we had to get you back to pay for your crime, fuck knows why, but anyway, we volunteered to come over to ask you to return with us.

'We knew, Harry, that from the start it was a dumbfuck, political idea, and it had no chance of working, but we thought, well,…hey, let's do it and say hello to Harry, enjoy a holiday and then tell the dumb pricks back in Canberra that we couldn't find you' Barry Upton concluded'.

'Is that really the truth Barry?' Asked Harry pulling his Glock from his pocket and aiming it at Barry's head.

'No No…..no Harry' said Nick, 'there is a much better way' and taking the Glock from Harry he asked him if he had just happened to get this gun from Crispy, Colin Crisp? Harry looked at Nick quizzically then replied that he had, yes but why?

Max Barrington

Nick did not answer Harry but removed the ammunition magazine from the grip of the Glock and then went up to Barry Upton and forced his, uncuffed hand, around the Glock, he then returned with the Glock to the table and reinserted the magazine, then placed the Glock on the table. Nick then looked at Harry's copy of the local directory and made a phone call on his mobile.

'Sí, necesitamos a la policía en Cala en Bosch-Serpentona 46, intento de secuestro' spoke Nick in very good Spanish, he then ended the call and calmly told Harry that he police are on their way to an attempted abduction at this address. We have thwarted their attempt by overpowering them and disarming them of their ACT police issue Glock and have secured them with their ACT issue handcuffs. I think Harry, that these two super sleuths may be in the shit and I think that it will be a long time until they are returned home to their families.

'Fucking brilliant mate, just fucking brilliant' Harry exclaimed.

'You've got it all wrong Harry' called Barry Upton.

'Good luck Barry and you too John, you fucking pair of arseholes' replied Harry. 'Remember when the Federal Police tried to do the same with Skassie? I think those cops are still in Madrid somewhere'.

The Spanish police were there within seven minutes and quickly took in the scene, they took possession of the Australian issued police gun and exchanged the Australian issued police handcuffs for those of Spanish issue and marked these items as evidence, they arrested the two trespassing Australian police officers and asked Harry and Nick if they could please come to the police station tomorrow, at any time that may be convenient, to make statements. Harry and Nick assured the police that they would be at the police station in the morning and bid them goodnight.

Both Harry and Nick were struggling to contain their laughter throughout the ordeal and now, both were almost uncontrollable.

'You are a fucking legend Nick' said Harry in between laughs, 'I am so glad that you came to visit and forgot to go home'

"Mate, I was thinking the other day how vulnerable you are here and then I thought of Skase and remembered that he got abducted by the Fed's but it all went wrong. But, just looking at this scenario, I reckon there is a way we can we make you become reincarnated' Nick was saying as his mind was going into overdrive.

Harry stopped laughing and looked deadly serious at Nick.

Nick said to Harry that, 'Those pair most likely won't be the last, and they may even be more vengeful now these pair have got nicked, haha, nicked, pardon the pun, he then asked Harry what was his plan, did he want to return to Australia?'.

'Yes Nick, I would like to go back to Oz, this place is great, don't get me wrong, but I do miss Australia'.

The next morning they both fronted up at the 'Guardia Urbana' and each made a statement which took absolutely ages to do, they had both assumed an hour or two at the absolute most but it had to be written in Spanish and the guy typing the statements was not too good at English.

The 'Guardia' had already established that Upton and Simms were working for the Australian Federal Police and that, officially, they were both on annual leave. The Glock had been identified as the property of the Australian Federal Police - ACT Policing Division and had been reported as stolen some years ago. The handcuffs were also identified as AFP and in current issue to a Senior Constable Robert Sharp. It was a common occurrence that cuffs got moved around between officers during the course of arresting suspects and adding additional cuffs to transfer them.

Upton and Simms had already appeared in court that morning and had been remanded in custody to face trial on a date to be announced, the local Official de Policia, told Harry and Nick that their case would not come up until about the middle of next year as there was a huge backload on the courts. More sniggers from Harry and Nick and they were free to go and 'muchas gracias'.

'What would you say Harry' Nick said in between drinks of his beer, 'if I told you that Skassie is actually in his mid seventies and is living in Australia?'.

'Well', replied Harry, also sipping a beer, 'I would say, no more beers for you old son'.

'If you don't ask too many questions, I will tell you what we did for Skassie and I reckon it would also work for you'.

'Who is 'we' and what the fuck are you talking about'.

'Too many questions already Harry' laughed Nick and told Harry what he had mean't and how it was done and could be done again. Harry told Nick that it all sounded pretty good to him but he would wait until the morning to have a think about it.

Harry was already in the pool at seven thirty the next morning when Nick came out to cook breakfast, Harry climbed out of the pool and wrapped a towel around him and said to Nick,

'Sound's good to me, let's do it'.

'We have not yet discussed the fine details Harry and it won't be cheap, nobody is going to help us for nothing you know'.

'What sort of a cut would you want Nick?'.

'I have thought about that Harry and what I want for my 'cut' as you call it, is your house here on the Island..'.

'Fuck off.......'.

'At least wait till I'm finished,......Your house, this house, for the price that you paid for it, I think you mentioned around the $750.000 mark? It would be at least a million Australian dollars on today's market, and....besides, aren't we good mates?'.

'You are a good mate, Nick, you really are. Thanks mate'.

The first thing that Harry got onto was a new identity and the only person he knew was Crispy. When he told Colin Crisp what he was going to do, Col took over the conversation, 'Let me see, passport, driver's license, medicare card, credit card and a tax file number, I can only do an ACT drivers licence, so if you go to another state you will have to change it, same as your bank account, but that is a piece of piss to transfer, both are really. Now roughly that will cost you....around the sixty grand mark all up and that will include ten grand in your new bank account'.

'Fucking do it Crispy, go for it you champ', was Harry's response.

The sale of Harry's house was just so unbelievably simple thanks to Marko, the real estate agent who had sold Harry his house when he first came to Spain, he had simply organised everything so swiftly including the permit for Nick. Nick had paid Harry in part Australian and part Spanish cash for the value of the house as he knew that was what Harry needed the most just now. Harry had told Nick that if he could not handle that amount of dollars for the house then they could sort it out later. Nick had told Harry not to ask questions but thanks for his concern towards his financial position, but the truth was that if Harry needed a couple of million dollars in a hurry, then Nick could accommodate him. Harry was impressed.

It wasn't hard to find an undertaker who knew of a man that would be dead within a month due to a failing heart and it had been diagnosed that the next heart attack, would sadly be his last, this man was told not to drink any alcohol of any description and the undertaker could organise a bottle of grappa for him at any time. His family could not care if the funeral for their esteemed grandfather included a body in the coffin or not for €1000,00 and the same for the undertaker to deliver the body to Harry's house, that price would also include shaving all the hair of the corpses head and to dress into Harry's clothes to make it slightly resemble Harry.

It was deemed by Nick to be just too risky to try to bribe the local doctor for a death certificate but that any doctor that had never met Harry would really do.

Next was Harry's will, it wasn't very difficult as he was leaving everything to Nick, which included the house and the contents plus the balance of Harry's bank account, a very simple matter done at the local village with the local solicitor.

Once Harry had a new name and identification then he would set up a bank account at the same bank where he presently had an account. Nick would also set up an account with the same bank, that way, Harry's 'will' money would be an internal bank transfer to Nick. Once Harry's new account was established Nick would simply transfer to that account a fixed amount on a weekly basis that would result in Harry's account balance being equal to that of his total will value. Harry would also organise a weekly rent payment to Nick's account just to add a little confusion. Very simple and the weekly transactions within both accounts are unlikely to be noticeable as it was an internal bank transfer.

So it was all set, a new ID was being set up for Harry with a passport showing an arrival in Spain, for this Harry had to send his legitimate passport to Colin Crisp in order for him to transfer his page with his arrival stamp for Spain to his new ID. Harry was dying to find out what his new name might be, but Crispy had told him that 'dying' was actually the crux of the matter as he needed someone to die that was around Harry's age and, fairly soon!

The undertaker had contacted Nick and had asked what day did he want the body? as to get the body, still warm, as it were, he would need to know what day so he could organise a drink for the victim. Nick had asked the undertaker to wait on the phone for a moment and called out to Harry and told him that tomorrow he would die, OK? He then told the undertaker to go for it and he would have the cash ready for him when he arrived tomorrow afternoon with the body. Done.

It was the worst day that Harry could ever remember, Nick told Harry to relax, he wasn't really going to die, someone else was doing it for him, and this made Harry worse. The undertaker had arrived at three o'clock that afternoon with the body and had proceeded to shave the face and the head of the body. The undertaker had gone to the man's house at nine o clock that morning with a bottle of very bad grappa, the man had enjoyed the grappa and had thanked the undertaker, his old friend from school days, for the excellent grappa. He had drunk half of the bottle and suffered a major heart attack, as advised that he most likely would if he drank alcohol by his doctor, who was called instantly and consequently issued his death certificate on the spot to allow the undertaker to remove the body and prepare it for burial.

Now the dead man was shaved and dressed in Harry's favourite floral shirt and his best Colorado shorts and was lying next to Harry's outdoor fridge where he kept his home brew beer. First, the ambulancia was called and attended within a remarkably short time, they attached an oxygen mask to the body and tried resuscitation but without any favourable result, it seemed that Harry had suffered a massive heart attack and was unconscious. The ambulancia had taken Harry to the hospital where he was pronounced dead on arrival. Poor Harry. Meanwhile Nick had closed all the window shutters at Harry's, now his house, as a mark of respect for the passing of his old mate Harry. This also assisted in the real Harry to move around the house without being seen by any inquisitive eyes. Harry would have to remain in hiding for at least two months, Nick had estimated. He had also suggested that he grow a beard and wear a hat, a thing that Harry never did, and just remain quiet and calm. Harry had told Nick that it seemed to be easy for him to say,

'You're not the one that's dead' said Harry and burst out laughing and so did Nick.

'This is going to work Harry, no worries'.

Harry's death certificate was issued by some intern at the hospital and Harry's funeral took place three days later, not allowing time for any relatives or friends to attend from Australia. The only people at the funeral was Nick and the undertaker, who was now well known by the late Harry. Nick had the undertaker contact the Australian Central News Agency for an obituary insertion which was quickly picked up by AFP and Harry's son, Scott who had alerted Harry's friends of his sad passing, some of which were members of the AFP. This really hurt Harry, that his son would think that his father was dead, but as Nick had said, no one could fake being sad at a funeral and the cops would be watching his son Scott and Scott's wife Zoe, like a hawk. It just had to be.

About seven weeks after the funeral, Nick had received a package in the mail from Fernandalio Cruzimorsz from Melo in Uruguay, it contained Harry's new identity with a letter from Colin Crisp. The letter contained very strict advice from Colin, Nick read out the letter;

It is imperative that this letter is destroyed once you have read it.

You will find in this package (1) a current Australian passport in the name of Dennis Harold Sutton, male, born in Victoria Australia 1959, the person described on the passport and photograph are of Harry Croft, the passport also showed an entry into Spain two weeks prior. (2) State of Victoria Drivers Licence, complete with date of birth and photograph of Harry Croft. (3) NAB Visa card issued to Dennis Sutton with an attached saving bank account, the balance on the Visa is $20,000 available credit, the balance on the savings account is $10,000.(4) Australian Tax File Number.

It is important that you do not enter any Australian Casino's or rail transit centres as these establishments will most likely have a photographic facial recognition description of Harry Croft and the AFP will be immediately alerted if any of these devices are triggered by a photographic scan of you. These devices recognise facial features and the growth of a beard will not prevent identification, so unless you want to undergo cosmetic or plastic surgery, stay away from any type of these devices.

Residential address should not be popular tourist areas where there may be a chance of someone holidaying from the ACT who may recognise you, well populated cities should also be avoided due to the widespread use of facial recognition camera's. Nor are small towns advisable due to the close knit of these people who seem to take delight in finding out exactly who the 'newcomer' may be and also a bored local police officer.

Rather a regional centre with a population of around 60,000 to 100,000 would be a better and safer place to live anywhere in Australia, or overseas for that matter.

Good luck Harry, or Dennis, whichever you chose.

'That man is nothing short of a genius Harry,... I..mean..Dennis' said Nick with a grin.

'It's all done, just like that, unreal...just..unreal, I mean like,..how on earth', responded Harry. 'But I think I will stick with Harold, Harry, yes,...Harry Sutton, I can get used to that'.

Harry was quite intrigued with the way that Nick had organised his change of identity and quizzed him on his knowledge of how such things can be done. Nick had told Harry, in confidence, that he was the one who had planned the escape for Skassie. Nick had worked for him in Port Douglas as his personal bodyguard after Skassie had bailed him on manslaughter charges and then had supplied Queensland's top barrister to defend Nick.

Nick had left Australia with Skassie and is wife and had come to Santa Ponsa at Majorca where they had bought a villa. It had been Nick's idea to create a new identity for Skassie after a few failed attempts to abduct him and return him to Australia, so he had done basically the same thing that he had just done for Harry, with the exception that Skassie had paid Nick five million dollars for his efforts,. Skassie had remained in Spain for seven years following his fake death and then moved back to Melbourne in Australia where everyone had forgotten about him, Nick assumed he was still living there as at 2022.

'Five million from Skassie, yet you want nothing from me?' Harry said feeling a bit confused.

'Skassie was a fucking thief mate, he was a criminal, you are not, you helped solve a big problem with juvenile crimes in the ACT, it's something the coppers there should have done and long time ago but were too gutless to even try. They let those punks run circles around them, they are embarrassed Harry of what you have done and they didn't even try, they just followed the book, 'you can't strike the youths as you will be put on report and it will be *you* that gets a kick in the arse' and that was their way of thinking. You are a hero mate, what Upton was saying about that would be true and they are all fucking jealous'.

Harry had been growing a beard for the last six weeks and had made this go permanently grey by the use of bleach when showering, he had shaved his head of hair and he had also lost about twenty kilograms in weight and now looked remarkably different. He had decided to test his new looks on the neighbour who had shown him how to brew beer.

He had knocked at the neighbour's door and when the neighbour had opened the door, he had not shown the slightest recognition, he had said to the man that he was looking for his late cousin, Harry Croft's former home and the neighbour directed him to the house next door and told him to ask for Nick.

Harry was now convinced that he had taken on a new identity that had certainly worked with the neighbour whom he had known fairly well since his arrival in Spain, he now felt confident to return to Australia, all he had to do was plan where to go to make a new start with his new name. But there was no rush now he had altered his appearance and he could easily get by as Harry's cousin, who was also called Harry. Well, it happens!

Harry was in deep thought about returning to Australia, it was now almost ten months since his new ID and the demise of the old Harry, he was homesick, true, but for what? He no longer had a home in Australia, he no longer had a wife, and he couldn't look up any of his old mates. His only real connection with Australia was his son Scott and his wife Zoe and of course his grandson who was about nine by now Harry guessed.

One afternoon while sitting and enjoying beers with Nick, Harry had decided to ask Nick for some advice.

'Nick, my old son, you....being the man of the world, which you surely are,......how would you suggest I go about contacting my boy Scott?'.

'I was actually wondering when you would come around to this, you have lasted longer than I thought you would, it's not that hard to do Harry but it must be done carefully, you don't want to blow all the hard work that has been done on your new ID. One wrong move mate and it's all been for nothing', Nick then also reminded Harry that , 'as he should know quite well, the cops would still be watching Scott like a hawk. Also remember Harry, that you have been out of the force for over twenty five years, that my friend is a fucking long time and lots of things have fucking changed. For instance, as an example,.....if you called Scott on his mobile, the cops would instantly know that a call from this area we are in now was received by Scott, they may even have a warrant to record all his

Max Barrington

telephone conversations and the same could also be true for Zoe'.

'So you are saying that it is out of the question'

'I didn't say that! Harry, no,…it's not out of the question, but it's still risky,…..what we do is get Scott to call you'.

Nick told Harry that the first thing they would do tomorrow was to organise Scott to call him, 'You'll see'.

The next morning they went into Cittadella on their moto's and went into the Telefónica store and bought two Galaxy A24 mobile telephone's complete with a sim card and international roaming. They then placed the number of each phone into the relevant contact section of each phone, in order for each phone to be able to contact the other. They then went to the Cittadella Correos (post office) and bought three different sized padded envelopes. Nick then asked Harry to write Scott's address onto a padded postage envelope that was just big enough to accept one of the Galaxy telephones. Nick then wrote a name and Canberra address onto a larger padded envelope and placed Harry's envelope inside this, he then took yet another larger padded envelope and addressed it to a person in New Zealand and placed the second padded envelope, which contained Harry's padded envelope inside it, he then went to the desk and paid for the postage to New Zealand and dropped the package in to the mail receiving bin.

'You now wait for a call from Scott', said Nick, 'Scott will recognise your hand writing on the envelope that he will finally receive, well should recognise your writing, I suppose, then he will see the number stored on the phone and hopefully will call it'".

'Sound's like a lot of 'ifs' said Harry, but he was quite impressed with the way Nick had set that up so simply and quickly, this man was definitely the man to keep on the right side of him. As it had been said about Nick previously, 'He had no enemies, they were all dead', Harry could well believe that.

It was just over two weeks that they had sent the telephone to Scott that the other Galaxy telephone had rung. It was eleven fifty on a Thursday night that the Galaxy had started to ring, fortunately Harry was just on his way to his bedroom when he heard the telephone's distinct tone that they had set, he raced down stairs and just missed the call. He had immediately called the number back but it gave the busy signal, as he was trying to call the number again the telephone rang , it was Scott.

'Is that you dad,....really......really' called Scott, his voice starting to stutter.

'Mate, I know I have a lot of explaining to do, I understand that it must be a great shock'

'Oh dad, I can't believe it, it's unreal'.

After a lengthy conversation, during which Scott admitted that he had strongly suspected that Harry, his father was not in fact dead, and a friend of his at his work, who happened to know one of Nick's sons, had told him not to be surprised if he discovered his father was still alive. They had lots to talk about as it had now been just over a year since Val had died, it seemed that in no time Harry's phone was giving a low battery warning and Scott had replied that his was also, they quickly made another time and day to make contact again.

During the many conversations that Harry had with Scott and also Zoe and young Morgan, the possibility of an actual meeting was discussed in great length only to decide that the risk was just too great. During one conversation with Zoe, she mentioned that things were not too good with Morgan and that they had discovered that the local priest had interfered with

Max Barrington

him whilst he had been at alter boy practice. She had told Harry that Scott had not wanted Harry to know as he he knew just how wild that you would get if you found out and that there is nothing now that can be done as the priest has now been moved along to another Parish.

'Zoe, listen to me', Harry was instantly at boiling point, 'what do you mean there is nothing that can be done, how is Morgan reacting to all of this'

'He refuses to go to church and he didn't want to go back to his private school, we have enrolled him into the local public primary school and he is just starting to settle down and get back into school interests,...hang on Harry, Scott wants to talk to you.....'

'Dad, don't worry, everything has been taken care of, everything is fine now, the priest has gone and.......'

'Bullshit everything is fine Scott, fucking bullshit Scott, who is this mongrel, what the pricks name.....'

'Dad, please, let it go'.

'You know I won't' and Harry finished the call, he was ropable, it was almost midnight when he went outside to pull a schooner of his brew, he was still there when Nick found him at about eight o clock the next morning, just brooding.
Harry told Nick about the priest and his grandson, Nick shook his head in disbelief.

'What would you do Nick?'

'Harry, if it was me, and I am glad it's not, but if it was, then I would go over and put the pricks lights out'.

'I reckon that's what I might do Nick, I'll have to work out a bit of a plan'.

'NO, HARRY.....WE'LL work out a plan, a good plan'.

Nick had suggested to Harry, for starters, piss off that useless iPad and go and buy a decent laptop computer, get a MacBook Air and get the top of the range, make sure it has the M2 chip in it. Nick had already upgraded the internet connection at the house with Balear WiMax and with that combined to Harry's MacBook he shouldn't have any problems doing his research.

Harry's first task, set by Nick, was to find out the priests full name and a bit of background, he told Harry that the catholic church are very talented when it came to hiding priests as they have had so much experience at it.

Harry had started on Facebook for any social pages on the priests former church, so simple to make up a false name and email address on Facebook. Harry had used the name of Denise Potter for his account together with a 'G' mail address. He had to go on line at night as Palma was nine hours behind Australian time, he had found a Woden Valley Church group and had placed a request to join the group and while waiting to be accepted read whatever he could on the Vatican and it's comments and views on pedophile priests and could not believe the reports that are available through Google.

One report estimates that 216,000 children were abused by priests between 1950 and 2020, and that accounting for abuse by other church employees increases the total number to around 330,000. Around 80% of the victims were boys.

Harry found that there were virtually hundreds of documents on the web in respect to priests., but there did not seem to be very many clues on how to bring it all to an end

Another question on Google was;
How many priests have been accused in Australia?

Max Barrington

Between 1950 and 2010, more than 1,200 Catholic clergy in Australia were the subject of child abuse allegations. As an indication of the extent of the abuse, the Commission calculated that, over the same 60-year period, seven percent of all the country's Catholic priests were alleged perpetrators of child sexual abuse.

And on May 9, 2019, Pope Francis issued the Motu Proprio Vos estis lux mundi requiring both clerics and religious brothers and sisters, including Bishops, throughout the world to report sex abuse cases and sex abuse cover-ups by their superiors.

Well, thought Harry, 'That will work'.

Harry's request to join the   Woden Valley Church group was accepted and he was permitted access to their page, he immediately began to scan the page and went back into the pages history and actually found a section welcoming the new priest to the group;

From the group committee, we extend a warm welcome to Father Jeremy Ironside, formally from Bendigo Victoria.

That was all Harry wanted, armed with the priests name and a landline phone number for the church, both Harry and Nick approached one of Nicks friends, a very pretty Spanish lady, Carmen, who spoke quite remarkable English.

Timing it correctly to around eleven o clock in the morning in Canberra, Australia, Carmen called the church twice before an answer;

'Hello,....Saint Francis Xavier Parish, this is Gwen'.

'Good morning Gwen, this is Carmen from the Civic Library. May I speak with Jeremy Ironside please'?

'Oh,..good morning, Carmen,..sorry but Father Irons is no longer our priest here, can I help you'?

'I hope so, Gwen, we have a rare book that Jeremy ordered some time back and has finally arrived, he has all ready paid for it but he did not leave a postal or delivery address, just this phone number'.

'Oh dear,...look the Archdiocese does not tell us where the priests go when they get promotional transfers and we have to direct any enquiries through them, if you just send it the the Diocese of Canberra and mark it for his attention, it should get to him'.

'I don't really know if I can do that, you see he has paid over five thousand dollars for this rare, collectors item book and I don't just want to send it to a generic address'.

'Oh wow, he loves his books, I know that much,...look....you did not get it from me but,....just two secs..it's here somewhere on my......stupid mobile..yes, The Presbytery at 41 Dargreaves Street, Bendigo. If you send it there he should definitely receive it'.

'Why thank you so much Gwen, I will get it away to him today, Thanks again, goodbye'.

'Well done Carmen, thank you very much', Nick said, 'Harry, find that number for the Bendigo Presbytery, it will be lunch time there and we'll get Carmen to do another call, but no book this time Carmen, tell them you are returning his call, it he answers just pretend its a wrong number, got it?'
Harry found the number and wrote in down for Carmen, she dialled.

'Presbytery, Robert speaking, may I help you', a very polished voice answered.

'Robert, this is Carmen, I am just returning a call from Jeremy, is he there please'?

'Father Ironside is no longer at this Presbytery Carmen, you will need to contact the Diocese, sorry goodbye'.

'Fuck it', said Harry, 'that's it'.

'Not at all, did you really think you would find him so easy, I have always had the opinion that priests are dumb, but not that fucking dumb, replied Nick., we will use the book idea, we will find him, get ready for a trip Harry'.

Nick and Harry had revisited the Telefónica shop and this time bought a 4g compact tracker with a sim card. This tracker, to extend battery life up to six months, could be turned on or off remotely with the telephone that it is paired to, simply by dialling the trackers sim card number and adding ##*, then turned off the same way but by adding #**.

An old relic of a book called The Five Saints of Spain that they found in the village was used to carve out a neat fifteen by fifteen x seven millimetre crevice about three quarters of the way through the book and close to the spine, that way if somebody flipped through the pages of the book, the tracker would not be discovered. The book was then carefully placed in a suitable box and then in a padded post bag and then addressed to Father Jeremy Irons at the Presbytery in Bendigo, They had tested the tracker in and out of the packaging and had discovered that the signal was reading in the tens on the receiving scale and about four when in the package, this would allow Harry to know when the package had been opened.

This package was not placed in the mail though, this package was going to accompany Harry to Australia.

Harry had also needed to contact Colin Crisp, another Galaxy M24 was purchased and sent the same way as the Galaxy for Scott was sent.

'What the fuck are you up to now Harry', the voice of 'Crispy' echoed through Harry's Galaxy at one am on a Sunday morning,

'And I hope you are well to Col', Harry jested Col.

'I have a little unfinished business back in Oz and I need something light and quiet'.

'What sort of distance are you looking at Harry'?

'I would estimate ten metres max, but it needs to be a terminator, and…quiet'.

'The only thing that I have that might suit is a Margolin .22 target pistol, it's an auto 10 shot mag, it has a silencer and can fire a subsonic forty grain projectile at enough muzzle velocity to kill a big Rottweiler dog with one head shot and you won't hear a thing, you can upgrade the ammo to Winchester super x with twice the power and just a little muzzle blast noise, very faint actually'.

'Sounds good', said Harry, 'how can you deliver though, I will need it in Victoria'?

'There is a home brew shop at Frankston that does a twenty four hour collection for items using a locker system with an access code, I'll send you the code but you will need to pickup within twenty four hours of my call, so let me know prior'.

'You've got it Col', and they hung up. All sorted thought Harry and pretty easy so far.

More Justice

'How do people ever live in Melbourne'? Harry thought to himself as he collected his hire car from the car park. He set the cars GPS for the Home Brew Store in Frankston, but before leaving the Melbourne city area he found a postal receiver and deposited his padded package. He then found the Home brew store and the contents of the locker, in the locker that Col had advised him

The Shamrock was a comfortable Hotel that Harry had stayed at before when he and his wife, Val, had visited friend's and Val's relatives in Country Victoria. There was a good bar and an excellent restaurant, the hotel was basically in the middle of the city and was an easy walk to other venues.

On day two of being in Bendigo, Harry assumed that the package would have been scanned by now and should be in transit so he dialled the trackers sim card and added ##* to turn it on, he then opened the scanners app on his mobile and after a few seconds the scanner was showing it's location on the app, it was showing the location to be 16 Deborah Street Bendigo. Harry checked the address and it showed it was the Bendigo mail centre. So the tracker had arrived in town, now he just had to wait for it to be delivered. 'You'r one smart cookie Nick', Harry was thinking as he headed to the restaurant for dinner.

The tracker had moved from Deborah Street to 41 Dargreaves Street the next day and had remained stationary inside the property and just to the left, it seemed inside the main entrance, for the next day. The package was then moved to number 47 Dargreaves Street and seemed to be to the far right of the building.

Harry thought he might call around to Dargreaves Street, doing the tourist thing and take a few pics and wander around. He was somewhat confused and needed to check out the lay of the land, as it were.

Number 41 Dargreaves Street, appeared to be a private residence. 'Hmm' thought Harry, wrong address and he drove on to number 47 Dargreaves Street, where the tracker was reporting as its location, this address also looked to be a private address. Harry checked the location again on his phone app and could not believe it, the package was now back at 16 Deborah Street, the mail centre.

After some consideration, Harry had concluded that the package was being redirected, Jeremy Irons was not in Bendigo. Harry's only course of action was to wait and watch where this tracker was going to from here.

Harry watched as the scanner went back to Melbourne and stayed there overnight, the next day it was out of range and remained so until late that evening and the location was Sydney Airport, the following morning it was still in Sydney but now at the suburb of Chullora where it remained for two days and then returned to the Sydney airport, the following morning the tracker was out mobile service until late in the evening when it arrived at Coffs Harbour. Harry was quite amazed how he could follow the tracker although he did become concerned when it showed that it was out of mobile service on a couple of occasions. It was a Sunday morning when the tracker finally left Coffs Harbour and started to travel south towards Kempsey, where it stayed overnight.

Monday morning and Harry checked the location before going down to breakfast, the tracker was at a small town beside the Macleay River called Scillons Flat.

Harry had waited, impatiently for another whole day to see if the package was still in transit or stationary. Harry had again checked it's location before going to bed, not only was the tracker still at Scillons Flat but the signal strength had increased by about thirty percent, indicting to Harry that the package had been opened, he assumed by Jeremy Irons.

Harry checked out of the hotel the following morning and had set his GPS from Bendigo to Scillons Flat, some   1260 kilometres. Harry had broken the trip up into roughly four hours driving each day and thoroughly enjoyed the trip and the hotels that he stayed at on the way, not to mention the different quality foods at the hotels, and the beers.

It was around five o clock when Harry finally pulled into Scillons Flat, population 3221, the sign had read.

He drove past the first motel, which he thought looked a bit dilapidated, and drove on into the little village to see what else was on offer, nothing, not in the way of motels anyway but, the local pub looked tempting for a cold beer before he looked any further. It was a fairly large looking, typical two story pub, 'The Flat Hotel' it was simply called, painted white with federation green window sills, trims and corrugated iron roof it looked as though it was straight out of the past and walking into the bar was like going back at least a hundred years, if not more.

Harry walked up to the traditional looking timber bar with polished timber handrail and continuous stainless steel ashtray running along the bottom of the bar, a newer addition, maybe forty years ago he supposed, that also worked as a footrest and an ashtray.

'Good day, looks like you could handle a cold drink' asked the young lady behind the bar.

'I do believe you are correct Madam, a schooner of Carlton might be the plan' Harry replied whilst sitting on a bar stool and taking a look around the bar at the three seperate, lonely, drinkers.

The barmaid brought Harry's drink to him and Harry handed over a fifty dollar note, the barmaid rang up $8 on the till and returned his change.

'Is it a quiet day'? He asked.

'Normally a bit busier than this, never really know here, It could get busy around sixish', the barmaid replied.

'Whats the chance of a room for a few days'?

'No worries, it's $60 a night for a standard double room, or $75 for a queen room with ensuite'.

'I'll take a queen with the ensuite, thanks', Harry took his credit card out of his wallet and passed to the young lady, 'make it five nights please'.

She took Harry's credit card and disappeared into the next room to return a minute later with a key and an eftpos receipt. The key's label read '4'.

'The dining room opens at six this evening for dinner, if you like and also at six in the morning for breakfast, and believe me the food here is second to none' she said handing the key and the receipt to Harry.

'I'll vouch for that', one of the morbid looking drinkers at the bar said, 'the steaks are the best in NSW', he continued and now standing and moving towards Harry, 'Monty Graham, mate' he said now extending his arm towards Harry.

Harry shook his hand and said 'Harry Sutton'.

'What are you drinking Harry'? Monty asked putting a $50 on the bar.

'Schooner of Carlton, thanks Monty'.

'Are you here for long Harry'? Monty asked whilst holding his hand up and summoning the barmaid.

'Don't know yet, just looking around for somewhere to settle down'.

'Theres nothing around here Harry, not many people ever leave here once they arrive and get settled, the only place around here for sale is this pub'.

Monty's words struck Harry like a club, 'well' thought Harry, 'might be an idea'

'I didn't see any 'for sale' signs when I arrived'.

'Na, Sue reckons the 'for sale' signs will turn the customers away, not that there are many customers these days thanks to the local law man'.

'Sue'?

'The owner, you'll see her around shortly'.

'And how does the local copper keep the customers away' Harry asked inquisitively.

'He sits in his car, not the police car, his car, parked just up a bit from the pub and then swoops on anyone leaving the pub who's driving. He's a dead set arsehole'.

'Are you talking about my best friend again Monty'? Called out a graying, but attractive woman who had just entered the bar.

'G'day Sue, how are you doing, this is one of your guests, Harry' replied Monty.

Max Barrington

'Hello Harry, I'm Sue, are you staying here? That's good, need all the guests I can get just now'. Sue responded.

Harry smiled and nodded as he said hello to Sue.

Harry enjoyed a few more beers with Monty, whom he had discovered was actually born here in Scillons Flat and lived on his five thousand acre property on his own since the death of his wife some seven years prior. Monty lives in the splendid homestead and leases two thousand acres of the land to a sheep farmer and three thousand acres to a cattle and horse breeder. Monty walks the one and a half kilometres from his home to the pub each afternoon for a few beers and dinner, then he walks home. Monty told Harry that he used to drive until the prick of a copper nailed him one evening.

The dining room at the pub was like going back in time with it's polished   spotted gum floors and wainscoting panels around the walls to the chair rail mouldings and then semi gloss, white painted vertical tongue and groove timber from the high, ten foot (three metre) ceilings also of tongue and groove timbers, but painted in a more relaxing matt, off white finish and a polished spotted gum Scotia finish around it's perimeter, just beautiful, thought Harry.

Monty had invited himself to dine with Harry, and as he sat there looking at the menu, Harry could see that Monty had had a hard life, he had the appearance of a worker in days gone by and it now took it's toll on Monty's physique.

Harry had instantly like Monty upon meeting him in the bar, he had that sort of charisma that made you feel that you wanted to be in his circle.

'What sort of dollars would Sue be looking for in the hotel sale Monty', Harry asked.

'I have no idea old chap, I do know that they paid around the half million mark eight years ago, but they have done a lot to it'.

'They'?

'Yes, Sue and Brian, her husband, you won't get to meet him as he is in goal, thanks to our local copper. It's a bit of a story actually', Monty replied.

'I am all ears, old son', was Harry's response and Monty told Harry about Brian, that he and Sue had a panel beating business in Sydney somewhere and decided to sell up and move somewhere quieter and sort of semi retire. They found this pub on the market and came to have a look, fell in love with the pub and the area and the rest, as they say, is history. They were very busy renovating and painting and putting on special days for the patrons, all was going quite well until this prick of a copper started to stalk the patrons coming out of the pub at night and put the breathalyser on them resulting in people not coming to the pub, or not as many people, for drinks and meals. The pub started losing money and Sue and Brian were under financed, old story, so they had to do something to get the customers back.

Brian comes up with an idea and goes to Sydney to the Government surplus vehicle auctions and arrived back in town with a Volvo bus that was formally used to transport police around, a thirty nine seater. He had it resprayed and sign written with the pubs name and set up a time table to cover most of the town and ran it every hour from five thirty to midnight on Friday, Saturday and Sunday. All was going really good and the pub was packed every Friday through to Sunday until, the copper decides to pull Brian over in the bus one night to breathalyse him. Brian of course blew negative, but then the police constable claimed to observe some tablets in a plastic bag in the storage shelf near the side window, he immediately arrested Brian and got all of the passengers off the bus and called for back up from Coffs Harbour. Brian was taken to Coffs police station and the tablets were found to be MDMA (ecstasy) and Brian was charged with supplying and dealing, he was sentenced to ten years goal and the bus was confiscated as being a means to transport illicit drugs. Brian had never touched drugs in his life.

'Well fuck me', said Harry, he could not prevent his pommy accent from emerging, 'the rotten twat, he needs a fucking bullet'.

'That's why Sue is having to sell the pub' Monty concluded.

Harry had a lot of trouble trying to sleep that night, he knew he had a job on hand but he was thinking that buying this pub would be a good cover and maybe a good way to spend his retirement. It was two in the morning and Harry worked out that it would be just after midday in Mallorca Spain, he called Nick.

'Mate, how are you going' answered Nick, recognising the phone number, 'Don't tell me you'r not coming back'.

'I'll be coming back Nick, but not for a while yet, no dramas but just a couple of ideas that I want to pass over you'.

'And they would be'?

'Do have a million to go halves in a pub, might be cheaper that that, could be a neat little investment'?

'And the second thing is'?

'Knock a badge, not permanent, just so he gets wheels', Harry replied, knowing Nick would understand'.

'The second item should be easy enough , what state'? Nick needed to know.

'The first state', Harry said quoting the slogan on the NSW motor vehicle number plates.

'Piece of Piss Harry, you know how to get the details to me, but Harry, buying a fucking pub? Why the fuck would I want a fucking pub Harry'?

'It's only half a pub, I'm buying the other half, it'll work out Nick, if it does not then I'll buy you out'.

'Yeah, ok, just do it, tell me where to send the mil, the other bit will cost you around the fifty 'g' mark'.

'We'll be going halves in that too Nick, it's for the pubs sake'.

'You crack me up Harry, you really do' Nick was laughing, how did you go with the communion at church'?

'It will be fine, plenty of time for that, this pub could also work as a good cover for me'.

Harry turned off the light in his room and decided to talk to Sue in the morning and buy the pub.

Harry asked Sue what were the chances of a fillet steak for breakfast with an egg and tomatoes, tinned if possible and some chips. Sue had replied that it sounded just like a breakfast her husband Brian would order, less the tomatoes.

'Hope you enjoy, Harry', said Sue serving the breakfast.

'Do you have a few minutes for a chat Sue'?

'Yes, should be ok, I'll just get a coffee, would you like one Harry'?

Harry declined with the coffee and after a while Sue returned and sat opposite Harry.

'What price do you have on the hotel Sue'?

'The old Monty said you might be interested', Sue replied instantly with somewhat brighter eyes, 'nine hundred thousand plus stock, that should come in at about one hundred and fifty thousand, plus bits and pieces say one point one all up'.

Harry stopped eating and looked squarely at her, 'Sold' he said 'but I would want you to stay on and run it, at a good negotiated price of course and still live in here'.

Sue could not speak and could only mutter, 'are you serious and you haven't even seen the place yet, or the books'.

'I have seen something that I like, I was looking to buy a house around the area and I like this place and so be it. I am happy to stay in the room that I am in and you can remain in your residence'.

Harry finished his breakfast and continued to discuss the sale of the hotel with Sue who, by now was quite relieved and excited although somewhat sad that she had to sell the hotel, but she found it was getting harder and harder to satisfy the mortgage that she and her husband, Brian, had on the hotel as she now had to pay extra wages as Brian was no longer there to help, plus the downturn in patrons to the arsehole copper.

Harry had told Sue that he was going into Coffs Harbour today to take back the hire car and organise another car for his transport and that he would also transfer the deposit for the hotel to her solicitor and that he would engage a solicitor for the conveyancing.

It was a pleasant one hour drive into Coffs Harbour from Scillons Flat, Port Macquarie is a little closer but lacked some of the facilities that Coffs could offer. He found the car hire company, dropped off the car and then walked to the main road that goes through Coffs and found the Coffs Harbour Subaru dealer who just happened to have an Outback turbo, demonstration model. Harry took the dealers details and the price of the car into the local branch of his bank and organised a bank cheque for his new Subaru Outback Turbo. Whilst at the bank Harry also organised the deposit for the purchase of the hotel to be transferred to Sue's solicitor, he also set up his account for internet banking and noted with delight that Nick's deposit of one million dollars had already been credited to his account.

Harry had then found a solicitor to act as conveyancer and also had an employment contract drawn up for both Sue and her husband, with a blank space where it stated remuneration.

On his way back into Scillons Flats he decided to visit the local, infamous, copper and pulled up in his new car in front of the police station and walked in knowing that it was most unlikely that face recognition camera's were employed in NSW police stations.

'Harry got quite a shock when he saw the young constable at the desk as he thought that there was only one officer at this station, and this officer looked much too young to be the 'famous' one, although he knew nothing of the country police station setups as when he was in the ACT police they only manned four police stations around the ACT and all had a crew of not less that thirty officers on duty.

'Good morning', Harry announced himself, 'are you the officer in charge'.

'Good morning sir, I am temporarily filling in, the acting sergeant is Bradley Moran but he is in Port Macquarie today, how can I help you'?

Harry introduced himself to the young constable and announced that he had just moved to the area and had just bought the 'Flat Hotel', to this the constable raised his eyebrows and said to Harry.

'Your'e kidding? We didn't even know it was for sale, Bradley will be pissed off' the young constable stated.

'It wasn't advertised, it was a private treaty, is there a problem'?

'Bradley has been sweating on that pub coming on to the market, that pub was his retirement plan' the young constable went on, volunteering more information than what he probably should.

'Oh', Harry replied, 'Will Bradley be back today'?

'Yeah, it's just his fortnightly staff meeting, he is generally back at around seven pm, they all normally have a couple of drinks following the meeting'.

This young copper was a treasure with his free information, Harry noted the day was Tuesday, hmm, good information. Harry told the constable that he would call in and see Bradley a bit later in the week and said 'Good day'.

Back at the hotel, Harry found Sue and told her that he had paid the deposit, which she already knew, he also told her that he had instructed his solicitor to proceed with a settlement as soon as practicable to both parties as he had the cash to make settlement. Sue was beside herself and even happier when Harry told her about the work contract that he had prepared for both her and Brian, as, he said you never know, Brian just might get an early release.

Sue had then apologised to Harry saying that they had moved him from room number four to room number one as that room was much bigger as it had two bedrooms and an a lounge. Perfect Harry had replied and then asked if there was a lock up garage that was available for him as well, which it was, plus a private office was also available.

Things for proceeding smoothly for both the hotel transition and Harry's plans, Harry had just walked into the drive through bottle department when a police landcruiser drove in, the police driver exited the vehicle and approached the sales counter, the police officer, a senior constable, identified Harry as a new face and assumed him to be the new owner and called out to him.

'Are you the new owner'?

'Almost, as good as all done' responded Harry.

'Acting sergeant Bradley Moran' the officer said approaching Harry with his hand outstretched.

'Harry Sutton', Harry replied, ignoring the police officers hand.

Meanwhile the barmaid, who also kept her eye on the bottle department, had been getting a carton of Tooheys Dry Lager from the cool room and had passed it to Bradley Moran, who in turn had placed it inside his vehicle left hand side back door, he then proceeded to get back into the drivers side door when Harry spoke.

'You have forgotten to pay for the carton of beer, acting sergeant'.

'Sue will explain it to you', the officer smirked towards Harry.

'I don't think so, the stock has all been transferred and I have paid for it, that is my beer and if you wish to take it with you, then you need to pay for it'.

Acting sergeant Moran, got back out of his car and approached Harry. Harry regarded Moran as a weedy looking specimen to be a member of the police force, unlike his days when a height and weight requirement kept shit like this out of the service.

'You need to learn Sutton, that I run this town and in return and out of respect many business owners offer me gratitude in the form of small gifts', the acting sergeant was becoming annoyed.

'You'll get no gratification in the way of gifts from me, you either pay for the carton of beer, or hand it back and if you don't I shall report you', said Harry as he pulled his mobile phone from his pocket and started to dial 000.

The astonished acting sergeant was now clearly becoming wild and turned back towards the rear passenger door and withdrew the carton of beer and threw it onto the ground beside the sales counter, smashing the contents.

Using his mobile phone that was already in his hand, Harry simply took a photograph of the scene which included the acting sergeant, the police car and the smashed carton. He then calmly told the officer to get off the premises and don't come back, Harry then took a video of the police car smoking up it's tyres as it accelerated out of the bottle shop driveway.

Harry immediately looked up the email address for the NSW police media and issues, public affairs branch and forwarded the photograph and the video with a full explanation of both, together with a formal complaint.

'Round one' Harry said to no one in particular.

Once Sue had heard about the bottle shop incident she became concerned and spoke to Harry and told him to be careful. He had responded and reassured her that there was nothing to worry about, 'you don't just keep stepping over weeds in the garden, they become annoying, so you simply remove them', he told her.

It was just about two weeks since Harry had decided to buy the pub from Sue that sensational news was broadcast from all the major television station's on the Wednesday evening news.

It stated; *The two major NSW newspapers received a tape recording of a full confession from a police officer in relation to false drug charges of a hotel co owner, the tape revealed how the police officer had used drugs that he had taken from the evidence safe of a different case and planted them on a bus that the accused was driving at the time. The news report went on to say that the officer involved had claimed that he had arrived back from police matters in the nearby town of Port Macquarie and when alighting from his police vehicle at his home he was seized by at least two men who placed a head cover over him and strapped both of his arm's around his body making him totally immobile. He was then forced, through excessive violence causing great pain to make the verbal statement on an audio tape. He was then held captive for about 24 hrs until the tape was made available to police and the press. Although the officer has stated that he made the statement under extreme duress and had also falsified the statement in an effort to be set free, police have confirmed that evidence, that is very similar, to that used in the hotel owners case, is missing from another case.*

It is further reported that the officer received extensive injuries to both of his knee's and may not be able to return to normal activities.

The following Friday morning, just two days after the spectacular news report, Brian Huntley was released from prison and Bradley Moran was charged with various, serious charges that would see him serve a lengthy term in prison, he is now also confined to a wheel chair resulting from injuries from his alleged attackers.

The Bradley Moran story is now emerging right across Australia as a warning to corrupt police officers as it seemed that a well trained team of experts may have been responsible for the Moran abduction and it should not be ruled out that it won't happen again.

That Saturday, all weekend for that matter, was a very joyous occasion around the pub, the bus had been returned on the same day that Brian was released and a casual driver had been engaged to drive the old weekend roster to collect and drop off the pub patrons who could also join in Brian's home coming celebrations.

Many patrons also drove their cars to the pub and were very mindful of how many drinks they could have, but at least they knew that they would no longer be subject to a breathalyser that would include vehicle checks, or so they hoped.

Harry got on well with Brian, who was about a similar age to him, they were both very thankful for Harry taking over the pub and having them run it for him and at a generous remuneration.

Both Sue and Brian were convinced that Harry had a hand in the demise of Bradley Moran as Sue had first hand information about what had happened in the drive through bottle shop and knew that Harry had filed a formal complaint against Moran. Harry had not quite denied any involvement but had also claimed his innocence, but when they asked Harry how they could possibly repay him, he did say that he may be in need of a favour one day.

Harry had been maintaining his grey beard and his shaved head and had now bought a collar length grey wig online. He had been a resident in Scillons Flat for almost three months and was settling in, he had also been attending Sunday mass at the Sisters of Mercy Parish in Scillons Flat. Harry had been making it a habit for the last month or so to take the worn pathway from the pubs beer garden across a vacant block of land to the main shopping centre of Scillons Flat.

This path led past the rear of the the parish church and Harry had actually made contact with Father Michael Wright, the local priest of the Scillons Flat Parish on a number of occasions and had no problems with taking several photographs of the good priest, unbeknown to him of course. He had also witnessed the priest signing a reference for a fellow parish member with his left hand.

These photo's were sent back to Nick in Spain who forwarded them to Harry's son Scott, with a letter asking for positive identification of the photographs to be that of Jeremy Irons. The confirmation that the photographs were definitely that of Jeremy Ironside eventually came back to Harry, via Nick in Spain.

So, not only had the church made a cover up of the reports of child molestation in respect to Father Ironside and relocated him, but they had also changed his name to Michael Wright.

The town of Scillons Flat has a population of approximately 3221 according to its last census, it had two hotels, 'The Flat Hotel' and the 'Scillons Flat Hotel'. The latter burnt to the ground in the early 2000's and was never rebuilt.

There are two motels at Scillons Flat, an IGA supermarket, two butcher shops, two ladies hairdressers, one chemist, one newsagent, one fish and chips shop, one Chinese cafe, called Happy's (how did you guess) and course the Post Office. Education consisted only of a public primary school, Catholic children travelled the twenty odd kilometres
into Kempsey as with the high school aged children.

Other than the Sisters of Mercy parish church was the Anglican Church of all Saints. It was an idealist retirement village where nothing really happens, or very rarely. The confessional at the parish church was open only on each Saturday between seven pm and eight pm.

Wearing his new wig and a pair of disposable kitchen gloves, Harry had arrived at the church at seven thirty on the Saturday night to find it empty and had gone into the confessional, it did not take long until Harry could hear the priest entering the other side.

'Welcome and may God, who has enlightened every heart, help you to know your sins and trust in his mercy'. Said the priest. Harry was hoping to God that it was Irons as the voice was a little muffled coming through the grill.

'Amen' said Harry, 'Bless me, Father, for I have sinned. It has been ten weeks since my last confession'.

Harry then pushed the rolled up document through the grill of the confessional to the priests side and said,

'Father you need to read this and then sign it, or you will be meeting your maker this evening'.

Harry stormed from his side of the confessional door and into the priest side of the confessional door with the Margolin target pistol in his hand, he took aim at the priest,

'Jeremy Ironside, sign that confession or I will shoot you dead' said Harry to a shaking, almost hysterical priest who was in no condition to read the document.

'Here, sign it now' prompted Harry passing a biro to the priest who was like he was about to pass out, he took the biro from Harry and without taking his eyes off Harry, he signed the document, Harry leaned down and placed the muzzle of the silenced Margolin into the priest's ear and pulled the trigger.

The priest seemed to collapse to the floor before the almost soundless hiss report of the Margolin was heard, the priest made no noise as he fell but the chair clattered quite loudly. Harry quickly placed the Margolin into the lifeless left hand of the priest and carefully moved the fallen document out of the path of the blood that now streamed from the priest's head.

Harry exited the confessional and closed both of its doors, the church was empty as he left and returned in the dark to the pub, once there he removed his wig and went directly behind the public bar.

'Sorry about that fellow's but I had to take that leak', Harry said, 'who's next'.

The news of the local police sergeant had made Scillons Flat famous as far as news went and for about a week following the revelations of the made up drug charges and the assault on the corrupt police officer. Just as the town was getting back to normal, the next Monday morning it made national headlines again.

'Scillons Flat Priest found dead in church clutching signed confession'!
The report stated that the police at this stage did not suspect any foul play and it appeared he was actually assuming a fictitious name as Father Michael Wright. Although police did not release the contents of the confession, leaked sources would indicate that he was being shielded by the church from charges relating to acts of child molestation at a church in a Canberra suburb.
This time the news reports failed to bring a caravan of reporters as it did with the Bradley Moran saga and the town soon settled down, a new priest was installed within a matter of days and Harry resumed his visits for Sunday mass and joined the other members of the congregation in pointing at the confessional and whispering what they had heard and that the word was out that it should be a warning to other priests that the lord works in mysterious ways.

Things were going very well at the pub, 'just like it used to be' said many of the locals who were sometimes three deep at the bar and there always seemed to be a packed carpark. A new police sergeant had been installed in town and he was busy assisting the police special investigations team that had been sent up from Sydney in relation to Bradley Moran.

Harry Sutton decided that it was time for him to retire and enjoy his pub, he couldn't wait for Nick to come over for a visit, but that will be a little while yet.

'Good morning Harry' said Sue as Harry went into breakfast, 'don't forget we have the live jazz on this weekend'.

'No, I won't forget, I am really looking forward to this, especially to see how it goes, if it works we'll do something similar every week', Harry's mobile interrupted him, 'sorry Sue', he said as he answered his phone.

'No worries Aitch, I'll get your breakfast' replied Sue knowing full well that he would have a steak and chips with eggs and tinned tomatoes for his 'usual' breakfast.

'Sorry to get you out of bed mate' was the reply.

'It's nine o'clock mate, of course, I'm out of bed, who is this'?

'Your fucking partner, dickhead, can you come and get me from the airport'.

'Nick?.....you are kidding me, where are you?

'Coffs airport mate, when you are ready!' Nick replied, 'no rush, I expect it will take you an hour or so to get here, I'll wander around and find a pub for lunch, give me a call on this number when you get here'.

Harry told Sue to cancel brekky as he had to go to Coffs and he went upstairs to his room to get his car keys, he came back down and was out of the back door heading to his car when he suddenly had a thought and returned to the dining room looking for Sue.

'Sue!.......Sue!, are you still here'?

'I'm in here Harry, eating your breakfast'.

'We will need another room tonight for a mate of mine.'

'For tonight and tomorrow is fine, but we are booked up for the weekend Harry.'

Harry nodded OK and went back outside to get his car and head off to Coffs Harbour. He was quite excited that Nick had finally decided to come and have a look at their pub and a hundred questions were going through his mind.

It was ten forty five when Harry got into Coffs after getting stuck behind trucks and road works, he pulled over to the side of the road and looked at his mobile for the last call and pushed 'dial'.

'I'm at a place called the 'Green Horse' tavern Harry, I haven't a clue where it is really, but it's on a busy road.'

'I'll find it, see you soon.'

Harry found the tavern about ten minutes after hanging up the phone and he walked into the public bar, and looked around at the dozen or so people that were in there, no Nick. Harry saw a sign that said 'thru to bistro', but still no Nick and hardly anyone in there, he looked around more and found the gaming room, but no Nick., 'Maybe he is having a leak' Harry thought as he walked back to the public bar.

He sat on a stool near the bar and took out his phone and redialled the last number, it started to ring and Harry could hear a 'Bohemian Rhapsody' ringtone somewhere behind him and he turned around.

'Here,...dickhead' called a familiar voice from a total bald headed and bearded stranger wearing coke bottle glasses and giving Harry the 'bird' with his centre finger on his right hand.

'No way, ...no fucking way, fuck me, how the fuck are you Nick' Harry could not believe Nick's appearance.

'It's 'Mick' Harry,..' Mick', Mick Marsh, responded a totally different looking Nick. 'Two more schooners of Carlton, thanks love' he said to the girl behind the bar.'I did a Skassie Harry, just like you.

'Well, it's good to see you...er, Mick' Said Harry picking up his beer from the bar, 'how long are you here for?'

'Couple of days here, then up to Brissy for a week or so, got a little job to do, I'll tell you about it later, Cheers!'

On the drive back to Scillons Flat, Nick told Harry how easy it was to change his identity and come back to Australia. He had placed all his assets, which included his home on the Island and his bank accounts to his various brothers. The reason he was back was to assist three of his cousins who are roof tilers around Brisbane and was hoping that Harry might be able to assist.

'I am not quite sure how I could assist Nick,..sorry Mick, I am too old to do any roof tiling' Harry stated.

'No, no tiling required,' Nick Laughed, 'just need a building surveyor, a QBSA inspector, that is, a fake QBSA building inspector', Nick then went on to explain the situation with his cousins.

They have supplied and installed the roof tiles on three unit blocks in Rockhampton, around five thousand square meters and they went in at $155 m², $775,000 for the whole project which was about $250,00 for each unit block.

They completed the first block and submitted their account for that and started on the second block, they had almost finished the second block and they had still not been paid for the first block so they gave the builder twenty four hours to pay for the first block or they would stop work.

'At this stage', said Nick they had already paid for the tiles for the first two blocks which was around forty five dollars per square metre, so around one hundred and fifty grand out of pocket plus the cost of labour which was about the same value again, say three hundred thousand dollars they had put out and the builder had not paid within the twenty four hours, so they stopped work until the builder came good with the money

The builder threatened them with a clause in their contract that basically stated, that if they failed to complete their contract, then the builder could bring in another contractor to complete the works at the expense of the original contractor. And that is what he did for the balance of the second block of about thirty per cent and the third block at 100 per cent,' Nick went on to say, 'The builder back charged my boys with the cost of the replacement tiler who happened to be two hundred and seventeen dollars per square metre, that is forty five per cent more of their original price. For the part of the second unit and all of the third unit, plus liquidated damages for lost time, less the work that they had completed, my boy's bill from the builder was a total of two hundred and fifty thousand dollars.'

'And all legal,' added Harry, 'your boys, they signed the contract which had that, fairly standard clause, that they should have been aware of and it was your boys that stopped work on the job, so the sneaky builder took advantage of that clause and turned your boys project into a loss of two hundred and fifty grand, what a bastard he must be'.

'It wasn't just my boys, Harry, he did a similar thing with some of the other trades as well on this and other projects'.

'It does stink, Nick and sadly the builder has the law behind him through the legitimate, but scandalous acting, contract', Harry stated and then said, 'What do you have in mind for this builder, Nick?'
Nick passed a Queensland Building Services Authority identification card across to Harry as he was driving, a quick glance at it showed a photograph in the top right hand corner of the card, of Harry wearing thick rimmed glasses.

'Hmmm' said Harry, 'from our friend 'Chrispy' no doubt, and the plan?'

Nick was pretty stoked when he saw the pub, he couldn't believe that they had bought it so cheaply and he shuddered when he thought that the copper who was sending the previous owners slowly broke, had intentions of buying the pub for even less.
Sue had placed Nick in room three for the next two nights and Harry had told her that he and Nick would be leaving on Friday morning but returning possibly the next Friday so as to keep the room for Nick.

The next day, Thursday, was a catch up day for both Nick and Harry and many beers were enjoyed, they had planned to drive up to Brisbane on Friday morning and then to Rockhampton on Saturday with a meeting of Nick's cousins on Sunday, a busy weekend coming up.
It was an uneventful trip to Brisbane of some six hours and we stayed at the Casino in the old treasury building. After good entertainment and good food, we had an early night for the trip to Rockhampton.
Nick's cousins seemed to be extensions of Nick, all Russians must be of solid build judging by these fellows, Aleksandr was

Max Barrington

the eldest of the four Romeril brothers then Mikhail, Bogdan and Radimir, Nick called them all by nicknames after he had introduced me to them. Alex, Mick, Dan and Dimmy.

The builder, John Jeffries had been sent an email on the previous Friday morning with a forged heading of the Queensland Building Services Authority and also with a fictitious return address which returned a response to Alex. The email had requested an inspection of a section of tiled roofing in the company of the tiling contractor and the builder for the following Monday morning at ten thirty am.

Harry was the QBSA representative and he met with John Jeffries on the Monday morning at ten thirty, normally Jeffries's building supervisor would handle this type of random inspection but he was enjoying a day off and had gone fishing with one of his friends, who just happened to be Mick Romeril.

Harry had gone into the site office and introduced himself to a very agitated and somewhat entitled John Jeffries who responded to Harry with.

'Haven't you blokes got anything to do, fucking me around like this'?

Harry simply replied, 'Where is the tiling contractor'?

'He should be out there organising the scissor lift, I hope, let's go'.

Harry and Jeffries went around to the first unit block and found Alex and Danny with the scissor lift that was set up next to a six metre rubbish hopper, Dimmy was near the hopper collecting pieces of broken roof tiles and throwing them in the hopper. There was no one else present on this site as it was almost complete.

Harry and Jeffries put on safety harnesses and joined Alex and Danny on the scissor lift, Harry got on before Jeffries, as they had previously planned and they clipped their safety lines to the scissor lift then Jeffries closed and locked the entry door as he was the last one in and standing next to the door. Alex pulled the elevate lever and they rose the four stories, approximately fourteen metres to the roof level.

Unbeknown to Jeffries, as he was glancing across the site, Danny and Alex had changed places with Harry and were now standing next to Jeffries, Danny quietly unclipped Jeffries's safety line and as he did so, Alex reached across and unlocked, then pushed open the door resulting in Jeffries falling from the scissor lift. Alex lowered the scissor lift and let Harry off the scissor lift, Harry immediately proceeded to his car and left the site. Alex called triple zero and asked for an ambulance, he then moved the scissor lift to the other side of the rubbish hopper with the scissor lift door in the opposite direction of the hopper giving the impression that Jeffries had fallen from the roof, he went to the rubbish hopper where Jeffries lay, the broken tiles had made Jeffries landing far worse and were most likely a contributor to his death. Dimmy had climbed into the hopper, removed Jeffries's mobile phone from his pocket and deleted the bogus email from the QBSA. The three brothers waited for the ambulance to arrive.

The three brothers had each made sworn statements to the Workplace Health and Safety officers who attended the accident site. Each statement read precisely the same, Jeffries had called them to rectify a defect in the tiling and had taken them up onto the roof to show them, everyone had connected their safety lines to the roof anchors, but it seemed, except for Jeffries who slipped on the tiled roof. The brothers expressed their grief of losing a workmate and friend.

The building project was placed into the hands of receivers and administrators were appointed, a complete site safety audit was carried out as was a complete contract audit that revealed some illegal contract variations that resulted in the Romeril brothers being paid all of their contractual commitments from Jeffries's now defunct company, as with some other contractors.

It was also revealed that Jeffries's building licence had been cancelled by the QBSA two years prior to him commencing this unit project, this resulted in an internal audit of the QBSA.

Weekdays were slow and easy for both Nick and Harry at the pub, weekends, however, were hectic, but fun.

'How long do you intend to stay here, Harry' asked Nick.

'Probably forever Nick, I think it's time to retire, and you'?

'Yeah, it's a pretty good lifestyle here, I'll probably stay until something comes up' said Nick just as his mobile phone rang. 'What.....you are fucking kidding me,...Mate...I'll grab Harry and we'll be right down there.

'Plenty of time to retire down the track, I suppose' thought Harry.

Max Barrington

THE NEW MARCH

Max Barrington

Max Barrington

The Shooting in The Bar

It was well over 34°c when Mitch had bought his first beer at the bar of the Sovereign Hotel in Cooktown, it was around one o'clock and the bar was quiet with just about a dozen Aboriginal people scattered around. He had just arrived in town and he was about to do some grocery shopping for the housekeeper at the property and then head home when he had a sudden urge for an icy cold beer.

He had never had a drink at pubs as he brewed his own beer at home from ingredients that he had shipped from Brisbane and it was collected for him by the properties accountant from the local freight company in Cooktown. It was the first time he had been to town in about two years.

Mitch ordered a stubbie of beer and had drank about half when he placed it on the bar and then visited the men's room, as he entered the room an Aboriginal man was coming from the room and for no apparent reason 'headbutted' Mitch, he reeled backwards and fell to the floor with blood streaming from a fresh cut between his eyebrows, the Aboriginal had simply walked away.

The girl working behind the bar had slammed the roller door above the bar shut as she saw this happen.

Mitch regained his feet and looked around him towards the bar, it seemed that every Aboriginal male at the bar was looking at him in anticipation of his next move, there were no other white people in the bar and Mitch thought that he had recognised the person that had struck him, he was a thick set male who looked dissimilar to the others, he looked more like a Kalkadoon man rather than the slimmer looking local Kuku men. Mitch took his handkerchief from his pocket and wiped the blood from his face as he walked out of the bar and to his 78 series Landcruiser tray back utility, he opened the passenger side door and reached under the seat and retrieved his Winchester model 94 30-30 carbine and walked back to the hotel, as he walked through the door to the bar a large aboriginal man approached him saying,

'What have you there brother, don't be silly bro give him here to me' and reached towards Mitch in, what Mitch thought, was an attempt to take his rifle.

Mitch quickly worked the lever action on the Winchester sliding one of the five 30-30 150 grain cartridges into the chamber and cocking the rifle ready to fire, he then instantly brought the rifle up to his shoulder and fired the round into the man who was instantly thrown backwards and dropped heavily to the floor.

The noise from the rifle was shattering and everyone in the bar seemed to freeze with their eyes on the now dead man.

Mitch with his rifle still at his shoulder looked across the room towards the Kalkadoon man who was standing at the bar with an amazed expression on his bearded face, Mick rapidly took aim at the bearded face but in his haste pulled on the trigger, rather than squeeze, resulting in the heavy projectile travelling on a slightly lower trajectory and striking its target in the throat which all but decapitated the man. Everyone in the bar stood motionless and the silence was shattering until a woman standing close to the, almost, decapitated man started to scream as the blood was pooling around her feet, she ran across the bar room to the side door which was like a starters signal for everyone else to try to get out of the side door at the same time, another small group of men were huddled to the left of Mitch hoping to get out through the door that Mitch had just entered.

The Cooktown police station is located opposite the Sovereign Hotel and the local police officer in the company of another police officer just happened to have arrived back at the station and were getting out of the police car when they heard the shots from the direction of the pub just 9 metres from them. With their Glock 9mm handguns drawn, they both ran towards the hotel bar where they assumed the sound of the shots had come from, the first police officer entered the bar door just meters behind Mitch and screamed for Mitch to drop the rifle, Mitch had pivoted and fired the next round instinctively, the projectile missing the police officer but hitting another man who was halfway exiting through the door behind the officer, the police officer fired one shot at Mitch which missed him totally but Mitch had already reloaded his rifle and fired almost point blank at the policeman striking him in his high chest area. The other police officer had entered the side door of the bar amid the people trying to rapidly exit and seeing the other officer had been shot dead, he just stared in disbelief at what had happened, Mitch took careful aim at the police officer and shot him somewhere in the middle of his face, Mitch reached down to the floor and collected the four empty cases, the fifth case was still in the breach of the Winchester, he then walked to the bar and picked up his stubbie of beer and took it with him, he had no intention of leaving fingerprints.

By the time that Mitch had replaced his rifle in the Landcruiser and started to drive away, the street seemed to be empty. Mitch was thinking about what a mess he had made, he was asking himself 'Why oh why did that prick have to do that?', but it was too late to think about it now, he had to get out of the area and quickly.

The one and only road that leads out of Cooktown is the Mulligan Highway to Lakeland with a turnoff to the Bloomfield Track which leads to Wujil Wujil and eventually into the Daintree which, due to road conditions can be up to a five hour drive. This road was blocked by the police within a matter of an hour of the reported shootings.

The roads leading from Lakeland are one heading north to Laura and then on to Weipa, which the police had blocked at Laura. The other road is south to Mount Carbine where another roadblock was established by the police.

With only three roadblocks the police had effectively sealed off an area of approximately seven thousand five hundred square kilometres and were confident that the person they were seeking in connection with the five deaths remained in this area and that with reinforcements being sent from Brisbane and other surrounding areas it was only a question of time before an arrest would be made.

Mitch had taken the same route out of Cooktown as the one he had taken into Cooktown earlier that day, he had travelled on the Mulligan Highway for a distance of thirty six kilometres west of Cooktown and turned left onto the Kings Plains Road and had crossed the Annan River and on to the Shiptons Flat Road and over the unnamed creek bridge and left onto another track which after a short distance went directly into the unnamed creek for a shallow causeway crossing, it was almost halfway over the crossing that Mitch turned right into the creek itself and weaved around the boulders, some higher than the Landcruiser, for almost one kilometre and then turned to the left again onto a rocky landing beside the creek that went between two large bounders and then turned right onto a gravel track which led to Mitch's home.

Fergus Laird

Mitchell's (Mitch) father, Fergus was the only son of Harris and Olivia Baird, he had a strict upbringing on their dairy farm which neighboured the adjoining property of the Campbell's famous property known as Duntroon which was later to become the Royal Military Colledge Duntroon.

Upon Fergus completing his higher school certificate he was looking forward to a 'gap' year but his father would hear nothing of it and he was enrolled at the Australian National University and studied to become a civil engineer which he achieved at the age of twenty two in 1962.

Following his father's wishes he then enrolled as a cadet at The Royal Military College and due to his degree in engineering emerged as a Luitenant Specialist Service Officer just eighteen months later and became attached to the Royal Australian Engineers.

In 1965 Fergus went to serve in Vietnam in 3 troop of 1 field squadron, RAE. To be known later as 'The Tunnel Rats' where he served three tours. He became most proficient in jungle warfare and left the army as a major following the end of the war in Vietnam in 1975.

Both Fergus's mother and father were to die in a car accident on the Monaro Highway later that same year on their way to the New South Wales ski fields. Fergus was to inherit the family property and he promptly sold it to the Federal Government and became enormously wealthy and embarked on a one year holiday to Scottland where his parents came from.

Whilst there he met a young lady named Amelia whom he married in Ayrshire Scotland and they returned to Cairns, Queensland in 1978 to make their home on a small property in the Little Mulgrave Valley, in 1980 Amelia gave birth to Mitchel Harris Baird.

Mitchell was aged ten when accompanying his mother on a shopping trip into Cairns, a police car that had another car pulled over and had just finished booking it had left rapidly and pulled in front of their car that was travelling at the speed limit of one hundred kilometres per hour, his mother swerved to the right to avoid a collision and went off the right hand side of the road and into a tree causing a catastrophic accident in which his mother was killed and although Mitchell was witness to what had occurred, the police placed the blame on Mitchell's dead mother. Mitchell was a witness that none of the police wanted to listen to, 'He's just a ten year old kid'.

The police officer in the car had stated that he was still with the offending driver that he had pulled over when Mrs Laird and ran off the road. His notebook containing the offending driver's details had gone missing.

Following the death of Fergus's wife, Fergus became withdrawn from society and seemed to have a huge hate towards the police or anyone else for that matter, with of course the exception of Mitchell.

Mitchell however, could not understand why the police officer that he had seen with his own eyes had lied and had said that he had not been driving his police car when his mother's car had left the road. Why had he lied and why did the other police who had questioned Mitchell had told Mitchell that he was lying to them about the other police officer driving his police car in the path of Mitchell's mother's car and that if he kept on saying that then they would put him in prison for lying. Mitchell knew that he would never trust the police again.

On the day of his mother's funeral at Saint Monica's Church in Cairns City, his father had booked them into a room at the Cairns International Hotel that was within walking distance of the church, later that night his father had left Mitchell in the company of some family friends who were also staying at the hotel following the funeral. Fergus was so depressed and just wanted to be alone and maybe also drunk. He had walked from the hotel across the street to the Great Northern Hotel and had bout a bottle of Johny Walker scotch whisky and had then proceeded to a quiet vacant bench down on the Esplanade to drink his whiskey. He was seeking solitude and was toasting his beloved wife with tears in his eyes when he was set upon by three Aboriginal males telling him that he was white shit and to get out of their country and a squat man with a broad bearded face took the bottle of whiskey from Fergus's hands and spilling the contents during the process. The other two Aborigines were shaping up to punch Fergus, for what seemed like an eternity the two men were punching at Fergus and then the squat Aboriginal started to strike Fergus with the empty whisky bottle, Fergus had turned to the man with the bottle and had instinctively used one of the fighting techniques he had learned in Vietnam, his right hand did one chop across the bridge of the nose of the assailant with the bottle which broke his nose bone and then with his other hand fully open pushed the heal of his hand up and onto the black man's nose which drove the broken nose bone into his brain killing him instantly.

One of the other men had picked up the dropped bottle from the, now dead, man and had struck it full force onto the top of Fergus's head, the bottle shattered and lacerated his head and he fell to the ground.

Fergus awoke in the Cairns Hospital sometime during the following afternoon to discover that he had suffered a fractured skull and three broken ribs, he also discovered that he was under arrest for murder and that he would be taken into custody upon his discharge from the hospital in approximately three days. The nurse, at Fergus's request, had organised for a telephone to be plugged into the phone socket by his bed to enable him to call his solicitor and friend, Brian Haptu to fill him in on his somewhat startling discovery this afternoon upon waking.

The day of his discharge was also the day of his court appearance and he was granted bail as he was a respected

Cairns citizen and had a very poor possibility of flight risk, he had some three months until his case was likely to go hearing.

Brian Haptu had warned Fergus that regardless of the outcome he would certainly be looking at some gaol time, sadly as it seemed for self defence. The Aboriginal legal office was seeking a murder conviction and had plenty of Government money to spend on the best of the Queens Council Barristers, whereas Fergus would have to dip into his own pocket to defend his actions and would plead guilty to manslaughter.

Brian Haptu had become power of attorney over Fergus's affairs and had sought caretakers to look after Fergus's property in his absence and Fergus had organised that Mitchell attend St Augustine's College as a boarding student. Brian was hoping for a three to five year sentence with parole at one year but even Sir James Whitby QC could do no better for Fergus than seven years with early release at five. 'That is justice'? Thought Fergus not looking forward to his interment and wondering what this country, that he fought for, was coming to. He was rapidly losing faith in the way the country seemed to be run.

It was 1993 when Fergus was released from prison and Mitchell was now fifteen years old with only three more years left of school, he was looking forward to becoming a day pupil at the college but that was not to be, his father had announced that he was selling the Little Mulgrave property and moving north near Cooktown and that Mitchell would join him up there once he had finished his education at St Augustine's, he would however, be able to spend his holidays up north with his father.

Whilst in prison Fergus had befriended an elderly cove with the name of Stephen Murray but everyone only knew him as 'Stez', he had got on really well with Stez and had become 'cellmates'. Strez had shown Fergus the ropes and had shown him who to avoid and how life can be survivable in prison. Stez had come from Shiptons Flat, he was born at the Cooktown Hospital, 'If you could call it a hospital' he said, his father had tried a bit of grazing around the area but the crocodiles and Aborigines had taken their toll on the cattle to the point of it being worthless effort, he also had a few gold mines in the area that once had good payable gold.

Stez told Fergus that there were a great many mines in that area from Shiptons Flat to Cedar Bay and then down to Wujal Wujal and the Bloomfield River, some were Tin, some Wolfram and some Gold. Stez had a huge holding in that area, a lot of the mines were on leases and as soon as the lease expired the area was not released and it became part of the Cedar Bay National Park. Stez's 110,000 acres however was freehold and it almost split the national park in half, the Government dearly wanted this part of his block to turn into national park, the other two thirds of his property went towards the west where it was no longer jungle and rainforests and turned into lighter timbered areas with scattered clearings and plenty of scrub. Stez's Father had expanded the property buying out from either farmers or miners who just could not make a go of it, there was quite a collection of buildings scattered throughout the property

Strez was becoming quite ill during the last two years of Fergus's time in prison and just before Fergus's release Stez had succumbed to his illness and had passed away, It came as a great shock to Fergus to lose his one and only real friend in prison, but it came as a far greater shock to learn that Strez had willed everything that he owned to Fergus, including his 110,000 acres at Shiptons Flat and now he was about to go and explore his new property.

Fergus had gathered whatever information and council plans and boundary maps for his new property which he had decided to simply call 'Stezland' he had also acquired every topographical map of the area that he could get his hands on.

For his first look, he had decided to take Mitchell with him and as a long weekend was imminent it seemed the perfect timing for them both to do daytime recce and stay in motel accommodation in Cooktown which was only forty five kilometres from Shiptons Flat.

During the week leading to the long weekend, Fergus had bought a new Land Rover Defender 90 TDI which he thought would be perfect for looking around Stezland, he was aware that there were multiple buildings scattered around the property with the main house just across an unnamed creek. Stez had been in prison for twelve years when Fergus had met up with him and Fergus had known him in prison for at least four years which meant that no one had been to the house for at least sixteen years, it could be interesting he thought.

On the Friday before the weekend, Fergus had everything packed and collected Mitchell, or Mitch as he seemed to prefer these days, from college and they headed to Cooktown.

Fergus was telling Mitch all about Stez on the drive to Cooktown, about how he had really looked after Fergus and helped him survive in prison and finally how Strez had left the huge property to them.

'You are joking Dad?' Asked Mitch.

'Hard to believe isn't it, god knows what it may be worth and god knows what we will find when we get there'

'What was this guy, Stez in prison for Dad?'

'I have no idea, Mitch, he would never tell me, I asked countless times but he would never say'.

Fergus was travelling on the inland way to Cooktown as there had been a lot of rain and king tides were also running which may have made it awkward at the Bloomfield River crossing and could have resulted in a lengthy wait to cross.

They had arrived at the Motel overlooking the Coral Sea at about seven thirty, the delay mainly because of the traffic of people wanting to get away for the weekend. The motel was good and the restaurant was fully booked so they walked the four hundred metres to the RSL club and enjoyed an excellent meal, sadly on their return to the motel they were accosted by Aborigines firstly wanting cigarettes and when told that they had none they were asked for money and when told that there was no money for them they became very abusive with the most vulgar language and kept telling us in no uncertain terms to 'Get out of our country' which really pissed off Fergus and regardless of his parole conditions if Mitch was not with him, they would all be suffering from broken ribs by the morning.

Saturday morning and on their way to Shiptons Flat, Fergus was very impressed with the Land Rover Discovery but Mitch had said that these type of vehicles were regarded as poufters four wheel drives and that a Landcruiser was the only way to go.

'Is that right?' Was the only reply from his father, 'We'll see'.

Mitch was navigating and Shiptons Flat was the easy bit, they had to cross the Annan River and then there was another bridge over an unnamed creek and then they wanted a track to the right in about six kilometres but the wasn't one, they went further for another three kilometres and found a track to the right, Fergus stopped and looked at the map and then he looked at the council boundary maps and decided that they would take this track anyway as it appeared to be on their land, Stezland.

After following this track for about two kilometres they came across another track to their right which they both assumed to be the track that they could not find on the road, after a few minutes they came into a clearing with a house in the distance, as they grew closer they could see a wisp of smoke coming from behind the house, the house had certainly seen much better days, Fergus stopped the car and took out his council boundary map and also his topographical map and laid them on the bonnet to compare. He was certain that they were on their property and showed Mitch with his finger firstly the council boundary map and then confirmed with the topographical map, there was no doubt, Mitch agreed but it appeared that someone was living there. According to the maps and council drawings, there was also another homestead about seven kilometres north of this one.

They drove up to the house, it was pretty derelict and could certainly use some work done to it, there was an old looking Nissan four wheel drive ute parked at the front of the house and an old truck parked to the side, two dogs came running towards them barking as they ran and they did not appear to be too friendly. Fergus told Mitchell to stay in the car as he got out and ignored the dogs, the dogs sensing that this man was not afraid went quiet almost immediately and began to sniff at the air around him. It didn't take long for a man to emerge from the house and shout out 'Hello'. He was an average height man with dark hair and a pathetic looking beard, he looked very unkempt and quite scruffy wearing torn jeans and the remains of an ex military, khaki shirt.

'Are yous guys looking for something' he asked.

'We're just having a look around' Fergus answered.

'Well, don't go looking too far because you're on private property'.

'Oh, is this your property?' Fergus asked now becoming interested.

'No, not that is any of your business anyway, but I'm the caretaker for the owner' The man was not very friendly but was also being cautious.

'Do you know the owner?' Fergus asked the man,' Does he live around here?' Fergus could see another person inside the house and looking through the side of a curtain.

'Why? do you want him for something?'

'Yes, I would certainly like to know who he is and where I can contact him, It's quite important actually'

'Well, he's away in Cairns just now and he can't be contacted so it might be a good idea if you just get off the property now, the man was becoming irritated and Fergus had to keep his cool as he did not know if the other person inside the house had a gun or not.

'This will come as a surprise to you, but I am the owner of this property since two months ago and I think you are lying' Fergus began to get firm with him, the man just stared blankly at Fergus, who opened the back door of the Landrover and took out his folder containing council copies of his tiles and boundary plans. He placed these on the bonnet of the Landrover and told the man to come over here to which he slowly started to walk towards the Landrover, as he got closer Fergus turned towards him and held out his right arm and said,

'I'm Fergus Baird and this is my son Mitchell, the man hesitated and then slowly shook the hand of Fergus and nodded towards Mitchell in the car.

'Rodney Hadrick' said the man sounding somewhat confused, 'and this is me mate Jason' as he turned slightly towards a second man now coming from the house. Jason waved and said good day as he joined the small group, 'I guess we had better talk', he concluded, looking at Fergus. Rodney suggested they come into the house and he would shout a cup of instant coffee, Fergus declined on the coffee but accepted the invitation inside. It was much cleaner and tidier inside the house than Fergus would have imagined, they went into the kitchen and sat at the table there which was also neat and clean, it was huge and looked like it was handmade from local hardwood, Jason asked Mitchell if he would like a Coke.

'Yes, thanks that would be good, Mitch is the name everyone calls me'.

Fergus laughed, 'I'm learning' he said towards Mitchell.

'No worries Mitch, here you go mate' said Jason passing a cold can of Coke from the ancient looking but functional refrigerator, 'Too early for a beer Fergus?' Jason quizzed.

'Why not?' Fergus said as he sat down at the table, 'That's if everyone else is'.

'Make it three' said Rodney as he sat down also next to Fergus.

Fergus looked toward the door they had just entered through as he heard the sound of a vehicle pulling up outside.

'That'll be the missus and Jas'es girlfriend' said Rodney, 'Been to town shopping'.

They all waited until the two women came into the kitchen from outside and Rodney said,

'Belinda, this is Fergus, the owner of this property and his boy, Mitch, and then looking towards the woman with Belinda he added, 'Alison is Jason's girlfriend, meet Fergus and Mitch, did I miss anyone? Grab a couple more chairs Belinda and join in, do you girls want a beer?'

Both Belinda and Alison declined a beer and looked quite shocked at what Rodney had just said as they moved a chair each in toward the big table.

Fergus sensing the tension, said that he would start and told them that he had inherited the whole of the property and little while ago but did not go into detail, he told them that he was here today with Mitch just to do some exploring, he went on to say that he was unaware of anyone living on the, his, property and would like to know the full circumstances of why they were living here. The room was silent, the four residents just looked at each other and then Rodney explained how they had all arrived there.

It was about four years ago that he and Belinda had been travelling around Australia in an old motorhome that was fitted to a Ford Transit vehicle and had started from Geelong in Victoria, they had both been working as Chef's at a restaurant and that's how they had met and decided that a life on the road would beat working for the tight arsed prick that owned the restaurant and had started to plan a working trip around Australia and the first part of the plan was to look for a vehicle which they did and after looking at many, that they could not afford, decided on the Ford Transit which was affordable once they had both sold their cars and pooled the money.

It had been a great trip travelling up the West Coast of Australia to Broom where they spent over twelve months both working and enjoying the climate and the atmosphere of the tropics. They had discovered that on their trip so far they seemed to spend more than they earned and found that they had to try to save up money to move to the next town.

After almost three years of travelling and working they ended up in Cooktown with a blown engine in the Ford and no money for repairs.

They were both working at different venues in Cooktown and renting a place just out of town, they had sold the Ford motorhome to a mechanic in town and had caught the bus from Cooktown to Mareeba to buy the Hilux ute that they now had and returned to Cooktown with it.

Belinda had befriended an old fellow, George, who worked as a kitchen hand with her and he had said that he was going back to live in Brisbane and that she could have his house if she wanted it. Belinda and Rodney had made arrangements with George to go out and check out this house.

George had told them that it was his uncle's property and that he was looking after it for him and that it would be fine for them to take it over, rent free in return for keeping it maintained, it sounded good. The place was pretty well run down, as it still was, but it meant that they could save the three hundred and fifty dollars a week that they were paying in rent.

Jason had been working as a barman with Rodney and was looking for a place to rent for him and his girlfriend Alison. Rodney had suggested that they come and share the big house out at Shiptons Flat with them, rent free in return to help keep the place maintained.

'So, here we are and I must add, and loving it' concluded Rodney as he moved to the fridge for more drinks. 'So, what happens now?' He added as he passed another beer to Fergus.

'I have no idea', replied Fergus, 'I have no plans for anything at this stage, as I said earlier we are just out exploring at the moment, but I can't see why anything should change with you guys at this stage. When I do move out here I would most likely build somewhere around here so you guys are just fine here for now.

'There's a much bigger and better place just over the hill you know' added Jason.

'The council boundary plans show it as the homestead' said Fergus, 'but when I saw this place I thought I must have read it wrong, so this isn't the homestead?'.

'No, I think the other place was the main homestead and this was the manager's house' added Rodney, 'The other place is, or I should say was, quite a mansion in comparison to this'.

'And nobody living there?' Asked Fergus.

'No, there is no power out there, I think the lines all went down in a bushfire many years ago and plus it is really out of the way and hard to get to as the road is so rough, it's a fair way from here along this track' Rodney answered.

Fergus gave Rodney his contact details and his Little Mugrave phone number along with his mobile telephone number which was unreliable around where he lived and next to useless around here at Shiptons Flat. Mobile telephones had just advanced from car phones to the large brick size telephones with a battery life of around three hours. He took up Rodney's offer to show him the way out to the bigger house and both Rodney and Jason accompanied him and Mitchell in the Landrover. It was quite a good track for about two kilometres and then the track headed towards a deep gorge and became very rough with huge craters in the track causing Fergus to stop the Landrover and engage low range four wheel drive, the track went in between two hills that met each other forming a narrow passage with towering rocks and boulders on each side. A large boulder had rolled from higher ground and was now placed firmly in the centre of the track leaving just enough room to squeeze past in the Landrover.

Once past the gorge, the country opened up to lightly timbered hills and the track started to climb up and away from the gorge, here there was a 'Y' section where the track went to the left or straight through where they saw a herd of about thirty cattle that had been started by the noise of the car and were clamouring up a timbered incline out of view.

'Who's cattle?' Fergus quizzed.

'Probably your's, there are quite a few around and I have never seen anyone come past the house to check on them and I have never seen them mustered, but I am sure that there is no other way into this area other than past the house, you need to veer to the right, going left will take you over the mountain and down to the beach. There are some really nice beaches but you will want to watch out for the crocodiles, they are all over the place down there.' Rodney answered.

The track to the right came over a ridge and the country now levelled to an almost flat area of lightly timbered and well grassed with views to the left down to the Annan River, Fergus could now see that this track may well indeed be the only access to this area and soon the house came into view.

In the distance, the home appeared very impressive and with a commanding view which gave anyone approaching the house, the impression of being announced of their arrival.

'Well, you couldn't sneak up on it, could you?' Fergus announced as he looked towards the homestead.

It was set on a batter that had been cut into the slope of the hill giving it a majestic appearance, it's white painted walls stood out in the sunlight with its subdued pale eucalyptus green coloured corrugated roof adding to its dignity. It wasn't until they got closer that the decaying of the magnificent looking house became apparent. There was a full length verandah on all four sides of the home, the hardwood timber decking on this has deteriorated in places to the extent that it was a hazard just to walk to the front door which was locked. Rodney knew where the key was on the top of the front door toplight framing.

'An old bloke at the bowls club told me where this was, we've been inside and had a look but we didn't touch anything as we were advised not to by the old bloke as it is supposed to be a shrine of some sort, he told us that he'd tell us the story one day' Rodney said as he retrieved the key and unlocked the front door. 'Apparently, the old bloke used to be the manager here and lived in our,...your place back at the flat'.

As they walked through the front door into the entry vestibule onto the spotted gum timber floor they could see that the house was actually furnished and seemed to have at least five millimetres of dust cover everywhere and the dusty, musty dank smell was somewhat overpowering.

To the left of the entry the doorway led to a corridor that had a doorway to its left as the kitchen entry, the kitchen consisted of a large double oven fuel stove range halfway along the right hand wall as you entered, a large square table dominated the centre of the room and two kitchen sinks against the left hand side wall. Another doorway at the end of the room went into a small dining or breakfast, room with a large window looking back along the valley that they had just driven down, back out of the kitchen door and left down the corridor and an opening to the right which was about one point six metres by one point two metres and had a door on each side that led to powder rooms.

Further along the corridor, the next door to the left opened into a large rectangular room of about five meters wide by eight metres deep with a long dining table in the centre of the room with five chairs on each side. To the left of the room was an enormous fireplace and a large window at the front of the room, a doorway to the left of this dining room led to a room of similar dimensions with a full size billiard table in the centre of the room. Lounge chairs faced a large window on the other side of the billiard table and a bar located on the right hand side with a magnificent gun cabinet mounted behind the bar.

The other side of the entry led off to four bedrooms, complete with bed, furniture and ensuites, a fifth bedroom, the largest, also with an ensuite was void of all furniture and it could be seen that carpet had been pulled up from the floorboards. The rest of the house was a laundry, another bathroom and a utility room located behind the entrance vestibule with a door leading outside to the rear of the house

Where a two bedroom self contained caretaker's unit was situated. Woodpanneing and wallpaper were peeling from the walls and the ceilings were falling in some areas, at one area Fergus could see that the internal construction of the partition walls was 150 series concrete masonry block lined with 13mm plasterboard which made him presume that the external walls were most likely 200 series concrete masonry block also with plasterboard on the internal sides and cement rendered on the external sides, so the house was not that old, nowhere near as old as what it appears from first sight.

There were some other buildings that were showing advanced signs of deterioration that they did not go to investigate as it was starting to get late and they headed back to the first house, or, Rodney's as Fergus had called it for want of a better name.

'That place is amazing' Fergus said in a quite excited voice, 'It's quite a grand homestead and that's for sure, I'd love to know the story, there's just got to be a story here'.

'Well check out the bowling club, it's Saturday, there's a chance the old bloke will be there' offered Jason.

Rodney added ' his name is Colin, I remember now that the barman called him 'Crazy Col'.

They were back in Cooktown at about four o'clock and Fergus walked down to the Bowls Club while Mitchell had a rest at the motel and watched television.

There were no bowls on that day which seemed surprising to Fergus, what with it being a long weekend, as he walked past the two bowling greens to the main club entry he noticed a sign on the fence of the bowling greens *Whites Only on Weekends*' Fergus had a chuckle, he knew exactly what it meant but wondered how they got away with it. The Cooktown Bowling Club is like nearly, every other bowling club in country towns, windows full length looking onto the bowling greens, the bar at the back looking towards the bowling greens, stools around the bar and tables and chairs in front of the bar near the windows, kitchen and dining room on the far right and pokie room on the far left, even the people in the club all look the same.

As Fergus walked towards the bar he was pretty sure that he'd found the person that he wanted to talk to, the man was at the very end of the bar where it turns to meet the wall, he was at the corner sitting on a stool and he had a perfect view of the bowls greens and anyone coming into the club. He had a ten ounce glass of beer in front of him, the ten ounce beer glass in Queensland is called a 'Pot', in New South Wales it's known as a 'Midday', this 'Pot' was almost empty.

The barman had watched Fergus walk up to the bar in anticipation of him ordering a drink, he thought that Fergus looked like a 'Schooner', a fifteen ounce beer glass, as he took one from the fridge as Fergus got to the bar,

'Schooner?' Asked the barman.

'Sounds good to me' Fergus replied and taking a punt added, 'And a Pot for Col too, thanks'

Colin heard what the stranger had said and his brain went into overdrive, 'Who the fuck is this?' he was thinking. It was getting harder and harder every day to remember things, especially people's names who he hadn't seen for a while, but he was pretty certain that he didn't know who this bloke was and he knew that he was not from around here.

'My name is Fergus Laird and I was hoping that I might be able to have a chat with you'.

'Well', started Colin, 'it depends on what it is that you're after, I am pretty busy just now, as you can see' and added a chuckle.

'I was wondering if you know the name, Stephen Murray'? Fergus had hardly finished saying the name when the old man's face drained of blood and he stared questionably at Fergus.

'What if I do?' The hint of joviality had totally disappeared from the man's voice, 'You'll do a lot better for yourself by not mentioning that prick's name around here'.

'He died a little whil....'

'That's the news that I have been waiting to hear for over twenty years', interrupted the old man, 'that prick should have died twenty years sooner' The old bloke looked quite ecstatic, 'But, who are you to come here to tell me this, what's going on here?'

Fergus didn't tell the man that he had met Stephen Murray in prison, he merely had told him that he had inherited the property through some obscure business dealings of many years prior, but that he wanted to find out more about the property and had heard that Colin had once been the Manager there. Colin looked carefully and seriously at Fergus and said,

'For me, Fergus, it is a very painful story, one that I have not told for quite a while now, which perhaps is better to let go, but you have brought me great news today of that miserable bastard's death that I will tell you the story, but I will warn you that you may not have enough money to pay for the beers that it will take to tell you', then with a grin Colin said let's go and sit down at a table away from this nosey bastards ears', indicting towards the barman who had been hovering close by since Fergus had arrived.

Stephen Murray

As they organised another drink and settled down at a table by the window Fergus was starting to think that his old mate Stez may not have been all that he had seemed to be and he was mentally preparing himself for some information that might not be good news. Colin Freebody, it seemed, was about to give Fergus the full history of his newly acquired property that he had casually named 'Stezland', Fergus was beside himself.

'The old bloke was a good man', Colin had started, 'He'd done a lot for me, even when he only had the old original place of around three hundred acres, me an him were running cattle through the national park without anyone knowing the difference, more than just a few times did we raise eyebrows at the cattle sales for such a large volume of store cattle that we were selling and in such good condition from such a small acreage property'.

Colin went on to tell me more about 'Old Ron Murray' who had started his small cattle property at Shiptons Flat and had helped himself to using the crown lands in that area as his personal cattle run. Most of the land around the Cedar Bay mountain ranges had been set aside for Tin Mining back in the 1870's and in the 1970's the Hippies had moved into most of the abandoned Tin Mines and the Bjelke-Petersen Governments had sent in the police to move the Hippies on and destroy their commune. This was great for Ron who was blaming the Hippies for the loss of some of his cattle.

Max Barrington

The Government meanwhile was seeking the mine owners to effect a buy back system for their mines.

Ron was way ahead of the Government and had started tracking down the Tin Miners well before the Government had moved the Hippies on and had been buying the mines and other properties that were freehold.

Colin had a small acreage at Shiptons Flat and lived in a small cottage on their property with his wife, Marge and his son David. Both Colin and his son David had started to work for Ron Murray on a full time basis building cattle yards on various parts of Ron's extended property, Many of the leases that Ron had gained also had accommodation buildings of various types that were once used by the miners. Ron had recruited Aboriginal males from Wujil Wujil and had trained them to become stockmen and allowed them to live in these miner's cottages with their families in return for work each year for mustering and other work around the property, he also provided them with as much fresh beef as they wanted to eliminate cattle being stolen.

Ron lived alone in the 'Gatehouse' as it was called, where Rodney and company were now living, Ron had an estranged wife who lived with their son Stephen in the Cains suburb of Manunda. Stephen would come out to Shiptons Flat on school holidays to help around the property but most times it resulted in arguments with his father and he would always leave to return to Cairns vowing never to return, which happened every year.

Life was good and Ron had started to breed cattle that were better able to manage the heavily timbered slopes around the Cedar Bay Area by introducing the Aberdeen Angus to this area of his property, on the other side, to the west of the flat, he maintained the 'Droughtmaster' cattle. This way he had the best of both worlds and things just got better for him.

Ron had suffered a heart attack in 1955, he was just fifty years old. It came as a shock to everyone who knew Ron, especially Colin Freebody. Ron Murray's estranged wife had the funeral held in Cairns and his body was interred in the Cairns Cemetery. Colin often wondered if she would have bothered with his funeral at all had she known that all of Ron Murray's estate was willed to his son Stephen and that his estranged wife was not mentioned in his will.

Stephen Murray had approached Colin at the funeral and had asked if he would stay on at the property and manage it for him to which Colin had agreed. Stephen had said that he would move out there and live at the 'Gatehouse' and work with Colin to keep the property viable.

Ron Murray must have left a grand amount of money in his will besides the property as Stephen, having looked over the 'gatehouse' had decided to build a new house some distance away from the 'Gatehouse' on the rise where the big homestead stands today and told Colin that he could have the 'gatehouse' as his residence if he wanted. The 'Gatehouse' suited Colin as things were not good with him and his wife and it made his life much more pleasant to live there with his son David who was also working on the property.

Stephen had engaged a Cairns Architect to design and supervise the construction of his new home which was estimated to be completed in just under twelve months.

There was not a day that went past that a truckload of building materials did not arrive to drive past the gatehouse to the site of the new home. Meanwhile, Stephen was enjoying a holiday in the Philippines where he had met his bride to be, she was a 17 year old Filipino and her parents wanted the equivalent of Two hundred and fifty Australian dollars per month as her dowry which is worked on how much she was earning for the family. Stephen thought that for the price of thirty thousand dollars, he had better make sure that her health was good and had her see a doctor, the doctor's report showed that she had a heart murmur and that she may need heart surgery in the near future to correct this. Stephan had decided not to go ahead with the wedding and the girl's family was distraught at losing the monthly dowry and offered her younger 16 year old sister as a substitute to which he agreed pending a doctor's report.

At twenty five years old, a millionaire, it seems, and a cattle property owner Stephen Murray now also had a Filipino wife whom he just knew would cause jealous looks from his friends in Cooktown and Cairns.

He had bought a house in Cooktown and he and his new wife resided there until their new home beyond the 'gatehouse' was completed and ready to move into.

The 'Murrays' cattle property had never had a name other than 'The Murray Property'. Colin could never understand why the 'Gatehouse' was called the 'Gatehouse' as it was closer to being in the centre of the property rather than the start of the property until Ron Murray had explained to him that it was once the very end of the Murray property until Ron had bought the mining and other properties and it was now the gateway to the Cedar Bay Ranges part of the Murray property.

Stephen Murray thought he was 'the man', he had a lot of money and he owned a lot of land, he also thought that he had married the most envious woman in the world and she *was* pretty, there was no doubt about that but she looked like a child dressing in her mother's clothes and wearing her mother's makeup.

Whenever Stephen was seen around town or in the hotels with his bride he knew that people were talking behind his back and he suspected it was jealousy, but when he overheard on one occasion, a large Aboriginal woman shouting out to another woman 'Look, there's that Murray cunt with the slant eyed slut', which had caused a large group of men to burst out laughing, that was the last straw and he made sure that he wasn't seen in public with her again but he still received calls from people in the street shouting out to him 'Hey Murray cunt, where's your slant eyed slut' followed by great bouts of laughter. He would often hear the popular TV ad phrase 'Shouda gone to Specsavers'.

The new house was finally finished and new furniture, mostly from Brisbane had been delivered and installed, Stephen moved in with his Filipino wife. He had planned for a huge housewarming party but after hearing the comment and knowing that people talked behind his back, he had changed his mind and just made the moving in a very private matter.

Stephen soon became bored around the property and he began taking trips alone to Cairns, Townsville and even Brisbane, doing what, other than drinking, lord knows but he always left his young Filipino wife alone in the big house on the slopes in the Cedar Bay Range and he was sometimes gone for weeks. He would return to the property and talk with Colin about how the cattle were going and asking about other matters relating to the property but Colin could see that Stephen had no interest in the property whatsoever.

Stephen had gone into Cooktown one Saturday to the races that were held there periodically and had not returned until quite late that night as Colin remembered hearing a car that he thought was David returning home, he also thought that he heard another car again some hours later but he wasn't certain. Colin and David had both also been in Cooktown that day, Colin to the Bowls Club and David had gone to the races.

David was not home at the 'Gatehouse' when Colin had arrived and Colin had gone to bed quite early.

Colin had not been overly surprised that David was still not home when he got up on the Sunday morning as he assumed that he may have stayed in town after the races.

When David was still not home by Monday morning, Colin was becoming concerned and he drove into Cooktown to see if he could find David, he had gone to the Shell service station where a friend of David's works as a mechanic, his friend had said that he had gone to the races on Saturday with David and that David had left there quite early before the races had ended and he hadn't seen him since then.

Colin had returned back to the property and had resumed his work. By the Wednesday David had still not arrived back and Colin drove to Shiptons Flat to ask his wife if she had seen David, he was afraid that she would go ballistic when he asked her if She knew where David was, and she did and called the police to report a missing person.

The following Monday morning the police called at the 'Gatehouse' looking for David and had asked Colin if he had seen or heard anything about him. It just wasn't like David he had told them, they asked if Stephen was around and Colin had told them that he had no idea of where Stephen might be, Colin had told them how to find the mansion down the track about eight kilometres and that if he wasn't there then his wife would probably be home and she may know where Stephen was.

Colin was just about to leave in his ute when the police car returned from the direction of Stephen's house, the police car flashed its headlights at Colin indicating that they wanted him.

'We're going to have to seal this gate down to Stephen's house and not let anyone through here', the constable told Colin, 'There are two bodies down there, most likely a murder suicide'.

'What!.. Stephen?.....and.' was all Colin could say.

'Yes, we don't know too much just yet but it would seem to indicate it, I have left John down there while I go back to Cooktown to summon help from Cairns, I will be back hopefully before dark, don't let anyone go down there as it is a crime scene'.

Colin felt shaky and wanted to vomit, somehow he thought that he was not too surprised with Stephen committing suicide, he had been acting strange for quite a while now, leaving his young wife on her own while he goes travelling around the country on his drinking binges, 'Oh I wish David was here, he's missing out on all the excitement' he said to himself.

There were vehicles coming and going past the 'Gatehouse' all that night and as much as Colin would try he could get no more information, everyone he spoke to as they came and went would offer no information.

It was around ten o'clock the next morning when a flatbed truck with loading ramps appeared at the gatehouse with the driver asking for instructions on how to find the police crime centre. Somewhat puzzled Colin had told the driver how to get to the house which he presumed was now the crime centre.

Colin suffered a violent shock and collapsed to the ground when the truck returned an hour later with David's ute on the back.

A police car that was following the truck had witnessed Colin falling to the ground and had stopped to assist him and call for an ambulance from Cooktown.

Colin had regained consciousness the next day, Wednesday, at the Cairns Hospital where he had been transferred to by helicopter from Cooktown the previous day. He had suffered a stroke and was slowly recovering. Colin was totally lost, why was he here, what stroke, how could he have a stroke, then he remembered...David...... David's ute.......on the back of the truck.....David was missing.......it's David's ute, why was it at Stephen's house.....Stephen is dead, why is David there....what is happening? He saw the buzzer lying close to his hand and he tried to pick it up but his hand would not move, he tried again, but his hand would not move, he used his other hand and it did move and he got the buzzer and pressed.

The nurse seemed to arrive almost immediately, Colin looked at her and simply said 'help' as the tears welled in his eyes. He had been given a strong sedative and he had slept until early the next day and was given breakfast and advised that the doctor would be here to see him in about half an hour and then the police wished to talk to him and that his wife would also be here later this afternoon.

The doctor had explained to Colin that he had suffered a stroke and that he would recover to some degree but not fully and said that if he did not feel up to talking to the police then he did not have to, Colin had interrupted the doctor to say that he *did* want to talk to the police, he had many questions that would not wait and he asked the doctor what he knew about David, his son? But the doctor said he knew nothing other than Colin's medical condition but that he the police were waiting outside and that he would send them in.

The Cairns detective, Sergeant John Collins, entered the ward quietly and went up beside Colin to introduce himself but had hardly opened his mouth when Colin asked him.

'How's David, my boy David,? Is he in trouble? Did he kill Stephen?'

The detective was at an utter loss, he could not comprehend what Colin was saying.

'Er, Mr Freebody, I think you may be a bit confused' the detective answered.

'But is David OK'

'David is deceased I'm afraid to have to tell you Mr Freebody' the detective said softly and slowly so that there could be no mistake in what he was telling Colin. 'His body had been identified by his mother, your wife, from photographs of his two tattoos on the back of his calves'.

Colin was in shock and just stared at the wall behind the detective and although the detective asked Colin some more questions there were no answers from Colin, just staring at the wall. The detective called the nurse and then left.

Later that day Colin's wife had arrived, very teary, at the hospital and as soon as she looked at Colin they both burst into tears, Marge sat on the chair beside Colin's bed and after a while, Colin managed to talk to Marge.

'It was just horrible' she said, 'They would not let me see the body but only showed me two photographs of David's tattoos, they wouldn't tell me why I couldn't see him, they just said that it was for the better that I didn't'.

She had told Colin that she had been told that David's body and the body of another person had been found at the house on the property, they did not tell her anything other than that and asked if the person in the photos was David. She had responded that it was definitely David's legs because she knew the tattoos, one with her and Colin's name in a scroll on his left calve. Other than that she knew nothing else and she was in tears again.

When the two Cooktown constables had arrived at Stephen's house that Monday morning the first thing they saw was the Toyota Hilux utility parked at the front of the house. They had knocked on the door of the house several times on both the front door and the back door to no avail, they had then looked inside the Hilux ute which was unlocked and the log books in the glovebox showed that the car belonged to David Freebody.

While one constable was looking inside the car the other was going around the house on the verandah and trying to peer inside the windows that were all covered by netting curtains on the inside. It was during this that the constable first heard and then saw the huge amount of blowflies between the glass window and the curtain netting, he immediately called the other constable as he broke a window panel in the front door to gain entry to the house. Upon opening the door the smell was overpowering and the constable reeled back outside trying to get his breath. The other constable went inside the house to find the cause of the smell that was coming from the main bedroom where two bodies, covered in flies and maggots, lay in a pool of dried blood on the king size bed. Upon seeing this and entering the room no further than the doorway, he turned and ran from the building trying to suppress the vomit welling in his throat.

After recovering from the shock of their discovery, one constable remained guarding the scene as the other returned to the Cooktown police station to call for assistance.

Sergeant's John Collins and Chris Murphy were dispatched from Cairns Police Headquarters at eleven AM that Monday morning and arrived at the Cooktown Police Station at three PM that afternoon, two members of the forensic science section from Mareeba Police Station were already at the Cooktown station waiting for the detectives, having been briefed by the constable that had discovered the scene they all left together for the 'house on the Murray property' as it was known.

By around seven PM that evening, the conclusion of the identity of the bodies was, although not confirmed, that the female body was the wife of Stephen Murray, this was ascertained by various photographs from around the house. The body of the male was assumed to be that of Stephen Murray. Positive body identification of the male body by comparing photographs that were around the house was made extremely difficult owing to the disfiguration of the face by what appeared to be a shotgun blast. It was also assumed that the owner of the vehicle that was parked in front of the house, David Freebody was a person of interest.

The bodies were transported to Cairns that night and people were sought the next morning who may be able to identify the bodies, the condition of the male face was so bad that it was decided to ascertain a positive identification by use of photographs of the two tattoos on the back of the male bodies calves. The mother of Stephen Murray was shown photographs of tattoos taken from the dead body and emphatically stated that the deceased was *not* her son.

Colin Freebody was not in any condition to assist in body identification and his wife was later found in the waiting room at the Cairns hospital, she was shown the photographs and confirmed the body to be that of her son David.

The police had put together the scenario that Stephen Murray had arrived home from the Cooktown races on that Saturday night to discover David Freebody in his house with his wife, apparently in their bed as that is where the bodies were found and it was believed that is where the murders took place. It was assumed that Stephen had entered the house to discover the pair and had then taken a 12 gauge shotgun from the gun cabinet in the billiard room and returned to the bedroom and shot both of the victims with a shotgun. No spent shotgun cases nor the shotgun had been found at the scene but an autopsy report on both bodies had confirmed the presence of 9mm shot made from a mixture of pure lead and antimony that are consistent with 12 gauge cartridges known as 'Triple A's' which have a shot content of 9 x 9mm balls. David Freebody was shot in the face and the wife of Stephen Murray was shot in the back of the head.

The bodies were not discovered until eight after the shootings and rapid decomposition had set in due to the extreme temperature. The police were looking for Stephen Murray.

'And', concluded Colin, 'The police had searched Murray's house and had removed other firearms and ammunition that were in the gun cabinet in the billiard room, they then closed and locked the house and placed the police seals on it.

The house had remained locked until Stephen Murray was caught in a small country town in Victoria and was sent back to Brisbane for trial, just after this Murray's Attorney attended the house with removalists and much of Murray's possessions were removed from the house and taken away, the bed that the bodies were found on was taken from the house together with the mattress and the carpet from the bedroom and set alight beside the house'.

Fergus went back to the bar for about the fifth time and replenished their drinks and returned to the table with Colin.

'So what happened to the house after that' Fergus asked.

'Nothing,..nothing, no one had been there except the kids staying at the 'Gatehouse' and now yourself as you have told me, the place had just been slowly rotting away. I must admit that I was tempted to burn it but I would only have ended up in jail for it, not worth it. I left the 'Gatehouse' and went back with Marge, we both needed each other after the tragedy of losing our David.

It was half past seven PM as Fergus walked from the bowling club and went to the RSL club's restaurant to get a couple of takeaway pizzas and walked back to the motel amid the cries of the traditional owners of the land for cigarettes, beer and money, 'fucking cretins' he thought.

Mitchell and Fergus had decided to go back to the 'Murray's' house again the next morning to do some more exploring of the home with the thoughts of bringing it back to occupation status and move in as their new residence.

The second look at the home was a bit dismaying for Fergus as when a closer look seemed to reveal more deterioration, he only quickly looked at the room where the murders took place and he found that it didn't really phase him and that he would most likely turn this into his own room, Mitchell had already claimed his bedroom and had spent more time looking at the billiard table and trying to find all the billiard balls and pool ball that went with it as well as the cues. Although Fergus could imagine the cost of getting the house back to its former glory to be quite extensive, he decided that as he had got the place for nothing it was probably well worth it even though it would most likely cost almost as much as a new home.

That afternoon as they were leaving Shiptons Flat and had just turned onto a very quiet Mulligan Highway they were pulled over by a police officer who was up ahead on the side of the road and flagging them down, Fergus pulled up behind the police Landcruiser and wound down his window as the police officer walked up to them.

'Good afternoon sir, I'm Senior Constable Kirkland, Queensland Police, and I am conducting random breath testing and require you to submit a sample of your breath'.

'Good afternoon' Fergus responded.

'This is a breath testing device. To comply with my requirement, I direct you to place your mouth over the mouthpiece of the device and blow directly and continuously through that mouthpiece until told to stop by me'.

Fergus complied and leaned towards the device held by the officer.

'Commence blowing now,......keep going.....keep going,..stop!'

Fergus knew that he would be negative as he had nothing alcoholic to drink since Saturday night and had since eaten dinner, breakfast and lunch in the last eighteen hours, however, the officer had shown some concern with the reading and had quizzed him on what he had been drinking as he was close to borderline.

'I will have to arrest you for the purpose of conducting a breath analysis test at the police station, get out of your vehicle'

'Grow up' was Fergus's response, 'What about my son, are you taking him to Cooktown too, you can't leave him here on his own, he is only a minor and I am not leaving my vehicle here beside the road for very obvious reasons'.

'I,..I thought he was an adult' the officer said, not so sure of himself after the quick quip from Fergus and noting that he did not seem the least intimidated as most motorists are when confronted with this situation.

'Well, he is a child, so I suggest that you call for backup' Fergus said.

'I'll decide when and if I call for backup' the officer said now regaining his authority, 'I'll do a roadworthy check of your vehicle while I decide what I am going to do with you'.

'It's a new car, it has not got two thousand kilometres on it, there is nothing wrong with it' Fergus was starting to lose his cool and he tried to hold himself. It seemed to run in the family, his father also had a very short temper and Mitchell had also shown signs of a short fuse on occasions.

The police officer started walking around the car, Fergus looked at Mitchell and grinned, but Mitchell looked like death warmed over, he was just glaring at the road ahead.

'What's wrong Mitch?' He said but before Mitchell could reply there was a smashing sound at the back of the Landrover and the constable walked back to Fergus's window quickly.

'You have a broken tail light and I am giving you a vehicle defect for that and I am also booking you for exceeding the speed limit by fifteen kilometres per hour, hand me your license'.

Fergus somehow maintained his calm, he was biting down on his lower lip hard enough to make it bleed slightly.

He refused to sign the officer's booking page and the constable just tore it off and threw it into the vehicle beside Fergus. The constable sensing that Fergus was about to blow his top got into his police cruiser and left.

Fergus just sat in his seat and regained his posture, he looked at Mitch and asked him what was wrong.

'That's the same cop that killed Mum' was all that he replied.

Senior Constable Stanley Kirkland had arrived back at the Cooktown Police Station with an irking feeling about what had just transpired, there was something with the name, Laird, it was not a run of the mill name and it suddenly hit him, Amelia Laird, the woman in the car whom he had pulled in front of near Cairns about five years ago.

He remembered the day very well and he would never forget it, he was leaving the scene of booking a driver for speeding and he didn't even look behind him as he pulled back onto the highway, thank god the woman driving the car had seen him and had suddenly swerved and missed him but had gone head on into a tree on the other side of the road, he remembered seeing the kid looking out of the passenger side window at him as the speeding car went past him and into the tree. The kid survived to tell investigating police that the police car had pulled in front of his mother's car causing her to swerve and hit the tree killing her instantly. Kirkland was a witness and he testified that he was booking another driver and both cars were well off the road when this crazy woman simply crossed to the wrong side of the road and then drove into the tree.

Kirkland's testament was believed, the testament of the ten year old boy was not.

Could this bloke he pulled up today be some relative? Doubtful, even if he was so what? Kirkland had been cleared of all involvement in that accident, but just as an afterthought, he destroyed the infringements that he had issued to Fergus just in case the guy was to jump up and down as Kirkland did not want to open up old wounds regardless of how well he had covered himself back in that incident of five years prior, he was lucky that his superiors did not question him more on his missing notebook to find the identity of the driver that he had pulled over that day who would have witnessed the whole accident.

The New March

In medieval Europe, a march or mark was, in broad terms, any kind of borderland. More specifically, a march was a border between realms

Fergus and Mitchell had arrived back to Little Mulgrave.

Mitchell had resumed boarding school as he and his father had planned to allow Fergus to get their new home at Shiptons Flat refurbished and ready for their occupation, Mitchell would be joining his father during each school holiday to assist with the set up of the property for grazing cattle. The event of his father inheriting the property that his father was calling 'Stezland' had caused Mitchell to consider doing Veterinary Science after he completed school rather than Medicine which was his earlier intention, anyway, he had plenty of time for that as he would be taking a 'gap year' following his completion of school in just over two years time.

Fergus had an uneasy feeling following the altercation with the police constable near Cooktown, this copper certainly did seem like a troublemaker and if what Mitchell had said was true, that he was the cop involved with Amelia's accident. He had the constable's name on the infringement notice and he now called his solicitor, Brian Haptu who was involved with the accident and he confirmed, after checking his file that the police constable who was a witness to the accident was in fact Senior Constable Stanley Kirkland.

Fergus was now thinking that this Kirkland had now annoyed him and may become a nuisance to him, back in his jungle warfare days in Vietnam if there was a hazard along ones march, then one did not detour around the hazard but removed it and then the march continued, perhaps, thought Fergus, that he should consider removing Kirkland.

Fergus had looked up an old friend from his army days, Geoff Fawkner, Geoff was these days working as a Building Surveyor for the Cairns Council and was very excited when Fergus asked him if he would be up for a trip to Cooktown to look over a house for refurbishment and to perhaps write up a scope of works for the whole project.

'I'll pay you for it of course' Fergus had told Geoff Fawkner, 'It's much too rough to camp out there just now so I'll look after accommodation, meals and, of course, drinks at a pub in Cooktown'.

'Mate, I should be paying you for such a holiday, just say when and I'm ready…and don't offer me money ever again'.

'What about next Friday arvo, I can pick you up from work if you like', Fergus suggested.

'Mate, how about pick me up from home on Friday morning, I'm not working that day and June is going to Innisfail for the weekend with her mother'? Said Geoff.

They had arrived in Cooktown at midday and had checked into the hotel, following lunch and a couple of beers they had headed out to 'Stezland' just for a quick look around the house to get a few ideas going for a full on day of design for Saturday.

Geoff was most amazed at the extent of deterioration but soon realised that most of it was actually ascetic mainly due to the appearance of the wallpapered walls and parts of the plasterboard ceiling collapsing.

Geoff soon discovered the reason for the ceiling collapse at various areas of the home but in particular the larger sized ceilings seemed to be the lack of ceiling back blocking of joints and it appeared the ceiling adhesive had failed on the rather cheap looking pressed metal ceiling battens, the roof trusses were manufactured from Redwood hardwood and there were no signs of termite intrusion. The roof sarking and metal roof cladding were all in excellent condition.

All the internal timber flooring was of Australian Spotted Gum and had been carefully laid over a membrane placed on the concrete slab and was in perfect condition and would require only a sanding and sealing to bring them back to as good as new, the veranda decking however, was not so lucky as the bearers being made from treated Hoop Pine had failed and in turn the Spotted Gum decking had also failed.

All the external walls and partition walls being constructed from 150 and 200 series concrete masonry block were all in excellent condition.

The only real major items were the plumbing which was HDPE and had been eaten by rates in many areas, the septic tank seemed to filled itself in and collapsed and to get power back to the house, a direct distance of around eight kilometres would be a costly effort.

By Saturday night, Geoff had handwritten a full scope of work and told Fergus that he would get it typed out sometime next week and give him some good contractor names. It was then on to dinner at the hotel and then around to the bowling club so Geoff could meet Colin Freebody who was there that night with his wife Marge.

Before Fergus could get any tradies onto the home site at Stezland he needed to upgrade the track that passed the gorge as at present only a four wheel drive utility could squeeze through and Fergus's contractors would require material supplies by trucks.

A quote by an electrician to reinstate the power lines and reconnect the house came in at a staggering twenty three thousand dollars per kilometre for a single phase connection from the 'gatehouse' to the refurbed home and the track upgrade all the way from the 'Gatehouse' to the refurbed home at around the same value. Fergus was looking at around three hundred and seventy five thousand for both, 'No way' thought Fergus and decided to start his own civil works company instead.

A call to another ex army comrade, Tim Abbott, who the last time Fergus was talking to him was running an earthmoving company based in Yass New South Wales, he had left his message for Tim on the answering machine and was about to leave his house in Little Mulgrave when the telephone rang, It was Tim who was pretty excited about hearing from Fergus and they had a great chat about the past. When Fergus got around to asking Tim about how his business was going there was hesitation from Tim and he finally told Fergus that sadly his business was no longer operating, his wife had left him, his house and block of land in Yass was on the market and he really did not know what he was going to do.

Without any hesitation, Fergus suggested that he get on a plane and came up to Cairns to have a talk about setting up a civil works operation in the far north. Tim told Fergus that he hardly had the price of a pack of cigarettes at the moment as he had just paid out his ex wife for her share in the property but that would change soon as he had a contract on his place, Tim had said that once he had that sorted he would give Fergus a call. But Fergus would hear nothing of that and said that he would send two thousand dollars to him via the Yass Post Office and he could get himself organised to get up north by the next weekend. Tim jumped at the opportunity to get out of Yass and to see his old mate again and simply said 'I'm on my way', details were sorted and Tim would be in Cairns in two days time.

It was Friday morning at eight thirty when Fergus collected Tim Abbott from the airport and by nine o'clock they were on their way to Shiptons Flat, the usual four to five hour road trip seemed like only an hour with their reminiscing of days back in the RAE, it wasn't until they had actually arrived at the 'Gatehouse' that Fergus had started to tell Tim of Stezland and his plans.

'Starting from this gate here' Fergus said indicating the gate near the house, 'I need the track turned into a road all the way down to where we are going and also to reinstate the power lines that were burnt out a while back'.

Tim reached into the back seat and removed a notebook from his backpack, the only luggage that he had brought with him, and started to sketch the track as they drove it.

Like everyone who sees the house for the first time, Tim was blown away.

'Oh wow, that is some place, and what a location'.

On the drive back to the 'gatehouse' Tim asked Fergus to stop at various locations and he got out of the car and walked on the track making further notes for the road construction and also for the powerlines. After calling in to say hello to Rodney and company at the 'Gatehouse' they drove back to Cairns Stopping at the Hambledon Hotel in Edmonton for dinner and then on to Little Mulgrave where Fergus showed Tim his room and told him to make himself at home.

Not much happened over the weekend other than planning for the purchase of the equipment needed for the road construction, they were going to look for mainly secondhand and the budget would be around three hundred thousand dollars. Tim had said that the best marketplace would be Queensland as moving heavy equipment around was very time consuming and expensive and also suggested that they buy their own transporter as it would pay for itself with the delivery of their machinery and that the prime mover could also be used for a B Double tipping body for the road material deliveries.

Monday morning saw Tim on his way to Brisbane to source equipment and Fergus was organising transportable accommodation for five persons, amenities including kitchen and lunch room and an office to be delivered to the 'Gatehouse' as that was the closest site with power. These were all available ex Cairns and would be in place by the following weekend. It was all happening for Fergus and Stezland, he was aware that his bank balance would be taking quite a hit and although he still had sufficient funding back from the Canberra property sale he decided to place the Little Mulgrave property on the market as he would be living in one of the dongas on Stezland anyway and would be moving into his renovated home from the donga, equipment and gear that he wanted to retain could be placed in one of the many sheds on Stezland.

Fergus made contact with local Gordonvale real estate agents Les and Kay Walsh, and a property inspection time was organised for the following Tuesday morning with Kay.

Later that afternoon Fergus had contacted Rodney at the 'Gatehouse' on the telephone line that Fergus had Telstra install there and had organised for Rodney to assist him in marking out this coming Wednesday for the placement of the work camp at a location near the 'Gatehouse' close to electricity but not so close as to infringe on Rodney's group's privacy.

Fergus had estimated his property value at Little Mulgrave for the sprawling five bedroom home and outbuildings on forty, fenced, hectares to be in the vicinity of one point seven million dollars, he had paid one point two million for it sixteen years before.

Fergus was pleasantly surprised when Kay Walsh suggested that they place the property on the market for two point four million and be happy to settle for around the two, to two point two mark. Kay also suggested that her husband should look at the property as soon as practicable and Fergus said that he would be available on the coming Friday to allow Les to inspect the property.

The mark out of the portable buildings went ahead on Wednesday with the Building supply company, Fergus and Rodney. Two of the supply companies 'Bobcats' were already on site and three buildings were expected to be delivered and installed that day, Rodney had organised for an electrical contractor to be available for the installation.

As Fergus was leaving the property a Cooktown Council vehicle was approaching and Fergus stopped to see what he wanted. The council man was the local building inspector and said that he had been made aware that dwellings were being constructed without a building permit, Fergus told the inspector that his information was incorrect and that some temporary accommodation was being installed, not constructed, and that no permits were required.

'It's up to me to decide whether permits are required or not' replied the building inspector rather sharply, a little too sharply for Fergus though.

'It's up to me who comes on my property' Fergus responded in a tone to match that of the building inspector, 'Now turn around and get off this property instantly'.

'I have the right of entry on any property in this area' said the inspector, his tone worsening, 'I will return with the police'

'Fuck off now and don't come back' was Fergus's final words with the council building inspector, 'Why do people want to piss me off' Fergus thought to himself as the council vehicle turned to leave the property. Fergus went back to the 'Gatehouse' to warn Rodney that the inspector may return with the police later and not to worry as he would get everything sorted. Fergus then, for the second time that day, left to head back to Little Mulgrave.

Les Walsh, like his wife Kay, was most impressed with the Little Mulgrave property and together approached Fergus with a personal offer for his property of two million dollars which Fergus verbally accepted. The Walshes indicated that they would return later that day with a contract for the sale of the property with a thirty day settlement and a negative commission on the sale of the property, Fergus was very pleased with this as it meant that he could virtually move into a donga on Stezland this coming week, it was a busy month for Fergus but by the end of the month Fergus was now living on Stezland in a donga and Tim had returned to drop off a Caterpillar 336DL excavator using the 1988 second hand Mack Superliner MarkII and a transport low loader quad axle that he had bought from the auctions in Brisbane and had registered under Fergus's new company name of Stezland Civil and Earthmoving Contractors P/L.

Once unloaded Fergus joined Tim in the low loader and they both headed back to Brisbane to collect another Mack prime mover with a tipping body that had two Bobcat wheeled skid steer loaders on board that Fergus would drive back to Shiptons Flat and Tim was to collect a Cat 140M Road Grader with the low loader and bring it to Shiptons Flat.

Fergus had left Brisbane one day earlier than Tim, the idea had been to travel back together but the grader would not be ready to travel.

After travelling for twelve hours and in accordance with the Queensland Motor Transport regulations for heavy vehicles, Fergus had spent the first night at Fairview near Mackay as the motel there also catered for heavy vehicles and trailers. Whilst enjoying an early breakfast at the Fairview service station having just completed fueling up the truck, Fergus had struck up a conversation with a likeable fellow of roughly his own age who had a strong accent which Fergus was guessing was German.

It seemed that this fellow, who introduced himself to Fergus as 'Everyone calls me Wes' whose full name was actually Werner Fischer as Fergus found later, was driving a truck from Brisbane to Innisfail which had burst into flames the previous day and he was now finding his own way back to the truck depot at Tulley, a small town south of Innisfail to collect another truck to drive to Adelaide. Fergus did not hesitate to offer him a lift to Tulley.

Wes was comfortable in the passenger seat and suggested to Fergus that there was no need to stop for his required rest period as he, Wes could share the driving and added.

'Yar und I von't be grinding off the gearing as you are' Fergus cracked up laughing at this.

'Mate, more than welcome, I haven't even got a licence to drive this fucker, it's a first time truck driving experience for me' he told Wes.

'You are lucky that you have come this far' laughed Wes then asked Fergus if he held a car driver's licence and told Fergus that a car driver's licence also worked as a permit to learn to drive a truck providing that a licensed truck driver was also in the truck with him giving instruction.

Fergus felt very relieved as he had been very nervous about not having a license to drive a truck and was going to remedy that when he got back to Cooktown.

Wes had asked where the two Bobcat's on the back are going to and Fergus told Wes all about Stezland and how they were having to firstly make an access road to the house for renovations and to re establish the power poles down to the house. Wes then told Fergus that he had operated the American Bobcats before he had joined the army and had also done a lot of road and bridge construction and other earthworks including dams and drains, he had moved to Australia after he had left the army as he had a sponsorship from friends of his fathers who lived in Melbourne.

'I tell you, Fergus, fuck that Milburne, it is colder than Austria and they don't recognise my certificates to operate the machinery that I worked in Germany so I am driving these trucks instead'. Fergus could not believe his luck and did not hesitate to ask Wes if he would be interested in joining him and Tim at Stezland.

Wes thought that would be a good move but said that he would need to collect his belongings from Tulley and tell his boss there that he was finished driving for him. Fergus told Wes that he had enough time to do those things in Tulley and it was all set.

During the trip to Tulley Fergus was to discover that Wes had been in the German Armed Forces - Special Operations Command (Kommando Spezialkräfte, KSK), Fergus likened it to be similar to the Australian Defence Forces SAS and this further increased his respect for Wes, what a great find and he seemed to be getting on well with this guy from Germany.

They had arrived in Tulley and their first stop was the trucking company that Wes was working for, they said they were sad that he was leaving but held no malice towards him and told him that if things didn't work out, then his old job would be there for him.

Next, it was to his rented unit in Tulley Heads where his belongings also included his 1975 SWB FJ Landcruiser with a canvas top, it was unregistered which made it a problem to get it up to Stezland, Fergus had a thought, they would wait on the highway for Tim to come through which Fergus guessed would be just before midday the next day and they could fit his cruiser onto the back of the low loader behind the grader, it would also make it easier to put the rest of Wes's belongings into the sleeper cab of the Mack Superliner.

After spending the night at a motel in Tulley that offered truck parking and a great meal and drinks with his new mate Wes, Fergus was not far out with his anticipated arrival time of Tim at Tulley. Fergus had made contact with Tim by CB radio some distance before Tulley and Fergus had told him where to turn off for Tulley Heads and that he would see him at the turnoff.

There was more than enough room for Wes's FJ cruiser and Tim was introduced to Wes, Fergus explained to Tim that Wes would be joining them at Stezland which Tim seemed pleased with as it meant that both trucks could now head off from Stezland back to Brisbane to collect more gear.

It was only a seven hour drive from Tulley to Shiptons Flat and both trucks arrived at the dongas at the 'Gatehouse' at around seven pm that evening, it was decided to unload the trucks the following morning and they decided to drive the fifty kilometres into Cooktown for dinner as Wes did not drink alcohol and he was elected the driver which left it open for Fergus and Tim to drink a few beers which they did and also brought back a good supply of beer in stubbies.

They had unloaded both of the trucks the next morning and then spent the day checking the trucks and getting them ready for the return trip to Brisbane to collect more equipment. Tim had bought a Caterpillar D7 bulldozer which he would place on the low loader and an air track rock drilling machine and wheeled compressor they would place on a flat top trailer that they had yet to source in Brisbane and tow with the second Mack truck that would leave the tipping body behind at Stezland. It was all sorted leaving very little for Fergus to do until they returned other than get the dongas and office setup, have a telephone connected and practice driving some of the growing list of machinery that was now lying around about four hundred metres from the 'Gatehouse'.

Fergus had taken a drive past the 'Gatehouse' and had taken the left hand fork in the track that led towards the higher ranges in search of a suitable site to quarry road base materials. It was at a section where the colour of the track turned to a darker red than the track he was driving previously, it looked as though it was damp but was just as dry as the rest, Fergus followed this track and went off to the left where the ground rose until it was too rough to drive ant further, he then got from his vehicle his maddock and pick and started to walk towards the rising ground of red material and digging small samples as he went.

The decomposed granite was abundant it seemed to Fergus and could be relatively easy to extract and cart back to the road site, he thought he may bring the Cat excavator out here tomorrow and do a few sample diggings.

As Fergus arrived back at the donga camp he found that the building inspector from Cooktown Shire was walking around the dongas making notes on his clipboard in the company of a police constable.

'What can I do for you guys', Fergus asked as he walked up to them.

'I'm the building inspector for the Cooktow........'
Fergus cut him off abruptly.

'I know who you are, what do you want out here'?

'Do you have a permit for these build.......'

'I have told you that these are only temporary and the people whom I am hiring these buildings from have told me that I don't need permits, so now.....get off my property', Fergus was becoming very agitated.

'This man is only doing his job, you can speak to him in a civilised manner' the police officer butted in.

'And who the fuck are you? And what the fuck do you want?' Fergus's good day was being destroyed and he was losing it.

'I am Senior Constable Kirkland and you will show some respect or.....'

'Orr?......Introduce yourself FIRST next time and then tell me what you are doing here' demanded Fergus, 'You don't just butt into a conversation that does not have any business of yours'.

'I have had dealings with you before, haven't I? Driving with over the prescribed blood alcohol limit if I remember'.

'Well, I thought it was speeding and a vehicle defect' reflected Fergus.

'Actually all three but I decided to let you off'

'Because you are a fool or just too gutless'? Fergus wanted to know. The constable opened his mouth to speak but thought the better of it and turned to the inspector.

'I would seem that you should be talking to the owners of these buildings and not the lease'ee, it's time to go'.
The police constable, not even looking towards Fergus, got into the police car and was gone before the building inspector, who now had a very anxious look on his face, got into his car and started to drive off when he remembered something and wound down his car window.

'Who owns the buildings?' He shouted to where Fergus was standing watching the retreating police car.

'Who owns the buildings? PLEASE' said Fergus as he walked away towards his donga leaving the building inspector guessing, 'Fuck you' he thought to himself and was starting to think that there was something wrong with this local copper and it seemed that Mitchell was correct with his assumption that it was the same person who was involved with the death of Amelia.
Fergus had used the telephone in the 'Gatehouse' and enjoyed one of Rodney's beers, while he contacted the Cooktown Caltex dealer seeking a diesel tank on a stand and also asked if they knew of any second hand diesel

tankers, it did not have to be registered, just to run around his property he told them. The ten thousand litre tank was delivered the next morning and filled with diesel just after lunch.

Fergus had filled the excavator with fuel and started the slow trek towards his Deco (decomposed granite) site, it took him just over one hour to reach the site and he commenced to dig into the side of the hill. Once he had cleared the vegetation the digging into the granite was fairly easy for the big Cat excavator with the decomposed granite breaking up quite easily but Fergus thought that they would still need a portable crushing plant to make the material suitable for the road base.

As he was travelling back to the camp he was mentally going through a list of items that they would require, it seemed endless and now a crushing plant and they would also require a water tanker and a roller, where does it end?

The telephone had been connected to the office donga and Fergus had made some calls to equipment suppliers looking for the gear he needed, he found a perfect transportable crusher at Mount Isa and the guy selling it assured Fergus that he could get it delivered and set up for him within a couple of weeks, another box to tick, he then found an eight wheel, twin steer Kenworth that was an ex concrete truck and had been fitted with a flat eight metre long body and a six thousand litre water tank at the rear and a two thousand litres diesel tank upfront. It was located at Cardwell and was registered to drive on the road, just perfect, Tim and Wal could go and collect it on the coming weekend.

As Fergus approached the camp he could see that both the trucks had returned and they were unloading the bulldozer first as the airtrack and compressor that was loaded on the other truck would require a loading ramp to get it off the back and the dozer was required to build this.

Following the unloading of the equipment they had all showered and decided on the Cooktown RSL club for dinner and drinks and not necessarily in that order.

They had enjoyed a great meal at the club and had talked about going to Cardwell to collect the twin steer on the following Saturday morning. Fergus had shown them his new Nokia mobile telephone but sadly there was no mobile service around the Cooktown area as yet so it was quite useless, it had a recording feature that did not require mobile service and he demonstrated how it worked, it was too large to fit into a pocket and needed to be carried by hand, could be a thing of the future they all agreed.

It was around eleven thirty when they spilled from the club and into Fergus's Landrover, Wes was driving as he had drank only coke all evening.

They had just left Hope Street where it now became the Mulligan Highway and the speed limit sign changed from sixty kilometres per hour to eighty kilometres per hour, just as Wes had increased his speed from sixty to eighty a set of bright headlights, on high beam with two blue flashing lights above them, came very fast up behind them and Wes immediately slowed and looked for a safe place to pull off the road and the following police car also pulled off behind them, Fergus had his new telephone sitting in the centre console of the Landrover and decided to switch on the record feature.

'Well...well..if it isn't Mr Laird' said a voice from the person carrying a light and walking up on the right hand side of the Landrover to the driver's door, 'You won't be getting out of this one tonight........, who the fuck are you?' Said the voice now shining the light on the driver's face.

'I'm Wes mate, what can I do for you?'

Senior Stanley Kirkland's face dropped as he looked at the driver of the Landrover in the beam of the light and was trying to comprehend what was happening and then shone the beam on the passenger and realised that it was Laird's Landrover after all, he thought for a moment that he had pulled over the wrong vehicle. Recomposing himself he said,

'Any reason that you are doing eighty in a sixty zone?'

'I was doing sixty in the sixty zone and was just getting up to eighty in the eighty zone' Wes simply replied.

'Don't get fucking smart with me pal, you were doing eighty in the sixty zone, let me see your license'.

Wes leaned forward and placed his left hand behind his back to withdraw his wallet from his back trouser pocket when all of a sudden there was a police Glock in the side of his neck.

'Freeze, one more move and you're dead, put both hands on the steering wheel now and very..very slowly' Kirkland screamed at Wes in a limpid, highly excited voice without much authority.

'Whoa....whoa...hey...hey..stop, put the gun down' shouted Fergus.

'Mein Gott! I'm only getting my license, vhat is mitt you?'

Fergus had seen that Wes had not even flinched when the gun was put to his head, the next second Wes was in possession of the Glock, he had disarmed Kirkland in an instant and he could have quite easily killed Kirkland.

The blood had drained from Kirkland's face and he stood there as if frozen solid, Wes had opened his door and took hold of Kirkland and turned and held him over the bonnet of the Landrover saying 'Cool...cool, be cool and you vill be OK'.

'Vot the fuck ist wrong with this copper Fergus?'

'I don't know but I think we should call the police in Cairns or Mareeba, find his handcuffs and we'll take him with us, Tim can you go and turn off his car and lock it' Fergus instructed.

Kirkland was handcuffed and placed on the back seat of the Landrover next to Tim which made it very unpleasant for Tim as Kirkland had shat himself, Tim had to travel the whole distance with his head almost completely out of the window.

Kirkland had started to regain himself and had started to tell them that would all go to prison for kidnapping a police officer, Fergus had told him to be quiet or he would be gagged, this seemed to have some effect on him.

At the camp, Fergus was looking for the nearest police station but Tim advised that they would be in cahoots with Cooktown and that to go directly to Cairns would be a better option, it was twelve thirty am when Fergus called the Cairns police station.

'Cairns Police, Constable Wood speaking'

'Ahh, constable, we...we've had an episode at Cooktown and we had to make a citizens arrest on a senior police constable, we have him held at a property near Shiptons Flat' reported Fergus.

'Just a minute' was the reply and the phone seemed to go dead, Fergus had thoughts about hanging up and calling again when a gruff voice said to him.

'What is your location?, are you armed?, can we land a helicopter there,? how many of you are there? Stay on this line and do not hang up'.

For what seemed like an hour there was nothing on the line and then a voice announced that the police will be there in twenty minutes and to go out into an open area, take the police constable with you and lay face down and wait for the police, dod *not* look up at the police, remain motionless at all times until directed and then the line went dead. Fergus conveyed the message to the others and they went outside into an open area taking Kirkland, who was now trouserless, with them still handcuffed, Kirkland was silent and would not make eye contact with any of them.

They saw the spotlights before they heard the helicopters and as the spotlights locked onto them they lay on the ground as they had been directed but with their eyes clamped tight to stop the dust from being driven into them by the rotors of the three helicopters.

The helicopters remained hovering for what seemed like an hour when they could hear sirens arriving at the camp. Rough hands had placed them all in handcuffs while they were still on the ground and black material hoods were placed over their heads as they were loaded onto a helicopter.

They were taken from the helicopters after almost two hours and were escorted into a building whilst still wearing the hoods, they were then stripped searched and given paper overalls to put on, placed and shackled on hard chairs and then the hoods were removed.

They blinked and looked around, they were in a small unpainted concrete masonry walled room with a concrete ceiling and floor, two police armed with Heckler & Koch MP5 rifles in black SWAT type uniforms and wearing hoods were standing on each side of them, in front sitting at a large desk was a high ranking uniformed police officer and two men wearing suits.

'Start talking' said the uniformed officer staring at all three of them. Fergus, together with both Tim and Wes adding bits and pieces, explained exactly what had happened while the two men in suits were quickly writing notes in the books that they held.

'Which one of you disarmed the constable?' Demanded the officer.

'I did that' responded Wes, 'I thought that my life was in danger so I removed the danger'.

'What training do you have to do such things' the officer wanted to know.

'I was an officer in the German Armed Forces - Special Operations Command (Kommando Spezialkräfte, KSK)' Wes replied. The two plain clothes men quickly exchanged glances when they heard that and one of them asked Wes.

'Isn't that the same ranking as the US Navy Seals?'

'Yar, I think so only much better trained than the Americans' Wes said grinning which was contagious to all three police interrogators.

Fergus remembered the mobile telephone that he had started to record with the moment that Kirkland had approached the car and said that he had it in his hand when he was arrested at the camp and mentioned this to all three of the men at the desk to which the uniformed officer told him that they had discovered the telephone and had found and played the recording and that the telephone would be returned to him in due course.

Fergus had said that he would like to call his lawyer and was told that it would not be necessary as none of them were being charged with anything and that we were free to go upon signing a letter of confidentiality not to speak to anyone about what had transpired and that they would be issued with travel warrants for airfares back to Cooktown.

He went on to say that they do not apologise for the somewhat dramatic action by calling in a SWAT team to handle this incident as they take any actions like this towards their police team members very seriously.

The officer had concluded by telling them that the whole camp was searched last night and a number of firearms had been seized and taken to the Cooktown police station and can be released upon the sighting of the relevant firearms licenses.

It was just coming light at five thirty am when they walked from the police station and found a twenty four hour cafe. They had been left in the dark concerning what would happen to Kirkland.

'The man's a fucking idiot' said Fergus

'I am thinking that there is more to this man Kirkland, that means so much to you, I think you have a hatred for this person Yar?' Wes asked Fergus.

Fergus told both Tim and Wes about his wife Amelia and about Kirkland stopping Mitchell and him in the Landrover a few months back and also at the camp just days ago.

'I would have removed this man a long time ago' stated Wes to which Tim responded with,

'It seems that you don't fuck around Wes, you remained so calm when that prick put that gun to your head and before I knew it you had taken the gun from him, I certainly would not mess with you, my friend'.

They ate toasted sandwiches and drank coffee and Tim suggested that he may as well go to Cardwell and collect the twin steer truck as they were three quarters of the way there and that he could catch the Greyhound bus service that morning and would be back at camp that night. They all agreed it was a good idea if he could manage to stay awake and Fergus and Wes headed to the airport to get a flight on the Dash 8 service from Cairns to Cooktown.

Fergus called Rodney at the 'Gatehouse' and asked him to collect himself and Wes from the Cooktown Airport later that morning.

Rodney was full of questions for Fergus as soon as he saw him standing by the airport shed that morning, he told Rodney that they had been awoken by the helicopters last night and then the police sirens and that early this morning two police constables had knocked on the door of the 'Gatehouse' to complete an ID check.

'What the fuck is going on', Rodney wanted to know, 'What is it that you guy's are up to? We don't want to be put at personal risk'.

Fergus assured Rodney that they were in no danger whatsoever and told him about what had happened when they had left the RSL last night, Rodney could not believe it.

'You are fucking kidding me....right?'

'I kid you not' was Fergus's response, 'I'll tell you the background story tonight, call into the butcher on the way back and you can all come to the camp for a BBQ tonight and I'll fill you all in on the big picture, better stop at the bottle shop too'.

Fergus had dragged out his new Weber BBQ and brought out most of the furniture from the lunch room donga and placed it in front of the amenities building where the floodlights lit the whole area. He had sliced the two whole rumps that he had bought from the butcher this morning and had brought to the boil in the kitchen a large stainless steel boiler with chat potatoes. Tim had arrived back with the twin steer truck just as Fergus and Wes were setting the BBQ up.

'Good timing by the look of it' said Tim climbing out of the Kenworth and taking the stubbie of beer that Wes offered him.

'The kids from the 'Gatehouse' are coming over for dinner Tim, apparently, we scared the shit out of them last night so I'm putting on a feed and a few beers and tell em what happened' Fergus explained.

Rodney, Belinda, Jason and Allison had all arrived carrying eskies with drinks by walking over to the camp that was approximately four hundred metres from the 'Gatehouse'.

Wes and Tim were introduced to everyone and Fergus suggested that he explain what had happened that night before he had many more beers, they all sat around on the chairs from the mess donga and Fergus began from the beginning, being the accident that had killed his wife Amelia and ending with the proceedings of last nights drama to the extent that he was allowed under the confidentiality agreement that he had signed together with Tim and Wes, but they had all really got the full picture by the end, Fergus added that they won't see anything on the news or in the papers as it was hush hush as far as the coppers went.

Everyone was quite moved by Fergus's story and the girls were saying 'Poor Mitch' and that he must be carrying a huge hatred for the police and also for the Aboriginals that had been responsible for Fergus being committed to prison, Fergus had commented that it hadn't done much to himself either when it came to Police and Aborigines and to top it off with this prick Kirkland pursuing him.

Fergus had not been told what would become of Kirkland but he was confident that he would no longer be stationed at Cooktown, both he and Wes were going to the police station at Cooktown in the morning to reclaim their rifles that the police had seized last night.

A great night was enjoyed by everyone with the last to leave being Rodney at about one o'clock the next morning. Fergus was somewhat shattered as he had not slept for about twenty four hours, Tim had left the BBQ at about ten PM and Wes around eleven thirty. Once Rodney had left Fergus just went into his donga and did not emerge until eleven AM that morning.

Tim was up and doing some minor work on the Kenworth twin steer. After looking over the unit, Fergus was quite impressed. Fergus spoke to Tim and suggested that now we have the gear we need to find some operators, Tim mentioned that he had been talking to Jason at the BBQ last night and Jason had told him that he was operating an excavator, similar to theirs, down in Brisbane a while back and had his ticket for it, he had also told Tim that he knew the former council road manager at Cooktown, he was a good operator but he got the arse for drinking on the job, he is a part Aboriginal and a good bloke.

'What do reckon then Tim? Let's give Jason a job and the first thing he can do is find the former council worker and bring him out for a yarn' suggested Fergus.

'I was going to suggest the same thing to you Fergus'. Wes was in the mess donga having a late breakfast when Fergus found him and reminded him that they were going into Cooktown to the police station to get their firearms and not to forget to take his firearms license and rifle permits if he had any. Wes assured Fergus that he had all the necessary permits in force.

'Good morning' the young police constable had said as they entered the foyer of the modest police station.

'Good morning, my name is Fergus Laird and this is Wes,..sorry, Werner Fischer, we are here to collect our firearms that were taken from my property near Shiptons Flat the night before last'.

This made the constable stop and sit upright in his chair.

'Ahh....yes,...I'll just call Senior Sergeant Sutton if you could just wait a moment', the constable went into the next room and they could clearly hear the constable talking on the radio and then he returned and said that the sergeant would be only a matter of minutes and sorry to keep you.

Fergus assured the constable that was not a problem and they sat on the waiting room chairs, Fergus did notice that the constable gave a few inquisitive looks towards Wes.

The sergeant, who looked like he did not want to be here and had obviously been disturbed from resting, arrived through the front door and looked in the general direction of Wes and Fergus saying as he entered,

'Do you have your permits and license's there?'

They both stood and walked to the counter where the police sergeant now stood and put their documents on the counter in front of the sergeant who read from Wes's permits first,

'Mannlicher-Schoenauer M72 .22-250 Rem, number ZCX 567GF998 and a Mannlicher-Schoenauer M72 S/T Model .375 H&H number CBX554Ws87V, wait here while I get your rifles'.

He returned with the rifles in their respective rifle covers, undid each one and read off the serial number and then asked Wes to 'Sign here!' He had then asked Wes what he was using the massive .375 calibre for and Wes had told him that he was shooting camels with it in Western Australia and added with a grin, 'I am told that this is also very goot for shooting the pigs'. The sergeant ignored him and turned to Fergus.

Looking at Fergus's permits he read them out loud, 'Winchester Rifle model 94 Carbine number 7709hq1, Winchester Rifle model 94 number 7762298Za, wait here and I'll go and get yours' He returned with the two Winchester rifles, Fergus did not have covers for these and the sergeant read off the serial numbers and then asked why had one of the rifles been cut down?

Fergus explained that one was a rifle and the other a carbine which was about four inches shorter than the rifle, the sergeant looked confused and looked closely at the end of the barrel of the shorter version as though he did not believe what Fergus had told him.

'Why do you need a long one and a short one?' The sergeant quizzed Fergus.

'The carbine is for my son, when I bought it he was only nine years old and my rifle was too big for him to use'

Fergus had suddenly regretted being open and honest as the sergeant berated him and reminded him that the rifles are in his name and no one else is permitted to use them and that there is an age limit for the use of firearms, Fergus just replied 'Whatever' and signed the document and picked up his rifles and started to leave when the sergeant announced that he would be watching them closely and then sarcastically stated that nobody would ever take his gun from him.

'Let's hope we don't haff to find out yar' Wes openly grinned at the sergeant with a smile, not unlike the 'Mona Lisa' a secret half smile, half grin which Fergus had seen in photographs of surrendered German officers although proud in defeat and still commanding respect but still always makes the onlooker feel inferior. The sergeant recognised this expression on Wes's face and could not maintain eye contact with him.

They both left the station smiling with the sound of the sergeant telling the constable not to disturb him in future for such minor issues that he could have handled and when the constable reminded the sergeant that he had explicitly told him to call him when Fergus arrived to collect his firearms, he screamed 'Don't fucking argue with me, Sonny Jim!'

'You know Fergus, ve could dig a big pit at Stezland, big enough for that fat copper and his car and he could be a missing copper that nobody missed at all und would never be found, what do you think?' Wes said quite seriously and continued, 'I am thinking that this one will also make trouble for us'. Fergus just grinned at Wes's suggestion but also started to think of how easy that would be, the more he thought about it, with a little planning, the easier it seemed.

Excavation for power lines to be laid under the road had commenced at Stezland with road construction following and as soon as the road had reached the other side of the gorge it had allowed for construction materials to be brought in and the builder could start work on the house.

Road construction at Stezland came to a halt at this stage as it was no longer urgent, the builder did not need power as they used generators and the track from the gorge was pretty good when dry to enable the worker's vehicles and reasonable size delivery truck access to the home site.

Tim had secured a fairly large civil job from the Cooktown Shire to replace a washed out bridge and a three kilometres section of road, Fergus was happy with this as his bank balance had been eroding somewhat from his capital purchases of equipment and although this contract would require more equipment in the form of another compactor and roller plus a far more advanced grader that they had bought for Stezland, Tim had included these items costs on top of his price submitted to the council, it was a ludicrous price of over twelve million dollars as they didn't really need to have the job, the council had responded by asking how soon could they get the job done? as the Aboriginal settlement of Hopvale could be isolated during the wet season and that would not go down well in Federal Parliament.

Tim had engaged workers from Hopevale and had trained some to be machine operators, this had seemed to protect their equipment that had to be left on site overnight, another plus. It seemed the local Hopevale people knew not to shit on their own doorstep and the project was completed within the contract period and earned a huge bonus which Fergus had distributed amongst the settlement people.

Following the successful completion of this project, they were offered another project on the Rossville to Bloomfield road and here workers were recruited from the settlements at Bloomfield and Wujil Wujil.
Fergus had given control of the earthmoving side of things to Tim, he could handle it a lot more efficiently than Fergus could and it left Fergus and Wes more time to start organising a cattle muster as no one had a clue of how many cattle may be on Stezland.

Colin Freebody had told Fergus that there were three sets of cattle yards on the property but were in pretty poor shape when he last used them some twenty years ago, but they were constructed from good hardwood and may still be alright, he drew a rough map of where these yards were and said that they were only good for draughting, marking, ear tagging and dehorning, there were no scales or loading ramps at these yards as the roads were too bad for transports. Once the cattle had been mustered at these yards they were then driven down to the big yards that used to be located halfway between the 'Gatehouse' and the unnamed creek, but they had been burnt out when the big bushfire took all the power poles out for Murray's new house. Colin said that he could help set up a great system, that he had seen on a trip to Western Australia about seven years ago that he was sure would work here.

Fergus told Colin that he would be happy to pay the old man for his time in designing a system that would be beneficial to Stezland.

'You have the equipment to make it possible', Colin said, 'If you are prepared to invest some of your own resources into this it will work, it will be easier to get the cattle down to the main yards, that is, the ones you want at the main yards, before by droving them down we had a shitload of cattle down here that we didn't want and didn't have the feed for but by transporting them down you only bring the ones you want'.

The Muster

Colin's plan to improve the cattle yards to enable a good muster on Stezland was to firstly build a new set of cattle yards near the 'Gatehouse', where there is a good water supply from the unnamed creek, made from steel complete with a loading ramp. The existing yards should be modified as required, also in steel, as with any future repairs.

The next is to manufacture a *mobile* loading ramp that is combined with locks and draughting gates and a set of scales.

The loading ramp will have the turrent for a prime mover fitted just underneath the top of the loading ramp, just like a normal semi trailer coupling but instead of cargo decking it will have cattle loading rails this will make the loading height perfect as stock transport loading doors will be the same height as the turrent plus the deck thickness.

This decking will be two metres in length then ramp down for three metres and level off with a nine metre meter race for the crush locks, draughting gates and scales, a total length of fourteen metres. Three quarters along will be fitted with dual detachable wheels that can be removed with high lift jacks.

This ramp will easily be moved by a prime mover and easily attached to the cattle yard that is being used. Once set into its location at the yards the prime mover can be used for other trailers if required. Colin had done a scale drawing of the contraption and Fergus gave it to Tim to have it fabricated in the new workshops that he was building at the camp.

It had been two years since Fergus had stepped onto Stezland and in that time, although he had achieved a great deal, he seemed to have so much more to do.

Mitchell was seventeen years old now and was staying at the camp for the Christmas school holidays, Fergus had bought him an HZJ landcruiser for his birthday but had restricted him to use it only around the property until he was eighteen.

The house was all but complete and the power was connected, a Vietnamese couple had been employed as cook, housekeeper, maid, and gardener and had moved into the unit at the back of the house.

The three old cattle yards had been repaired and modified to 'self mustering' yards and to accept the mobile loading contraption which would become known as the 'Freebody" and was just completed and ready for its first test. The new, all steel, cattle yards had been constructed with two loading ramps and three holding yards for up to six hundred head and four water troughs being fed from both the unnamed creek and two bores.

Fergus had put pressure on Tim to get the roads to the cattle yards finished before the wet season for mustering between June and November. This caused them to buy a fourth Grader, this time a Komatsu, the biggest yet for use on council road rebuilds with a 426 HP engine, this allowed the on Cat grader that they bought initially to become a dedicated station grader and a Wujil Wujil man was trained as it's operator and he moved onto the camp.

The camp had been extended to a total of ten accommodation dongas, another double office donger, a bigger mess and kitchen donger and an additional amenities donga. Fergus had intended to maintain his office at the camp and the new offices were for Tim and Wes.

The first ever muster on the property for, officially, twenty two years took place that year, there had been unofficial musters at least every two years according to local gossip. Future musters would not be required as the yards have now been modified for 'self mustering' which involved setting a holding yard with one-way entry points, water troughs and feed handlers. Prior to mustering the troughs are turned on and the handlers filled with hay on a regular basis until the yards are holding all the cattle from the area.

But this year it was put out to a contractor who is based at Cow Bay and although Cow Bay is located just over one hundred kilometres from Shiptons Flat, Stezland's boundary where the muster was to begin is just East West of Wujil Wujil and only around thirty kilometres from Cow Bay the contractor wanted thirty dollars a head for all cattle mustered, they would help with marking, tagging, draughting and loading. Fergus took note that the contractor seemed to know the country extremely well.

The 'Freebody' loading ramp was set up at the first, or high, set of yards and the first muster put one hundred and four mixed head into the yards. Of these, there were twenty calves to be marked, tagged and let go, two bulls to be tagged and released and thirty cows and heifers with at least eleven in calf. The balance was fifty two bullocks for transportation down to the camp yards. While Fergus was organising this transport the second muster began for the number two yards resulting in a total of one hundred and thirty head with only one bull, eighteen calves, thirty seven cows leaving seventy four bullocks for transport.

The final muster at number three yards ended up with a total of one hundred and ten head being five bulls, twelve calves, twenty eight cows and sixty five bullocks for the camp yards.

Once all the bullocks had been placed into the camp yards the neighbouring properties were summoned to inspect the herd for any of their brand that may have been included in the muster, They were released back to the respective owners for a mustering fee of fifty dollars.

When all was done Fergus had a one hundred and ninety one bullocks which were transported to the cattle market at Charters Towers and sold for an average of nine hundred dollars per head $171,900, less his mustering costs of $10,320 and transport costs of from yards to yard $9000.00, from Shiptons Flat to Charters Towers he was charged $100.00 per head for the 800km trip = $19,100, Fergus was left with only $133,000 and had to pay his own labour costs and attribute some towards the cost of the yards, 'It was going to be much better next year' Fergus was thinking as he would not have the muster costs and he would buy his own cattle truck to transport from yard to yard, that in itself would save around twenty thousand dollars per year and that money can go towards the salary of someone who knew cattle as Fergus had discovered that when it came to cattle, he knew fuck all.

Restructuring

Fergus seemed to have a lot of money coming in but also seemed to have a hell of a lot of money going out, he had no idea if he was making or losing money and he knew that was not good. Accountants in Cooktown were almost non existent but Fergus did come across a former commercial construction accountant who had been serving a prison sentence of ten years for fraud, he saw him working behind the bar in the RSL club one night and the more he looked at him the more he was sure that he knew him and finally approached him.

He was very hesitant to speak with Fergus and told him that the past was the past and that he had chosen Cooktown as a place to live as no one should recognise him here, 'Well that was a fucking mistake, by the looks of it', he told Fergus.

His name was Ken Miller and he was formally from Brisbane, he had never actually done any official accountancy courses and was not registered or recognised as an accountant, but as he said, 'He knew his sums'.

'Would you be interested in a business proposition?' Fergus had asked.

'No fucking way my friend, no fucking way am I going back to jail, he had quickly responded, 'This is a shit job behind the bar because I should be on the other side of the bar, but at least it is honest money and I don't have to look over my back'.

'I meant something legit, everything that I do is perfectly legal, I am just not good at bookkeeping, that's all I want, an accountant, nothing more let me tell you' Fergus explained.

Towards the end of the night, Fergus had talked Ken into letting him collect him in the morning and take him out to his office at Stezland to explain the situation and let him look at his operation so he could have a think about it.

They had arrived at Fergus's office at around nine thirty, on the way there Fergus had shown Ken the new cattle yards, the 'Gatehouse' and then the the camp which was now starting to look huge with its fifteen buildings and now also a huge workshop and a storage compound for machinery, he pointed towards where his house lay some eight kilometres,

'Down that way, I'm finally moving in down there next week' and then asked Ken where was he living in Cooktown and was told that Ken was renting a 'shitbox' one bedroom flat in a dilapidated block of six and was presently looking elsewhere, but it was very limited accommodation in Cooktown.

Fergus explained briefly what he had inherited and what he had started to do and in a nutshell that he needed someone to set up some type of accounting system and maintain it for him. Ken having seen the setup now seemed more interested and started to ask Fergus some questions about what he had in mind and whether would it be a full time position and what sort of dollars was he thinking of paying for such a person and that he knew that he could do what Fergus required quite easily and would be interested in setting up a structure which would see his different activities become different companies under a major head office.

Fergus and Ken came to an agreement on a salary for Ken and Ken would also move out to the camp and take up Fergus's donga when he vacates it next week, it seemed that it would be a good situation and Ken could not wait to design a structure for Stezland. Fergus took Ken back to Cooktown and was dropping him off for work at the RSL when Police Senior Sergeant Sutton drove by very slowly and taking special note, so it seemed, of both Fergus and Ken.

Fergus had an inkling and when he returned to his office he called Brian Haptu, the solicitor was on another call and his secretary said that he would call him back, while waiting, Fergus went to the kitchen and made a cappuccino from their newly installed machine that Wes had organised and returned to his office just as the telephone rang.

After chatting about everything Fergus asked Brian about consorting laws and then told him about employing Ken Miller as his accountant and gave him Ken's full background and also told him about the interest that had been shown by the police sergeant this morning. Brian told Fergus that he would check on Ken's full prison term and find out if there were any obligations and/or liabilities still in currency and if there were not then there should be no problems as consorting is generally regarded as at least three people.

He had called Fergus back within thirty minutes saying that Ken was fully discharged and there were no obligations on him. Fergus had commented that this particular copper had been harassing them a fair bit for minor motor traffic infringements with their trucks and things and he wanted to make sure that everything was above board.

After only two weeks of looking at Fergus's operation at Stezland Ken had come up with the following suggestion. The principal company will be called;

Stezland Proprietary Limited and shall be the owner of the property known as Stezland with the exception of the subdivision of two hundred and fifty acres that will be privately owned by Fergus Laird where Fergus's home is situated and the owners and purchasers of all equipment used by other Stezland sub companies. Stezland is the administrator of all Stezland companies.

Stezland Civil Engineers and Earthmoving Contractors Proprietary Limited; will lease the camp, workshops, compounds and all equipment from Stezland P/L

Stezland Pastoral Proprietary Limited; will lease grazing pastures, cattle yards and water facilities from Stezland P/L

Stezland Raw Materials Proprietary Limited;

Lease the quarry from Stezland P/L.

Stezland Transport Proprietary Limited; will lease prime movers and trailers and rent premises from Stezland P/L.

By following these measures much money can be saved by avoiding taxation of well earned money and capital investments can be written off.

Ken gave one example to Fergus;

The Stezland earthmoving company earn one million dollars per year, outgoings are staff wages, materials from Stezland Raw Material, lease of equipment from Stezland P/L all amount to nine hundred and fifty thousand dollars equaling a taxable income of fifty thousand dollars which should result in about thirty percent being fifteen thousand dollars total in taxation for a turnover of one million dollars.

Similar situations will follow with each of the Stezland companies resulting in each company, including the principal company, of reducing its taxable income to only five percent of its turnover.

After studying Ken's proposal Fergus had sent it by facsimile to Brian Haptu for his perusal and legal opinion, Brian had in turn also forwarded the document to a taxation specialist chartered accountant who stated that the system was brilliant and within the laws of the Australian Taxation Office. Brian forwarded his findings to Fergus who set them in motion and had Brian Haptu register all of the Stezland companies.

After being the owner of stezland for just three years now everything was coming into place unexpectedly but nicely for Fergus. He was now living in the house on the recently subdivided two hundred and fifty acres he now called StezPark.

Wes, who had now become Fergus's personal assistant, and best friend, had also taken up residence at StezPark, he also wore the title of Manager of Stezland Pty Ltd.

Mitchell had completed his schooling and was also now a resident at StezPark and enjoying being at home with his father, he was also enjoying the cooking of the Vietnamese housekeeper. He had decided to study veterinary science following a year's break of working on Stezland and as a reward, his father would make him the Manager of Stezland Pastoral Pty Ltd.

Tim, at his choice, was still living at the camp in his donga and could not be happier, his official title was now the Manager of Stezland Civil Engineers and Earthmoving Pty Ltd.

Ken was also a full time resident at the camp and had taken over Fergus's office at the camp as the account for the principal company.

He had also started to make homebrew beer and was putting it into kegs and set up a beer tap in the mess donga which became popular with all the camp residents who placed money in a jar to help finance the next kegs.

Ken had also shown Mitchell how to make homebrew and Mitchell was keeping the house at StezPark well stocked with good beer.

The Vietnamese house staff had settled into things nicely, the woman, Bian, was very good at cooking Vietnamese food but Mitchell, Wes and Fergus had soon tired of eating that style of food and Fergus took it upon himself to teach Bian how to make beef roasts and how to cook steak and serve it with chat potatoes. She was a very fast learner and the food soon changed to a more palatable type for the men.

Bian's husband, Phúc, whom they all playfully called 'Phúcyu', had started a vegetable garden at the back of the caretaker's unit, Fergus had arrived home one afternoon to find Phúc attempting to dig a garden in the rock hard ground with a post hole shovel, Fergus had gone back to the camp and took the bobcat that was fitted with a rotary hoe that was being used to make firebreaks and had shown Phúc how to use it. The next day Fergus was amazed to find a huge vegetable garden of approximately five hundred square metres. It was only a matter of a couple of months and they seemed to be enjoying fresh vegetables according to the season.

The whole of the Stezland operation had just fallen into place nicely and they had created a much needed service for the local area with the earthmoving company which also created a pet hate from the local senior sergeant who took delight in booking every Stezland Civil

Engineering and Earthmoving vehicle he could find, most for incredibly minor issues that many vehicles around Cooktown also bore but were not booked for.

Tim, Wes, Ken and Fergus were put on the breathalyzer and their vehicles checked for defects almost every time they were in Cooktown, it was definitely getting past a joke and Fergus mentioned to Wes that he was thinking of sending a letter to the Queensland Police Commissioner in protest of this unfair treatment but Wes had cautioned him about it.

'Not a goot idea boss', Wes had said, 'because when he goes missing your letter may become a pointer towards yourself'.

'I thought you were joking Wes when you spoke of him disappearing'.

'I have thought even more about him disappearing, I have decided that the best place would be the quarry floor'.

'The quarry floor?'

'Yar! The quarry floor, a hole, a big enough hole to take him und his Landcruiser is dug here in the quarry floor und filled back in, no person is going to be looking for the bastard there'.

Fergus had laughed off Wes's suggestion and had taken it as a joke, later that evening after dinner, Mitchell was in the lounge watching a video on the television and Wes had set up the pool balls on the snooker table and called out to Fergus,

'I am on ze big wons und it's your shot' he said pouring two schnapps with coke.

'How could I say no?' Fergus took the glass of schnapps and coke and his cue from the rack and then asked Wes,

'How would the sergeant and his car get to the quarry without being seen?' Fergus asked.

'That is called, vorks in progress' Wes laughed, but Fergus had started to realise that Senior Sergeant Sutton had certainly stirred up Wes more than he had realised and Fergus knew from his own military training that Wes could be a very dangerous man to get on the wrong side of and with Sutton saying to Wes, at the station the day they collected their rifles, that no one would ever take his gun from him was taken as a direct challenge by Wes, the fool Sutton, did not realise t

It was time for their second cattle muster and they did not need contractors to do it this time as they installed the self mustering gates on the extended holding yard, all they had to do was to close the gates so that they opened in towards the enclosure, the spring on the gate would close it automatically, the gates would let the cattle in but not out. At this time of the year, just months before the wet season, most of the water holes and small creeks were dry and the cattle became familiar with drinking from the troughs in the enclosures which were being maintained periodically by Mitchell, the 'self mustering' enclosure gates were locked in the open position at this time of the year until muster time.

Now, at muster time, they would fill the handlers with hay, they did that for three days and the yards were slowly filling up and they counted each day, after four days the numbers did not increase so they assumed they had them all, there were more cattle this year as they freely walked in, not being chased by men on horseback so the cattle were not being evasive. Mitchell soon learned that even the small heifers were wild and would charge at him for no apparent reason.

Colin had told them to bring the bulls back this time and to buy six new bulls, two for each run to replace the old bulls, he said a maximum of two years for each bull at each run so look at changing every seven years

The 'Freebody' ramp was perfect and needed just a couple of more modifications to make it even better.

Fergus had bought a bogey drive R series Mack with a double decker cattle carrier B Double trailer with folding interlocking decks so both trailers could be loaded without disconnecting the trailers, this was to be used for transfers from each yard to the camp yard, the prime mover was also used to move the 'Freebody' ramp to each yard.

Mitchell had been to a neighbouring property to learn how to mark (castrate) the male calves so this became his job plus the dehorning and Wes did the ear tags.

This years bullocks for the market was just slightly up at 201 and the sale price was also better at $1006.00 per head with the same transport costs to Charters Towers at $19000.00 leaving a gross of $183,206.00 before offset charges to other Stezland companies at approximately $175,000 leaving a taxable nett profit of about $10,000.00, just below the tax threshold.

Fergus was looking seriously at a fleet of B Double trailers and prime movers to save on his cattle transports and to make money on other work as there seemed to be a shortage of stock transports and he had to book these trucks six months earlier. He lost interest when he did his research to discover that the cattle could only travel a maximum of 48 hours and even less in the Far North Queensland temperature and then they have to be unloaded for a break and then reloaded to continue the journey. The biggest problem was finding suitable and dedicated drivers who also had to be good cattlemen, apparently, there were plenty of transports without good drivers lying idle.

A Plan

Wes and Fergus were playing pool, which was becoming quite a common occurrence on most evenings, it also seemed to go better with a glass or two of schnapps and coke which Wes had introduced to Fergus.

'Ve need a back gate, what do you think Fergus?'

'A back gate for what'? Fergus mused.

'You cannot drive here into this home without everyone at ze camp or za 'Gatehouse' seeing you'

'Does it matter if people see you driving past the camp?'

'If you are driving a police car up to the quarry, then yar!'

Fergus laughed, 'Are you still thinking of that copper disappearing?'

'Und you are not?' Wes seemed puzzled, 'You are not thinking of it seriously Fergus?'

'I don't hate him enough to kill him, but he is a real pain in the arse, I wish I had killed the other mongrel Kirkland when I had the chance a couple of years ago, I have a lot to hate him for'.

'Yar, maybe you will get another chance now he is back in Cooktown'.

Fergus stopped taking his shot and turned to Wes, 'What!..what are you saying'?

Wes told Fergus that Sutton had passed him on Charlotte Street yesterday and Kirkland was his passenger and it also looked like Kirkland now had three stripes on his arm.

Fergus found it hard to believe that Kirkland would return to Cooktown.

It was late afternoon the next day when they took Fergus for a drive in his FJ40 down behind the house, weaving around trees and rocks until finally, they arrived at the unnamed creek that was just below, but out of view from the house, about three kilometres he guessed. They got out of the Landcruiser almost at the waters edge and Wes brought with him a topographical map and walked to the edge of the flowing creek.

'The camp cattle yards are just around there, about a kilometre' Wes said.

Fergus looked to where he pointed and shook his head,

'No way'.

We walked the few steps back to the Landcruiser and opened up the topographical map,

'Look here' Wes pointed to the map showing the creek and the hill to their right when facing the creek, 'See, just around this hill here Yar?'

'Can't be......can it..well fuck me' Fergus was quite astonished, even more so that he had never really realised that the house was actually back behind the hill towards the camp and the 'Gatehouse' but when you drove past the 'Gatehouse' you went through the gorge and then veered to the right and as you came up upon the house that was on a rise the hill behind the house was also the other side of the creek but it gave the impression that the house was at the base of the huge hills. Once you left the 'Gatehouse' you were doing a big half circle back towards the 'Gatehouse' without realising it as it seemed you were in a different valley as you could not see the creek.

'Now, Komm look at this boss', as Wes walked to a huge boulder that was about three metres high and five metres wide along the bank of the creek and partly in the creek, they approached it on their right and after walking past the boulder and looking across the creek the view was cut off by another boulder just a bit bigger in the same dimension as the first in height with the exception that the length was more like seven metres long.

'You Vill need to take off your boots here, and socks and roll up your trousers' Wes suggested.

'Is this necessary'? Fergus began to complain.

'Komm und look' Wes said with his boots already kicked off and his trousers rolled up to his knees.

Fergus followed suit and walked into the water behind Wes, the gap between these two huge boulders was about two point five metres, they walked upstream until they were clear of the longer boulder and here you could see the bank on the other side.

Wes kept walking almost to the bank on the other side of the creek, he stopped and turned waiting for Fergus to come up to him then told him to turn around. Fergus turned and was amazed, the two boulders looked to have turned into one huge boulder and the passage between the boulders could not be seen, Fergus walked up water to his left for about thirty metres and still, the gap could not be seen due to the unique angle that the first boulder covered the second and then yet another boulder on the bank also seemed to become part of one huge boulder.

'Now komm this way' Wess called to him.

Walking down water past the boulders with water up to their knees they started to approach a long bend and about one kilometre further, Fergus could see the shallow crossing of the unnamed creek which is about one kilometre from the 'Gatehouse' and camp. Fergus was just amazed when Wes said grinning to him 'Das will be our back gate, yar?'

Fergus thought it would make a great back gate but it may take some work to do it. He had been thinking for some time about turning the creek crossing into a low level concrete crossing which would mean not having to get the vehicle tyres wet and cause the dust to turn to mud on the wheels and the underside of the wheel arches. Fergus had completed a design and had done an indicative estimate to construct the concrete crossing and thought that it was just too much money for what it was but then remembered the time when he had bought a new Toyota Prado as a company vehicle and had given it to Ken for his trips to Cooktown and sometimes Marreba and Cairns rather than him having to take Fergus's Landrover.

Ken was just over the moon to receive the Prado as his company vehicle and had told Fergus that he had the best job in the world and lived in the best place in the world.

It was only two days after he had given Ken the car that Ken had returned from doing the banking in Cooktown, he had found Fergus down at his house and he looked so miserable as he told Fergus that he was sorry but that he had to leave his job. Of course, Fergus was shattered by this news and asked the reason for this sudden decision to leave his job.

Ken had told him that Sutton had pulled him over in Cooktown that morning and had told him that he was going to get his parole revoked as he was consorting with another convicted criminal, meaning Fergus.

Fergus had told Ken that was bullshit and that it was not consorting if it was only two people concerned and that it had to be three people minimum who are convicted criminals. Ken was not convinced and had told Fergus that he would have to leave as he did not want to go back to prison, there was no way was he ever going back to prison.

It had taken Fergus hours and had included telephone calls to Brian Haptu who had also given Ken the phone number of a Barrister who had finally convinced that it would be most unusual for him, especially in the position that he was now serving, to have his parole revoked, it had been a very close thing, not only would it have been a disaster for Fergus on the business side but it would have been heartbreaking and soul destroying for Ken.

Having remembered this, not so long ago incident, Fergus finished the design for the low level concourse and gave it to Tim to get it underway ASAP and he would survey for a temporary creek diversion tomorrow which would also allow construction of 'the back gate' underwater road construction which would be a top secret part of the concourse project.

Fergus had found Wes and had told him that they would be surveying the creek for a temporary diversion tomorrow.

'Fucking ripper' was his reply and suggested a game of pool after dinner.

'Due to the wide, approximately twenty metre, width between the banks of the creek, it was a fairly simple diversion and one of Tim's best operators from Hope Vale operated the big Cat excavator at Fergus's request to dig the diversion channel as he did not want Jason, the usual excavator's operator, to see the boulder formation where the StezPark 'back gate' was going to be built. Fergus had thought that it was most likely not necessary but just to be sure, as the fewer people that knew about the 'back gate' the better.

A portable 'dry batch' concrete plant was leased from Mount Isa together with two concrete agitators fitted to Mack R600 6WD ex army trucks. Fergus bought a Michigan articulated 4WD front end loader with a three metre 4 way bucket to service the concrete plant with sand and gravel taken from below, down the waterside, of the proposed concourse.

The concrete plant and agitator trucks were operated by Fergus and Wes, much to everyone's amusement, who sometimes worked late afternoons, when everyone else had finished work, to make and pour about seventy cubic metres of concrete directly onto the course river bed filling in swirl holes about two metres in width from the centre of the concourse span and up towards the giant boulders. They would return early the next morning before other workers had even risen from their beds and use the two bobcats to spread a light covering of river gravel and sand over the newly poured concrete of the previous afternoon making it invisible to a glancing eye.

'So my friend' said Fergus to Wes, they being the only ones still up and playing pool after dinner with more than a few of Mitchell's beers and a couple of Schnapps, 'The 'back gate' is now finished, tell me more of your plans, how does our target get taken'?

'He lives in his house on Flinders Street, it's a very leafy, almost bush, street and although only about three hundred meters from the police station he drives to and from the station daily and at, almost, the precise time..five forty five pm...' Wes was cut off from Fergus.

'Sounds like you have been stalking him'?

'It was not hard to find these things out, It did not take very much time, but it is here, at his home in the evening, that I would shoot the victim while he is still in his vehicle and then drive him about five hundred metres further along Flinders Street where it is only bush and where I have parked our 'tilt tray' stock truck, drive onto the stock truck and then out of town and back to our causeway where I will unload the police vehicle and come in the 'back gate', up to the quarry and down into the hole, fill the hole und..wallah'.

Fergus just stared at Wes, 'Fuck me Wes, you have got it worked out haven't you, you are really serious aren't you'?

'He is spoiling things for us Fergus, he has challenged me personally, he has upset Ken.....soon he will be picking on Mitchell...he is just a cunt,...he just has to go' replied Wes, 'But I think we should also get rid of the other prick at the same time.....if we could come up with a plan, there is plenty of room in Sutton's police car'.

'Where does Kirkland live'?

'That's the problem, he lives out of town', said Wes 'And I have not yet managed to come up with a plan,..but I vill'.

'So, the copper arrives home in his car at five forty five and then what'? Asked Fergus while pouring them both another of Mitchell's kegged beer.

'The moment that he opens the car door I shoot him before he gets out, that is very important because if he gets out and I shoot him he vould be very hard to put back into the car, I estimate that fat prick vould be weighing vell over the hundred kilo mark which would take some getting from the ground and back into the car, so...he must be shot in the car' Wes explained.

'And,..no body would hear the discharge of your rifle,..shotgun,..perhaps'?

'I have a special vepon dat ist made for such assassinations, I have kept it from the KSK and smuggled it into Australia by disassembling the vepon into many parts and placing them all through my luggage, I'll show you', said Wes leaving the snooker room and returning shortly with polished timber box that he placed on top of the pool table and carefully opening the box revealed a Russian manufactured Margolin .22 target pistol set into a red velvet moulding amongst an array of other items.

We took the pistol from the box, worked the cocking slide and then handed it to Fergus.

'Wow,....looks impressive', Fergus said then handed it back to Wes who unscrewed a knurled cap, that was very un noticeable, from the top of the barrel; that revealed a fine thread, he then took a small cylindrical object, that appeared to have a bore through the centre of it, from the box as he murmured 'Suppressor', he then took on of the two, fully loaded, magazines from the box and inserted it into the hand grip of the Margolin, he then cocked the pistol so it was ready to fire, walking to a lounge chair he picked up one of the hand sewn red leather cushions that Bian had made, placed the barrel of the Margolin against the cushion and had fired.

Fergus had thought that the weapon had misfired as there was no sound other than an audible click but he had seen the ejection of the empty .22 case which had confused him. Wes held up the cushion for Ferguss to see the tiny entry hole of the .22 projectile and although the cushion was now very distorted, and would probably never regain its once oval shape, there was no exit hole, the projectile was still within the cushion.

'Fuck Me'! Exclaimed Fergus looking at the cushion and then back at the pistol, he himself was somewhat an expert in firearms but he had never seen the like of this and..so quiet..and no mess. This was a very sinister weapon indeed.

Wes explained that the Margolin was a standard issue in the KSK along with a Walther 9mm, the Margolin was used for silent close encounter combat.

It was at this point that Fergus was convinced that Wes was fully intent on carrying out his plan and he almost had everything in place. It was also obvious that the man had planned every minute detail, it did not seem to matter what question Fergus asked him about his plan, Wes had a perfect answer, as just now, with the question of a weapon, he seemed undefeatable.

The formworkers had completed the laying out of the causeway form around the five three hundred millimetre diameter pipes that ran through the centre of the causeway to keep a dry top surface under normal conditions.

Fergus and Wes had completed making and delivering the concrete for the causeway and now the contract concrete placers were busy finishing the surface of the causeway.

The owner of the mobile concrete plant and trucks was on his way to collect and transport the items back to Mount Isa and Wes decided that it was time to dig the hole in the quarry.

There were now two quarries on Stezland, the first was now only used for crushed deco with lay in two large stockpiles, the second quarry which was roughly one kilometre from the first, where the crushing plant was presently installed, was producing a much better road base that conformed to council requirements.

It was the first quarry that Wes had chosen was to become the grave site of Sutton and his car, along with Kirkland if he could somehow combine them both.

Wes had told Tim that he wanted the Cat excavator for a couple of days and a tip truck, Tim could not really afford to lose the excavator again as Fergus had just had it for over a week digging his creek diversion channel and the contract works that Tim had lined up for the excavator could not really wait any longer than they had already.

Tim knew that he could not say no to Wes as Wes was not only Fergus's right Hans man but he was also treated as Fergus's brother, but the excavator needed to be used on Tim's other projects first so he approached Fergus.

Tim had briefly explained to Fergus the issue with allowing Wes to have the excavator and Fergus had simply told Tim to acquire another excavator as Wes wanted to use the Cat excavator for some project of his own and that was fine with him.

Wes had marked out for his excavation and had dug to a depth of about one half of a metre in the decomposed granite and had been piling the removed material close to the excavation for later backfilling, the ground material had suddenly now changed to a lighter coloured clay material and this Wes placed onto the tipper truck and took it to place over the refuse at the landfill area near the camp that was being used as a rubbish tip for the camp, the 'Gatehouse' and now also the house at StezPark. This was certainly helping the land fills appearance. Tim could not understand why Wes going to all this trouble in covering the rubbish in the landfill area but also admitted that it did certainly help the aesthetics of that area and most importantly, seemed to keep Wes busy and amused.

Fergus had asked Wes casually whilst taking a pool shot one evening, 'What's the idea of covering the garbage over at the land fill? Not that I don't think it looks good, just curious'.

'Well,…if one is searching for something that seems to have disappeared and comes upon a large pile of earth, then it may seem suspicious' Wes's answer was like it was just a natural thing. Fergus was again amazed at this man's exactness, he was now convinced that Wes's plan would be complete and would most probably succeed and the sergeant, or, sergeant's may never be found.

Mitchell had turned eighteen whilst he was working on the property and looking after the interests of Stezland Pastoral Pty Ltd, it was the middle of December and the wet season was expected to commence at any time which would eliminate his bore checking duties at the cattle yards and enclosures. He had enrolled at the James Cook University for a Bachelor of Veterinary Science which would be at the Townsville campus and also at Fletcherview Station west of Townsville. It was for a five year, full time, term.

He would miss being at Stezland but he would be able to come home regularly as it was only a six hundred kilometre drive. Now he was eighteen he was allowed to take his Landcruiser off the property and had decided on a drive into Cooktown, he had mentioned to Bian that he was going into town and had casually asked her if she needed anything brought home from there. To his surprise, and slight annoyance, she had given him a list of items. It was already hot at midday and looked like it would just get hotter as he drove past the camp and the 'Gatehouse' waving at Ken, and then a little later at Rodney and Jason, it was just after twelve o'clock when he crossed the new causeway.

The Aftermath

At 35°c and deciding that it was just too hot to be outside today Fergus and Wes had just returned from the bull sales at Mareeba and had finished lunch and were talking at the bar in the snooker room when Mitchell had entered the room seeming very distressed.

'Dad!....Dad,.. I have fucked up big time' and he hugged Fergus around his shoulders and started to shake and sob. Wes rose from his seat and started to go and Mitchell said,

'Wes, don't go,...just listen first' Mitchell always had a feeling of security and safety when Wes was near and he felt that he needed much security and safety now.

Mitchell slowly composed himself and then quietly and calmly told both his father and Wes of what had just happened in Cooktown.

Wes and Fergus had not said a word while Mitchell was speaking, for some reason or other Fergus thought that Mitchell was just making all of this shit up and he could not understand why, they all just looked at one another for what seemed like a minute or two and then both Fergus and Wes asked the same question at the same time, 'You have killed both of the police sergeants'?

'I don't know if they are dead! I only shot them once each, I only shot all of them once.........oh..fuck me...what have I done,....please help me, dad, I'm so sorry, I don't know what to do now, what should I do...' Fergus cut him off and said that getting upset is not going to help anything, he told him to settle down, have another drink and tell them again what had happened.

Mitchell had told them both the story more than three times now and it had not varied much, Fergus and Wes had asked him so many questions and his answers had never varied. It just seemed incredible, what had caused it? they both had asked, heat and a bad temper from something or other seemed to be the answer but that was the very least of the problem. Are they all dead was the big question that they had no answer for but then they realised that it did not matter if they were dead or not, it would still be the same fate for Mitchell.

The more they all talked and thought about it the more logical the discussion turned.

'You fired how many shots?' Wes asked

'Five'

'Are you sure?'

'Yes' said Mitchell pulling four empty .30-30 cases from his pocket, 'There is another empty in the breach, there was only five in it. If I had missed with the last shot he would have got me'. Mitch said, meaning 'he' to be Kirkland.

Regardless of the whole mess, Wes was somewhat impressed and he also thought that Mitchell's father was also. The kid took down five people with five shots with a .30-30 lever action rifle, that is legendary for starters.

The questions did not stop for Mitchell, all afternoon both Fergus and Wes grilled him on who saw him, who did he see, and on and on, and then Mitchell suddenly said

'I came in by the the 'back gate' '

Fergus jumped to his feet and asked Mitchell if he had the air conditioning on in his cruiser when he left here and Mitchell had replied yes as it was so hot,

'So your windows were wound up when you left quickly,...quickly..call the Cooktown police station and report that your car has been stolen from here, do it now quickly...quickly'.

'Yes'! Said Wes, on the same line of thought as Fergus 'Hurry,...do it now'. As Fergus was on the phone by the bar and Fergus was looking in the telephone book for the number,

'Here it is' said Fergus calling out the number as Mitchell dialled and added 'Stay strong and talk calmly'

There was no answer and they tried again but the number just rang out. Fergus looked up the Mareeba police station and said try this as he called out the number.

'Can I report a stolen vehicle, please' Mitchell said as the phone was answered, 'It was stolen from our property near Shiptons Flat, yes it is near Cooktown...Mitchell Laird....The property is Stezland on the unnamed creek road, Just now..I just went outside to go somewhere and it's gone...OK..our number is.......'

Mitchell told Wes and Fergus what the constable who had answered the phone had told him that the Cook town police were busy just now but he would take the details and get it to them.

Fergus looked at Wes and said 'Put his car in your hole Wes'

'Where is your rifle, Mitch?'

'It's under the seat, Dad'

'Good, it stays there, I'll follow you up there Wes with the Komatsu Loader, Mitchell stay here and don't answer the phone if it rings, tell Bian that you didn't go to town today as your car was missing but don't say too much else, to anyone OK'! Fergus was saying as he was leaving the room.

The excavation was about three plus metres deep with a very steep ramp that would allow a vehicle down but there was no way it would come out again, as per the design.

Wes drove Mitchell's one year, old fifty thousand dollars plus, Landcruiser down into his excavation and climbed back up the steep ramp to the quarry floor just as Fergus arrived with the Komatsu articulated front end loader and commenced to fill in Wes's excavation hole, after about fifteen minutes no one would know what was buried below the quarry floor and never would.

The story was, that Mitchell went to the Mareeba Bull Sales this morning with his Father and Wes and returned at about two o'clock that afternoon, he had gone to get his car to drive into Cooktown to get some things for Bian at about two thirty but his car was not there, he reported his car stolen at two forty.

The three of them then moved a small herd of bullocks from the camp paddocks into the paddock behind the house to take care of any tyre marks coming from the creek.

Fergus had driven down to the camp later that evening and had dropped in to see Ken, he told Ken that Mitchell's car had been knocked off at some stage today while they were at the Bull Markets in Mareeba and asked if he saw anything. Ken said he saw the cruiser at around midday and had presumed that it was Mitchell driving it, he couldn't be sure as the windows were wound up and it was glarey.

He then visited Rodney and told him the same thing, he also said that he and Jason had waved as they thought it was Mitch but couldn't be sure but just assumed.

Dinner that night was a conversation of anything other than what had happened, they all acted casual and happy so as not to alert the Vietnamese staff, following dinner they all adjourned to the snooker room and the conversation changed dramatically.

'You have to realise Mitchell that if the police discover it was you at the pub today who shot those people, and it doesn't matter if they are dead or not, you will go to prison for life, your whole life will be ruined and I am not going to let that happen and neither is Wes. If you follow our lead and play it cool then you may escape going to prison, it will be a lie, a very big lie, that you can never mention to anyone, never,....do you understand'?

'But I don't think that I can live with myself Dad after what I did' Mitch was becoming tearful.

'It doesn't matter if you want to feel guilty but it will be easier to get over out of prison than in prison, sure you have made a monster of a mistake but going to prison is not going to make those five people better, let me tell you'.

'You will never forget what has happened Mitchell if you are in prison as they won't let you, we will' added Wes.

It was agreed that they would all just get on with life as though they knew nothing other than the theft of Mitchell's car.

There was a knock at the snooker room door, they always kept it closed when in the snooker room as the language sometimes became loud and quite blue.

'Yes,' called Fergus and Bian's head poke around the door.

'Misters need anyting more for evening, oi I going bed'

'No we are fine, thank you Bian, goodnight' said Fergus.

'OK, night....you hear news of big shooting at Cooktown today?' She asked opening the door a bit wider.

'No,....what news Bian,...come in and tell me please' Fergus sounded very surprised and Bian entered the doorway and in her broken English said that five people had been shot dead in a hotel bar at Cooktown this afternoon and the police are blocking roads in and out of Cooktown and are conducting searches, she then added that it was good that Master Mitchell did not go to town today.

They all feigned shock at her news and as soon as she left they got more drinks and Wes said, 'It begins'.

Fergus looked at Wes and realised that both of them were wearing the bright green 'Cattleman' with the embroidered name Stezland Pastoral above the lefthand side pocket, Fergus had bought three each for Wes and himself and now he had a sudden thought and went to his bedroom and brought back one of the other 'Cattleman' embroidered shirts and handed it to Mitchell.

'Wear this tomorrow and every day until I can get you some of your size, if anyone wants to know it is what you have been wearing every day all week, you've been working up at the yards and no one has seen you so they won't know anyway' Fergus instructed Mitchell.

Wes offered to give one of his shirts to Mitchell also and Fergus said that as Mitchell had not been to Cooktown for at least the last two years it would be doubtful if he had been recognised by anybody and anyone offering a description to the police would be a khaki shirt.

All that they could really do now was wait and see what transpires tomorrow.

Wes gave Mitchell a very stiff schnapps and Coke and made him drink it with another two of his homebrew beers so he would sleep tonight rather than have nightmares.

Fergus said that he would go to the camp office in the morning on the pretence of some business with Tim and see if any news had come in from some of the workers who lived in Cooktown.

No one other than the Vietnamese staff slept that night, Fergus woke up just before midnight and could not get back to sleep so he dressed and went to the snooker room to get a drink only to find Wes and Mitchell in there playing pool.

The next morning the camp was abuzz with the news of the shootings, the news was hazy and second hand but it seemed the police were looking for a white Landcruiser driven by a slim man but there was no real description of him and that he had shot dead five people in the bar including two coppers.

'Fuck' said Fergus to Tim and everyone else that may be able to hear, 'Might have been the prick that knocked off Mitch's ute yesterday morning',

'Fucking could be the same bastard that shot them poor cunts in the pub, better tell the coppers boss!' Called out one of the plant operators from Cooktown.

'Yeah, we tried to call yesterday but no one answered the phone' Fergus responded, 'I think I'd better go into town and see them'.

Fergus then had a thought and went back to the house and told Mitchell that he was going into Cooktown with him, Mitchell seemed hesitant and Fergus told him,

'Probably the best thing we can do is have you front up to report your stolen car, and you'll have to look angry and then totally shocked if they tell you it may have been taken by the same person that they are looking for, good to see you are wearing the 'Cattleman' shirt'. He then called out to Wes who was still in bed, 'You want to come into town Wes?'

All three were in the landrover heading into Cooktown and just over the bridge at Shiptons Flat was a police car parked in the incoming lane with two police officers standing by it, Fergus slowed as he got to the police car and sked what was going on to one of the police officers.

'Just checking all vehicles coming from the North' was his reply.

'Any particular reason?' Fergus asked

'You haven't heard the news?'

'Some of the workers were talking about a shooting at the Cooktown Pub last night' Fergus offered.

'Bit more than that, but if you are heading to Cooktown you will probably find out all about it'

'Yeah, we are going to Cooktown to report a vehicle theft from our property yesterday morning'. Replied Fergus.

'Just pull over there please sir' the other police officer who had been listening, a senior constable, said.

Fergus pulled over and glanced at Mitchell in the back seat who seemed to be holding up just fine, so far.

He filled out a full report, including a complete vehicle description, which also included its last known location for the senior constable. The constable then told him that there was now no need to travel to Cooktown and that he would handle the report and that the detectives may want to see him.

'Suits us as we are flat out just now trying to get organised before the wet and now we are a vehicle down' replied Fergus and they made a three point turn and drove back to the camp.

Tim had the full news as they went into the camp office.

'That mongrel Sutton was killed yesterday in that shooting'

Now Fergus was shocked, seriously shocked and Wes looked sick. Tim continued to tell them that some other police sergeant, doesn't know the name, was also shot but he didn't know who that could be as he thought there was only one sergeant at the Cooktown Police Station. There was also three Aborigines shot dead but two of them were out of towners, Kalkadoon's from Mount Isa, apparently.

Tim said that no one knew who the white guy was, he hadn't been seen around Cooktown before but a few people saw his truck and said it was a new looking Landcruiser ute.

They had left the office and were heading back to the house to get some breakfast, Wes let it slip,

'Bet it was fucking Kirkland'.

''That's what I was thinking' Fergus said, 'Mitchell did one of those coppers yesterday look like the one you think killed your Mum?'

'Dad, I only saw police who were shooting at me, they were trying to kill me, Dad, I honestly don't know what they looked like other than police firing their guns at me and I just knew that if I did not kill them then they were going to kill me' Mitchell said losing his voice halfway through what he was saying.

'It's OK son, let it go, don't worry, remember that you *have* to stay strong…OK'

They hadn't long finished breakfast when the house phone rang, it was Tim telling Fergus to expect company, two plain clothes coppers were on their way down, Fergus thanked Tim and hung up the telephone and it immediately rang again, Rodney this time announcing that it looked like 'D's' coming down to see us and then asked 'did you hear the news'? to which Fergus said yeah bits and pieces and that the coppers are probably coming about Mitch's stolen ute.

Fergus let the police in the door and into the lounge, Mitchell and Wes were already in there waiting.

The police introduced themselves and Fergus, quite casually, asked if it was about Mitchell's missing ute.

The older looking detective told them that the first thing they all needed to do was to tell them where they were yesterday between noon and two o'clock.

'On our way back from Mareeba, from the Bull Sales' Fergus simply stated then added that Mitchell didn't realise that his ute was missing until about two thirty, or there abouts.

'We are not talking about the ute Mr Laird, can you prove that you were all in Mareeba yesterday and at what time' The senior detective snapped at him.

'I have the receipts for four bulls, but it won't show the time of course, just yesterday's date' Fergus then remembered something that could be important, when they had smoko yesterday in Mareeba they both had fish and chips each and Wes was starving and also had a burger, Fergus had paid for this on his credit card, three meals, you ripper he thought as he told the detective that he had a credit card meal receipt for three meals and it was probably still in his shirt pocket from yesterday. He went to his room and returned with the receipt from yesterday at 10:46.

The discussion then moved on to Mitchell's ute, Was it locked? - No, Were the keys in it - Yes, What else was in the ute the detective wanted to know.

'Handheld GPS, two way handheld radio, machete, Akubra hat, and a rifle' Mitchell had replied
The mention of the rifle made them sit up, and they asked Mitchel for a description of the rifle.

'30-30 Winchester'

'Was it loaded'?

'Yes, five rounds'

'Any more ammo in the car'?

'No, just an empty box lying in the glove box, I think'

'When did you report the vehicle stolen?'

'About,…three o'clock'

'To who'?

'I tried the Cooktown Police Station telephone number but there was no answer, so then I rang the Mareeba Police Station and they told me to report it in person to Cooktown tomorrow,..that is today'.

Fergus interrupted and told them that they had left to go into Cooktown this morning and had met the police at the roadblock who took the details of the stolen vehicle and they had then returned home, here.

The police told Mitchell that he would be reprimanded for not locking his vehicle and not securing a weapon but that would be about all and to learn a lesson, the senior detective told Mitchell that he did not hear this from him, but when making a claim to the insurance company for the loss of his ute, to make sure you tell them that it was *locked,* as they rarely read the police report in detail and those thieving pricks will cancel your insurance if they know it was unlocked, he then said good luck mate! And they left.

Epilogue

Mitchell filed a claim with his comprehensive insurance company and as the vehicle was under two years old it was eligible for a full replacement.

He received a reprimand from the Firearms Licensing Police and his firearm license was suspended for one year.

The two police sergeants did not seem to be missed by anyone and they both had very low key police funerals, they were definitely not only missed by Wes, Fergus and Tim but by quite a number of the local habitants.

The local Aborinine male who was shot by accident was sadly missed by his family and mob but no malice was held towards the unknown white male that had shot him as it was all the fault of the visiting Kalkadoon men who were known troublemakers who had started the whole thing.

No one has yet been charged for the Cooktown shootings.

End

.

Max Barrington

BAD COMPANY

Max Barrington

Max Barrington

Prologue

The year was 2016, the place was the Mareeba Police Station.

Police were interviewing two witnesses to a shooting murder at a remote area on the banks of the Mitchell River in Far North Queensland.

'Right, let me get this clear' exclaimed Detective Sergeant Cameron Jamison of the Mareeba CID, 'You were all at the camp on the river on the Saturday night at the Mitchell River with the intention of fishing on the property, you were all aware that you were trespassing'

'No!' Interjected David Barnes (Barnsy), 'They don't own the river, the river's not their land, we were camped on the dry riverbed'

'But to get to where you were you had trespassed, and to go fishing the next day you would be further trespassing', quipped the sergeant, 'Right? So you left the camp at five o'clock the next morning and then, tell me again what happened?

The Detective Sergeant was not at all happy with what these fellows were telling him. It seemed to change around a bit the more times that they told it, and he knew that he had to get it right.

The call had come in late the previous afternoon at five fifty four PM, that there had been a shooting out at a location on the Mitchell River, it had been witnessed by two of the missing man's friends.

The distance from the nearest police station at Laura to the location of the reported shooting was two hundred and thirty kilometres but, it was a one manned station and the Senior Constable in residence was away on that day, so the call went to the next nearest major station being Cooktown.

Two constables had been despatched that evening to travel the three hundred and seventy kilometres, on mostly unsealed roads, from Mareeba to the alleged shooting incident near the intersection of the Mitchell and Palmer Rivers.

Senior Constable Franko Casselis and Constable Owen Jones arrived at the address of the phone call at two AM the following morning. They had collected the caller, Terry Andrews who took him to the campsite on the river. They had arrived at the campsite at two forty seven AM and listened to what both the witnesses had to report about the shooting and their missing companion. They then secured the area and the witnesses and made a call via their satellite telephone to Mareeba Police Station.

Backup teams of police arrived the next morning from Mareeba and investigated the alleged shooting site.

Later that same day, police arrested David Watson and Stan Strauss and transported them to Mareeba Police Station for further questioning.

Terry Andrews and David Barnes were escorted to the Mareeba Police Station to furnish statements to the police on the events that had happened the previous afternoon.

David Barnes again told the Detective Sergeant that at about five thirty am on the Sunday morning, they had all walked along the river towards the homestead which was about a kilometre away and had separated to start fishing in the river, he explained that they liked to separate when fly fishing for Barramundi as it involved transversing up and down the river banks and you needed good space around you.

They had passed a couple of good looking gullies with creeks entering the river and then broke from the river and went over a slight rise and then crossed a track then back onto the river, they were all about one hundred or so metres away from each other and the missing group member, Mark, was last seen starting to go down onto a riverbed, he was wearing headphones that were connected to his mobile telephone that he was using as a music source of pre recorded music, he was the only one wearing headphones whilst fishing.

The other two of the group were on the opposite bank around a bend in the river and David Barnes had left Terry and had gone back down the rise towards the river when he heard the sound of a vehicle with a diesel engine and assumed it would be the property owner Stan Strauss so he quickly found a place to stay out of sight from the vehicle that was heading his way, he assumed the others would also hear the Landcruiser and take similar action which they did with the possible exception of one member, Mark, who was wearing headphones. Barnsy had seen the Landcruiser go along the track that they had crossed earlier and he could make out its occupants to be the owners of the property, Stan Strauss and David Watson, although he could not see Mark he knew more or less exactly where he was and he shuddered when he saw the vehicle stop and one of the occupants get from the vehicle with a rifle in hand and fire a shot towards where Mark would have been fishing.

Barnsy was about to bolt when the person re entered the vehicle and the vehicle made a detour down the rise towards the river, he waited and watched and although he could no longer see the vehicle he heard it stop and he

Max Barrington

heard another gunshot followed by some other indistinct sounds.

Barnes was out of there and kept the tree line between him and the vehicle so that he could not be seen.

Terry Andrews told of a similar story with the exception of only hearing the vehicle and the gunshots, he too as soon as he thought it was safe bolted into the bush but became somewhat lost.

It took him an hour or so to return to the camp to find Barnsy waiting for him, he didn't think that he seemed to look too worried about the events of the day as they were having a beer and a chat, he had casually asked him had he seen Mark and when he replied in the negative Barnsy said he should be back soon and added, 'I hope those pricks didn't shoot him.'

It seemed the general consensus with Barnsy and Terry Andrews that Mark should show up later but Barnsy had suggested contacting the police so Terry had driven their Nissan Patrol back to another nearby property that had a telephone and contacted the police and they were now at the Mareeba Police Station making statements.

It appeared to be a pretty straight case as far as the Detective Sergeant could see and he organised to detain the property owners and a search of the property.

Both Stan Strauss and David Watson denied even being in that area of their property that day and told police that they were in the other direction of where the police claimed that Mark had gone missing, they were marking and ear tagging calves at the cattle yards a long distance from there.

Extensive searches of the property failed to find Mark or his body, some items with signs of blood were found on the river bank and DNA from samples taken, later revealed it to be the blood of Mark Crampton.

A firearms license search had shown that Watson was licenced to hold a Tikka .270 Rifle and that Strauss was licensed to hold a Marlin 30-30 lever action repeating rifle and a Savage pump action shotgun.

A search of the homestead and the vehicles on the property could only find the Tikka .270 rifle that was licensed to Watson, Strauss had stated that his shotgun and rifle were in his bedroom, if they weren't, then he had no idea where they were.

Tests were performed on the clothing of Strauss and Watson for both blood and gunpowder residuals but none were found. They appeared in the Cairns Law Courts and were both found guilty of murder under circumstantial evidence as the body of Mark Crampton was never found.

They both pleaded their innocence but were both convicted to life imprisonment for the murder of Mark Crampton and in accordance with a new law that had recently been passed, 'No Body, No Parole' they would never be released unless they would reveal the location of Mark Crampton's body.

Some say that it was the fastest murder case on record in Queensland law, as far as the police were concerned it had been a pretty simple case based entirely on circumstantial evidence and they had successfully obtained a conviction for the murder.

Detective Sergeant Cameron Jamison was amazed at the result, he had warned the prosecutor that the evidence from the two prospectors was flimsy and seemed to change every time they repeated it. He was also doubtful about other physical evidence, or more the lack of it, that they were implying in this 'circumstantial' case but the prosecutor told him that the jury would not have knowledge of it and he doubted that the defence would pick up on it. 'Ah well', thought Jamison, 'A conviction is a conviction.'

The 'No Body, no parole' law was introduced into Queensland in 2015, this law would apply to Srauss and Watson.

Strauss & Watson

David Watson was born on Watsonville Station in 1974. He was raised, educated and worked on the property all his life, he had one younger brother, by two years, who was also born and educated on Watsonville but who had decided at the age of sixteen to leave the property and move to Chillagoe, a small town, some one hundred and eighty kilometres to the South East.

His parents had taken up the lease of 400,000 acres just to the west of Mount Mulgrave on the Mitchell River where it is joined by the Palmer River, in 1968.

Benjamin and Doris Watson had both worked and had been married in the Wimmera District of the State of Victoria and worked a small property that produced wool from wethers when they had heard from a friend of a lease available in Far North Queensland.

They had decided to leave the cold behind and had sold their small property to their closest neighbour for a modest price.

Less than half of the money from the sale of the Wimmera property enabled the purchase of the Far North Queensland lease of 400,000 acres, or 161,874 hectares.

They were aware that the country was rough and that the cattle carrying capacity was around one head per fifteen hectares and that the accommodation on the property was pretty sparse.

The property also had a passive income from mining leases that were along the riverbanks.

Tragically both Ben and Doris Watson were drowned whilst attempting to drive through a river crossing in their Landrover in 1994.

David Watson was the sole heir in the wills of Ben and Doris. The younger brother of David, named Jeffrey, had been cut from the will once he had left home in 1992.

Stan Strauss was born in Innisfail in 1972, the only son of the local Police Sergeant and School teacher. Stan had entered into a life of being in trouble with the law for some reason or other but only in a minor capacity.

He had found work in the canefields and had saved his money until, at the age of 20, had enough money to buy a cattle property of 100,000 acres, 40,468 hectares, that adjoined the Watson's property.

For the two years before the tragic drowning of Ben and Doris, Stan had a great working relationship with them, they would assist him when required and he would assist the Watsons in return.

Upon David's inheritance of Watsonville, both he and Stan Strauss had decided to combine the properties and become fifty-fifty partners in Watsonville.

Both being fairly young at twenty and twenty two, they had decided to modernise the property and aimed to maximise beef production at Watsonville and had taken out a small loan using the property as collateral, with this money they had purchased two second hand Robinson R22 helicopters for mustering and hired pilots for the mustering periods until they had both become proficient in flying them. The helicopters, together with a system of fixed cattle races installed in strategic places around the property allowed for more efficiency, with a better yield of up to thirty percent, annual mustering using a total of only four people, rather than the usual twelve. A drawback of Aerial mustering was that it took a considerable time for the cattle to settle down before drafting and loading on transports.

Both Stan and David were annoyed that they seemed to be plagued with trespassers on their property, it was either camping, shooting, fishing or metal detecting but it seemed to be a consistent problem that they both took exception to and started to go out of their way to detect and remove trespassers from Watsonville.

They even used the helicopters to check out boundaries and favourite fishing holes looking for trespassers.

The biggest problem it seemed with trespassers was the lighting of fires that sometimes became uncontrollable and became bushfires, the rubbish left behind at fishing holes in the rivers and creeks and huge damage to the roads and tracks from people becoming bogged and recovering bogged vehicles, but what seemed worse of all, was the bullets zipping past them whilst they were working around the property.

They had become known for terrorising trespassing people and had been accused of taking overhead shots at them and rigging wires and other obstacles across gazetted roads. They had been visited by police on a number of occasions in respect to complaints from people merely travelling through their property on gazetted roads.

They, of course, denied any wrongdoing, and when confronted with bullet holes in vehicles, they blamed the shooters that came onto the property that seemed to fire indiscriminate shots anywhere and everywhere, hence that is why they were against roads throughout their lands being gazetted.

The police knew that Stan and David were not being truthful but they could not prove anything on them and only notes were recorded against the complaints that were received by the police.

But it seemed that the actions of the Watsonville Station owners were working and the roads became quieter as articles appeared in such publications of *Camping, 4wd Driving, Fossicking and Fishing*, with warnings to people travelling around the area of Watsonville Station.

It became well known in later years to avoid any roads in and around Watsonville and even council and electricity workers were known to take long detours around the property.

Annual Board Meeting 2015

'We are running out of development sites, it's as simple as that, we have taken just about all of the caravan and camping ground sites that have become available, we have bought council members of small rural communities and have gained their parks and reserves, we have bought up all the cane farms that have become available, I reiterate, we are running out of development sites in Queensland' the 'chair' for Juliet Consolidated Enterprise Proprietary Limited (JCE) had just announced at the company annual general meeting of its six directors.

JCE was a very successful development company that specialised in acquiring suitable land, or properties, for commercial or residential purposes. Its commercial development consisted of manufacturing and/or warehouse facilities at a suitable location or region that was considered prime for development.

JCE very rarely purchased the land or property but rather entered into a partnership, or deal, with the landowner and quite often another company would be formed to engage JCE as the developer.

This acquired region was then labelled as manufacturing decentralisation and the idea was either sold or implanted in the minds of the local council and chamber of commerce as yet another possible source of income.

This was often achieved by the careful selection of one or more councillors who may be sympathetic towards JCE in return for a possible future position with either JCE or one of its many offshoots or even become a benefactor of one of its surplus properties.

Following this, then various major Australian manufacturing or assembly companies were approached with the idea of relocation or decentralisation or even a new business opportunity with generous rebates on rates and charges available from the council, not to mention construction and capital gains assistance from the developer.

Once such a project was underway, a residential development would follow as the infrastructure would be there for employment.

The 'chair' was none other than the Queensland Premier, Ms Fiona Gibson, the daughter of the mining magnate Horace Rimshaw The other five directors of JCE in attendance were;

Mr Eric VanDerstatt a grazier from Toowoomba who was also a local councillor. Eric VanDerstatt was the founder of VanDerstatt Constructions a well known building construction company that was busily engaged in providing residences to many of JCE's development projects in various Australian States. Mr VanDerstatt was also the President of the Building Construction Association of Queensland, a voluntary building standards self regulator made up of its members who also formed a strong building materials buying group.

Doctor Christopher Dunwoody MLA (Lib) Qld was formerly a director of a Brisbane Hospital and the resident surgeon, he now spends most of his time enjoying life at one of his three Gold Coast Resorts where he resides with his wife. His two sons run the three resorts between them together with their wives.

Christopher enjoys being a Federal Member of Parliament and is currently 'The Speaker of the House'.

Roz Dagleish is a partner of Huey, Cheetham and Dagleish, Barristers and Solicitors that has chambers in almost every capital city in Australia. A good friend of Fiona Gibson, Roz was also once a colleague of Fiona when she was once a member of State Parliament and enjoyed being the Qld Attorney General.

She has many political and business interests in both Queensland and Western Australia. Accepted to the bar as a King's Council, but these days she is rarely seen in court.

Carl Stephenson formally the Queensland Police Commissioner, the resignation of Carl Stephenson, who once served as the Chief Superintendent of the Queensland Police and then later became commissioner, was triggered by allegations that lacked any credible evidence or corroboration.

Carl is the owner of several Queensland country hotels (pubs) and spends most of his time either at country race meetings or visiting one of his pubs. Since retirement things have been hard for Carl as many of his so called friends turned their backs on him once he had lost his powers in the police force. Unlike the others, Carl relied heavily on his dividends from JCE and it showed.

The sixth and final director on the board was Father Damien Downes, an ordained priest who was now an administrator in the church's financial department and who also undertook church investments in the form of real estate and commercial ventures.

The church kept Father Damien out of the public eye these days due to some unfounded allegations of inappropriate language whilst conducting masses and condemning fellow priests with respect to very publicised unusual activities and he narrowly missed being charged, on a number of occasions, for physical assault on some of these priests. Father Damien did not seem to have a care in the world and lived in a luxury apartment in Brisbane's exclusive Teneriffe that was valued at over twenty million dollars, Father Damien shrugged that valuation off as a joke suggesting that one hundred and twenty thousand would probably pull it up. Father Damien enjoyed a drink and openly displayed this fact at board meetings by demolishing at least one full bottle of scotch whiskey.

That concluded the makeup of the Board of directors for JCE, the company that, generally, had a vision of at least ten years ahead was not looking good after the next five years as they seemed to be running out of viable areas of land and developers cannot develop without land.

True they had a very high criteria as far as properties went but they were also very open to diversification.

JCE had recently suffered a huge loss of some thirty seven million dollars through a failed project that would have been the saver in the five years that was now of contention. It was not unusual for JCE to suffer a loss from time to time but this particular one had hurt for two reasons, the huge amount of money lost with no possible salvage and secondly, there were no other projects to take its place to maintain the steady income stream.

The other five directors had their attention fixed on Fiona and were waiting with bated breath for the resumption of her announcement which they all knew would contain a solution to the issue at hand, but in this instance, instead, she fell silent.

'And the solution..........'? Asked Carl Stephenson.

'I was rather hoping that some of you may have some thoughts that you may want to expand with us all' was Fiona's response.

They just all looked at each other and did not appear to be too concerned, Fiona observed this and added,

'You may feel relaxed at the present, but in five years time when the dividends get smaller, or disappear, then you may feel very concerned. Sure, we may have a solution at the next meeting in a year's time, but we need to be onto it now!... Not in a year's time, at least start something in some direction today'.

'Diversification' Father Damien Downes suggested, 'We always seem to be looking at the same thing, either residential housing developments or commercial developments, what about something other than those'?

'Such as Father' smiled Fiona.

'He's right' uttered Roz Dagleish, 'We've done the housing development to death, it's been good to us but maybe it's time to change'?

'We have mentioned the greatest requirement that exists on earth in the past, but we have never pursued it' Father Damien answered.

'Enlighten me, please' Fiona was not a quick thinker, she didn't have to be in her position as Premier, she was just the figurehead, so to speak, she enjoyed advisors for all types of situations and had no requirement to be smart.

'I am talking *FOOD* madam, we have but briefly discussed it from time to time, but we have never really got very serious about it, we all agreed the world can't go on without it but we seemed to have totally ignored it'. Continued Father Damien.

'Are you talking 'Cereal Farming''? Asked Dr Dunwoody, 'could be good, but I think we might have left it a bit late though'.

'That yes and maybe livestock' was the Father's response.

'And why not the whole deal with abattoirs and butcheries?' Asked Roz becoming interested in the good Father's suggestion.

'Order..order, let's come to order, let someone put a motion forward' Fiona had regained the meeting and a motion was accepted to look into a food supply venture and Father Damien Downes had accepted to provide an indicative viability assessment on areas of food production for the next meeting.

The meeting came to a close and the bar was opened, the caterer was informed that dinner would be taken at six thirty that evening and Doctor Chris Dunwoody complimented Father Damien Downes on his excellent suggestion and offered to help in the viability research as he handed him a glass of scotch and ice.

Eric VanDerstatt was, understandably, not too happy that JCE would not be seeking an extensive construction type of future project as his company was starting to struggle to maintain its extensive knowledgeable team of project engineers and managers. Soon some of the better ones would be on a sizable retainer with no projects to oversee, he approached Father Damien and jovially suggested he concentrate on a project that would be without any infrastructure so they could start from the ground up.

'Much too early to even consider what I am seeking Eric'

'I suppose that I mean,..we don't want to look at buying someone out to improve an established food chain, you know'? Added Eric.

'Do you have any ideas on what we should be looking for, Eric'?

'No, but I do have some good scout contacts in the Western Australia broad acre farming regions, they would know who is doing it hard and they could analyse them for you'.

'I was looking more towards the frontier of Far North Queensland', but Father Damien was rudely interrupted by Carl Stephenson,

'There's fuck all up that way old son'!

A silence descended on the room as it was a strict protocol that swearing would not be tolerated at meetings.

The 'Dinner Gong' sounded.

'Saved by the bell old chap' beamed Dr Dunwoody as they gathered towards the dining room where the traditional board meeting 'Roast Beef' was being served with traditional baked vegetables and horseradish sauce.

Carl Stephenson was sitting next to Father Damien and Father Damien was receiving an uninvited report on the state of conditions in the Far North Queensland territory with advice on staying away from the area as it was a disaster waiting to happen,

'I tell you the Queensland Department of Agriculture has rated the cattle production north of The Palmer River at around fifteen hectares per head' Carl enlightened the good Father, 'Which, that alone, puts a halt on any grazing in the area, not to mention the huge costs associated with mustering the cattle and transporting them to the nearest markets. Do not even consider the area, Father'.

'I remember reading about you and your drug operations around that area' exclaimed Roz Dagleish, 'All rather colourful I thought'.

'And all above board Madam, I can assure you, we broke up a huge cultivation ring up there that had apparently been running for many years undetected' replied Carl.

'Yes and I'll bet it's still happening up there too' added Doctor Christopher Dunwoody.

'I know it is Chris, believe me, but until you see just how wild and extensive the country is out there then you have no idea, the country is just so vast and now with modern technology, the cops get busted by satellite detectors as soon as they go on to a property and the cultivators are long gone into hiding by the time the crops are discovered. It takes about a week or so to collect the crops and destroy them on site with a huge contingent of men and three weeks later the cultivators have a new crop coming up. It's just impossible'.

Carl went on to tell of one occasion where the police used their drones in an attempt to locate the offenders on one of these plantations but the perpetrators were in possession of much better technology than that available to the police at the time and they took out the police drones by overriding the drones communication systems,

'The drones just dropped from the sky' he said

More than one of the directors were of the opinion that Carl Stephenson seemed to be going to great depths to turn Father Damien away from Far North Queensland and of course made a joke out of it.

'Sounds like you still have a strong interest in the plantations up there Carl' suggested Fiona, 'Should we be looking at getting into cultivating up there'? This created laughter around the table and soon the subject was forgotten, much to the relief of Carl Stephenson.

Following dinner, Carl did offer his help to Father Damien and implied that with his extensive local knowledge of the area, it could make things a lot easier with his assistance, but Father Damien firmly declined his assistance and assured him that he had a very capable person on hand to undergo a complete feasibility study of that area.

'During the after dinner drinks, Carl maintained a pleasant conversation with Father Damien which after some time revealed the name of Father Damien's exploration scout to be a Mark Crampton and other than him running a market analytics company based in Canberra nothing else was revealed of him.

The meeting, dinner and evening drinks had concluded and all had agreed on the date for the following month's meeting.

The following morning the official JCE manager was instructed to appoint Mark Crampton of MCA (Mark Crampton Alanyctics) with a charter to survey and perform a feasibility study in an area north of The Palmer River where it meets with The Mitchell River on a broad range of activities from mining to food production and to report directly to the board of JCE, the tenure was for twelve months.

Father Damien Downs had commenced his task issued by the board.

Mark Crampton

Mark Crampton had received the email from the JCE manager and had no idea what it was about, he reread it for the third time;

Mr Mark Crampton

MCA Pty Ltd, Canberra ACT.

I have been instructed by the board of directors of Juliet Consolidated Enterprises Pty Ltd, to confirm your appointment for the purpose of conducting a feasibility study as per the attached scope of purpose and topographical maps.

A full brief is enclosed for your perusal, if you require any additional information please contact Fr Damien Downes on 049951014.

The tenure for this study is twelve months at the agreed remuneration, including all expenses and associated costs, of six hundred thousand dollars, fifty percentum of that value will be deposited in your nominated bank instantly and the balance after completion.

Mark had never heard of JCE and had no idea what the letter meant other than the six hundred thousand dollars, but he certainly knew who Father Damien Downes was as he dialled the number listed on the mail.

'Hello, Father Downes speaking'

'What the fuck is going on 'Damo''?

'Ahh…Mark, I was just about to give you a call to warn you about the email, but it seems I might be too late'

'Yeah, I just got it, but what does it mean'?

'Mate, a little job came up at the board meeting and naturally, I just thought of you as I know you are at loose ends just now, Father Damien explained to Mark.

Mark Crampton had been the victim of sexual abuse at Saint Edward's Boys College, Canberra in his early teen years as a boarding student.

As it happened a Bishop was visiting the college and Mark and his friend George had been selected by the college to become the Bishop's personal assistants during his stay. Unfortunately, the Bishop had taken the opportunity to abuse Mark and Mark had vigorously fought off the Bishop's advances and had threatened to go to the police to make an official complaint.

Father Damien was the physical education teacher at the college at that time and was very popular with the boys as he was also the school team's rugby league coach and he not only turned a blind eye to the boys smoking and drinking but also joined them in the occasional drink and smoke.

Fortunately, Mark had told Father Damien all about the incident and Father Damien was able to persuade Mark not to report the matter to the police and that he would ensure that Mark would be well compensated in return, he also promised Mark that the Bishop would be well and truly punished for his actions, much more so than the consequences of reporting the Bishop to the police. Mark reluctantly agreed to keep the incident quiet and to act as if nothing had happened.

It was a very strained week for Mark to pretend that nothing had happened and finally, the Bishop's last day visiting at the college had arrived. A farewell dinner was planned for the Bishop aboard the floating restaurant, MV City of Canberra.

It was known that the Bishop was not feeling well due to the choppy water conditions on the lake that night and had visited the restrooms which are located out on the rear lower deck.

Indeed it was Father Damien Downes who had assisted His Grace to the restroom where he had left him in private to recover from his bought of illness.

It was about an hour after he was last seen going towards the restroom with Father Damien that the alarm was raised that His Grace was in fact, not in the restroom, he seemed to have disappeared and a search of the boat failed to locate him. The ACT Water Police were immediately notified and a search of the area the next morning revealed his body floating in Lake Burley Griffin, such a tragic accident.

The church although saddened by this tragic event was also somewhat relieved as the stories about the Bishop were becoming too numerous and it was becoming harder to suppress the reports of child abuse by the Bishop.

The Arch Bishop was shocked at what Father Damien Downes was telling him and asked him to repeat himself,

'If it pleases your Grace', Father Damien with confident composure again settled in the visitor's chair that was placed in front of the Arch Bishop's desk, 'I do have first hand evidence of the Bishop's activities during his visit to Canberra and also a full dossier of the Bishops previous sexual abuses on students'. The last part was a lie, he had only heard of rumours but the Arch Bishop would not know that.

'And you feel a reward of twenty five million dollars for advising the church, and *no* other persons or entities of these activities, would be in order'?

'Yes, I do your Grace' Father Damien replied calmly.

'The office will be in touch with you Father, you are excused', were the last words that Father Damien ever heard from the Arch Bishop. The Arch Bishop's office contacted him the following day seeking his banking details.

On the day following the Bishop's disappearance, Mark had developed the utmost respect for Father Damien and they had remained very good friends and had stayed in contact.

Father Damien was forever giving gifts to Mark such as cars and even an apartment and Mark knew enough to not ask any questions.

Mark now listened intently to what 'Damo' was saying to him, true he was at loose ends. Following college he had applied to the Australian Defence Force Academy to become a fighter pilot with the Australian Airforce, he attended and passed the YOU session, the assessment session, the officer selection board and finally the Flying training school at at Williamtown, just north of Newcastle, this training course which he completed together with a degree in physics, in around four years only to discover that he suffered chronic air sickness and was unable to continue training as a jet pilot but could continue as a military drone analyst and controller, same as being a pilot, they said, except you don't leave the ground.

Mark had continued in drone analytics and found it very challenging, especially when a drone failed to destroy its target.

Once a drone failed on a mission a full examination of the mission was analysed and scrutinised.

Why? Did the mission fail, had the drone arrived at the destination on time, if the answer was no, then a check of all four motors was conducted starting with the electrical supply rate measured to each motor, the revolutions of each motor, the pitch of the rotor blades. The wind speeds and directions, the moisture content of the atmospheric pressure.

Everything about that drone flying on that mission was double checked to ascertain if the drone had been where it was calculated to be at the time that it should have been there.

Once that had been checked then it was onto the weapons function, was the projectile's coefficiency checked, was the charge a tested component, was the ignition spontaneous, and check and check and check, until a solution appeared which was in most cases some minor item that had caused the mission failure. Such causes were found to be a slight difference in rotor speed to cause the aircraft to cause drag to one side and that the automatic yawl compensator would correct this but in doing so may cause a slight lag in airspeed to lose a millisecond in coordination time when the projectile is fired to cause the projectile to miss its target.

It was when no such instances of malfunction could be detected, then a complete takedown and analysis of the drone was required.

It was during one such scrutiny that revealed a component of the drone's motherboard was extraneous to its ADF specification, in other words, this drone had something other than that of its Australian Defence Force Specification fitted to the drone.

After extensive investigation, it could only be assumed that the Chinese manufacturer of the drone had placed a device into the drone to report back the drone's location and flight data but was only activated when the drone was at cruising height and speed. This would report the drone's direction and possibly its target.

It was not believed that the device could interfere with the drone's operational functions, it was simply a reporting device, a spying device.

All other drones were immediately checked to find several of the newer model drones were also equipped with this device.

A solution to remove the device was established as a priority and all new drones being received from the drone manufacturer were also found to be fitted with this device.

It was decided by the ADF in conjunction with ASIO (Australian Intelligence Organisation) not to approach the Chinese manufacturer of the drones in this instance as it was assumed their response would be, that the device was merely a quality assurance tool for possible future device failure.

By not advising the manufacturer and by building an add on to the drones operational application, the ADF was able to use a drone fitted with this device as a decoy to anyone that was monitoring the drone to assist in any future drone missions.

This meant that if someone monitoring the drone was advising a group of an impending drone attack, they would be advising an all clear, or stand down, situation as the drone was off course to the target, but the drones without the device fitted would be on target for an imminent attack.

As things went quiet on the international front and the US Military had pulled out from Afghanistan, Mark had decided to opt out of the airforce, he didn't really need to be working on 'scenario' cases rather than real ones and definitely did not need to be regimented any longer.

He had gained a degree in physics and had acquired great analytical skills, he was sure to find some sort of work.

A close friend of Mark's late father, who had been like a second father to Mark since his father's tragic death when Mark was only nine years of age, had come up with a suggestion that Mark should start his own company as a business analyst as there seemed to be a call for them in these harsh commercial times and as fate would have it, another friend of his who owned a Pioneer Plasterboard Franchise at the South Coast of NSW was losing such an amount of money at the franchise that he was considering closing it down. Mark may be able to assist by looking at the company's operation and checking it for obvious flaws.

Mark would have nothing to lose and it would also help out his friend. Mark took on the job and even though he knew nothing of business acumen, or very little, the Air Force had taught him analytical skills that he could apply to how this business was being run.

It was quite a simple situation with the plasterboard franchise that it was stupid, the manager engaged to run and operate the business was obviously a fool when it came to common sense trading. Mark likened him to the two brothers who bought watermelons from a farmer for $2 each, they set up a stall by a busy road and sold them for $2 each, at the end of the day they calculated their sales and one brother said to the other;

'Didn't make much money today, what do yer reckon we should do'?

'Get a bigger truck,' answered the other brother.

And that is exactly what this franchise manager was doing, as his price was so competitive and he had great volume sales of plasterboard he had also employed extra staff and paid overtime to get the high volume of the product out, but he had not considered his trading costs and sadly the franchise ended up closing.

It had been a great experience for Mark but had resulted in very little money for him in return for his efforts as the owner had little money left following his venture into Plasterboard.

Mark now worked as a casual coach driver doing Canberra to Sydney Express three times a week for three hundred dollars a trip and it suited his lay back sort of lifestyle. Three days of work and four days off was just perfect, he could work up to seven days if he wanted but he declined the offers from the bus company.

On the days that he didn't work he would eat out at different restaurants and bistros and soon discontinued going to the places where the food was either pretentious or just plain shit.

It amused him to watch people, especially lunchtime groups usually made up from, he guessed, office workmates who would buy exotic foods, that they could not afford, and pretend to eat them with relish. The most obvious were the oyster eaters who simply swallowed them without ever getting a taste of them.

Mark would spend at least one day each two weeks, cleaning his unit, or more accurately Father Damien's unit, as it was not yet in Mark's name, Damo kept on saying 'Must get that transferred' but he never seemed to get around to it.

It was a large, three bedroom, three bathroom unit with a large kitchen, formal dining room, family room and very comfortable lounge. Mark kept two of the bedrooms and bathrooms closed as with the dining and family rooms, he didn't need such a big unit, Damo had some stuff in one of the bedrooms and he would, very, occasionally come down to Canberra for a visit but he never stayed for too long as it was either too cold or too hot for him and he would always comment, that he didn't know how he once lived here?

'You only have to study the area before you go and make a plan, get up there and just look around in that area as nominated and find out what's happening, for fucks sake Mark, you are not an idiot, you are an educated man and you know what JCE is looking for out there, just do it, Mark'. Father Damien was convincing Mark quite easily.

Looking at the maps, the areas to the north of the Palmer and the Mitchell Rivers don't reveal the rough and harsh terrain. It was evident to Mark that the best base would be Cooktown but it would be a six to seven hour drive, depending on the road conditions, from Cooktown to the intersection of the rivers which would mean having to camp out somewhere.

Mark added to his growing list of items 'Camper Trailer', he already had a Landcruiser 70 series dual cab utility at the start of the list and now he would research camper trailers to find a suitable one as well as various items of camping gear, his list was now looking at around the one hundred and fifty thousand dollar mark which left him half of his advancement left for fuel, food, other accommodation and other consumables.

The following morning Mark was at the ACT Toyota dealer looking for a 70 series dual cab and as fate would have it they could offer a Merlot Red model that had diff locks, tow bar, high lift body kit, UHF radio and heaps of other accessories including a lock up metal canopy that was also painted in Merlot Red, it was a demonstration model and had only twelve thousand kilometres on the speedo and they were keen to do a deal of around ninety six thousand dollars and offered Mark and excellent price for his Tesla.

Next was a camper trailer, he had in mind what he wanted but when he had looked at a few he was losing interest, they were just too much work to set up and back again but when he saw the MDC X10E which presents as a small compact caravan with everything that he would need he changed his mind from camper to a small caravan, plus it had a much more comfortable bed. By the end of the following week, he had everything that he thought he would need and was ready to head north.

David Barnes

Meanwhile, Carl Stephenson had left a message for Kirill Nikolaev, 'Nick' on his home phone near Gladstone in Queensland, to contact him as soon as practicable. He did not have a mobile number for Nick, the system was, according to Nick, he leave a message on the landline number and Nick would get back to him either sooner or later. Each time that Nick had called him back it was on a different mobile number.

David Barnes had spent fifteen of his thirty three years in Far North Queensland. He had left his birthplace of Martha Cove on the Mornington Peninsula in Victoria, along with his parents, to seek a better lifestyle, and also to get the Victorian Police off his back for minor drug offences. He had chosen to head north for no other reason than a friend of his fathers was driving a 'B Double' truck from Dandenong to Townsville and a lift was available.

Townsville had not appealed to David with its dry tropical climate and after only a few days he ventured along the coast north to Cairns spending a few months along the way at Tully and Mission Beach.

Finally arriving at Cairns broke with nowhere to stay he met up with two young deckhands, Adam and Troy, at Gilligan's Backpackers in the city. They had told David about the good conditions on board the prawn trawlers and although it was short, seasonal work, the pay was good enough, sometimes depending on the catch, to last over until the following season. Plus, you get accommodation and meals.

They had explained that the Banana prawn season would be starting next week at the end of March and would go to mid June. There would be a break for about a month until the Tiger prawn season would start from August to September. Now was the time to get on a boat if he could find one and they told him that their boat had a full crew but other boats were still taking on crew and where to look for work.

He was on the wharf at Portsmith, the Cairns waterfront area, early the next morning with his possessions in one small backpack and was lucky enough to get a berth on the prawn trawler 'Rag Top', an independent twenty two metre long trawler with a crew of seven and about to head to Bamaga later that morning.

Rag Top's skipper was a huge Isander looking man with maybe a little Malayan added with the name of Isaya.

He had told David, in no uncertain terms, that he would be paid very little until he was useful, and that if he was of no use to the trawler, then he would be put ashore in either Bamaga or Karumba. The choice was his, take it or leave it?

Rag Top had left Cairns at ten thirty that morning with a strong south easterly wind causing a two metre swell, by the time Rag Top was north of Port Douglas David was lying on the stern deck as sick as a dog.

'You are not on the payroll until you can work 'Barnsy' and that goes for your tucker and bunk too, so I'll have to deduct your board from your pay until you can work, OK?' Isaya told David.

David could only nod his head in agreement, he wasn't game enough to open his mouth for fear of another bout of vomiting.

By the time they had reached Bamaga, two days after leaving Cairns, David, or now 'Barnsy', as everyone called him, was feeling much better and the trawler's cook, Chongy, assured him that he would now have his sea legs and that he would cook fish chop suey for dinner tonight and it was guaranteed a tonic for weak sea legs.

Rag Top was running a prawn trawl double rig with one 'warp wire' on each of the booms on either side of the vessel. These warp wires led to a bridle that connected to the otter boards that were designed to keep the nets open like a funnel. The ground gear, made from heavy chains that are connected to the bottom edge of the net causes the net bottom to skim over the seabed and encourages prawns living on the sea floor into the trawl mouth of the net.

While the trawl was down Barnsy was put to work cleaning the hopper and the sorting tables, when the first trawl came up he was shown how to sort bycatch and to allow the prawns through to the prawn sorting belt, he was then shown how to sort the prawns and what to identify to eject unsatisfactory prawns and then how to perform dipping of the prawns into the solution of metabisulphite prior to packing and freezing.

Prawning was more complex than David had thought and he found it interesting but hard work, by the end of the day he was looking forward to knocking off but that didn't happen. The crew had their evening meal while the trawl was down and then it was back into bringing up the trawl and sorting under the halogen arc lights that are placed above the working deck.

Sleep was taken in shifts by the crew and the prawning continued all night and into the next day until the nets came up almost empty and then it was off to another fishing ground searching for prawns.

After two weeks the trawlers freezer was full and David assumed that they were now heading back to

Cairns to unload the catch and it was back to lazy days of net mending.

To David's dismay, the Rag Top was rendezvousing with a barge to offload the catch for transit to Cairns and then it was back to the twenty four hour shifts.

Rag Top was in the Gulf for just over two months and had made a monster haul in prawns much to the crew's delight as it meant a big pay packet of about sixteen thousand dollars for the two months of work, about two thousand dollars per week.

They would now return to Cairns and the trawler would be readied to head back for the Tiger prawn season which was twice as long as the Banana prawn season that they had just completed and Isaya invited 'Barnsy' on for the Tiger season.

Other than David, there were only three of the Banana season crew aboard the Rag Top when it left Cairns for the Tiger prawn season and three new crew members, they still had the same skipper, Isaya, and the cook, Chongy, along with, Grumpy Bob. Of the new crew, one was a large muscly Pommy who seemed to complain quite a lot and had a run in with Isaya, who threatened to put him off at Bamaga if he 'didn't pull in his head'.

It was about two months into the season and the Pommy's whinging was getting worse, he was getting on everyones nerves, his voice was starting to make David nauseous and he would not stop talking. It was during the night trawls that suddenly David seemed to realise that the Pommy had stopped talking and after a while noticed that the Pommy was not with him on the sorting table but had been replaced by Grumpy Bob.

'Where's the Pommy?' David asked Bob.

'He's in the head, he's crook'. Was Bob's unemotional answer.

It wasn't until about ten o'clock the next morning that David, noticing that the Pommy was still not present at the sorting table again spoke to Bob,

'Is the whinging prick still sick, Bob'?

'Fucked if I know, just shut up and do your fucking work. It's not good to ask too many questions on a trawler'. Bob seemed unphased.

It was later that afternoon when Isaya announced to everyone on board that it looked like the Pommy must have fallen overboard during a trawl at some stage last night and that he had conveyed a message to the barge who would convey a message to the police at Bamaga and that we would be spending the rest of the afternoon and evening searching for the 'man overboard', the Pommy.

To David, it did not seem to him, like searching, more just like prawning with Isaya occasionally flashing the spotlight around on the water.

David could not help himself and said to Bob,

'Wouldn't it be better to stop prawning for a while and head back to where we were last night?'

'Suggest that to Isaya mate, and we'll be looking for you tomorrow' grinned Bob and it suddenly dawned on David that the Pommy had gone missing by design. It didn't pay to have a run in with the skipper on a prawn trawler.

When the police interviewed the crew at Bamaga a few days later it seemed that David was the last one to see the Pommy.

'He was working with me on the table one minute, and then the next time I looked up, he was gone!' David had truthfully told the police.

David stayed on board the Rag Top for three full seasons of each Banana and Tiger prawns and had saved over two hundred thousand dollars from prawning alone.

There had been no more loss of people onboard the Rag Top but two other trawlers had reported losses of a total of three deckhands who had gone missing, presumably, fallen overboard.

It was on his last, and final, prawning trip that he met up with a new deckie on board Rag Top, Terry Andrews from New Zealand. Terry had just been released from prison where he was serving an eight year term for cultivating and supplying drugs.

Terry had bitterly complained to David after he had received his first pay for two months' work of only sixteen thousand dollars and had explained to David that he could make this amount of money in a week by harvesting Coca and turning it into cocaine. David was instantly interested and wanted to know more about this crop.

They spent many hours on that last return trip to Cairns on board Rag Top, talking about setting up a plantation and that they would look for a suitable place as soon as they got back on shore at Cairns.

Terry was aware of an area just north of where the Palmer River meets with the Mitchell River it was rugged and the natural vegetation would camouflage a crop from the satellite surveillance used by the police and water was in abundance.

He had also been warned that the area formed part of a four hundred thousand acre cattle property that was owned by a man named Stan Strauss who was renowned for going out of his way to find trespassers on his property.

Terry had got to know some members of a Russian bike gang whilst he was serving his term. The gang operated many illicit businesses from near Gladstone in Queensland. They had told Terry that, if he was ever interested in growing for them up north, they would teach him how to cultivate a product from Coca and would buy as much as he produced. They had given him a landline phone number to leave a message on if he was ever interested.

Terry had also learned from another source that it may be possible to buy a mining lease in that area to give him an excuse for being there. This person had also given Terry the address of a gold buyer in Cairns who may know of any mining leases for sale in that area.

'What do you's want the lease for?' The man at the shop that was selling metal detectors, fossicking equipment, topographical maps and books on how to find gold and other mining items. 'Do yous want it for growing drugs or looking for gold?'

Both David and Terry looked at the man in horror.

'You's don't have to look too shocked', said the shop owner. 'That's what they do up there, it's either fucking drugs or gold, you wouldn't be the only dicks growing Hemp or Coca and setting up a lab, or do you's think you've invented something new? Come on, show some fucking respect'.

They bought one of the five mining leases that was available and it was carefully selected by viewing a topographical map of the area situated on the cattle property that appeared to give good cover from vegetation, water and remoteness.

A bargain they thought at Nineteen thousand dollars and the shop owner wished them luck and grinning, said,

'If you should accidentally find some gold, bring it in and I'll give you a fair price for it'.

A rough map showing how to get to the lease, along with a couple of keys for gates and the shed at the lease, was issued to them and they set about organising to buy a reasonably good four wheel drive vehicle and some camping gear before setting out to find their new lease.

Although the lease was approximately six hundred kilometres from Cairns it seemed that it would be an all day trip to get there from Cairns by travelling via Mareeba, Lakeland and Laura. Although they set off early in the morning they were still around one hundred, or so, kilometres from their lease at four o'clock that evening and decided to camp along the track on that first night. That was the night that they met the landowner of their lease Stan Strauss and his partner David Watson.

'And what the fuck do you jokers think you are doing here?' Came a voice from behind them in the treeline that was close to the road. 'And,… you can put out that fucking fire before you fuck off out of here'.

'I can explain' Terry quickly responded. 'We have a mining lease on this property and that is where we are heading'.

'Is that so? Well, you are not on any lease here pal so get moving'.

David then butted in, 'Settle down mate, let us explain' but was cut off by Strauss,

'I'm not your mate! Now fuck off before I get serious'.

That was enough for Terry, he was tired from driving all day and most of it had been on extremely rough tracks, he didn't need this.

'Just fucking calm down and stop being a fuckwit' was Terry's reply and as he said that he could see that this person was carrying a rifle, but unfazed went on. 'Just who the fuck are you anyway, even if we are trespassing you have no right to threaten us like you are'.

The man in the shadows moved closer to Terry and David and not sounding quite as authoritative said that he was the owner of the property and that he was fed up with people trespassing on his land. Terry and David assured him that they were not intending to trespass and assumed it was a gazetted road they were travelling on which gave them a right for passage.

'The stupid council think that it is a gazetted road but I can assure you fellows that it is not, I'll let you camp here tonight but make sure you put the fire out properly when you leave tomorrow and in future.....let me know if you need to camp on my land'.

'You're a fucking joke mate' Terry had had a gutful of this bloke and wasn't afraid of him, 'We don't even know who the fuck you are, let alone your fucking contact number, grow up mate'!

'The contact number should be on your lease agreement'. Quipped Strauss sounding even less unsure, he wasn't used to people standing up to him and he didn't like it.

'We haven't even had time to read the fucking lease agreement', added David, 'Don't worry we'll be gone at first light'. With that, the man in the shadows, and the person with him, turned around and went into the trees where they could no longer be seen. A short time later

David and Terry heard a diesel engine start and then they heard the sound of a vehicle on the dirt road heading away from them.

'What a fucking arsehole' mumbled David getting a couple of beers from the car fridge.

'Well, that's what those blokes in Cairns were telling us about, that prick doesn't worry me, mate, fuck him, at least he'll keep others away from our lease'. And they both laughed a relief as they drank their beers.

They found their lease the next morning and had used the keys they had been given to unlock the gate, there was another padlock connected to the padlock that their key operated and they assumed it belonged to the station owner whom they had met last night. Terry made a mental note to get rid of the other padlock.

Another key on the ring opened the front door of the shed that was located next to a roller door, it was very dark inside the shed but David found his way to the inside of the roller door, unlocked and then raised it so that it was fully open and allowed them to see inside the shed.

It was a standard looking six metre by six metre pressed metal shed with a corrugated iron roof, there was a very rough concrete floor which appeared to have been made from river gravel from the huge creek bed close to the shed. There was an old cast iron cooking range on one side of the shed with its chimney of unprotected sheet metal pipe going up through the roof. A small table with four chairs was beside a kerosine refrigerator and a set of concrete laundry sinks, or wash troughs, were set on besser concrete blocks. Three beds were at various locations around the shed as were various items of equipment including picks, shovels and a maddock. A

Honda 2kva generator was beside the concrete wash troughs and looked to be quite new.

Another door at the rear of the shed and to the right hand side revealed a second shed of about half the size of the first that ran, sideways along the back of the main shed. This too had a roller door to the right hand side but it was too dark to go in and open it and Terry had to go and get the LED lantern that they had bought.

The lantern showed the smaller shed to contain even more mining and sluicing equipment including another generator and a small front end loader, a coil of rope, three 44 gal fuel drums, three 9kg gas bottles, two Honda powered pumps and various other equipment including four folding tables. Terry opened the roller door on the smaller shed to allow them to see the equipment in daylight.

'Better than what I thought' stated David.

'This'll make a good processing shed' said Terry nodding at the smaller shed, 'I'll see if I can get this fridge working to keep our beer cold and then we'll get this loader out and see if it works, it will come in handy'.

A busy day exploring and getting set up for camping in the shed and then to the planning of getting a crop happening.

Terry had already established a source of Coca Erythroxylum seeds and they would plant these in small plastic pots of approximately fifty millimetres in diameter using a quality potting mix and once watered and fertilised, these would be placed into small zip tie plastic bags which would be opened up and watered twice a week until they have sprouted, usually within one to two months, these can then be planted around a sunny protected area amongst other vegetation but will require watering every day. For this, an irrigation system would be required. A pump at the creek where previous dredging had taken place would be an ideal spot for pure, chemical free, water which the plants would thrive on.

Planting the seedlings out, amongst other vegetation, would also help camouflage the plants in their later growth as it would be unlikely that anyone would even notice what species the plant was, in fact it would only be recognised by a person who was familiar with the plant, to most it would resemble only a wild blackberry bush.

Terry and Barnsy were heading to Cooktown the next morning to buy a car box trailer from a local manufacturer and to source some irrigation equipment. It was Friday early afternoon when they arrived following the four hundred and fifty kilometre drive of mainly bush tracks and roads.

They collected and paid for the trailer which the manufacturer had also registered for them and then they collected other items that they had on their list.

They booked into the Central Hotel on Charlotte Street and enjoyed a few beers and a meal, they had gone to their room at around seven pm to get some rest before their planned early start of two am the following morning.

By two fifteen the next morning they were at the Cooktown Country Club green keepers workshop and store and were busy loading irrigation fittings and coils of water pipe onto their new trailer by torchlight.

By three am that same morning they were breaking into the Cooktown Garden Centre and loading pot plants and bags of potting mix and fertiliser onto their trailer and by four am that morning they were on their way back to their mining lease.

It would take a full twelve months before the plants could be lightly harvested of leaves and the fruits would be collected to retrieve the coca seeds which would be propagated in the same way as they had started from scratch.

Twelve months went very quickly as they had found so much to do around the lease. They had found some good fishing areas around the property that they had now discovered to be called Watsonville, it was named after the original owners of the property and Stan Strauss's partner in the property, David Watson was a descendant of the original owners.

They had encountered Strauss a number of times within the first twelve months that they were living on the mining lease at various locations on *his* property, Watsonville.

On every occasion, although Barnsy and Terry attempted to be friendly, and they were hoping to establish some form of a mutual relationship with Strauss, it just did not happen and resulted in an altercation between them and Strauss with Strauss threatening to have them charged for trespassing and Terry challenging Strauss to a fight and telling him to fuck off before he gets hurt.

After a while, the boys thought it was quite amusing to have a Mexican Standoff, type of situation, with Strauss, though they were very wary of him nonetheless.

They had tried using the gold dredge and pump that they had found in the shed but found the work very hard for such a small return and had bought metal detectors from the gold buyer in Mareeba. These had proven to be both interesting and profitable and they wandered along the creeks and river beds finding some good nuggets and some junk like remains of old tins and odd metal items, even out in the middle of nowhere.

It was almost time for their first harvest and they had bought a Childs canvas, wading pool with an aluminium, bolt together frame, and had it set up in the small shed as their mulching area for the leaves. The selected leaves were then placed into the wading pool and with the aid of a whipper snipper, the leaves were mashed into a pulp, the pulp was gathered and placed onto the fold up tables that had been placed together and the extract was squeezed by hand from the pulp and placed in the sun to dry on another table.

The final result of their first yield was just under two kilos of the white powder and they sold it to their Russian friends for three hundred and sixty thousand dollars, less their minder fees', as they were called of twenty five percent.

They were quite happy with their first result which gave them an annual salary for each of one hundred and eighty thousand dollars, much better than a deckie on a prawn trawler and much less work.

Selling the product to the Russians seemed a complex operation, and they could only sell up to one hundred thousand dollars at a time, their first yield had to be sold in four transactions.

The only way to contact Nik was to call him on a number that he had supplied to them and let the number ring three times then hang up and Nik would contact them generally within an hour. The sale of the product was strictly only on the third day of every month between ten o'clock and noon they should contact the number and wait for the callback. They would tell the caller the weight of the product and the caller would tell them where and when to drop off the product.

Sometimes it was Cooktown, sometimes Cairns or Mareeba and even in between the major towns.

The product was packed into a laptop bag that had been supplied to them by Nik and the drop off was normally in a pub, club or busy cafe, they would go to exactly where they had been told and a person with an identical laptop bag that contained the payment, less the minder fee, in cash for the product, would be waiting, it was then simply a matter of exchanging the laptop bags.

It seemed that it could be a good lifestyle but they had to watch out for Strauss who was becoming more and more prominent around their mining lease area.

The small harvest had also resulted in a collection of around one hundred and fifty seeds from the coca fruits they had collected and these were propagated as were the seeds before them, resulting in the plantation being extended by one hundred and fifty plants. They were well away in their new venture and set off for a shopping expedition in Cairns.

The shopping list also included bags of potting mix and fertiliser which they bought from several shops to avoid any suspicion.

During the next two days, food and drink supplies were also loaded onto the trailer to take to the lease, and just as they were about to leave Cairns for the long trip back to the mining lease a call came from Nick Sabott, their Marreba contact with the Russians in Gladstone,

'Stay away from Watsonville for a couple of days, the cops are hitting it as we speak' and the call promptly ended.

Terry tried to call the number back but the message said that the number was not connected.

'Fuck,....now what?' David wanted to know.

'We just hang loose around here for another couple of days I suppose' Terry answered, 'Nothing else we can do I suppose'.

'Try calling Nick back' David suggested.

Terry pushed the redial on his phone and the line was immediately answered.

'Hang up,..I'll call you back' said the voice, presumably Nick's.

After what seemed like hours, Terry's phone rang.

'Nick?'......answered Terry.

'Some arse dobbed you pricks into the cops, I don't know who it was, my source won't say, but I'm guessing it's the prick that owns the place. The cops are destroying what they can find but they are not staying out there, give it a day and you'll be right, just watch out for the mongrel Strauss in future'. Nick then hung up.

They had arrived back at the mining lease two days after Nicks's phone call and they nervously entered the shed, other than it being unlocked and all the beer drunk and the empties left lying around the floor, you wouldn't know anyone had been there, nothing seemed to be missing?

They gingerly checked up the slope where the plantation was to find about a dozen marijuana bushes, that they had planted for their personal use, pulled from the ground and left out lying on the ground to die, but that was all, some raid they thought and shrugged.

'Let's get that prick' said David, 'And fix him for life'

'Sure, growing dope is one thing, but I think the cops might get a lot heavier with us for murder' replied Terry heading to the trailer to bring in some beer for the fridge, ' We'll just have to watch out for him, or try harder to make friends with him'.

'Fuck that, I'd rather just shoot the prick, there are so many places to hide a body around here,... he would never be found!'

Feasibility Study

The furthest Mark had been from the ACT was Sydney in New South Wales and Melbourne in Victoria, he had never ventured into Queensland even though Damo had kept at him to 'Come on up and thaw out' he had just never found time in his laid back style of life.

Mark had worked it all out on Google Maps, it was two thousand and eight hundred kilometres from his unit in Kingston in the Australian Capital Territory to Cooktown in Queensland.

Not that far when you look at it, he thought, and he knew that if he had to he could be there in three days by going hard and driving for ten hours each day, but he had decided to take all the time in the world.

Damo had told Mark that the tenure of his job was for twelve months and Mark had decided to spend at least a month to get from Canberra to Cooktown.

The western town of Dubbo was to be his first stop, it was only around four hundred kilometres, or a five hour drive, which suited him so he could become familiar with driving his cruiser, which was quite packed with gear, and towing his small caravan.

He had found a caravan park that was located almost in the heart of town and began his tutorial in setting up his van, he had meant to go 'somewhere' around Canberra to have a practice at setting it up but for some reason, or other, had never found the time, so now here at this park with an amused audience he commenced to teach himself.

It didn't take long before an elderly, and quite experienced, caravaner had sided up to him with the offer of help.

He demonstrated to Mark how to quickly get the van levelled and to connect his waste tank and water inlet and then also the power cable. He indicated towards the direction of the amenities block and mentioned that they were the filthiest he had ever seen and to make sure that Mark wore thongs in the showers there so as not to catch some horrible disease.

It was only a few minutes walk to the RSL club and Mark thought that would be the best place for dinner that evening. It wasn't, the beers were cold but the food was very ordinary and a bit canteen style which was not to his liking, so he decided to look elsewhere for future meals whilst staying there.

The next day was a look around Dubbo for a business that could install airbags to the suspension of the Landcruiser as Mark had thought the cruiser had seemed to sway a fair bit on the trip from Canberra. By late that afternoon the airbags were fitted with a gauge on the dashboard and an onboard compressor for adjustment.

Dinner that night was at the cattleman's restaurant and a very good rump steak was served, the next morning with the caravan hooked up and ready to go, today's destination being St George in Queensland which was around six hundred kilometres.

The difference that the airbags had made to the Landcruiser's suspension was quite amazing and made the vehicle feel much more stable when towing the caravan. Following one night at St George it was onto Emerald, another six hundred kilometre drive. Here the difference in temperature was very noticeable.

Travelling from Emerald to his next stop at Charters Towers and noting the signs for other cities and towns such as Townsville and Mt Isa which Mark wanted to visit but the vast distances between these towns would mean planning another trip in the future.

He had fully planned on his route to Cooktown to be through Cairns where he was planning on checking out the Great Barrier Reef and other attractions in the area, but when the signpost at Mareeba indicated Cooktown at two hundred and seventy kilometres he decided to travel straight through and bypass Cairns on this trip, plenty of time for Cairns a little later he thought.

Stopping at the Palmer River Roadhouse for fuel, Mark saw that it was also a camping ground and decided to stay over and head for Cooktown the following morning.

After reading the sign, whilst paying for his fuel, he asked the lady at the servo there for a powered site. She handed him a key to the amenities building and said,

'That's thirty five dollars, and the power is only from seven in the morning, if he gets up on time, and ten pm at night, unless it's quiet in the bar when we might shut it down early, park your caravan wherever you can find a place behind the tavern, you'll see the power posts'

He thanked the lady and took the key while still wondering what she meant about the power and it wasn't until he set up his caravan that he noticed the drone of a motor. He followed the direction of the engine noise down towards the Palmer River and discovered the 58kva generator being run by a Cat C4.4 diesel engine.

Mark had spent about two hours wandering along the Palmer River. When looking at the flow of the river he lost his bearings and turned to look at the sun starting to go towards the west yet this river was flowing towards the west, away from the coast to the east. He had just assumed that the river would have flowed towards the coast, about seventy kilometres to the east, but had discovered later that it ran to the Gulf of Carpentaria some three hundred and sixty kilometres to the west.

When checking in earlier that day Mark had noticed a paperback book for sale, 'River of Gold' written by Hector Holthouse in 1994. That afternoon Mark settled in his folding chair under the pullout canopy of his caravan and started to read his book. He was amazed at the descriptions of the savage Aboriginals attacking the miners and cannibalising the miners' dead bodies and also their horses. What an amazing story, a true story.

He had walked the few metres to the tavern at around six o'clock that evening and had ordered a chicken parmigiana for dinner which was excellent, following dinner he sat at the bar and ordered a xxx gold stubby. It wasn't long before he had entered into a conversation with a local prospector named Ivan Karabanoski who said he was camped down towards Maytown.

Ivan had described Maytown to Mark as the relic of a once thriving gold rush town.

Mark was enthralled with his stories about the town and about gold finds and, just having read the book 'River of Gold', Mark asked Ivan if there were many Aborigines around that area.

'Aborigines?…around Maytown?…Fuck no, why would you ask that? Ivan wanted to know, 'There's fuck all for them down there, no pubs or poker machines and no banks or post office to collect their dole'.

'I have just finished reading the book 'River of Gold' by Hector Holthouse and he tells of many Aborigines that were in the area back in the 1870s and that they were a real threat to the miners and that they also ate the bodies of the miners that they had killed' Mark replied.

'Yes, true, I have also read that book and, I might add, also another book that has been written about this area', I have also heard many stories of around this area, but, he added, 'You won't find many Aborigines around here these days, they all live in the towns, well most of them anyway, they enjoy the white man's way of life these days'. Ivan spoke in a well polished English voice.

He continued by saying that the modern day Aborigines now enjoy spending the money that the Government give to them and wearing the white man's clothing, drinking the white man's grog, living in the white man's housing, eating the white man's food and playing the white man's Rugby League.

Speaking of rugby league, have you noticed at the matches where *white* Aborigines are doing the so called smoking ceremony, that the real Aborinine players give them strange looks?

'The only Aborigines that whinge and bitch about the white man and the white man's Government are the 'Faux Aborigines' and you will find a lot of them in Federal Parliament, they are hard to pick out from the others as they look just like us, very rarely are these fellows black. It's not until they start talking that you can recognise them by the bullshit they speak about Land Rights and they need more money'.

Ivan went on to say, 'I mean like really, some of these blokes are a fucking joke, they stand up in parliament and say they are a 'Kalcadoon Man' or some other fucking tribe, and they are fucking whiter than me and you, for fucks sake old chap where have you been?'

'I was born and bred in Canberra, this is the first time I have ever been to Queensland, the only Aborigines that I have seen were the ones manning the 'Aboriginal Embassy' opposite the old Parliament House. Was Mark's response.

'Well,..you'll soon get used to them around these parts mate and it's not a good idea to walk around Cooktown on your own after dark and never ever, go to an ATM on your own. You'll see them in the supermarkets walking around the isles whilst having a feed of chips, or having a drink of milk, or something and discard the wrappers on the shelves so they don't have to pay at the checkout.

Generally, if they want to talk to you it's to ask you for money or smokes.....or they are offended by you and they want you to leave *their* country'. Ivan continued his summing up, 'You see, they don't have to go to work and the kids don't have to go to school, so....look, there are some good ones and I have worked with some really top Aborigines....it just seems that when they get together they don't give a fuck..and you know, when you look at it,..we would most likely be just the same if we were given everything that we needed without having to work for it'.

Mark offered, 'I spent a few years in the airforce and I must admit that I never came across any Aborigines in the armed forces, not saying that there wasn't any'.

When Ivan heard where Mark was heading he suggested a nice little caravan park in Charlotte Street he might like and it was only a short walk to town, and, make sure you check out the museum, some good local history in there'.

Mark had thanked Ivan for the good company and conversation and had said goodnight as he headed to his caravan. He had not quite made it there when suddenly the hum of the Cat diesel stopped and the place was plunged into darkness, and it *was* dark.

It was so dark, and as it happened Mark remembered turning around, he now slowly made a half turn back again, hoping that he was back on the course that he was when the lights went off.

He placed his right arm out in front of him and slowly walked forward, it was very eerie as he could not see anything at all.

He was thinking that surely someone around here would have had some sort of light on, but there was nothing but blackness when suddenly his hand touched something metallic at about the same time that his legs also touched something metallic and he fell forward striking his head on the bullbar of his Landcruiser.

He finally found the door to his caravan and flicked on the 12v LED light and sat down at the little table, he took his telephone out of his pocket and looked at it stupidly, it has a torch and he didn't even think of it. He turned on the camera of his phone and reversed it so that he could check out the condition of his head, it was quite bruised and would look even worse in the morning he surmised.

He had a great breakfast at the bistro the next morning, then he headed towards Cooktown which was about one hundred and ten kilometres.

He was in no hurry and stopped at Lakeland, a small town with a population of three hundred people and after wondering about the town for an hour had discovered the local history of Lakeland that went back to 1877. Over time the larger properties had been divided into many smaller farms and the largest surviving property of 140,000 acres, which was within Mark's selection criteria, was bought by the Queensland Government in 2016 and added to the states protected area network. Sadly, Mark had ruled out any activity in this area for the magnitude that JCE was interested in.

He found the small caravan park in Charlotte Street Cooktown that Ivan had told him about and had booked onto a powered site for two weeks. A perfect place for a base he had thought. Besides a visit to the museum, Ivan had also recommended both the RSL and the Bowling club for meals, both around a one and a half kilometre walk.

During his walking down to the clubs and the time that he had spent there he was starting to doubt Ivan Karabanoski's advice with respect to Aborigines, the people he had seen so far were quite friendly and only a few of them had asked him for money.

He was on his way back to the caravan park at about eight o'clock when he was asked by an elderly Aborigine if he could spare two dollars, as Mark was looking for change in his pocket he was struck from behind with great force, something had hit him in the centre of his back and had taken the wind from his lungs and before he could turn around he was struck again.

It was just after eleven o'clock pm when Mark opened his eyes and saw the dim light gleaming down on him. It was the light that was mounted on the power pole that was three metres to his right. He had no idea where he was, he sat up from the strip of grass that he was lying on, it hurt, his back was very painful just above his buttocks. He looked across at the building in front of him and could just make out in the feeble light that it was the Post Office.

Unable to stand, he crawled towards the Post Office and used the white timber railing in front of the building to pull himself to his feet. As he got to his feet he remembered the great pain he suffered in his back whilst talking to the Aborigine, he checked for his wallet, but it was gone! His car keys were also gone.

It took a while for him to realise what had happened as he slowly began to walk towards the caravan park, each step brought pain to the area around his kidneys but he finally made it to the park and his caravan and he saw that his Landcruiser was not there.

'Fuck it….no'! He called out to no one, and as he went to open the caravan's door, he then realised that he did not have the key to his caravan and was locked out. Placing his hands on each side of his head he slumped to the ground, the pain shot up his back and he again passed out.

It was daylight when he opened his eyes and he realised that he was lying on the ground looking towards the driveway that exited the caravan park as his memory slowly came back.

He sat up and the pain in his back also reminded him of last night's events, remembering that his Landcruiser was missing he quickly looked around and saw the caravan but the Landcruiser was not there.

Slowly getting to his feet amid the pain around his kidneys, he also remembered that he had no key to enter his caravan.

Stumbling up to the caravan he gently lowered himself to the ground and crawled underneath the caravan to where the water tank is installed, reaching up the the chassis cross rail above the water tank he retrieved the magnetic key holder, which also had a safety chain attached, and removed the two keys, that were connected with a keyring, inside the holder.

Mark had finally got inside his caravan and he lay on the bed and again passed out.

It was almost three o'clock in the afternoon when he had again awoken and the memory flooded back to him as he slowly got from the bed. The back pain had subsided somewhat and he was able to walk a lot easier as he contemplated his next move.

'The Police' he exclaimed to himself as he opened the caravan door to yet again confirm that his Landcruiser was not there.

'What time was it when you left the RSL club?' The senior constable of a force of ten stationed at Cooktown was asking Mark.

Senior Constable Jason Walsh was on his second posting since graduating from the police academy in Oxley, Brisbane. His first posting had been Townsville where he had served for three years and he had just been promoted to Senior Constable after serving in Cooktown for two years.

Jason Walsh was born in Queanbeyan New South Wales, just south of the Australian Capital Territory.

Jason was a sole child and his parents were both public servants and both worked for the Department of Supply at the offices in Constitution Avenue in Canberra.

The family home was in Cameron Road, just down from the Queanbeyan South Public School which Jason had attended, then later schooling at Karrabar High School which was just one block away from the primary school.

Following attaining the HSC Jason left school and decided to join the army, it was a spur of the moment thing as his best friend from high school was also joining the army, but it had been his friend's lifetime wish. His parents had tried to talk him out of it but to no avail.

Jason joined the 1st Recruit Training Battalion and was sent to do his training at Kapooka, his school friend failed his medical and was refused entry to the army.

It was a whole new experience for Jason, he had never taken communal showers and slept in a barrack with other males, nor had he ever had to queue for his meals and be denied a selection of foods.

He thoroughly enjoyed the rigorous training and the training with weapons but found the unarmed combat training to be a bit too tough for him as it was something that he had avoided all his life, he was the sort of person to avoid confrontation at all costs, most likely from his bringing up and being an only child with no siblings to play and fight with.

On his third night of sleeping in the barrack, someone had shorted his bed sheet which had upset Jason greatly and made him feel that the rest of the platoon was ganging up on him.

Another recruit named Les Morton, who was part Aboriginal, had befriended Jason and had told him,

'It was that arshole Bryan Bennet who did that bed thing to you, do you want some help to get back at the prick?'

'Do you mean, do the same to him?' Jason had responded.

'Fuck no! That won't work, he'll only do it to some other poor prick, no, we'll fix the bastard properly, OK?'

Jason had no idea what Les had meant but he agreed to go along with him.

The next day after training he accompanied Les to the kitchen at the mess where Les asked the 'dishie' for a small freezer bag.

They then went towards the training area in the bush and Les found a 'bull' ant nest, then taking a small stick he placed it on the nest, and the stick immediately became covered in ants. Les then picked up the stick and quickly placed it inside the small freezer bag and tied the opening.

'This'll fix that fucking Bryan, fucking Bennet' Les said laughing in anticipation.

'He'll know its me' said Jason nervously.

'So what? Just stand up the prick, you're not frightened of him,....are you?'

'He's a pretty big bloke, and he does well in the unarmed combat training' said Jason.

'Well..bro, you need to learn to stand up for yourself, generally, big blokes like Bennet are all piss and wind, you know..they are all bluff, once you stand up to pricks like him they usually back down pretty quick', Les went on to give Jason some confidence, 'If he has a go at you, then you need to get in the first hit, but..after you hit him, don't just stand there looking to see what effect it had, you need to hit him again and keep hitting him until he either backs off or, goes down..got it?'

'He'll fucking kill me' Jason was really getting worried now.

'Kill you! Fucking bullshit, you can sort that dude out bro, believe me, anyway, if it goes wrong I'll be there to administer first aid. Nar only joking, you can clean him up, no sweat.

The scream that night, just after lights out, was indescribable, Bennet had lept from his bed brushing ants from him as he cried out with each ant bite. Then he looked straight across at Jason.

'Walsh....you fucking prick...you did this, your fucked' said Bennet as he started to approach Jason.

Without answering Jason walked towards Bennet and Bennet stopped, it would seem that he didn't expect Jason to approach him. Jason came up to Bennet and hit him fully in his face as hard as he could, Bennet fell to the floor unconscious.

Bennet was transferred to the Kapooka Hospital and Jason was charged by the military police with assault and discharged from the army. Les had said, sorry brother, to Jason and added that he had no idea there would be such consequences.

Jason was pretty pissed off but did not hold a grudge against Les, Les in return gave Jason his home address in Townsville, Queensland, and told him to keep in contact.

Jason did not want to return to Queanbeyan and thought he would check out Les's hometown Townsville.

He fell in love with Townsville, the weather was just perfect and the people were friendly.

He found a job at the 'Purple Pub' on The Strand, as a cellar man and quite enjoyed it. He also discovered that the job also gave him plenty of opportunities to practice his new found pugilistic skills, much to the satisfaction of his employer.

It didn't take Jason long to earn a reputation for his ability to quell fights and clear bars and he was in demand around town as a bouncer at many events.

It was actually a somewhat drunk, off duty local police sergeant, that he had bounced one night at a function that he later became friends with, who talked him into joining the Queensland Police Force. The rest was history!

Mark's case was like a breath of fresh air to Jason as the only cases that he had been involved in since being in Cooktown had been domestic violence which seemed so repetitive and quite often, the same faces. It was for this reason that he had applied for a transfer to the Highway Patrol which now had two full time officers in Cooktown.

'About eight,..eight thirty' Mark replied and grimaced in pain.

'Mate, I think that it might be best if I run you around to the hospital and get them to check you out before we get into the full details' Jason said as he stood up from the front desk and told the other constable to watch the fort for a while.

There was no waiting at the hospital, it seemed that Constable Jason was quite popular there with the doctors and staff, Mark was ushered into the triage room almost straight away once they had his details and his Medicare card number.

The check revealed severe bruising around his upper torso and lower back but nothing that would not heal within a week or so with the aid of some Panadol Forte pain killers which they gave to Mark. Mark accompanied the senior constable back to the police station where Mark completed his statement and report.

The constable then offered Mark a lift back to the caravan park but Mark had declined the offer and suggested that a walk may be helpful in the healing process.

Upon arrival at his caravan, Mark used his MacBook Air to cancel the two credit cards that had been in his wallet and his insurance company to notify them about his car. He then went to the hiding place he had in the Caravan and checked that he still had the ten thousand dollars cash that he had stored there and placed one thousand in his back pocket. He felt a bit naked without his wallet, it was now six thirty and Mark headed to the RSL Club for his first meal of the day. He would call Father Damien with the news later that evening.

As soon as Mark had walked into the club he recognised the old Aboriginal that had asked him for money last night and he didn't hesitate and walked up to where he was sitting with a group of other Aborigines

'Hey you black prick' Mark called out to him, 'Are these your accomplices from last night'? he said indicating to the other's at the table.

'Ay don't know whut you are talkin bout brother' he replied.

None of the other people at the table looked up but Mark noticed that there were quite a few empty stubbies, as well as full stubbies, on the table.

'You don't seem to need a couple of dollars tonight though?' Mark said as he walked away from the table and went to the bar to order a meal.

'Hey!...feeling better'? It was the constable, Jason who was standing at the bar, now wearing civvy clothes, just about to order a drink, 'Can I get you a beer'?

'Thanks, Jason, a xxxx gold stubbie will be nice' Mark agreed.

'Y'reckon that's your man?' Said Jason nodding towards the old bloke.

'That's the one that asked for the money before I got hit, it wasn't him that hit me, it must have been one of the younger blokes sitting at the table' Mark replied

'They all know that there is not a thing we can do about it, it's pretty sad but you didn't get to see who hit you, you can't identify any those clowns sitting there,..can you?'

Mark agreed that he only really suspected that the person, or persons, who hit him were there at the table, as he didn't see who it was and it seemed a coincidence that they seem to have money to spend tonight.

'Are you eating here tonight?' asked Jason, 'I often have a steak here during the week'

They both ate their steaks at the bar and drank a few stubbies, Jason asked Mark if he would like to get even with the brothers later tonight, he told him that it wouldn't get his wallet or car back, but it would make him feel better.

'These blokes are usually the last ones to leave the club, especially when they are cashed up, and they will buy take away's, and it would seem that they are cashed up, and I just happen to have some Covid masks at my house just up the road along with a couple of six hundred millimetre lengths of one inch HD poly pipe, Jason went on, 'So,..if you are keen we will leave just on closing and don the masks and the poly pipe, what do you reckon Mark? Might find out where your truck is'.

'I'm in Jason,..fucking oath mate, I hope you're for real?'

Jason responded by holding his hand out to shake and said that no one is to know and that *is* important and to try not to kill any of them as it might get complicated. Mark shook his hand and said,

'Just say when mate!' Mark did not hesitate to shake Jason's hand and ordered two more beers.

They left the RSL just before ten o'clock as the barman called for 'Last Drinks' and walked over the road and up the hill for about two hundred and fifty metres to Jason's Qld Police residence.

'Come on in Mark', Jason called whilst opening the front door, 'You don't have to be quiet, there is no one else living here except me, my wife couldn't handle Cooktown and moved back to Brisbane and lives with her mum. Here, grab this' Jason said handing a piece of poly pipe to Mark and then he opened a drawer and took out two face covid masks.

They went back towards the club and stood in the shadows on the opposite side of the road. They did not have to wait very long before the Aborigines came out of the front door carrying two cartons of beer in cans.

There were seven males, including the old man, and two females, Jason told Mark to watch out for the 'Ginns' as they would most likely attack them, but a whack on the backs of their legs with the poly would generally change their minds.

The group moved from the entrance of the club and headed towards the river where they settled at a park picnic table, Jason and Mark were following behind them in the shadows and Jason said to Mark,

'Not too hard Mark and don't hit any of them in the face or head, just around the shoulders is the best, we can't kill any of them remember, and leave the old bloke alone for questioning, don't hit him'.

They advanced up to the group rapidly, they had a radio playing 'Life Goes On' by Ed Sheeran, it was very loud and the group did not hear their attackers until almost half of them had been struck and were on the ground. Contrary to what Jason had said about the Ginns, they just grabbed one carton of beer and ran away screaming.

It hadn't taken long to put them all on the ground and Mark just knew that he had broken ribs on at least two of them.

They lay on the ground in submission and begging for mercy and Jason said to the old fella,

'Where's that white fella's wallet bro?' As he jabbed him in the ribs with the poly pipe.

'Dow know what you mean boss'.

Another, much harder jab in the old fella's ribs and this time he screamed out,

'He's in the river boss, with all dem cards too, we only tookem money boss'

'And where is the white fella's truck' asked Jason giving the old fella a very hard jab in the ribs making him suck air which made it impossible for him to answer straight away. Jason asked him the same question again, but this time he used his poly pipe to hit the nearest man to the old fella across his shoulders making him scream out in pain. The old fella said,

'Fella in Hopevale buy him boss'

'Which fella in Hopevale?' And Jason gave the nearest man another whack.

'The fella Goodwin, Thomas, yeah he's the Thomas Goodwin, he buy him boss, too right boss'.

'If I find that you fella's are telling me the bullshit I'll fucking kill the lot of you and burn your fucking homes'.

Having said that, Jason indicated to Mark that it was time to go and they disappeared over the road into the darkness.

Mark handed a cold tinny (can of beer) to Jason from one of the two six packs he had taken from the Aborigines. They walked back to Jason's house and drank the rest of them as they talked about investigating this man at Hopevale called Thomas Goodwin, Jason said that he would check out the name on police files and they would go and talk to him tomorrow afternoon at Hopevale. They both agreed that it had been a great night and Jason had told Mark that he would pick him up tomorrow afternoon at about two o'clock, and added,

'For fucks sake, don't breath a word of this to anyone'.

Mark walked back to the caravan park feeling much better following the bit of exercise he had performed with his new mate Jason.

The next morning Mark had made a call to Father Damien's home and was lucky to catch him, as he was about to leave for his office. He told Damo what had happened but had omitted the interviewing of the old Aboriginal man last night.

He had told Damo about Jason and how helpful he had been and that he had contacted the banks about his cards and said that the insurance company would not do anything about his car for a while until the police found it, but they had offered him a hire car for use in the interim.

Father Damien suggested that Mark move down to Cairns to get everything sorted, he could collect his cards from the respective banks and put pressure on the insurance company in person, 'That always works' insisted Father Damien, 'And you can collect your new vehicle in Cairns, doubt there would be any dealers in Cooktown'.

Mark agreed that would be the best bet, he would leave his caravan at the caravan park and find a short term unit rental in Cairns.

At exactly one thirty that afternoon Jason arrived at the caravan park in his police Landcruiser and found Mark and gave him one of his police shirts to put on for the afternoon to avoid any one that they would talk to today becoming suspicious of Mark, they would assume him to be just another copper.

Jason had an address for a Thomas Goodwin at Hopevale and they were on their way to pay him a visit.

It is close to fifty kilometres from Cooktown to Hopevale, on the way there Jason asked Mark what it was that brought him to Cooktown and Mark had told Jason about the feasibility study that he was conducting for a business conglomerate.

'So you are buying up cattle properties around the area?' Jason asked

'Maybe, it just depends on what size the properties are and their carrying capacity and, of course, what price the property will be available at. There are a lot of variables involved and it is still early days, but this sort of shit, losing my car, will set me back a bit'. Mark also went on to tell Jason of his plan to move down to Cairns until he can get another vehicle.

Hopevale is an Aboriginal Shire and has alcohol restrictions of 1 x carton of 30 cans of 375ml beer, a total of 11.25 litres of beer or one bottle of 750ml unfortified wine, per person on foot or per car and per boat, regardless of how many people are in the vehicle.

This means, as there are no liquor stores in Hopevale and the nearest is at Cooktown, then to bring alcohol into town by vehicle means only one carton of beer per trip.

This restriction is for all public and private areas, one of the reasons so many of them frequent Cooktown.

They found the address that they were looking for and a pregnant woman inside the house with two young children claimed that she had not seen or heard from her husband, Thomas Goodwin, for about six days but believed he was in Weipa visiting relatives. Other random interviews with people around Hopevale came up with similar stories, or some just did not know him, but, knew of him.

A description of the missing vehicle had gone Australia wide and, as Jason said, 'It would be only a matter of time'.

It was four days after the Landcruiser had been stolen when a truck driver returning from Weipa had noticed a reflection that was well off the road in the bush on the Northern side of the small township of Coen. He had decided to investigate and saw skid marks on the bend in the road heading into the scrub, he had followed the skid marks for about twelve metres and came across an Isuzu Pantech Truck, the truck was upside down with a body trapped inside the cab. Inside the Pantech, was a Landcruiser utility. It wasn't Marks Landcruiser, it was, however, another stolen late model Landcruiser that had been reported missing from The Archer River Roadhouse some two weeks previous.

Mark had taken the Dash 8 air service from Cooktown to Cairns and had found temporary accommodation in the form of a three bedroom, three bathroom, unit in Digger Street, just a short walk from the city.

His motor vehicle insurance company had told him that if the vehicle was not recovered within twenty one days then it would be written off, if it was recovered after that period, then it became the property of the insurance company to dispose of it as they wished. It looked like a two, to three week stay in Cairns for Mark, plus the time to get a new vehicle organised.

It was a good time to research what he could with respect to rural properties as described in his brief from JCE.

Cooktown was to be considered the most northern geographical cut off point for rural properties for the purpose of transportation.

The property area is required to carry a minimum of 50,000 head of cattle with a forecast production of 25,000 bullocks per annum after 2 years with a target of 750kg live weight per head, or approximately 18,000 tonnes.

With the aid of data made available from The Queensland Government Department of Resources, he was able to make a list of properties in the area west of Cooktown and obtain an indicative land valuation as per the Valuer General where possible. With this list, he was able to link properties until the required carrying capacity was achieved and then calculate his budgeted property value of ten million dollars against the possible combinations of indicative value. It was not going to be easy, especially when it came to approaching the landowners.

As the residing Police Constable from Laura, being the closest station to the fatal accident of the truck rollover, was away attending court, Senior Constable Walsh, was assigned the task of investigating the accident and submitting a report to the coroner. The forensic traffic police had attended the scene and had forwarded their findings on the fatality to Jason.

Jason discovered that the deceased man was the owner of the Isuzu Pantech truck that was involved in the single vehicle accident and had collected the vehicle that was being transported in the back of the Pantech from an address in Weipa. The address of the collection point was sent to the Weipa Police Station and was confirmed to be the parking area on John Evens Drive at the Weipa Airport.

The deceased man's address was found, via the trucks registration details, to be a Manunda address in Cairns.

Jason had contacted the Cairns Police to visit the man's home and interview the man's wife or partner.

The Cains Police had to reject the request due to staffing shortages caused by sickness, the Cooktown Officer in Charge directed Senior Constable Walsh to transfer to the Cairns Police Station on a temporary basis to enable him to conduct his investigation into the deceased truck driver and the stolen vehicle and to investigate if the vehicle stolen in Cooktown was in any way connected.

Jason had contacted Mark in Cairns and had told him that he was coming down to Cairns for about a week and that they should catch up,

'Where are you staying?' Mark asked

'Haven't found anywhere yet, most likely the Colonial Club is where they recommend' Jason Replied.

'Well I'm staying in Digger Street and I have two spare bedrooms and bathrooms if you want to go halves?'

'Done' was Jason's reply, 'I should be there about three pm and I'll have to report to the operations officer in charge and I can meet you at around four thirty. What do you reckon, a few beers and a feed at the 'Rattle n Hum'?'

It didn't seem to take more than ten minutes to walk from Digger Steet to the Esplanade where 'Rattle n Hum' are located, the beers were cold and at a good price and the food was just excellent.

'So,..you haven't told me why you are in Cairns' Mark asked

'I'm here on business, investigating a fatal accident that happened on the Peninsula Development Road near Coen. A truck ran off the road into the bush and killed the driver.'

'You have to come to Cairns to investigate a prang?' Mark queried.

'There is a bit more to it, there was a stolen 78 series Cruiser on the back of the truck that was, presumably, heading to Cairns......' Mark interrupted him.

'My truck...?'

'No, sadly, Mark, it wasn't. But it was another Cruiser about the same as yours but this one was a single cab' Jason explained, 'And I am checking to see if they, the vehicle thefts, might be linked, the Cairns coppers are short on staff so I have a transfer down here to investigate. I'm in the boss's unmarked car and I'll work in plain clothes'.

Following dinner, it was a stroll to the Reef Casino, a few more beers, and a hopeless game of blackjack, then back to the unit at around one thirty that next morning.

It was a late start the next morning with a walk down to 'La Pizza' on the Esplanade for breakfast, Jason left Mark at the restaurant and went back to the unit to get his car, Mark went down to Woolies to get a couple of things.

Jason had found the address and a talk with the occupant of that address had confirmed that her partner had received a call from someone to collect the car from Weipa and drop it off at an address in Portsmith, she wasn't sure where it was but her partner had often picked up cars and taken them to this address where the cars were put onto B Doubles that were returning empty to either Brisbane or Sydney. That is all she could tell Jason.

It was after four hours of sitting at a desk and making telephone calls to local Cairns transport companies and asking about empty B Doubles transporting vehicles down to either Brisbane, Sydney or Melbourne, that one company receptionist mentioned that a really nice looking 'red' Landcruiser was put onto Steve Brown's B Double truck just last week to be taken to Melbourne,

'I assume the Landcruiser was going to Melbourne as that's where Brownie's next pickup was'.

'When will Brownie be back in the depot?' Jason casually asked.

'Actually,...Hmm,..tomorrow,...tomorrow morning at around five am' the lady said.

'How would I recognise him?' Jason wanted to know.

'You don't have to be here at that time, I'll see him at about nine o'clock, and I can tell him to contact you if you like?'

'No...no, that won't be necessary, I would rather you didn't say anything about this call please, not to anyone'. Jason added quickly.

'I hope I haven't gotten anybody into trouble' she said resentfully. 'Brownie drives a green Western Star with the name Brown Transport written on each door'.

'I assure you, you have not got anyone into trouble, please don't speak about this conversation, goodbye...and thank you'.

Jason hung up the telephone, 'Can't be right' he thought out loud, 'Too fucking easy, much too easy'.

'What do you reckon Jase, we have dinner at the Casino tonight?' Suggested Mark just after Jason had got in and was on his second beer. Jason had declined the offer telling Mark that he had to be gone at around four in the morning and then he told him a little about the day's activities, but he omitted the part about the 'red' Landcruiser.

The boys enjoyed A quiet night that night, if you can call a quiet night a full carton of xxxx Gold Stubbies and half a bottle of Makers Mark Whiskey with two delivery Pizza Hut pizzas.

Well, it was Friday and there were two games of NRL on the TV that night.

Jason, with fellow Police Officer Constable Neal Hardy from the Cairns Police CID, had arrived at Fearnley Street, Portsmith, at just after four o'clock, there were three B Double trucks pulled up just before the transport company gates that were still closed.

Jason slowly drove past the trucks and saw that the last truck had the name Brown Transport displayed on the door.

It was still dark as Jason parked the car behind the last truck,

'You go to the passenger side and I'll go to the driver's side', Jason commanded, 'He may be asleep, but if the passenger door is unlocked then open it and I'll do the same with the drivers side door, just play it by ear'.

The man was not asleep, but looking at his phone as Jason opened his door and showed the man his badge. The expression on the man's face was that of pure shock, it changed to worse when the passenger door was flung open by another person showing a police badge.

'Relax....relax,....just want to ask you some questions' said Jason with his hand resting on his holstered Glock.

'What the fucking....hell!' The truck driver was lost for words in his sudden shock.

'We just need to ask you some questions, now please step down from the truck....please' said Jason with his hand still on his Glock.

'Fuck you,..get off my truck, fucking arseholes' as the truck driver attempted to push Jason away from him through the driver's side door.

'OK, have it your way' said Jason quickly as he grabbed the man's arm whilst jumping backwards off the step tank of the Western Star truck, bringing the driver falling after him and landing on his back on the ground beside the truck, meanwhile Jasons colleague had got down from the passenger side door and was already at the drivers side when the driver had landed on the ground. The constable went straight down with his knee landing on the driver's throat as Jason started to put handcuffs on his wrists. Following a brief struggle with lots of shouting from the truck driver, the truck driver was sitting on the ground with his hands cuffed behind his back.

The driver's shouts had brought the drivers from the two trucks parked in front of the Browns Transport truck.

'What the fucks going on here then?' called one of the drivers.

Jason held up his badge and said 'Police,..stay back there!' As his colleague was starting to put the driver into the back of the police car.

'Leave the poor bastard alone fuck yers, what's he done?' The other truck driver called.

'Just mind your own business and stay back there' Jason repeated to the other truck drivers.

The handcuffs had been removed and Steve Brown had been placed in a small interview room that contained only one small table and three chairs. He had briefed the interviewers, Detective Sergeant Rohan Scott and Detective Senior Constable Howard Fergusson on the case and the events leading up to detaining Steve Brown. Within two and a half hours the interviewers had the names of the stolen vehicle receivers in Melbourne and had learnt of their spare parts operation.

The Victorian Police, Melbourne CID had been advised of the events that were discovered in Cairns and within twenty four hours they had exposed a major stolen vehicle operation that was receiving vehicles from all Australian states and turning them into spare parts for the busy Australian vehicle spare parts market.

The information pertaining to the Cairns incident was that the Melbourne car theft operation's Far North Queensland's operative was a male suspect named Antonio Calabishi.

He was known to offer indigenous people in remote areas, ten thousand dollars cash, for late model four wheel drive vehicles with no questions asked. The man Antonio Calabishi was the deceased Isuzu Pantech truck driver in the accident near Coen last week.

Jason remained in Cairns for the next three days completing his report on Steve Brown and appearing at the formal charging and remanding in custody of the offender. Jason had said to Steve Brown that had he just got down from the truck in a nice manner, then he would most likely have been granted bail, his aggression had not done him any favours.

Mark had already been looking for a replacement vehicle and had found one on '<u>carsales.com</u>' located in Brisbane, it was a similar vehicle to the one he had lost, including some of the accessories.

Mark had contacted Father Damien and had asked for an advance of one hundred thousand dollars to pay for the replacement vehicle, he could repay Father Damien once the insurance company had compensated Mark, if necessary.

The money was in Mark's bank account the next day and Mark made arrangements to fly to Brisbane to collect his new ute.

The seller of the 78 series Landcruiser had collected Mark from the airport and had driven him to his home in Brisbane North where the vehicle was garaged. Mark was beside himself once he saw the condition of the 'Midnight Blue' coloured car, it was immaculate with a matching coloured metal canopy, it had a polished stainless steel nudge bar, an adjustable, front and rear, high lift kit, front and rear diff lockers, rear airbags with internal air pressure gauges and onboard compressor, a four tonne capacity electric winch and was fitted with Recaro leather seats.

The only thing it needed was a towbar, which Mark had organised to be fitted on his way back to Cooktown at Redcliffe in Brisbane North.

It was almost seven o'clock when Mark returned to the caravan park at Cooktown and he had decided on a steak at the RSL for dinner that evening, on his way to the club he walked across the road to Jason's house, he found Jason sitting on his front verandah with a stubby in his hand.

'Well, fuck me, your back, I'll get you a stubby, have a seat'.

Mark sat down and asked   Jason if he wanted to go to the RSL for dinner.

'Mate!..I was given a whole rump today by the sarge and I was just about to slice a steak off it for a feed, why not stay here and have a steak with me, I'm nearly out of piss though if you wouldn't mind grabbing a slab from the pub while I get the steaks cut?'

'You're on' said Mark as he headed across the road to the Sovereign Hotel's bottle shop.

After dinner and a few stubby's, Jason was telling Mark about the investigation in Cairns,

'It seems that the Pantech truck driver from Cairns, Antonio Calabishi, had put the word out to the Abbo's that he would pay ten grand cash for late model Landcruiser's and it's a good bet that our friend, Thomas Goodwin from Hopevale, has ten grand in his pocket.

Watsonville Station

Mark Crompton had left Cooktown and was towing his caravan on his way to meet the station owners that he had been in contact with by telephone with a view to the purchase of the property, he had made arrangements with them to camp in his caravan on the stations for the duration of his visit to allow him time to look over the properties.

It had taken him a little over four weeks to inspect five properties that may have fallen within JCE's criteria but sadly none of them did, mainly it was the price wanted by the owners of the properties that eliminated them.

Even though the price of some of the stations was within the criteria, the beef carrying capacity was not and the property would need to be linked to another property, but the then combined price of the properties would exceed the JCE criteria.

There was but one property in the district left that Mark had yet to visit due to the fact that he had been unable to contact them, so he had left that property until last and now was the time.

He had tried calling the telephone number that he had, but to no avail, so he decided to make an unannounced visit.

He had left Laura on Palmervale Road and then turned onto Kiamba Road, after travelling for just over five hours his odometer showed he had travelled three hundred and thirty kilometres, he estimated that he still had approximately forty kilometres until he would reach the homestead of Watsonville Station, it was five fifty in the afternoon when he saw a turnoff to his right and decided to turn onto it and find a place to camp for the night, he had proceeded all of thirty metres along this track and was pulling off to the right hand side of the track where there was room beside the track for a campsite, the vehicle was almost stationary and suddenly his steering wheel spun to the left knocking his hand from the steering wheel, he simultaneously heard a loud bang.

Mark had completely stopped the car once this happened and got out to look at what might have caused this, walking from the driver's side door and around the front of the vehicle he immediately saw that the left hand side front tyre was completely flat.

Whilst bending down for a closer examination of the tyre Mark noticed what seemed to be a metal spike protruding from the centre of the track, then looking closer at the spike he saw other spikes that were almost completely across the track.

Luckily for him as he had almost stopped the vehicle to turn right, the right hand wheel had just missed one of the spikes in the track but the left hand wheel had struck another, it was fortunate that he had completely stopped otherwise all four tyres on the Landcruiser and the two tyres on the caravan could have been spiked.

Leaving the Landcruiser exactly where Mark had stopped it, in the centre of the track he commenced to jack up the front left side of the vehicle, as the wheel came clear of the track it exposed the metal spike that had penetrated the tyre.

Mark removed the wheel and then realised that he could not put on one of his two spare wheels until he removed that spike from the ground, grabbing the spike with his hands he realised that it was firmly in the ground and using a hammer started to strike at the spike to loosen it in the ground surrounding it.

The spike did not move with a hammer blow but rather it repelled the hammer with each blow,

Strange thought Mark, they must be driven in very deep. He then took the small maddock-type pick that he had bought for prospecting and attempted to dig out the spike.

Whilst digging around the spike with the hope of loosening it, he struck something else that felt and sounded like metal, beside the spike on the side towards the other spikes, he then realised that the spikes seemed to be connected together with a metal bar, or something, under the ground.

Giving up his attempt to dig the ground around the spike, he took a beer from the caravan's fridge and sat down in front of the Landcruiser, drinking his beer and staring intently at the spike. Finishing his beer, he then fitted the spare wheel to the front of the Landcruiser and then jacked the front up higher.

Looking around Mark found two large rocks that were just a bit higher than the spike and placed one rock on each side of the spike, he then carefully lowered the jack so that the left hand wheel now sat on top of the rocks that were either side of the spike.

Moving the Landcruiser very slowly backward away from the spikes, Mark then reversed the caravan off the track and stopped just adjacent to the spikes and decided to camp there for the night.

The next morning whilst surveying the track section that had the spikes, it became obvious to Mark that where he had reversed the caravan into and spent the night, was in fact, a by-pass for the section of the track containing the spikes.

'Well fuck me' Mark said aloud to no one and then prepared some breakfast.

He had just begun to eat his breakfast of toast and coffee when he heard the sound of a vehicle in the distance, he guessed it was on the Kiamba Road as it got louder and closer to the track that he had turned onto and he assumed that it would go past him. The vehicle, however, slowed and turned onto the track where Mark was parked.

David Barnes and Terry Andrews both got quite a shock seeing a caravan and Landcruiser ute parked in their by-pass on the track leading to their lease and they had to stop to avoid the spikes that they had installed to keep out unwanted visitors.

Mark Jumped up from sitting on the caravan steps with both arms in the air about to scream out 'STOP!' But the vehicle had already stopped in the middle of the track just in front of the spikes.

'Doing a bit of camping mate?' Asked David while getting from the Nissan driver's side.

'You just stopped in time mate! there's spikes in the road there' said Mark pointing to the track with the visible spikes.

Before David could reply, Terry said 'Yeah, it's the pricks that own the property, they're trying to keep people out for some reason or other, they're a fucking nuisance'.

'I'm Barnsy Mate, this is Terry', said David holding out his hand towards Mark', 'We've got a mining lease up the road here'.

'The spikes are a real prick, they caught us out when we first arrived', lied Terry, 'We dug the fuckers up but Stan put them back in, so we just drive around the pricks now, just where you're camped is our detour actually'.

'What brings you out here?' Asked David.

'I'm on my way to see the owners of Watsonville' replied Mark.

'Well they mustn't know you're coming' interjected Terry, 'Cos they're on their way to Chillagoe, we passed em earlier, and they usually stay overnight'

'Well, I haven't been able to get them on the phone so I thought I would just call out there'.

'It must be important, travelling all that way on the spec of meeting up with them?' Terry was wondering why this bloke would be looking for Stan Straus and David Watson. 'You can camp up at the lease with us if you want, it's only about twenty four Kays up the road'.

Mark appreciated the offer and thought why not, more county to see and he would have to camp somewhere tonight.

Terry said to move his rig forward so that they could get past with the Nissan and then to follow.

The three of them were enjoying a beer at the mining lease, Mark had noticed a few Marijuana plants growing amongst the Coca bushes but he didn't recognise the bushes as Coca, like most people wouldn't.

'Do you mine much gold?' Mark asked.

'Fuck all' said David, not thinking.

'We get enough to get by on and a little extra' Terry quickly put in, 'we also do a bit of detecting around other parts of the river and get some good nuggets from time to time, at around three grand an ounce you can get a good days pay on some days'.

'Wow!' Whistled Mark, 'I didn't realise that gold was that price these days'.

'The next morning as Mark was getting ready to leave, Terry had told him that the owners wouldn't be back at the station till the afternoon and that he and Barnsy were going fishing at a good spot that was on the way to Watsonville if he wanted to join them and they would have a feed of Barra for lunch.

'Sounds good!' answered Mark, 'I really do appreciate you guys thanks'.

It was a top spot on the river that Terry and Dave had shown Mark. The fishing was excellent, they asked Mark to keep it to himself, and then laughed,

'As if' said Barnsy, 'Those pricks would shoot anyone they saw fishing just here, it's their favourite spot too,' meaning the Watsonville owners.

Barnsy had a disk from a plough that he used as a hotplate and they cooked barramundi and drank beers beside the river, it was a great afternoon.

Terry told Mark to keep in touch as he was preparing to leave for Watsonville, he also told Mark that they would be leaving for Mareeba the next morning to collect some gear and then he gave him his Iridium satellite phone number and said to give him a call next time he's out here.

It was three o'clock when Mark had arrived at Watsonville, it was not what he was expecting. Compared to the properties that Mark had been inspecting during the last few weeks Watsonville looked like a dump, to put it mildly.

His car had been surrounded by barking dogs as soon as he had driven into the driveway, more of a track, to the house, which looked like more of a shed than a house. He waited in the car to see if anyone would come from the house out to him.

It was not long before a man emerged from the door at the front of the house and yelled at the dogs to 'Get Back', he then walked up to Mark, as Mark would down his window.

'Are you lost and blind?' Asked Stan Strauss.

'No, not lost, I am looking for the owner of Watsonville' Mark answered the man who looked very upset to see someone in his driveway.

'Well this is private property, you have driven past about a dozen signs telling you that, so why are you here?'

'To see the owner of the property, is that You?' Mark tried again.

'Your trespassing' said the man, 'And you must be fucking blind because you would have driven past a dozen signs that say No Trespassing!'

Mark saw that this was going nowhere and as Terry had told him that 'This bloke was a total fuckwit and not to let him put it over him', remembering these words Mark said to the man,

'What are you? A fucking idiot or just fucking deaf. Can you not hear that I am here to see the owner'. Mark could see the man did not look so confident when he spoke to him in this tone.

'Are you police?' Asked the man.

'Do I look like a fucking copper? doe's this look like a fucking police car? for fucks sake, are you the owner!' Asked Mark becoming agitated.

'Are you from the Government?' The man now wanted to know.

'Mate, whoever you are, I am just a private person with a proposition for the owner, or owner's of this property, if you don't want to hear me then just say so without all of this fucking around and I will gladly go because I do not need this sort of bullshit'.

'Yud, better come inside then', the man said to Mark as he slowly walked back to the wide open house door.

Mark followed the man back to the house, he could see another person inside the dimly lit house.

The man stopped at the door and told Mark to go in, the other person in the house looked at him and just nodded his head.

The man who let him in the door said,

'I'm Stan and that is Dave,..David' corrected the man in the form of an introduction without any indication of a handshake.

'I am Mark Crampton, I am working for Juliet Consolidated Enterprises, and to cut it short, my company want to buy your property'.

'Not for sale' was the simple reply from David who was still standing back in the shadows.

'You haven't heard the offer yet' said Mark wondering what planet these dudes were from.

'And you have the nerve to call me deaf, It's not for sale' said Stan.

'What sort of dollars was your company going to offer?' called out David.

Mark felt like responding with, fucking Australian dollars you fool. But he said calmly,

'What sort of dollars would you consider?'

'Tell your Company that fifty million would get us to the table for starters' said Stan.

Mark slowly shook his head and said that fifty million dollars would be way out of contention, to which Stan

Strauss suggested he leave, but that he was welcome to camp by the river just down by the road, but no fires.

Mark thanked him and suggested that if they think of a realistic price by the morning and let him know. Stan Strauss just told him to 'fuck off'.

Mark arrived back in Cooktown quite late the next afternoon only to find that the caravan park was totally booked out due to the annual 'Cooktown Discovery Festival' held every June. Not knowing where to head he drove to Jason's house.

Jason was happy to see his friend Mark and when he heard about Mark having nowhere to park his caravan he insisted that he park it in the backyard and that he stay inside the house in the guest room.

They went over to the Sovereign Hotel for dinner but the place was packed and the restaurant was booked out they tried the RSL for dinner and the place was also packed out but as the manager knew Jason quite well he said he would organise a table for them.

Waiting for their meals to arrive and having a beer, Jason asked Mark if his trip had been successful, Mark told him the disappointing result he had as far as finding a property, and then laughingly told him about the two strange, to say the least, people that he had come across at a property called Watsonville and went on to tell him about the spikes that they, the Watsonville owners, had put into the track at one location and had been told that these spikes were also in other locations and that the owners did it to discourage trespasses on their property.

To Mark's amazement, Jason said that he had heard all about the strange vehicle traps and things like that around Watsonville and that he, when relieving at Laura Police Station, had actually visited Watsonville on more than one occasion following complaints about road spikes and bullet holes found in vehicles that have travelled along the gazetted roads across their property and that one of the owners, Stan Strauss had blamed the spikes being installed by organised gangs, as with the bullet holes, that were growing drugs around the area. Strauss had also told Jason that there were rumours of tents burnt at campsites. Stauss also said that both he and David Watson were fearful for their lives on occasions.

The next morning Jason had told Mark that he would be working extra hours that day due to the festival crowds and would not be home until about eight PM,

'The pub's and club's meal will be finished by then but I'll get a couple of rump steaks out of the freezer, what d'you reckon?'

'Fine by me, thanks Jason, I have a phone call to make and a report to write, and that's about me, a lazy day, but I will get some beer organised for this evening' replied Mark.

'You're a fucking legend mate! I'll see you later today' said Jason heading out the door.

Mark called Father Damien,

'Mark! How are you?' Asked the good Father.

'I'm good, Damo, but my news isn't great', Mark told Father Damien about his past weeks inspecting properties and the sad results, he told him about Watsonville and how ideal the property would be due to its size of around five hundred thousand acres and location with access from two directions, although it is only rated at fifteen acres per head of beef it could be improved quite easy to twelve or maybe ten. The Surveyor General has valued the leasehold at only just under one million dollars'.

'Well! That sounds very good Mark, have you offered a price to the owner?' Father Damien asked.

'They don't want to sell,' Mark replied.

'Everything is for sale my dear boy, it's just a matter of price, you need to find their price, it sounds like you have done all your homework on the property, at five hundred thousand acres, then maybe you should be offering up to the max, ten million isn't it? Do you think it would work at that price, Mark?'

'They were pretty adamant that it is not for sale' Mark emphasised, 'but' he continued, 'One of the owners said the negotiating start price would be fifty million'.

'Fifty million is five times the maximum amount that JCE is prepared to pay Mark, even if you got down to half of that price, as the property is around one hundred thousand acres more than what we are looking for, it may still be much too expensive, but at least you have a negotiating start price, that's something. Go back and talk to them and call me when you start negotiating.' Father Damien wasn't fazed at all.

'I can't call you from there unless I use their landline and that wouldn't be good, mobile phone reception ends out here almost as soon as I leave Cooktown' Mark advised.

'Can't you get a satellite telephone, don't they work up that way?' Father Damien asked.

Mark remembered that Terry had given him his Iridium phone number and to call him the next time he was around the area, so they must work out there.

'I hadn't thought of that', Mark replied, 'I'll get one organised and get back out there.'

Father Damien told Mark not to waste too much time, it was already over six months that he had been on the project and that JCE may get itchy if they don't get any reports and the next annual board meeting which is drawing close.

Mark advised Father Damien that he would get back out there ASAP and get back to him.

Mark called all three locations around Cooktown in the hope of obtaining a satellite telephone but to no avail, It seemed that the closest place he could get one was Cairns.

Mark started to put together his report on the property Watsonville Station.

It was around two o'clock that he remembered to get some beer for this evening, he walked up to the Sovereign and noticed the heat, even in June the temperature was twenty eight degree's centigrade, he decided he would have a schooner in the bar and then get a slab of stubbies from the bottle shop.

Owing to the festival there were quite a few people in the bar as Mark sat at the bar sipping his beer, a fellow sitting next to him who was dressed in denim jeans and a kaki Gundwana shirt asked Mark if he was 'up for the festival', Mark had replied no, that he was doing a bit of work here, but he didn't go into detail. And then, more of a courtesy Mark said to him.

'And you, are you up for the festival?' Knowing full well that he wouldn't be.

'Nar just finished mustering, I'll have a few weeks off and then probably do a bit of maintenance and a bit of work for Ergon, checking poles' the stranger said.

'Checking poles?' Mark queried.

'Yeah, with me chopper', helicopter that I use for mustering, I do contract mustering for a few places around here, generally start from April and finish up about now, before the wet and then there's typically a bit of work from the power company checking power poles in the hard to get at areas, it's a quid I suppose,' the stranger went on, 'Warren's me name, but everyone calls me Jacko' he concluded and reached out his hand.

Mark shook his hand and introduced himself whilst thinking what an interesting fellow this person seemed, then said.

'Another beer?' Mark asked, raising his empty glass.

The stranger picked up his almost empty schooner glass and said 'Why not, thanks' then drank the small amount of beer remaing as Mark ordered two more schooners from the lady behind the bar.

'Do you do any work for Watsonville?' Mark asked while waiting for the drinks to be served.

'Yeah, just finished mustering with the boys up there, d'yer know Stan, Dave?' Warren replied.

Mark told Warren that he did not know them but had met them just the day before yesterday when he was out there on a bit of business, he didn't say what business, but he said that he found them most unfriendly.

'They're alright, those boys,' was Warren's reply. They have been doing it tough up there and have been having their fair share of problems with people trespassing on their place and people growing plantations if you know what I mean'. Warren took a drink of his beer, 'Once you get to know 'em, you won't find nicer people. What sort of business do you want to do with them, are you a cattle buyer?'

'No…no, not a cattle buyer, I had a proposition to put towards them, that's all', Mark thought what the hell, this bloke might be able to help him.

Warren told Mark that they didn't like people to just 'drop in' and he said that he didn't blame them and told Mark that the only way to get around them, especially Stan, was to call them first, they are hard to get onto but just keep ringing until you get them.

Then, when you get them on the phone and you say you will be out there at such and such a time, ask them if they need anything bringing out and have a pen ready cos they will have a list of things. Then you will be right as they will be looking forward to seeing you as you will be bringing the stuff they need out and it saves them a big trip and time away from work.

'Oh, and they are very partial to a good bottle of scotch whiskey, My shout' said Warren ordering two more drinks.

As it turned out Warren had known both Stan and David for quite a long time, Warren's parents had a property close to theirs when it was owned and run by David's parents, then not long after Davids's parents had drowned in that tragic crossing, they had sold up and moved to Mareeba, much to Warrens disgust as he really missed living out there.

Mark finished his drink and said farewell to Warren and thanked him for the advice, Warren had told him that he was more than welcome and told him to just persist with those boys out at Watsonville and he'll be right.

Mark bought a slab of stubbies from the bottle shop and headed back to Jason's house, it was almost five o'clock and Mark was surprised to see Jason was home.

Jason said that it had been a fairly well behaved day and as extra coppers had been sent from Cairns his boss said that he could knock off for the day.

They sat at the outside table with a beer each and Mark told Jason that he was going to Cairns in the morning to buy a satellite telephone and that he would return in the afternoon then asked him if there was anything that he wanted bringing back from Cairns.

Jason asked Mark why he wanted a satellite phone and Mark told him that he needed to contact his boss while he was out in the field to get approval of things.

Jason had put down his beer and gone inside the house, he returned moments later with an Idium Extreme 9575 satphone.

'Here, you can borrow this for as long as you need to' Jason said as he passed the phone to Mark. 'You'll just have to set up your own account with Telstra, you can do that over the phone, your normal mobile that is'.

The next day Mark set up a Telstra account for the satellite telephone that Jason had loaned him. He then spent almost the rest of the day trying to call the landline phone number of Watsonville on his mobile phone but to no avail.

It wasn't until that night at nine o'clock, just after Jason had gone to bed for an early start the next morning, that when Mark tried calling the landline number again that it was answered.

'David speaking' said a mild voice

'Hello David, It's Mark Crampton, I was out there earlier this week with respect to making an offer on your property' Mark rushed to avoid letting David to get a word in, *such as* 'not interested', he continued 'I will be out there tomorrow at around three o'clock and wondered if you needed anything brought out from Cooktown?' There was an extended pause and then,

'Just a moment', David said and then laid the telephone handset down. Mark could hear footsteps and a door open and then distant voices, after quite some time just as he was about to hang up, he heard a distinct OK, and soon after David returned to the line,

'Do you have a pen?' He said.

'Yes' replied Mark anxiously. It was just like Warren had said.

The list of items that David had given to Mark was quite extensive and would require Mark to visit a number of Cooktown locations to fulfil the requirements.

It was almost eleven o'clock by the time Mark had finished running around Cooktown for the items on David Watson's list, there was only one item that was not available.

He was on his way to Watsonville and he calculated that it would be at least four o'clock by the time he got there, one hour later than he had told David, so be it! Mark thought, it was the best he could do. In his rushing around to get all the items, plus a bottle of Johnny Walker black label scotch whiskey, he had almost forgotten his purpose of the visit to Watsonville.

He had hooked up his caravan and had arrived at the Watsonville homestead at four thirty that afternoon and to his surprise, the dogs were on their chains. He opened the back of the canopy and started to take out the boxes containing David's items, there were four of them, the front door opened and Stan came out to the Landcruiser to help with the boxes. They both carried the four boxes into the house and placed them on top of the kitchen table, David appeared and asked Mark how much did he owe him and Mark replied he would get the receipts from the car.

He went back out to the cruiser and got the receipts and the bottle of Johnny Walker and returned to the house.

'Would anyone care for a drink?' Asked Mark lifting the bottle above his head.

'Suits me' David said, 'Just as soon as I fix up paying you, I'll need your bank details as I can only pay by phone banking, the internet is shit out here.

'You can count me in too' Stan said in a much better mood as he got three glasses from the bench.

Mark opened his bank account on his mobile to reveal his BSB number and his account number which he showed to David who wrote it down.

They all went outside in front of the house where a table and chairs stood under a big Flame Tree that was not in bloom at that time of the year. Stan poured two fingers of whiskey into each glass and passed a glass to Mark and then David, then holding his glass to chin height said 'Good Luck; as he sat in a chair, he looked at Mark,

'Thanks, Mark for bringing out that gear, much appreciated believe me and thanks for the drink too, you'll be staying for dinner I hope?'

Mark could not say yes fast enough and was thinking 'Thanks Warren' when Stan added,

'But firstly, get it straight, this place is not for sale for any amount of money to anyone...OK! So don't even ask and don't make any offers and we can all be really good friends'.

Mark was quite shocked, but on one hand, not really, Stan had put it straight forward to him, which in a way he respected, but he did feel a bit deflated and had no idea of what to say except OK.

'Look, Mark, if the property ever did go on the market, which of course it won't, then we would give you the first option to buy it' David added to Stan's comment. 'We want the lifestyle, not the money'.

What would we do with the money, live at the Gold Coast in a high rise apartment and drink ourselves to death?'

The barbequed tomahawk steaks were absolutely brilliant, David told Mark how he prepared them two hours before eating them by salting them generously with rock salt on each side to cause osmosis inside the steak which makes them very tender and does not make them taste salty.

Mark enjoyed the evening with Stan and David, they had a lot of yarn's to tell and also told him about the drug growers which they could do nothing about and it also seemed that the police couldn't either.

Stan told Mark he could camp by the river like he did last time, but reminded him 'No Fires!'

Mark asked Stan if he could fish in the river and Stan instantly said 'No!'

'We don't own the river, I know, but we own the land that you 'Have' to walk on to get to the river, that's the way it is, we just don't want anyone on the property and we don't think that is a lot to ask, and sorry, but we don't make exceptions and that includes you'. The change in Stan was incredible, he was becoming quite chatty and seemed even friendly over dinner, but now he had reverted back to the person that he was when he had first arrived at Watsonville Station.

David added 'If we catch anyone fishing we will have a writ of trespass issued, we have the right to ask them for identification for that purpose'. David was also becoming unfriendly and for no apparent reason.

'If we see a car parked anywhere on our property we have a writ of trespass issued to the car registration address' Stan concluded. 'If we let you go fishing today it will be shooting tomorrow and then bringing your mates up here and before we know it there are people up here everywhere and bush fires all over the place, no way!'

Mark decided that it was time to say goodnight to this pair.

Mark camped by the river that night, he went to bed thinking that this pair of station owners were certainly different, strange people indeed he thought.

The next morning Mark called Father Damien and told him briefly about the conversation last night and told him that it seemed that they would not be able to buy Watsonville for whatever price JCE put on it.

Father Damien also thought that these people must be a bit strange to knock back such an offer on a somewhat, from what Mark had described to him, run down property and homestead.

He told Mark to get it all in writing to him and to start looking at properties further west of Cooktown.

Mark headed back to Cooktown feeling somewhat disappointed but on the other hand he was looking forward to exploring new territory to the west.

Father Damien had called the other member of the board who was assisting him in seeking properties suitable for JCE's new venture.

Carl Stephenson was not overly surprised when he heard the results of the negotiations with cattle stations in the Far North and most particularly in the response from Watsonville Station.

'I'm sure that you will have a trick or two to pull out of your bag Carl' father Damien had said as he hung up the telephone.

Carl Stephenson called Kirill Nikolaev, he let the phone ring for about three rings and then hung up waiting for a call from 'Nik'.

The Fishing Trip

Mark had returned to Cooktown later that day and had again parked his caravan in Jason's backyard, Jason had returned home from work at around five PM and they both went over to the Sovereign for a few beers and then a meal.

Mark had told Jason the result of the proposition that he had put to Strauss and Watson and mentioned that he thought they were different sorts of blokes and he told of the mood change when he asked if he could go fishing on their property and the savage reaction by both of them.

Jason was aware that they went out of their way to keep trespassers out of the property, even to the extent of using their mustering choppers to find them and chase them away.

Jason told Mark that he had to go to Cairns the next morning to attend the preliminary hearing on the car theft gang and the truckie Steve Brown and that he may be gone for about four days, but he reminded Mark that he was more than welcome to stay in the house while he was gone.

Mark thanked him and said it would be easier to use his kitchen table to write his reports to JCE. He also said that Jason's Iridium sat phone was in his car, locked in a concealed, safe place, and he would grab it for him on their way back to Jason's place as he had no need for it anymore.

Both drinking a stubby and talking on the way back to Jason's, they forgot to get the sat phone out of his car for Jason that night.

It was the second day that Jason had been in Cairns that Mark got a call from Terry asking if he would be interested in a fishing trip, Terry had said that they would go tomorrow, Saturday and be going for about two days and would be camping on the river bank so he would need his swag.

Mark thought that would be a great idea, he had just finished and sent off his report to JCE and a fishing break would be just perfect, It was Saturday tomorrow and Jason was due back on Sunday. Mark told Terry he would be there tomorrow just after lunch.

Terry Andrews and David Barnes had parked their Nissan Patrol just far away from the Watsonville Station homestead so they could see that the old Nissan Ute that Stauss and Watson used to get around the property was not parked where it usually was near the machinery shed. Terry had assumed that they would be pretty busy drafting cattle up at their yards which were about fifteen kilometres away from the homestead.

David waited in the Nissan while Terry walked down the track to the homestead, David had a view of the track behind the homestead for roughly two kilometres, should the Strauus-Watson patrol come down this track heading towards the homestead he was to sound the horn, just one quick blast.

There was only one dog that had been left at the homestead and it was fast asleep and as Terry could see was on a chain.

He went to the front door and reached up above the door and onto the top of the door frame where they left the key each time they locked the door. Terry had seen them do this purely by accident when he was scouting around their place one afternoon and they had returned from around the property somewhere and had unlocked the door, one of them had gone into the house to collect something and then when leaving the house had relocked the door and replaced the key.

Terry was now inside the house and looked quickly for the firearms that he knew had to be in there somewhere.

He found the bedrooms and in one bedroom a Tikka .270 rifle leaned against the wall in one corner opposite the unmade bed, he checked the next bedroom which had only a mattress on the floor without bedding, lying on this bed were all sorts of things, fishing rods, landing nets, a sleeping bag and a singe barrel twelve gauge shotgun. In the next bedroom on a wall mounted gun rack were a Savage pump action shotgun and a Marlin lever action 30-30 rifle, The shotgun was loaded with four AAA shot cartridges and the rifle seemed to be loaded but he could not see how many rounds were inside the tubular magazine.

Terry worked the rifle's lever over the unmade bed and ejected five 30-30 rounds, he quickly reloaded them back into the rifle and then left the house carrying the shotgun and the rifle, leaning them against the wall outside the front door he carefully locked the door and returned the key to the top of the door frame in the exact place that he had found it, picking up the weapons he returned to David waiting in the Nissan.

'That was fucking tense mate, sitting here watching, it seemed that you were gone for fucking hours', Barnsy said.

'It was no fucking picnic in that fucking brothel of a place either pal', replied Terry, 'It fucking stank inside that house and that fucking dog would not stop barking, I was expecting to hear you on the horn at any time, plus the fucking stink inside that place, I don't know how they live in there.

The next day, Saturday, Mark met David and Terry at their lease and it was decided to take only Terry's Nissan Patrol wagon as it was big enough for all of them plus the tree swags on the roof rack with the fishing rods, leaving plenty of room in the back for the three esky's and gas cooker plus various bits and pieces.

They were all enjoying a stubby as they drove along the road back in the direction towards Laura for about nine kilometres where they found a hardly visible track to the left.

The track was extremely rough and overgrown and Terry became lost several times and told Mark that he had not been down here in a while.

Mark was of the opinion that no one had been down this way for quite some time but he kept it to himself as these guys seemed to know what they were doing and had said that it was well worth the effort to get to this place as the fishing was great and it was out of the way with little chance of being seen.

They were now going down a very steep and very rough section and Mark was glad that they weren't in his Landcruiser.

They had arrived at the bottom of the track and the river was just in view. Terry had said that they could go no further and that they should all walk down to the river and look for a campsite.

They were ready to go when Terry slid the rifle from behind the back seat and Mark gave him an enquiring look,

'Crocks mate, the pricks lay around the banks and I don't want to be their dinner' responded Terry.

They walked down to the river bank and turned to walk upstream of the river toward a towering rocky outcrop on both sides. It wasn't long before it turned into a gorge and they had to leave the river to climb up the slope to go around a point in the river.

Mark had somehow become in the lead in front of Terry and David was last in line, Terry lowered the loaded 30-30 rifle level with the back of Mark's neck and pulled the trigger.

The explosion of the rifle shot reverberated around the gorge, at around one hundred and seventy decibels it was quite deafening, but Mark would not have heard it, he was dead before he hit the boulders they were climbing over.

Terry, wearing disposable gloves, had taken a hand towel from his pocket together with a freezer bag, he dabbed the towel in the puddle of blood that had formed next to Mark's throat and then placed it into the freezer bag. They then went through his pockets and took the keys to his Landcruiser. Then they removed his R M Williams boots,

There was a large hole that had been formed by three large jagged rocks just near where Mark's body lay and it was little effort to push his body head first into the hole where the body fell for about three metres or more. It was deep enough decided Barnsy and Terry dropped the rifle down into the hole.

They returned to the Nissan and, still wearing disposable gloves, took one of Mark's fishing rods and from his backpack took his mobile telephone, one of his iPod earphones, a fishing knife in a sheath, his hat and a pair of leg gators together with the shotgun. These items were also dropped into the hole containing Mark's body.

Other items, the remaining iPod earphone and a small pocket knife they took with them

Terry Andrews and David Barnes had then driven to the fishing spot where they had enjoyed fishing and lunching with Mark Crampton a few weeks prior and, again wearing disposable gloves, they set up camp being careful to place Mark's swag in position near the fireplace unroll it and make look like it had been slept in. His esky was also placed in the camp as with his backpack with some clothing removed and placed on top of the backpack his spare fishing rod was laid on his 'slept in' swag along with some clothing from his bag.

David Barnes had gone fishing while Terry made a campfire and, wearing gloves, set up utensils and plates for three people, it was just starting to go dark by the time they had eaten a feed of fish and canned baked beans ensuring all three plates had been used but not cleaned, as with the utensils.

Six of Mark's beers were drunk and the empties were placed in a pile with Terry and Barnsy's empties.

They spent a quiet night camped beside the river and the next morning, leaving the campsite undisturbed they drove to their lease and unlocked Mark's Landcruiser to look for any valuables and money. Wearing disposable gloves they found Mark's wallet locked in the glove box, there was approximately two hundred dollars in his wallet which they left intact as with his credit cards. They also found in the glove box three thousand dollars in one hundred dollar notes and a sat phone, these items they took and then relocked the Landcruiser and took the keys with them for disposal.

They had driven back to the river just after lunch and had parked close to their camp, Barnsy, wearing Mark's boots and carrying his own boots with him, then walked up and along the river making sure to make footprints in the sand with both pairs of boots and then with Mark's boots only up and over the track beside the river and down a gully where a creek meets the river he stopped at a grassy area and removed Mark's boots.

Wearing his disposable gloves he took the blood soaked towel from the freezer bag and carefully wiped it on and around the grassed area, he then carefully placed the pocket knife onto the grassed area that was covered in blood ensuring that some blood went onto and into the crevices in the pocket knife, he then did the same with the one iPod earphone but well away from the pocket knife.

He then set fire to the grassed area which burned very rapidly being dry, taking off his shirt, he wafted the flames over the blooded area so they extinguished before completely burning the area.

Carrying Mark's boots and wearing socks only on his feet Barnsy very carefully moved off the grassed area and onto the creek gravel and down to the river back toward the camp where he could then safely remove his socks and walk barefoot back to the camp.

It was about five o'clock in the afternoon that Terry had driven to a neighbouring property that was about an hour's drive and had used the property's landline telephone to report the shooting to the police.

Jason had not become aware of the shooting until he had reported for duty at nine o'clock on the following Monday morning when he read the brief about the shooting call last night, he didn't relate the shooting with Mark and wasn't until later that day when Mark had not returned to Cooktown that Jason had informed his sergeant that his friend had gone fishing and that he had not returned as yet although a note that he had left in Jasons' house had indicated that he would be back at around five PM Sunday, yesterday. His name, he told the sergeant was Mark Crampton.

When the sergeant informed the officer in charge of the investigation, Detective Sergeant Cameron Jamison, at the Mareeba Police Station the officer had confirmed that the missing man's name was Mark but that his surname was unknown to his friends. The missing man's vehicle had been left at his companion's mining lease and a crew from the scene were going there this morning to get an identification on the vehicle's owner via the number plate.

The sergeant told Jason that the missing man's name was Mark but that a surname was not available at this stage.

'Looks very much like it's your mate', the sergeant told Jason, they want two more of our boys out there this afternoon to help with the search and I was going to send you, but that can't happen now for obvious reasons'.

Jason was now feeling quite shattered and even more so towards the late afternoon when it was confirmed that the vehicle left at the mining lease was registered to Mark Crampton.

Jason had at about five thirty that afternoon received a call from Detective Sergeant Jamison asking what was his relationship with Mark Crampton,

'I met him about two months ago when he came in to report an assault and the theft of his vehicle here in Cooktown' replied Jason and continued with a brief report about the exposure of the stolen vehicle group operating in FNQ. He didn't hear back from the detective again.

After a few weeks and the talk about the shooting and the missing person had died to almost no mention.

A tilt tow truck had taken Mark's caravan from Jason's backyard and Mark's vehicle had been collected from the mining lease, these had been relocated at the police storage yard in Mareeba and would be held in evidence.

As the search for a body continued at Watsonville the whole of the property was declared a crime scene and any movement with the property was under the supervision of the police.

The mustered cattle in the yards had been released back into the property by a caretaker who had been appointed to look after the stock on the property for the time being.

In the following few months It was basically back to normal for Jason except for being promoted to sergeant and being transferred to Officer in Charge at Laura Police Station which quite suited him and served there for just over twelve months when he had a win on the 'Oz Lotto' of a little over four million dollars.

Jason had resigned from the Queensland Police and bought a unit on the Gold Coast in Queensland following his win.

The Alleged Shooting Aftermath

The court case for Strauss and Watson was held as a combined case and had been to the Supreme Court of Queensland at Cairns listed as R v Strauss & Watson.

Jason Walsh was subpoenaed to attend the trial at the Cairns Court as a witness for the prosecution, it had been over a year since the disappearance of Mark Crampton and both the accused had been remanded since the day of the alleged shooting at The Lotus Glen Correctional Centre located just eighty six kilometres from Cairns.

Jason was asked how he had met Mark Crampton and how well did he know him, he was asked if Mark had told him why he was in Cooktown and Jason had said that he was a property scout for a company called JCE and was looking at properties in the area with a view to purchase.

'Did Mark Crampton ever visit Watsonville Station in respect to his business?' asked the prosecuting barrister.

'Yes he did' Jason answered

'On how many occasions?'

'Err..two,.. I think, or maybe it was three' Jason was trying to remember.

'Was it two, or was it three?' Queried the prosecutor.

'It's quite a while ago now and I am not sure, it was no big deal, I knew he was just busy with his work', answered Jason.

'Did he make any comments about the owners of Watsonville Mr Walsh?'

'It was following his last visit that he thought they were a bit strange and from being quite friendly towards him they had turned quite aggressive when he had asked if he could fish on their property. They had told him that he could neither fish nor shoot on their property and to keep off their property or he would receive a writ of trespass from them'. Jason replied.

'Have you met the owners of Watsonville Mr Walsh?' The prosecutor then asked.

'Yes, on a number of occasions' replied Jason.

'And what were the circumstances of those occasions?'

'It was when as a member of the Queensland Police that I had cause to talk to them in respect to complaints from people who had been chased by them, the property owners, from their property where the complainants had suffered personal or property damage' Jason recalled.

'Did Mark Crampton ever mention to you the names of Terry Andrews and David Barnes?'

'He did mention them, but only their given names, I don't think he told me about their surnames and I think he referred to David as 'Barnsy' once or twice'. Said Jason trying to remember.

'Did Mark Crampton tell you how he had met with these two, Terry Andrews and David Barnes?'

'Yes, Mark Crampton's vehicle had got stuck on a spike, as I recall, and they came along and helped him I think and he must have kept in touch with them as far as I know. Again trying to remember Jason had said.

'Did he tell you that he was going fishing with Andrews and Barnes?' The prosecutor then asked.

'No, I was in Cairns when he decided to go fishing with them, he was staying with me at that time and he had left a note saying that he was away fishing and would return on Sunday afternoon'. Jason explained.

'That will be all thank you, Mr Walsh'. Said the prosecutor.

The defence did not wish to cross examine Jason and he was free to leave, he decided to sit in the public gallery and listen to more of the evidence against the accused.

The next witness to take the stand was Warren Jackson.

'Mr Jackson, did you ever meet Mark Crampton?' The prosecutor started.

'I did yes, one time only you mind, at the Sovereign Hotel in Cooktown, sir' he answered.

'And are you familiar with both of the accused?'

'I am, yes sir'.answered Warren Jackson

'What capacity do you know the accused Mr Jackson?'

'I fly with them and help at mustering time, we, Stan and David and meself, all fly choppers and do the mustering for most of the properties around that area of Watsonville, for a price like!' Offered Warren Jackson.

'Did Mr Crampton enquire to you about the accused, the owners of Watsonville Station?' The prosecutor wanted to know.

'He did, he said that he had tried to approach them at their property, unannounced mind you, and thought that they were arseholes, pardon your honour,' said Warren glancing at the judge.

'Did you advise Mr Crampton how to approach the accused at their property?'

'He wouldn't tell me exactly what it was that he wanted to talk to them about but said it was very important to him so I told him how they appreciated people calling them on the telephone before going out to the property and that they would welcome the offer to collect supplies for them from town to bring outwith them. I also told him that they were very partial to good scotch whiskey' Warren Jackson told the court.

The next witness was Father Damien Downes.

'What is your relationship with the missing man Mark Crampton?' Asked the prosecutor.

'I was Mark's school teacher in Canberra and had been more like a second father to him in his growing up and had lately engaged him with employment in the company that I am a board director', the very well spoken Father Damien replied.

'In what capacity was Mr Crampton employed and why was he based in Cooktown?, Father'. Asked the prosecutor.

'Mark was employed as a consultant analyst and was engaged in a feasibility study of the area west of Cooktown.

'Did Mr Crampton's job involve meeting with the owners of Watsonville?'

'Yes, and other property owners in the district, my company was desirous to do business with property owners in the region'. Said Father Damien.

'Did Mr Crampton mention to you about his meeting with the accused?'

'Mark had said that one minute the Watsonville Station owners were quite receptive and then the other minute they became quite aggressive and I advised Mark to discontinue any negotiations with them'. Father Damien answered.

'That will be all thank you, Father'. Was the prosecutor's response.

It was obvious to Jason that the prosecution was portraying both Watson and Strauss as agressive and using these witnesses, including himself, to confirm this.

He knew the rest of the court case would be too boring and too long for him and it would bring back sad memories so he left the courthouse and before flying back to the Gold Coast he decided to hire a car and visit his old friends in Cooktown.

Things had not changed in the eighteen months since Jason had been in Cooktown with the exception that a new Officer in Charge had been installed at the police station. The Senior Sergeant when Jason was stationed there was a great fellow named Ken Marsden who had retired from the police and was now working as a ranger and was based at Coen.

It had been an accidental 'meet up' with Ken at the RSL club. Ken had come into Cooktown to get a few things, one of them being a satellite telephone which he could not get anywhere around Cooktown, he was staying the night and thought a few beers and a meal at the club before an early night was the plan.

Jason had said to Ken that he had a sat phone which he hadn't used for yonks and that he was welcome to have it and that he would send it to him once he returned to his unit, that's if he was in no rush.

Ken had thanked Jason for the kind offer, but he had that afternoon ordered one from Brisbane and he would have it sometime next week.

Ken had told Jason that he was really enjoying his job as a ranger as there was very little pressure attached to the job, unlike the police force, he was, however, amazed at the amount of drugs that he had found growing around the district.

The police had seized the entire property known as Watsonville Station and the Public Trustee had organised a cattle muster and sale, the trustee then had the property evaluated and valued by the Valuer General.

Due to the complexity of the situation, it was a further two years before the trustee placed the property on the market for public auction at a venue in Mareeba.

JCE had instructed a local real estate agent Vincent Villani to attend the auction and bid for the property on their behalf.

Villani placed the successful bid of six point three million dollars on the property on behalf of JCE.

JCE created a new company, Watsonville Pastoral & Mining Proprietary Limited, also known as WPM. This company leased the property of Watsonville Station from JCE for a staggering amount of ten million dollars per annum and took out a trading loan of twenty million dollars which was guaranteed by JCE. This loan was to introduce fifteen thousand head of breeding stock onto Watsonville Station and for pasture improvement including self mustering yards in various locations, the establishment of accommodation buildings and access roads.

Part of the Watsonville business plan was to produce and sell fifteen thousand head of beef cattle for a gross profit of thirty five, million dollars within twenty four months, this was achieved, and this figure would grow as more breeding areas could be brought online.

At the time of purchasing Watsonville, it was estimated to be able to carry breeders at fifteen acres per head, it was estimated to have increased the carrying capacity of Watsonville to twelve acres per head within two years of careful management and had now forecast an increase of beef cattle sales to twenty thousand head at approximately forty eight million dollars gross sales.

The board members of JCE were quite happy with the trading results of WPM, the lease alone was contributing one point six million dollars to each of the shareholders and the net profits were also now returning another four million to each shareholder.

The shareholders in this instance were the six members of the board of JCE and other companies under JCE were also contributing excellent returns for its members.

The loss of Mark Crampton had put a heavy shadow over the project and all were quite saddened about the event, but as Father Damien had expressed to them 'Life must go on'.

The Satellite Telephone

Jason Walsh had decided to move from the bustling Gold Coast to somewhere a little quieter and with a bit more room and no neighbours.

He had been living off the interest of the investments he had made with the lotto winnings and decided to change some of those investments into a small cattle property that he could manage on his own and his new partner Narelle, whom he had met about a year previous and had now been living with him in his unit for the past ten months, she too wanted to get out of the rat race and go bush.

They had found a small property of three hundred acres near a small town called Monto, which is about five hundred and fifty kilometres from Brisbane and were busy packing for the move.

Jason was taking things from his top drawer and packing them into a carton when he came across the note that Mark had left for him while he was away in Cairns.

He had kept the note, which said that 'he had gone fishing and would be back on Sunday' in case it was required for evidence, which it wasn't, but for some reason he had kept it.

Seeing the note had brought to Jason's mind the sat phone which he had offered to give to Ken Marsden in Cooktown, he now wondered where it was and made a mental note whilst packing to look for it.

Everything was packed and had been picked up by the removalist with smaller items placed in his car, but he did not recall seeing the sat phone and it now played on his mind.

They had moved into the home near Monto and everything was going well, they were about to commence stocking the property and working out a plan to visit cattle sales around the area when Jason suddenly remembered loaning the sat phone to Mark and it became more important to him to try to go back in his memory to what happened to the sat phone than to buy cattle, much to the annoyance of Narelle.

He had remembered loaning it to Mark just before his second meeting with Watson and Strauss as he needed to contact his boss whilst at Watsonville, yes he could visualise that quite clearly.

When Mark returned from the meeting he gave the sat phone back to Jason...yes..? 'No!...they were in the pub,...' Jason said aloud, 'We were going to get it from his Landcruiser on the way back to my house from the pub!'

The satellite telephone was in the Landcruiser, where did the Landcruiser go after it was picked up by the police?

Jason called the Mareeba Police Station and asked for Detective Sergeant Cameron Jamison.

'You mean Inspector Jamison' the lady had said.

'Yes, that would be him' Jason said.

'Who is calling please', he was asked.

'It's Ja...It's former Senior Constable Jason Walsh from The Cooktown Police,' Jason thought that it may be easier for Cameron to remember him by his old title.

After a short wait, 'Jason! How are you, mate? I heard you won the lottery and pissed off' bellowed the voice of Cameron Jamison.

'Yeah, and now you are an inspector, congratulations Cameron'.

They chatted about old times and then Cameron asked Jason the reason he had called him.

'Stupid question, but when you guys searched the ute of the missing bloke at Watsonville a while back, did you come across a sat phone?' Jason asked.

How the fuck would I know?' Laughed Cameron. 'Why? Would you want to know that?'

'I loaned Mark, the guy who went missing, my sat phone and I am pretty sure it was in the Landcruiser, just wondered that's all' said Mark.

'Yeah, they are pretty exy items, Jason, I can understand that you would want it back, there will be a complete list of items that were in the vehicle and I'll see if I can find it and send it to you. What's your email?'

Jason gave Cameron his email and after a little more reminiscing hung up.

The email arrived two days later, it was a complete inventory of items that were found in Mark Crampton's Landcruiser after it was brought in from the mining lease of Andrews and Barnes. The satellite telephone was not listed.

In the bottom right hand side of the inventory was the name, date and signature of the person that searched the vehicle and as fate would have it, it was a colleague of Jason's from the training days in Townsville. He called the Mareeba Police Station again and this time asked for Senior Constable Grant Simmons,

'Sergeant Simmons is not available just now, can I take a message, or get him to call you back' the lady asked, Jason left his name and mobile number and it was only a matter of minutes before he received a return call.

'Hey Jase, long time no see' said Grant eagerly.

They exchanged some banter about the Townsville Police Academy and where they had been and so on.

'Mate!' Said Jason, 'The Crampton Landcruiser you did the search on about four years ago.'

'That's going back, but I do remember that one, the salvage team had a lot of trouble getting it on the truck as the vehicle was locked and they had to spray silicone on the tyres to get it off when they got here.' Replied Grant.

'So, nobody got into the car before you?' Asked Jason.

'Don't think so, it was thought that the keys were with the missing owner, we ended up finding the spare set of keys in his caravan. Why do you ask?' Continued Grant.

'It's a bit of a story, but I actually knew the guy and he was staying with me when he went missing, the short of it is, he had my sat phone in his car when he disappeared and it now looks like it has also disappeared'. Jason told Grant and he had suggested searching for the sat phone through the phone's manufacturer, he had done it previously and if Jason could give him the information of the manufacturer, where purchased, what date and serial number, then they could search for it and tell you the last time it was used and it's location, and strangely they don't need the phone number to do it.

Grant gave Jason his email and said to send him the sat phone's details and he would see what could be done, he also gave Jason his mobile number so he would not have to go through the station switch which recorded all conversations.

Narelle had been patient while Jason had been doing his bit of investigation but now thought she should remind him that they were supposed to be buying some cattle and plans were made for the following Monday.

The next day Jason received a text message from Grant telling him that the sat phone had been used just three days ago from latitude 'sixteen degrees, five minutes and twelve seconds South, one hundred and forty two degrees' forty four minutes East. Where the Vehicle was collected from?

Jason immediately checked the coordinates that placed the location near the Mitchell River, he hadn't been to the mining lease on Watsonville but he knew it was around that location. He knew that Mark would not have sold the sat phone nor would he have loaned it as it was not his, had he left it at the lease accidentally and the lease owners Andrews and Barnes were using the phone. Jason thought about contacting the police but then decided that it was not really a police matter and he doubted that they would be interested, he would check this out personally.

Narelle was horrified when Jason said he was going up the Mitchell River to check on his sat phone,

'Surely…surely, it would be cheaper just to buy a new one' she said to Jason and her anger was starting to show.

Jason poured a couple of drinks and took her out to the front verandah where they sat in the sun and he told her the story of Mark Crampton.

She said that she completely understood and said that she would go with him, Jason had at first objected but when she said that she was not going to hang around here on her own, he changed his mind.

They only had a BMW X5 and a Hilux SR5, and decided to pack the SR5 for the journey from Monto to Laura, one thousand and seven hundred kilometres.

They were booked into the Lakeland Downs Hotel at Laura, they had come via Cairns and Cooktown where they had spent a night at each and Narelle just loved Cairns to the extent that Jason had promised that they would spend some time there on the way back.

Using his newly bought Hema X2 navigation system he had left Narelle at the hotel and had set off towards the mining lease on the off chance that Andrews and Barnes would be out there.

He had remembered Mark's warning about the spikes just after the turnoff and slowed to a snail's pace but it seemed that the spikes had been removed.

He didn't quite get to the lease when he met an old Nissan Patrol coming towards him and he pulled over to the left as much as he could and stopped.

The Nissan Patrol containing two people, who Jason guessed were Andrews and Barnes, pulled up level with him and the driver asked him if he was lost,

'I might be', Jason answered, 'I am looking for Terry Andrews'

'Never heard of him mate! what would you want him for anyway.' Said the driver.

'I think he has my satellite telephone and I want it back' Jason said, he had thought hard about how to approach these people and thought that going straight to the point might be the best.

'We aint got no satellite telephone up here' the driver' stated.

'Strange, the satellite company gave me this location, they said it was being used here!' Jason said quite calmly.

'He sold it to me!' The person in the passenger seat called out loudly and unexpectedly.

'Shut up dickhead' quipped the driver.

'Who sold it to you?' Jason asked quickly.

'A bloke that used to work for us, he owed us money and sold his phone to us, can't remember his name but I always thought that the phone was hot. Nicked it from you eh?' The driver took over the conversation from the passenger. 'We haven't got it anymore, Charlie here dropped it in the river last week!'

Jason guessed that he could be in a dangerous situation and cut the talk short, 'Ah well, no good going any further up then, seems that it is lost, so be it, thanks anyway fellers, I'll just find a place to turn around'.

The two occupants waited and watched until the stranger turned around and they watched as he returned down the track that he had come from.

'Where the fuck did you get that fucking phone from?' Barnsy asked Terry,

'I found it in his truck when I went through it' replied Terry.

'And you fucking kept it, you fucking drongo, I had just assumed it was your phone' Barnsy said shaking his head. "We'd better be careful now if this thing is linked to us.

Terry responded, 'The bloke didn't seem too upset when we told him it was now in the river'.

'And that's where it had better go' Barnsy said quite pissed off at Terry, he thought he was a lot smarter than that.

Barnsy told Terry that he thought that the bloke was a copper just scouting and that he probably recorded the conversation about the phone and that he would take it back to analyse it. Terry told him he was getting paranoid and not to worry.

Jason had recorded the whole conversation from when the Nissan driver had asked if he was lost. It was sad that he could do nothing more until he returned Narelle to their home in Monto, but it had been nearly four years now and a couple more weeks wouldn't hurt.

Once back home the first person that Jason called with the news of the sat phone was Inspector Cameron Jamison and he explained to Cameron that the phone may be linked somehow to the disappearance of Mark Crampton for the following reasons.

(1) Mark had told Jason that the sat phone was safely locked up in a concealed place in his Landcruiser

(2) Mark would not have sold the sat phone as it was not his and Mark was not short of money, he always seemed to have money as he was being paid exceptional money from his employment.

(3) How did Terry Andrews come into possession of the phone if Mark's car was locked and no keys could be found in his backpack and it was presumed that Mark had the keys on him when he disappeared?

Inspector Jamison had listened to Jason without once interrupting him, but once Jason had finished talking, Jamison told him that he was wasting both of their time as the the two people who were responsible for Crampton's murder, had been found guilty and were now both serving life sentences in prison, the case was closed some time ago and it is now history.

Jason had detected a tone in Cameron Jamison that was not there before when he had called him the other day, something was not right.

Jason then called Grant Simmons on his mobile, there was no answer and the call went straight to Grant's message bank.

Grant called back just minutes later.

'Jason..what the fuck is going on, Jamison revved the fuck out of me a couple of days ago about this fucking sat phone, apparently for some reason he had gone looking for our conversation through the station switchboard and told me not to communicate with you in respect to the closed case of the missing Crampton man and not to bring up this conversation with anyone. I don't think he is aware of the report that I received from the satellite telephone company just yesterday' said Grant.

'Yeah, I just spoke to him a little while ago and he sounded quite alienated, say,..what report from the sat phone company? Do you mean the location?'

'I also asked for a call record for the last five years and they sent me through a report on the numbers dialled and the numbers received, I suppose you would like a copy, I'll email it to you tonight from my home computer, got to go', and Grant ended the call.

The email showed all the calls made and received by that satellite telephone for the period before Jason had loaned the phone to Mark which showed some calls that Jason had made, it showed the only call that Mark had made according to the dates and then just after Mark's disappearance, it showed a number of calls made to a number that had never answered followed by a received call within an hour after making the call from the same regional communications tower as the unanswered calls.

The report also showed a call to the same number that was never answered at about the same time that Jason had fronted the guys in the Nissan and had then reported a call from the same communication tower just minutes later.

Jason thought he could understand what might be happening when he studied the report, but he wanted a second opinion.

Narelle's brother James, was visiting them next week and he was a communications technical engineer, Jason wanted James to have a look at the sat phone company report and see what he could make of it.

In the interim Narelle was pushing Jason every day to get the cattle thing happening as she was bored shitless.

Jason had no intention of leaving his newfound investigation and he suggested that she visit the Gym or something in Monto just while he got this thing of his sorted, she unhappily informed him that there was 'Fuck all' in Monto and that she may as well head back to the Gold Coast,

'You said you had had enough of the Gold Coast so we agreed to come here' Jason said.

'Yeah,..and you said we would get into growing beef cattle, not turning into a private fucking investigator' Narelle had angrily responded.

It suddenly came to Jason, 'Why not set up a gym in town, you said there was nothing there, could be filling a big gap, what do you think?'

'Wow!…that could be good, but… you are too busy' she said.

'I really meant You!.. You could do it and I'll bet you would enjoy it' Jason said as he thought that she sounded half keen.

'But once it is set up I don't want to hang around it all day' said Narelle sounding a little less positive.

'You would employ someone to run it, simple. Jason solved that one! And Narelle started research instantly on the internet.

James had arrived on Friday afternoon and by seven o'clock that evening, he was pouring through the sat phone report and was becoming as interested as Jason was.

It seems that since Mark had possession of the phone, he made one call, and he highlighted it on the copy that Jason had made, but then it seems that at least once a month this phone has called this unanswered number and that this phone has received a call from different numbers within one hour from calling the number that never answers and from the same tower that the unanswered call went to.

The number of the return calls is varied but only five times, so in this period each of the five numbers has called the sat phone nine times and the unanswered number has been called five times that amount, forty five times.

The unanswered call duration time hardly varies, which means it rings for the same amount of times with each call, like a code, Jason had asked James,

'Exactly, the number that the sat phone is calling alerts someone to make contact with the sat phone caller and they do, obviously with a different number but one that is not identified by caller ID' James explained.

'Can we find out where it is?' Jason asked.

'I can find out where the tower is and then we can look at the tower's range and the signal strength of the outgoing call to the unanswered number and calculate it by percentage on a map within the radius of the tower to determine its actual distance from the tower, but that's probably as far as we can go without a warrant from the police, can you get one Jason?' James outlined the system.

'No, I don't think that I can, the police are not the least interested' Jason told James.

James finished his drink and said that there are ways, but they are illegal.

James went into detail with Jason on how a scanner can follow the direction of a mobile phone from a transmitting tower but not so from a receiving tower.

Firstly you need the type of scanner and you need to know the transmitting mobile number and the receiving tower location, which we do, he added but then the hard thing is, it can only be traced while it is transmitting.

'You have a scanner! Jason asked excitedly.

'I do', answered James, 'But we would have to be in the tower's range area to use it'.

James had worked out the location of the tower which was in Gladstone and the signal strength of the outgoing call registered seventy eight percent, which would make scanning a lot easier than if it was lesser.

All they had to do was be in Gladstone at any location within twenty kilometres from the tower with all the Five numbers that had been recorded by the sat phone, locked into the scanner, if any of those numbers dialled out on a call the scanner would locate the equipment to within ten metres.

So all it will really do is tell you at what address the equipment is that is dialling out to the sat phone, for whatever that would be worth'. Commented James, 'Will that really prove anything for you?'

'Probably not', conceded Jason, 'But it won't hurt to have a look at the place that's communicating with the boys at the mining lease, which I would think is more of a plantation than a mining lease.

James looked rather confused so Jason got more drinks and then told James the whole story as far as he knew it and ended by saying that he thought that Strauss and Watson had been set up, he had no idea why, but he also thought that Andrews and Barnes may be the answer but he had very little to go on. He also thought that it was very strange that the police did not want to know about it, or that's how it seemed.

Looking back at the sat phone records it seemed around the third of every month and always between ten o'clock and twelve noon in the morning, very consistent they agreed. And decided to meet at a football field in Gladstone on the third of next month, which was a Tuesday, and see if they could get the scanner into operation.

The morning of the third day of the following month found Jason meeting up with James at the little park near the council depot which was close to the tower, it was almost ten o'clock and James had superimposed the Gladstone map onto his scanner and had calibrated the location to within five metres.

He had not long finished the map calibration when one of the five numbers registered and almost immediately the scanner placed a red marker onto the map. This was the location of the unit transmitting a call to the tower for a satellite transfer.

The address showing on the scanner was in the CBD on Chaple Street, they drove to the address to discover that it was an office building that housed one company, Northern Trading and Logistics.

As they drove past the office building, two bikies were parking their Harley Davidsons in the car park area that had a sign 'Staff Parking Only', they drove on innocently and found a Maccas for some breakfast.

Jason had only a one hundred and sixty kilometre drive to his home in Monto, after an hour and a half he was already doing a company search of Northern Trading and Logistics to discover that it was a subsidiary of The Northern Hotels Pty Ltd and the company director is Carl Stephenson.

A subsequent search showed that The Northern Hotels company is part of the JCE group of companies.

'Now that *is* interesting; said Jason to James who had followed Jason back to Monto to spend the balance of the week helping his sister put the gym together in town.

It just seemed to Jason to be a strange coincidence that this company, that Mark's employer was associated with, was in contact with the mining lease on Watsonville Station.

That evening following dinner the three of them, Jason, Narelle and James were sitting at the dining table enjoying a great bottle of Penfold's Max's *Pinot Noir* and the conversation was about the discovery of the company in Gladstone that morning and what connections the company may have with the owners of the mining lease on Watsonville Station.

Jason had already told Narelle and James about Mark being in Cooktown on behalf of JCE who he was engaged as an analyst for the purpose of feasibility studies.

Mark had told Jason that he was negotiating with Strauss and Watson for the purchase of their station and that they refused to sell their property point blank.

'Well that's all pretty simple' said James who had looked up the prospectus that afternoon for Watsonville Pastoral and Mining. 'They are envisioning a gross profit after only the second year of trading of around forty eight million dollars, that is big dollars when you consider that they only paid around six million for it and the prospectus shows a loan of only twenty million dollars for capital expenditure and breeding stock, that will reduce the capex to nothing after two years, pretty good deal'.

'Yes' said Narelle, 'But when Mark tried to buy it for JCE, it wasn't for sale, so they were going to miss out on those huge profits, so...Mark has put in his report to JCE like you said Jason, that the property is not for sale, then another subsidiary of JCE is in touch with the people on a mining lease on the same property, then Marks goes missing whilst fishing with the same people that the JCE subsidiary was talking to,....Hellooo?' She looked at Jason matter of factly.

'But where is the advantage to JCE by getting Mark off the scene?' asked James.

'JCE's advantage was exactly what has transpired, but it's not a fluke as it appears to be, but it was possibly by design' Narelle added.

Jason had suddenly sat upright with what Narelle had said, my god, she could be right he thought.

'That's it! if something had happened to Strauss and Watson, like death, hypothetically speaking, then the property would go into Strauss and Watson's estates and may still not be available for purchase by JCE,...but..by removing Mark and blaming it on Strauss and Watson by two witnesses, the police arrest the accused Strauss and Watson, once found guilty the police seize the property as a crime scene and then when convicted, the public trust take it over for public disposal..wallah!' said Jason quite confident.

JCE Pty Ltd

James then suggested that his girlfriend's grandfather was a retired company auditor and he may be interested in looking at these companies for us.

Jason pleasantly noted the 'us' in James' suggestion, thinking that at least one other person besides Narelle and himself suspected something was amiss with JCE.

The girlfriend's grandfather turned out to be a retired magistrate who the federal government of Australia once commissioned as an auditor for various government departments and when told the story of Mark Crampton by Jason was more than keen to have a look into the company of Juliet Consolidated Enterprises.

Jason had travelled the two hundred and thirty kilometres to Woodgate Beach, a small community near Bundaberg on the central Queensland coast, to meet Travis Lachlan the grandfather of Amy Lachlan the girlfriend of James.

At seventy five years of age and seemingly very fit and in good health, 'thanks to a good beer' as he commented he enjoyed living by the beach and brewing his own beer.

He and his wife, Wendy, also fit and active were keen bowlers and spent a lot of time at the bowling club and also enjoyed fishing.

Travis had listened intently as Jason told of how he had met with Mark Crampton in Cooktown until he had heard the news of his disappearance on the Monday morning following the events of the previous day.

Travis Lachlan could instantly see the logic portrayed by Jason in the instance of blaming a murder upon the owners of Watsonville Station to gain access to buy the property and he agreed to have a look at JCE and would get back to him with his findings. He also added that he would enjoy doing it immensely as he no longer came across the opportunity of this kind of exercise.

The report from Travis came swiftly and caught Jason by surprise at the expedience.

He had listed the six members on the board of JCE as joint owners of the company and listed their names with a brief description of the person including their personal history.

Of the six members, Travis had described three of them to be of doubtful character. He explained this as quite normal and it is usually the doubtful people that recruit the squeaky clean people to throw a smokescreen for any company audits and/or investigations.

In his report, he made mention of the members whom he had referred to as 'doubtful'.

Father Damien Downes as he was, and thought Travis, still may be a suspect in the drowning of Bishop Gillard at Canberra. Father Damien was acting as the Bishop's chaperone on the evening of his disappearance and witnesses have reported that the Bishop was last seen with Father Damien, but nothing could be proven at the time, the case, however, has never been closed nor the coroners reported concluded.

Carl Stephenson, who is also the chairman and director of Northern Hotels which also operated a subsidiary called Northern Trading & Logistics of which a Mr Kirill Nikolaev is nominated as the managing director.

Kirill is well known to the police as a leading figure in drug production and distribution. Travis Lachlan could not confirm that Kirill was an illegal migrant

Carl Stephenson stepped down from his position as police commissioner when he was accused in state parliament of being involved in drug production in Far North Queensland in 2014.

Fiona Gibson was also formally the Deputy Premier of Queensland and was basically sacked from that position when Stephenson stepped down as police commissioner.

She is currently being investigated by ASIC (Australian Securities & Investments Commission) for an alleged Ponzi scheme.

An unconfirmed report states that the company, JCE was struggling to meet some leasing commitments with some of its subsidiary companies as well as superannuation payout issues and was at that time desperately seeking a new venture.

Travis had also looked at the case against Strauss and Watson and thought that their defence was inadequate but not necessarily from its administer but possibly from another influence, and he left it to a guess in what capacity, in other words, the barrister appointed by legal aid may have been advised that by being successful in defence may not be prudent to further appointments.

As with the prosecutor proceeding with a case with such limited physical evidence and unreliable witnesses and with a heavy reliance on circumstantial evidence. Strange to say the least he thought.

The former magistrate also believed that the satellite telephone belonging to Jason could be used as new evidence but was most likely not good enough to get the case reopened, besides it probably would have been destroyed by now, looking at the scenario presented by Jason he did however feel that it would not take too much of a police investigation into Andrews and Barnes to come up with some compelling evidence, ideally, if the police could convince the pair to tell the truth, but sadly the police are very limited to the methods of truth seeking allowed to them.

Jason was now convinced that they had been right in assuming that Mark's fishing companions were his likely murderers, but how could he take it further when it seemed that the police had shut down any enquiries into the Crampton disappearance?

He thought that maybe he could get Andrews or Barnes to speak and tell him what happened, or even where Mark's body was, that would be better, especially with the evidence of the sat phone communications which is irrefutable. Jason had an idea and called his old mate from his army days, Les Morton, he called his mobile number.

'This is Les, leave a message' the phone said.

Jason left a message, 'Jason from one R T B Kapooka, call me back on this number.

Jason then called Warren Jackson, the chopper pilot at Cooktown.

'yellow', said a voice after the phone had nearly rang out.

'Jacko'? Said Jason, 'I'm Jason the copper friend of Mark Crampton, we met a couple of times at the Sovereign'

'Orr yeah,..yeah,..Jason and Mark, yeah I remember you'. Warren had said and Jason asked him if he would be in Cooktown in about two weeks' time as he might have a job for him, Warren had said that he should be, not much happening at the moment.

Jason's phone rang and it was Les returning Jason's call.

'Well brother, I was thinking that you might be dead' Les had said as soon as Jason answered.

When Jason had been kicked out of recruit training at Kapooka, Les had gone through training and went on to more training when he went into the SAS and he had only recently retired from the army.

'Are you busy Bro? Are you up for a drive to Cooktown, I can pick you up from Townsville' said Jason.

'When are you talking man?' Les asked.

'Couple of weeks, I can let you know maybe tomorrow'. Jason said.

'Sounds cool man, I've got fuck all to do these days anyway, except drink piss, just tell me when' Les was keen.

Jason's next call was to his former boss at the Cooktown police station, Ken Marsden. Jason had been unsure of whether to include Ken into his Cooktown meeting, but the more he thought about it the better the idea, he thought as Ken was pretty clued up to police operations and any advice that he may offer would be invaluable to Jason's plan.

Ken answered the phone almost immediately and listened to what Jason had to say which was basically if he could meet up with him in Cooktown one day and then he mentioned briefly what it was about. Jason had been careful to tell Ken just enough about the plan to the extent that if he agreed to meet up with Jason then he knew that he would help him.

Ken said that he would look forward to meeting up with Jason and just to give him a good day's notice.

Jason had collected Les from Townsville on his way from Monto and they were enjoying a get together talk on their way up to Cooktown. They had bypassed Cairns by turning towards Atherton at Mourilyan and towards the last part of the eight hours of the journey Jason had gone into more detail with Les and had said that if Ken wasn't too keen on the idea then it would not go ahead, Les was even more excited about the 'mission' as he then called it and hoped the other dude liked the idea.

Jason had booked two rooms at the Sovereign for five days as he had no idea how long they would need.

They had met up with Warren Jackson on the second night they were there and Jason basically had three questions for him

How many passengers could he take in his helicopter?

Did he know where the Andrews, Barnes mining lease was?

Could he fly Les and himself into the mining lease undetected?

Jason felt that he could detect that Warren was not too sure of what Jason was asking him to do and was about to decline, so Jason told him the theory of what he and his friends had put together about Strauss and Watson being innocent and that he was hoping that the boys Andrews and Barnes might help him to prove it.

Warren gave Jason an unbelieving look and after a little pause said that he was in and for free, there would be no charge for the chopper,

'Those fellers were me mates Jason, and I knew that they would not do that to Mark, they could be pricks for sure, but not fucking murderers, I'm in all the way' Warren committed. 'I can take both of yous in the chopper no worries and a bit of gear, I know the lease well and have flown over it a hundred times and I can land you just down river where the wind always blows down from the hut so no one will hear me coming'.

Warren said that he wanted only a day's notice to fuel up and was happy to do a recce out there first to make sure the pricks were there. 'Shit' Jason thought to himself, he hadn't thought of the possibility of Andrews and Barnes not being out there at the lease.

Ken arrived and had dinner with Jason and Les and they then had a few beers afterwards, it was at that time Jason exposed his plan of getting a confession of sorts from Andrews and Barnes.

Ken had at first said it was a stupid idea, and then he said it was stupid but with merit and then after a short pause, said that it would possibly work and then asked what did Jason want Ken to do to make this plan work, he then told Jason that these two arseholes had taunted him for quite a while.

Ken whilst a police officer had suspected a drug plantation out at the lease and after considerable investigation work had determined it to be an illegal coca growing operation and had contacted his boss at Mareeba to discuss his plan of a raid and to source backup.

He was told that a plan on a raid for marijuana could go ahead but to leave the coca alone as it would be part of a much bigger planned raid down the track to expose bigger drug operatives.

Ken, believing what he had been told had organised a raid with backup police from Mareeba and discovered that the growers were not there on the day of the raid, he suspected that they had been tipped off, and that coca plants were in abundance but very few marijuana plants to even warrant a raid. Then in the subsequent months when no raid on the coca plantation had happened, he questioned his boss with respect to this and was basically told to mind his own business.

To say that Ken was disillusioned was certainly an understatement and he thought seriously about blowing the whistle on his boss but thought about other people, for instance, a police sergeant in another Queensland town who had gone missing for no apparent reason and he was not the only one. Ken then retired from the police force.

The three of them were staying at the hotel and it was two am when the door to Jason's room was opened by two uniformed Australian Federal Police officers, who woke Jason up and placed handcuffs on his wrists behind his back whilst telling him 'To take it easy, he was being detained'.

He was taken downstairs and into the rear car park where a Landcruiser wagon was waiting, he was placed into the back seat to join Ken and Les, also in handcuffs.

The Landcruiser left the hotel and drove to the Cooktown airport on Endeavour Valley road about ten kilometres from town where a Gulfstream G280 jet aircraft was waiting. They were placed on board and were separated around the ten seat aircraft. The time from takeoff to landing was all of fifteen minutes.

Another Landcruiser wagon was waiting on the tarmac at Cairns Airport and took them to the AFP headquarters at the airport where they were placed into separate interview rooms.

'I'm Superintendent Peter James' the man wearing jeans and a polo shirt addressed Jason, 'I know that you are Jason Walsh and you had intentions of raiding the mining lease of Terry Andrew and David Barnes, is that correct?' Jason saw that there was also another man wearing casual clothes sitting on a chair by the office door as he answered.

'Yes,...but what is going on here'.

'Can you tell me your intentions for the raid' the superintendent asked, 'And relax! You are not under arrest, we just want to talk to you'.

Jason told Peter James about Mark Campton and his going missing and about the sat phone and his belief that Andrews and Barnes had something to do with Mark's disappearance and that he believed that somehow a company called JCE is connected with another company Northern Trading and Logistics who have been communicating with Andrews and Barnes at the mining lease.

'I suppose the bottom line is that I wanted to get some answers' Jason concluded.

Peter James was fully aware of the missing Mark Crampton and his department shared similar views to that of Jason Walsh, the AFP however was restricted in the deployment of truth extraction.

'What makes you think that these two guys are going to tell you anything?' Peter James wanted to know.

One of my team is an ex SAS linguist, he spent quite some time in Afghanistan talking with soldiers from the Taliban and if they can tell him what he wants to know, then I am sure that Andrews and Barns would also tell my man what I want to know'. Jason went on to tell the Federal police officer that he was hoping to find the location of Mark's body and then he would hand it over to the Queensland police, but he wasn't sure where as he believed the officer in charge at Mareeba did not want to know anything about it.

'We are aware that you are ex police as with one other of your group, and that you are well aware that what you intend to do is against the law and you could all be prosecuted for such an act' the superintendent told Jason.

Jason, looking at the officer asked 'What has any of this got to do with the federal police?'

Superintendent James told Jason that the AFP has been closely working with various state police in relation to a huge drug operation that extends to North Queensland and beyond.

They have been closely monitoring Northern Trading and Logistics and are also aware of its ties to a company known as JCE. They have been focused on the cultivation of drugs and not the disappearance of Mark Crampton, although they are fully aware of the case. Peter James went on to say that he was also aware that the company, Northern Trading also has a contact at a local police station and provides restricted information back to them in relation to police activities.

Peter James then shocked Jason by inviting him and his two colleagues along on the raid in a limited capacity, that is to interview the occupants at the Watsonville mining lease with respect to the disappearance of Mark Crampton. But if anyone asks, it never happened.

They were flown back to Cooktown with instructions to be at a designated place and at a designated time that morning where they were then flown by Polair to the mining lease.

The Watsonville mining lease was already under the control of a police swat team which included some members of the AFP when Jason, Ken and Les arrived.

An AFP officer met them at the helicopter landing zone which was about one hundred meters from the lease.

The officer told them that they had approximately fifty minutes to conduct their interview and that he would be just outside if he was wanted and gave them swat team masks to put on with the instruction 'not to remove them'.

The three of them went into the main shed to find both Andrews and Barnes handcuffed and leg shackled sitting on plastic kitchen chairs in the centre of the shed.

Les went in search of a bucket and a towel which he soon found, he then filled the bucket with water and within seven minutes Barnes had told them that he would show them where the body of Mark Crampton was, Andrews just glared at him. Jason had recorded the interview with his phone.

Jason spoke to the officer outside the door and he organised a vehicle to take one of the Qld police officers with two AFP officers and Barnes to the location and ordered Jason, Ken and Les back on board the helicopter where they were taken back to Cooktown.

It was early afternoon by the time they got back to Cooktown and they walked from the oval where the Polair helicopter had dropped them over to the hotel where they were staying and, still in a sort of shock from the morning's events, went into the bar for a drink.

They would all love to know what was happening just now at the mining lease site but they realised that they would most likely hear nothing for a while and that they could not talk about it to anyone.

Between them, they discussed what had happened that morning and thought what a fluke that had been with the AFP about to do a raid just before their planned attack on Andrews and Barnes, and how Barnes had broken before Les had even started to apply the 'water treatment' to him. And then Jason asked,

'How did they know, how did the AFP know that we were planning to go to the Watsonville mining lease?'

Jason ordered another beer just as Ken said that the only other person who knew was Warren Jackson.

Could it be that Warren was a member of the AFP, or worked for them? They came to the unanimous conclusion that was the case with his great cover of flying all over the properties with cattle mustering and power transmission spotting.

'He was spotting alright' said Les, 'And reporting it straight back to the AFP'.

Epilogue

It was more than two weeks since the morning of the AFP raid on the Watsonville mining lease raid and there was no mention in the media of a drug plantation raid nor any mention about the discovery of the body of Mark Crampton. Jason was becoming concerned that perhaps David Barnes had changed his mind about showing the police where Mar Crampton's body was hidden.

He was considering trying to contact the AFP officer Peter James but was wholly aware that he had been told that the Cooktown morning event did not happen, and he then realised that other operations were likely to be connected to that raid and it may be months before any public information may be released. It was never released.

Jason answered the call, it was James congratulating him,

'Congratulations?' said Jason, confused and asked James what was he talking about.

'On the news!' James replied, 'About Stan Strauss and David Watson being released from prison'.

Jason turned on his television and went to channel 22 for the ABC news but there was no mention of any prison release, he looked at the latest news on his laptop and 9News was reporting that *The two men who were found guilty of the murder of Mark Crampton over four years ago have been released from prison due to the discovery of new evidence and that no further details were available just yet.*

Just as Jason was about to close his laptop he noticed another news article, *'ACT Police cold case reopened' Police. Police have new evidence in the decades old case of the drowning of Bishop Gillard in Lake Burley Griffin. Father Damien Downe is assisting police with their enquiries.*

It was during the course of the next seven months that more 'breaking news' stories began to emerge about the resignation of the Queensland premier and following that by about a month, the resignation of the Queensland police commissioner.

It seemed to be well spaced out in the media releases and after six months came the news that a former director of the Queensland based company, Northern Hotels was jailed for fraud. Some months later, an article about a Russian nationalist who was charged with drug offences in Gladstone.

Jason and his friends must have all missed the press release of two men remanded in custody for the murder of a man in Far Northern Queensland and went on to say that they are expected to stand trial in two years' time.

It was all very quiet and low key, even the compensation payment from the Queensland Government to Strauss and Watson was only a snippet advising that the pair had accepted an undisclosed amount.

The End.

Max Barrington